SOLAR

SOLAR

Ian McEwan

WINDSOR
PARAGON

First published 2010
by Jonathan Cape
This Large Print edition published 2010
by BBC Audiobooks Ltd
by arrangement with
The Random House Group Ltd

Hardcover ISBN: 978 1 408 48665 8
Softcover ISBN: 978 1 408 48666 5

British Library Cataloguing in Publication Data available

Printed and bound in Great Britain by
CPI Antony Rowe, Chippenham and Eastbourne

To Polly Bide
1949–2003

‘It gives him great pleasure, makes Rabbit feel rich, to contemplate the world’s wasting, to know the earth is mortal too.’

Rabbit is Rich, John Updike

Part One

2000

He belonged to that class of men—vaguely unprepossessing, often bald, short, fat, clever—who were unaccountably attractive to certain beautiful women. Or he believed he was, and thinking seemed to make it so. And it helped that some women believed he was a genius in need of rescue. But the Michael Beard of this time was a man of narrowed mental condition, anhedonic, monothematic, stricken. His fifth marriage was disintegrating and he should have known how to behave, how to take the long view, how to take the blame. Weren't marriages, his marriages, tidal, with one rolling out just before another rolled in? But this one was different. He did not know how to behave, long views pained him, and for once there was no blame for him to assume, as he saw it. It was his wife who was having the affair, and having it flagrantly, punitively, certainly without remorse. He was discovering in himself, among an array of emotions, intense moments of shame and longing. Patrice was seeing a builder, their builder, the one who had repointed their house, fitted their kitchen, retiled their bathroom, the very same heavy-set fellow who in a tea break had once shown Michael a photo of his mock-Tudor house, renovated and tudorised by his own hand, with a boat on a trailer under a Victorian-style lamp post on the concreted front driveway, and space on which to erect a decommissioned red phone box. Beard was surprised to find how complicated it was to be the cuckold. Misery was not simple. Let no one say that this late in life he was immune to fresh experience.

He had it coming. His four previous wives, Maisie, Ruth, Eleanor, Karen, who all still took a distant interest in his life, would have been exultant, and he hoped they would not be told. None of his marriages had lasted more than six years and it was an achievement of sorts to have remained childless. His wives had discovered early on what a poor or frightening prospect of a father he presented and they had protected themselves and got out. He liked to think that if he had caused unhappiness, it was never for long, and it counted for something that he was still on speaking terms with all his exes.

But not with his current wife. In better times, he might have predicted for himself a manly embrace of double standards, with bouts of dangerous fury, perhaps an episode of drunken roaring in the back garden late at night, or writing off her car, and the calculated pursuit of a younger woman, a Samson-like toppling of the marital temple. Instead, he was paralysed by shame, by the extent of his humiliation. Even worse, he amazed himself with his inconvenient longing for her. These days, desire for Patrice came on him out of nowhere, like an attack of stomach cramp. He would have to sit somewhere alone and wait for it to pass. Apparently, there was a certain kind of husband who thrilled at the notion of his wife with other men. Such a man might arrange to have himself bound and gagged and locked in the bedroom wardrobe while ten feet away his better half went at it. Had Beard at last located within himself a capacity for sexual masochism? No woman had ever looked or sounded so desirable as the wife he suddenly could not have. Conspicuously, he went to Lisbon to look up an old friend, but it was a joyless three nights. He had to have his wife back, and dared not drive her away with shouting or threats or brilliant moments of unreason. Nor was it in his nature to plead. He was frozen, he was abject, he could think of nothing else. The first time she left him a note—*Staying over at R's tonight. xx P*—did he go round to the mock-Tudor ex-council semi with the shrouded speedboat on the hard standing and a hot tub in the pint-sized back yard to mash the man's brains with his own monkey wrench? No, he watched television for five hours in his overcoat, drank two bottles of wine and tried not to think. And failed.

But thinking was all he had. When his other wives had found out about his affairs, they raged, coldly or tearfully, they insisted on long sessions into the early hours to deliver their thoughts on broken trust, and eventually their demands for a separation and all that followed. But when Patrice happened across some emails from Suzanne Reuben, a mathematician at the Humboldt University in Berlin, she became unnaturally elated. That same afternoon she moved her clothes into the guest bedroom. It was a shock when he slid the wardrobe doors open to confirm the fact. Those rows of silk and cotton dresses, he realised now, had been a luxury and a comfort, versions of herself lining up to please him. No longer. Even the hangers were gone. She smiled through dinner that night as she explained that she too intended to be 'free' and within the week she had started her affair. What was a man to do? He apologised one breakfast, told her his lapse meant nothing, made grand promises he sincerely believed he might keep. This was the closest he came to pleading. She said she did not mind what he did. This was what she was doing—and this was when she revealed the identity of her lover, the builder with the sinister name of Rodney Tarpin, seven inches taller and twenty years younger than the cuckold, whose sole reading, according to his boast, back when he was humbly grouting and bevelling for the Beards, was the sports section of a tabloid newspaper.

An early sign of Beard's distress was dysmorphia, or perhaps it was dysmorphia he was suddenly cured of. At last, he knew himself for what he was. Catching sight of a conical pink mess in the misted full-length mirror as he came out of the shower, he wiped down the glass, stood full on and took a disbelieving look. What engines of self-persuasion had let him think for so many years that looking like this was seductive? That foolish thatch of earlobe-level hair that buttressed his baldness, the new curtain-swag of fat that hung below his armpits, the innocent stupidity of swelling in gut and rear. Once, he had been able to improve on his mirror-self by pinning back his shoulders, standing erect, tightening his abs. Now, human blubber draped his efforts. How could he possibly keep hold of a young woman as beautiful as she was? Had he honestly thought that status was enough, that his Nobel Prize would keep her in his bed? Naked, he was a disgrace, an idiot, a weakling. Even eight consecutive press-ups were beyond him. Whereas Tarpin could run up the stairs to the Beards' master bedroom holding under one arm a fifty-kilo cement sack. Fifty kilos? That was roughly Patrice's weight.

She kept him at a distance with lethal cheerfulness. These were additional insults, her sing-song hellos, the matinal recital of domestic detail and her evening whereabouts, and none of it would have mattered if he had been able to despise her a little and plan to be shot of her. Then they could have settled down to the brief, grisly dismantling of a five-year childless marriage. Of course she was punishing him, but when he suggested that, she shrugged and said that she could just as easily have said the same of him. She had merely been waiting for this opportunity, he said, and she laughed and said in that case she was grateful to him.

In his delusional state he was convinced that just as he was about to lose her he had found the perfect wife. That summer of 2000 she was wearing different clothes, she had a different look around the house—faded tight jeans, flip-flops, a ragged pink cardigan over a T-shirt, her blonde hair cut short, her pale eyes a deeper agitated blue. Her build was slight, and now she looked like a teenager. From the empty rope-handled glossy carrier bags and tissue paper left strewn on the kitchen table for his inspection, he gathered she was buying herself new underwear for Tarpin to remove. She was thirty-four, and still kept the strawberries-and-cream look of her twenties. She did not tease or taunt or flirt with him, that at least would have been communication of a sort, but steadily perfected the bright indifference with which she intended to obliterate him.

He needed to cease needing her, but desire was not like that. He *wanted* to want her. One sultry night he lay uncovered on the bed and tried masturbating himself towards freedom. It bothered him that he could not see his genitalia unless his head was propped up on two pillows, and his fantasy was continually interrupted by Tarpin, who, like some ignorant stagehand with ladder and bucket, kept wandering onto the set. Was there another man on the planet apart from Beard attempting at this moment to pleasure himself with thoughts of his own wife just thirty feet away across the landing? The question emptied him of purpose. And it was too hot.

Friends used to tell him that Patrice resembled Marilyn Monroe, at least, from certain angles and in a certain light. He had been happy to accept this status-enhancing comparison, but he never really saw it. Now he did. She had changed. There was a new fullness in her lower lip, a promise of trouble when she lowered her gaze, and her shortened hair lay curled on her nape in a compelling, old-fashioned way. Surely, she was more beautiful than Monroe, drifting about the house and garden at weekends in a haze of blonde and pink and pale blue. What an adolescent colour scheme he had fallen for, and at his age.

He turned fifty-three that July, and naturally she ignored his birthday, then pretended in her jolly new style to remember it three days later. She gave him a kipper tie in Day-Glo mint green, telling him the style was being 'revived'. Yes, the weekends were the worst. She would come into a room where he was, not wishing to talk, but perhaps wanting to be seen, and she would look about in mild surprise before wandering off. She was evaluating everything afresh, not only him. He would see her at the bottom of the garden under the horse chestnut, lying on the grass with the newspapers, waiting in deep shade for her evening to begin. Then she would retire to the guest room to shower, dress, apply make-up and scent. As if reading his thoughts, she was wearing her lipstick red and thick. Perhaps Rodney Tarpin was encouraging the Monroe notion—a cliché Beard was now obliged to share.

If he was still in the house when she left (he tried so hard to keep busy at night), he found it irresistible to ameliorate his longing and pain by observing her from an upstairs window as she stepped into the evening air of Belsize Park and walked up the garden path—how disloyal of the unoiled garden gate to squeak in the same old way—and climbed into her car, a small and flighty black Peugeot of wanton acceleration. She was so eager, gunning the engine as she pulled away from the kerb, that his *douleur* redoubled because he knew she knew he was watching. Then her absence hung in the summer dusk like garden bonfire smoke, an erotic charge of invisible particulates that caused him to remain in position for many pointless minutes. He was not actually mad, he kept telling himself, but he thought he was getting a taste, a bitter sip.

What impressed him was his ability to think of nothing else. When he was reading a book, when he was giving a talk, he was really thinking of her, or of her and Tarpin. It was a bad idea to be at home when she was out seeing him, but since Lisbon he had no desire to look up old girlfriends. Instead he took on a series of evening lectures about quantum field theory at the Royal Geographical Society, joined radio and TV discussions, and at occasional events filled in for colleagues who were ill. Let the philosophers of science delude themselves to the contrary, physics was free of human taint, it described a world that would still exist if men and women and all their sorrows did not. In this conviction he was at one with Albert Einstein.

But even if he ate late with friends, he was usually home before her, and was forced to wait, whether he wanted to or not, until she returned, though nothing would happen when she did. She would go straight to her room, and he would remain in his, not wanting to meet her on the stairs in her state of post-coital somnolence. It was almost better when she stayed over at Tarpin's. Almost, but it would cost him a night's sleep.

At 2 a.m. one night in late July he was in his dressing gown on his bed listening to the radio when he heard her come in and immediately, without premeditation, enacted a scheme to make her jealous and unsure and want to come back to him. On the BBC World Service a woman was discussing village customs as they affected domestic life among Turkish Kurds, a soothing drone of cruelty, injustice and absurdity. Turning the volume down, but keeping his fingers on the knob, Beard loudly intoned a fragment of a nursery rhyme. He figured that from her room she would hear his voice, but not his words. As he finished his sentence, he turned up the volume of the woman's voice for a few seconds, which he then interrupted with a line from the lecture he had given that night, and made the woman reply at greater length. He kept this going for five minutes, his voice, then the woman's, sometimes artfully overlapping the two. The house was silent, listening, of course. He went into the bathroom, ran a tap, flushed the lavatory and laughed out loud. Patrice should know that his lover was a wit. Then he gave out a muted kind of whoop. Patrice should know he was having fun.

He did not sleep much that night. At four, after a long silence suggestive of tranquil intimacy, he opened his bedroom door while keeping up an insistent murmur, and went down the stairs backwards, bending forward to beat out on the treads with his palms the sound of his companion's footfall, syncopated with his own. This was the kind of logical plan only a madman might embrace. After seeing his companion to the hall, saying his goodbyes between silent kisses, and closing the front door on her with a firmness that resounded through the house, he went upstairs and fell into a doze at last after six, repeating to himself softly, 'Judge me by my results.' He was up an hour later to be sure of running into Patrice before she left for work, and of letting her see how suddenly cheerful he was.

At the front door she paused, car keys in her hand, the strap of her book-crammed satchel cutting into the shoulder of her floral blouse. No one could doubt it, she looked shattered, drained, though her voice was as bright as ever. She told him that she would be inviting Rodney for dinner that evening, and that he would probably stay the night, and she would appreciate it if he, Michael, would stay clear of the kitchen.

That happened to be his day for travelling to the Centre out at Reading. Dizzy with fatigue, he began the journey staring through his smeared train window at suburban London's miraculous combination of chaos and dullness, and damning himself for his folly. His turn to listen to voices through the wall? Impossible, he would stay out somewhere. Driven from his own home by his wife's lover? Impossible, he would stay and confront him. A fight with Tarpin? Impossible, he would be stamped into the hallway parquet. Clearly, he had been in no state to take decisions or to devise schemes and from now on he must take into account his unreliable mental state and act conservatively, passively, honestly, and break no rules, do nothing extreme.

Months later he would violate every element of this resolution, but it was forgotten by the end of that day because Patrice arrived home from work without supplies (there was nothing in the fridge) and the builder did not come to dinner. He saw her only once that night, crossing the hallway with a mug of tea in her hand, looking slumped and grey, less the movie icon, more the overworked primary-school teacher whose private life was awry. Had he been wrong to berate himself on the train, had his plan actually worked, and in her sorrow had she been forced to cancel?

Reflecting on the night before, he found it extraordinary that after a lifetime of infidelities, a night with an imaginary friend was no less exciting. For the first time in weeks he felt faintly cheerful, even whistled a show tune as he microwaved his supper, and when he saw himself in the gold-leaf sun-king mirror in the cloakroom downstairs, thought his face had lost some fat and looked purposeful, with a shadow of cheekbone visible, and was, by the light of the thirty-watt bulb, somewhat noble, a possible effect of the sugary cholesterol-lowering yoghurt drink he was forcing himself to swallow each morning. When he went to bed he kept the radio off and lay waiting with the light turned low for the remorseful little tap of her fingernails on his door.

It did not come, but he was not troubled. Let her pass a white night re-examining her life and what was meaningful, let her weigh in the scales of human worth a horny-handed Tarpin and his shrouded boat against ethereal Beard of planetary renown. The following five nights she stayed home, as far as he could tell, while he was committed to his lecture and other meetings and dinners, and when he came in, usually after midnight, he hoped his confident footfalls gave the impression to the darkened house of a man returning from a tryst.

On the sixth night, he was free to stay in, and she chose to go out, having spent longer than usual under shower and hairdryer. From his place, a small, deeply recessed window on a first-floor half-landing, he watched her go along the garden path and pause by a tall drift of vermilion hollyhocks, pause as though reluctant to leave, and put her hand out to examine a flower. She picked it, squeezing it between newly painted nails of thumb and forefinger, held it a moment to consider, then let it drop to her feet. The summer dress, beige silk, armless, with a single pleat in the small of her back, was new, a signal he was uncertain how to read. She continued to the front gate and he thought there was heaviness in her step, or at least some slackening of her customary eagerness, and she parted from the kerb in the Peugeot at near-normal acceleration.

But he was less happy that night waiting in, confused again about his judgement, beginning to think he was right after all, his radio prank had sunk him. To help think matters through he poured a scotch and watched football. In place of dinner he ate a litre tub of strawberry ice cream and prised apart a half-kilo of pistachios. He was restless, bothered by unfocused sexual need, and coming to the conclusion that he might as well be having or resuming a real affair. He passed some time turning the pages of his address book, stared at the phone a good while, but did not pick it up.

He drank half the bottle and before eleven fell asleep fully dressed on the bed with the overhead light on, and for several seconds did not know where he was when, some hours later, he was woken by the sound of a voice downstairs. The bedside clock showed two thirty. It was Patrice talking to Tarpin, and Beard, still fortified by drink, was in the mood to have a word. He stood groggily in the centre of the bedroom, swaying a little as he tucked in his shirt. Quietly, he opened his door. All the house lights were on, and that was fine, he was already going down the stairs with no thought for the consequences. Patrice was still talking, and as he crossed the hall towards the open sitting-room door he thought that he heard her laughing or singing and that he was about to break up a little celebration.

But she was alone and crying, sitting hunched forward on the sofa with her shoes lying on their sides on the long glass coffee table. It was an unfamiliar bottled, keening sound. If she had ever cried like this for him, it had been in his absence. He paused in the doorway and she did not see him at first. She was a sad sight. A handkerchief or tissue was twisted in her hand, her delicate shoulders were bowed and shaking, and Beard was filled with pity. He sensed that a reconciliation was at hand and that all she needed was a gentle touch, kind words, no questions, and she would fold into him and he would take her upstairs, though even in his sudden warmth of feeling, he knew he could not carry her, not even in both arms.

As he began to cross the room a floorboard creaked and she looked up. Their eyes met, but only for a second because her hands flew up to her face and covered it as she twisted away. He said her name, and she shook her head. Awkwardly, with her back to him, she got up from the sofa and, walking almost sideways, she stumbled on the polar-bear skin that tended to slide too easily on the polished wooden floor. He had come close to breaking an ankle once and had despised the rug ever since. He also disliked its leering, wide-open mouth and bared teeth yellowed by exposure to the light. They had never done anything to secure it to the floor, and there was no question of throwing it out because it was a wedding present from her father. She steadied herself, remembered to pick up her shoes and, with a free hand covering her eyes, hurried past him, flinching as he reached out to touch her arm, and beginning to cry again, more freely this time, as she ran up the stairs.

He turned off the lights in the room and lay on the sofa. Pointless to go after her when she did not want him, and it did not matter now, because he had *seen*. Too late for her hand to conceal the bruise below her right eye that spread across the top of her cheek, black fading to inflamed red at its edges, swelling under her lower lid, forcing the eye shut. He sighed aloud in resignation. It was inevitable, his duty was clear, he would have to get in his car now and drive to Cricklewood, lean on the doorbell until he had brought Tarpin from his bed, and have it out with him, right there beneath the coach lamp, and surprise his loathed opponent with an astonishing turn of speed and purpose. With eyes narrowing, he thought it through again, lingering on the detail of his right fist bursting through the cartilage of Tarpin's nose, and then, with minor revisions, he reconsidered the scene through closed eyes, and did not stir until the following morning when he was woken by the sound of the front door closing as she left for work.

* * *

He held an honorary university post in Geneva and did no teaching there, lent his name, his title, Professor Beard, Nobel laureate, to letterheads, to institutes, signed up to international 'initiatives', sat on a Royal Commission on science funding, spoke on the radio in layman's terms about Einstein or photons or quantum mechanics, helped out with grant applications, was a consultant editor on three scholarly journals, wrote peer reviews and references, took an interest in the gossip, the politics of science, the positioning, the special pleading, the terrifying nationalism, the tweaking of colossal sums out of ignorant ministers and bureaucrats for one more particle accelerator or rented instrument space on a new satellite, appeared at giant conventions in the US—eleven thousand physicists in one place!—listened to post-docs explain their research, gave with minimal variation the same series of lectures on the calculations underpinning the Beard–Einstein Conflation that had brought him his prize, awarded prizes and medals himself, accepted honorary degrees, and gave after-dinner speeches and eulogies for retiring or about-to-be-cremated colleagues. In an inward, specialised world he was, courtesy of Stockholm, a celebrity, and he coasted from year to year, vaguely weary of himself, bereft of alternatives. All the excitement and unpredictability was in the private life. Perhaps that was enough, perhaps he had achieved all he could during one brilliant summer in his youth. One thing was certain: two decades had passed since he last sat down in silence and solitude for hours on end, pencil and pad in hand, to do some thinking, to have an original hypothesis, play with it, pursue it, tease it into life. The occasion never arose—no, that was a weak excuse. He lacked the will, the material, he lacked the spark. He had no new ideas.

But there was a new government research establishment on the outskirts of Reading, hard against the roar of the motorway's eastbound section and downwind of a beer factory. The Centre was supposed to resemble the National Renewable Energy Laboratory in Golden, Colorado, near Denver, sharing its aims, but not its acreage or funding. Michael Beard was the new Centre's first head, though a senior civil servant called Jock Braby did the real work. The administrative buildings, some of whose dividing walls contained asbestos, were not new, and nor were the laboratories, whose purpose had once been to test noxious materials for the building trade. All that was new was a three-metre-high barbed-wire and concrete post fence, with regularly spaced keep-out signs, thrown up around the perimeter of the National Centre for Renewable Energy without Beard's or Braby's consent. It represented, they soon found out, seventeen per cent of the first year's budget. A sodden, twenty-acre field had been bought from a local farmer, and work to begin on drainage was in the planning stage.

Beard was not wholly sceptical about climate change. It was one in a list of issues, of looming sorrows, that comprised the background to the news, and he read about it, vaguely deplored it and expected governments to meet and take action. And of course he knew that a molecule of carbon dioxide absorbed energy in the infrared range, and that humankind was putting these molecules into the atmosphere in significant quantities. But he himself had other things to think about. And he was unimpressed by some of the wild commentary that suggested the world was in 'peril', that humankind was drifting towards calamity, when coastal cities would disappear under the waves, crops fail, and hundreds of millions of refugees surge from one country, one continent, to another, driven by drought, floods, famine, tempests, unceasing wars for diminishing resources. There was an Old Testament ring to the forewarnings, an air of plague-of-boils and deluge-of-frogs, that suggested a deep and constant inclination, enacted over the centuries, to believe that one was always living at the end of days, that one's own demise was urgently bound up with the end of the world, and therefore made more sense, or was just a little less irrelevant. The end of the world was never pitched in the present, where it could be seen for the fantasy it was, but just around the corner, and when it did not happen, a new issue, a new date would soon emerge. The old world purified by incendiary violence, washed clean by the blood of the unsaved, that was how it had been for Christian millennial sects—death to the unbelievers! And for Soviet Communists—death to the kulaks! And for Nazis and their thousand-year fantasy—death to the Jews! And then the truly democratic contemporary equivalent, an all-out nuclear war—death to everyone! When that did not happen, and after the Soviet empire had been devoured by its internal contradictions, and in the absence of any other overwhelming concern beyond boring, intransigent global poverty, the apocalyptic tendency had conjured yet another beast.

But Beard was always on the lookout for an official role with a stipend attached. A couple of long-running sinecures had recently come to an end, and his university salary, lecture fees and media appearances were never quite sufficient. Fortunately, by the end of the century, the Blair government wished to be, or appear to be, practically rather than merely rhetorically engaged with climate change and announced a number of initiatives, one of which was the Centre, a facility for basic research in need of a mortal at its head sprinkled with Stockholm's magic dust. At the political level, a new minister had been appointed, an ambitious Mancunian with a populist's touch, proud of his city's industrial past, who told a press conference that he would 'tap the genius' of the

British people by inviting them to submit their own clean-energy ideas and drawings. In front of the cameras he promised that every submission would be answered. Braby's team—half a dozen underpaid post-doctoral physicists housed in four temporary cabins in a sea of mud—received hundreds of proposals within six weeks. Most were from lonely types working out of garden sheds, a few from start-up companies with zippy logos and 'patents pending'.

In the winter of 1999, on his weekly visits to the site, Beard would glance through the piles sorted on a makeshift table. In this avalanche of dreams were certain clear motifs. Some proposals used water as a fuel for cars, and recycled the emission—water vapour—back into the engine; some were versions of the electric motor or generator whose output exceeded the input and seemed to work from vacuum energy—the energy supposedly found in empty space—or from what Beard thought must be violations of Lenz's Law. All were variants on the perpetual-motion machine. These self-taught inventors seemed to have no awareness of the long history of their devices, or how they would, if they actually worked, destroy the entire basis of modern physics. The nation's inventors were up against the first and second laws of thermodynamics, a wall of solid lead. One of the post-docs proposed sorting the ideas according to which of the laws they violated, first, second or both.

There was another common theme. Some envelopes contained no drawings, only a letter, sometimes half a page, sometimes ten. The author regretfully explained that he—it was always a he—

declined to enclose detailed plans because it was well known that government agencies had much to fear from the kind of free energy that his machine would deliver, for it would close off an important tax resource. Or the armed forces would seize on the idea, declare it top secret, then develop it for their own use. Or conventional energy providers would send round thugs to beat the inventor to a pulp in order to maintain business supremacy. Or someone would steal the idea for himself and make his fortune. There were notorious instances of all these, the writer might add. The drawings could therefore only be seen at a certain address by an unaccompanied person from the Centre, and only with the involvement of intermediaries.

The table in 'Hut Two' consisted of five builder's planks set on trestles, supporting sixteen hundred letters and printed emails, sorted by date. To save the Minister's face, all would need an answer. Braby, a stooping, large-jawed fellow, was furious at the waste of time. Furious, but compliant. Beard was for forwarding them all to the Minister's department in London, along with a few model replies. But Braby thought he was in line for a knighthood and Mrs Braby was keen, and upsetting a minister known to be close to Number Ten could blow the gong away. So the post-docs were set to work, and the Centre's first project—designing a wind generator for city roofs—was delayed by months.

All the more time for Beard, not yet a refugee from the near-silent endgame of his fifth marriage, to study the 'geniuses', so named by the post-docs. He was drawn by the whiff of obsession, paranoia, insomnia and, above all, pathos that rose from the piles. Was he finding, he wondered, a version of himself in certain of these letters, of a parallel Michael Beard who, through drink, sex, drugs or plain misfortune, might have missed out on the disciplines of a formal education in physics and maths? Missed out, and still craved to think, tinker, contribute. Some of these men were truly clever but were required by their extravagant ambitions to reinvent the wheel, and then, one hundred and twenty years after Nikola Tesla, the induction motor, and then read inexpertly and far too hopefully into quantum field theory to find their esoteric fuel right under their noses, in the voids of the empty air of their sheds or spare bedrooms—zero-point energy.

Quantum mechanics. What a repository, a dump, of human aspiration it was, the borderland where mathematical rigour defeated common sense, and reason and fantasy irrationally merged. Here, the mystically inclined could find whatever they required, and claim science as their proof. And for these ingenious men in their spare time, what ghostly and beautiful music it must be—*spectral asymmetry, resonances, entanglement, quantum harmonic oscillators*—beguiling ancient airs, the harmony of the spheres that might transmute a lead wall into gold, and bring into being the engine that ran on virtually nothing, on virtual particles, that emitted no harm and would power the human enterprise as well as save it. Beard was stirred by the yearnings of these lonely men. And why should he think they were lonely? It was not, or not only, condescension that made him think them so. They did not know enough, but they knew too much to have anyone to talk to. What mate waiting down the pub or in the British Legion, what hard-pressed wife with job and kids and housework, was going to follow them down these warped funnels in the space–time continuum, into the wormhole, the shortcut to a single, final answer to the global problem of energy?

Beard devised a rubric inspired by the US Patent Office which advised the geniuses that all plans for perpetual motion and 'above unity' machines should be accompanied by a working model. But none ever was. Mindful of his ambitions, Braby watched over the post-docs closely as they worked through the piles. Every submission had to be answered individually, seriously, politely. But on the planks there was nothing new, or nothing new that was useful. The revolutionary lone inventor was a fantasy of popular culture—and the Minister.

With numbing slowness the Centre began to take shape. Duckboards were laid over the mud—a huge advance—then the mud was smoothed and seeded, and by summer there were lawns with paths across them, and in time the place resembled every other boring institute in the world. The labs were refitted, and at last the temporary cabins were hauled away. The adjacent field was drained, and foundations were dug, and building began. More staff were taken on—janitors, office cleaners, administrators, repair men, even scientists, and a human-resources team to find such people. When a critical mass was reached, a canteen was opened. And housed in a smart brick lodge next to red-and-white striped barrier gates were a dozen security guards in dark blue uniforms, who were cheery with one another, stern with almost everyone else and who seemed to believe that the place essentially belonged to them, and all the rest were interlopers.

In all this time, not one of the six post-docs moved on to a better-paid job at Caltech or MIT. In a field crammed with prodigies of all sorts, their CVs were exceptional. For a long while Beard, who had always had face-recognition problems, especially with men, could not, or chose not to, tell them apart. They ranged in age from twenty-six to twenty-eight and all stood above six feet. Two had ponytails, four had identical rimless glasses, two were called Mike, two had Scots accents, three wore coloured string around their wrists, all wore faded jeans and trainers and tracksuit tops. Far better to treat them all the same, somewhat distantly, or as if they were one person. Best not to insult one Mike by resuming a conversation that might have been with the other, or to assume that the fellow with the ponytail and glasses, Scots accent and no wrist string was unique, or was not called Mike. Even Jock Braby referred to all six as 'the ponytails'.

And none of these young men appeared as much in awe of Michael Beard, Nobel laureate, as he thought they should. Clearly, they knew of his work, but in meetings they referred to it in passing, parenthetically, in a dismissive mumble, as though it had long been superseded, when in fact the opposite was true, the Beard–Einstein Conflation was in all the textbooks, unassailable, experimentally robust. As undergraduates the ponytails would surely have witnessed a demonstration of the 'Feynman Plaid', illustrating the topographical essence of Beard's work. But at informal gatherings in the canteen these giant children became frontiersmen of theoretical physics and spoke round the Conflation, treated it as one might a dusty formulation by Sir Humphry Davy, and made elliptical references to BLG or some overwrought arcana in M-theory or Nambu Lie 3-algebra as if it were not a change of subject. And that was the problem. Much of the time he did not know what they were saying. The ponytails spoke at speed, on a constant, rising interrogative note, which caused an obscure muscle to tighten in the back of Beard's throat as he listened. They failed to enunciate their words, going only so far with a thought, until one of the others muttered, 'Right!', after which they would jump to the next unit of utterance—one could hardly call it a sentence.

But it was worse than that. Some of the physics which they took for granted was unfamiliar to him. When he looked it up at home, he was irritated by the length and complexity of the calculations. He liked to think he was an old hand and knew his way around string theory and its major variants. But these days there were simply too many add-ons and modifications. When Beard was a twelve-year-old schoolboy, his maths teacher had told the class that whenever they found an exam question coming out at eleven nineteenths or thirteen twenty-sevenths, they should know they had the wrong answer. Too messy to be true. Frowning for two hours at a stretch, so that the following morning parallel pink lines were still visible across his forehead, he read up on the latest, on Bagger, Lambert and Gustavsson—of course! BLG was not a sandwich—and their Lagrangian description of coincident M2-branes. God may or may not have played dice, but surely He was nowhere near this clever, or such a show-off. The material world simply could not be so complicated.

* * *

But the domestic world could. In Beard's tally of sheared wedlock, none was so foolishly prolonged—by him—and none so reduced him or engendered such ridiculous daydreams and weight-gain and unwitnessed folly as this, his fifth and last. During those long months there was never a time when he thought he was fully himself, and besides, he soon forgot that self and settled into a state of mild and extended psychosis. He was hearing voices after all, and seeing elements in the situation—Patrice's sudden, lambent beauty, for example—which he decided later did not exist. The somatic consequences had a textbook quality. A sequence of minor ailments mocked the immune system that was supposed to protect him. Pathogens swam in hordes across the moat of his defences, they swarmed over the castle walls armed with cold sores, mouth ulcers, fatigue, joint pain, watery bowels, nose acne, blepharitis—a new one this, a disfiguring inflammation of the eyelids that erupted into white-peaked Mount Fuji styes that pressured his eyeballs, blurring his vision. Insomnia and monomania also distorted his view, and on the edge of sleep, when it came at last, he heard a newsreader's voice reminding him of his sorry state, but not in words he could actually hear. Beyond this, he suffered the rational despair of a cuckold whose wife, despite her fading black eye, still moved about the house with a triumphal air, falsely cheerful, drifting away the moment he attempted a serious conversation. The mouth is famously over-represented in the brain, and he felt a tiny sore along a crack in the centre of his lower lip as a hideous cicatrice, the mark of his fate. How could she ever kiss him again? She would not be engaged or challenged or accused, she would not be loved, not by him.

Yes, yes, he had been a lying womaniser, he had it coming, but now that it had arrived, what was he supposed to do, beyond taking his punishment? To which god was he to offer his apologies? He had had enough. After morosely clinging to stupid hopes, he began to watch the post and emails for the invitation that would take him far away from Belsize Park and shake some independent life into his sorry frame. About half a dozen a week arrived throughout the year, but so far nothing had interested him among the inducements to give lectures on the shore of a plutocratic north-Italian lake, or in an unexciting German schloss, and he felt too weak and raw to discuss the Conflation before one more colleague-crowded conference in New Delhi or Los Angeles. He had no idea what he wanted, but he thought he would know it when he saw it.

Meanwhile, it was soothing, mostly, to take once a week the grubby morning train from Paddington to Reading, to be met at that Victorian station squashed in among the stubby tower blocks and be driven a few miles in a prototype Prius to the Centre by one of the indistinguishable ponytails. Leaving home, Beard was a tensed one-note vibrating string, whose oscillations diminished the further he left his home behind and the closer he approached the expensive perimeter fence. The vibrations came to rest as he acknowledged with raised forefinger the friendly salute of the security guards—how they loved a supremo!—and swept by, under the raised red-and-white barrier. Braby generally came out to meet him and even, with barely a touch of mandarin irony, held open the car door, for this was no cuckold arriving, but the distinguished visitor, the Chief, counted on to speak up for the place in the press, encourage the energy industries to take an interest, and squeeze another quarter-million from the blustering Minister.

The two men took coffee together at the start of the day. Progress and delays were listed and Beard noted whatever was required of him, then toured the site. In an off-the-cuff way he had proposed right at the start that it would be easier to procure more funds if he could claim for the Centre a single eye-catching project that would be comprehensible to the taxpayer and the media. And so the WUDU had been launched, a Wind turbine for Urban Domestic Use, a gizmo the householder could install on his rooftop to generate enough power to make a significant reduction in his electricity bill. On town roofs the wind did not blow smoothly from one direction the way it did on high towers in open country, so the physicists and engineers were asked to research an optimal design for wind-turbine blades in turbulent conditions. Beard had leaned on an old friend at the Royal Aircraft Establishment at Farnborough for access to a wind tunnel, but first there were some intricate maths and aerodynamics to investigate, some sub-branch of chaos theory that he himself had little patience with. His interest in technology was even weaker than his interest in climate science. He had thought it would be a matter of settling the maths for the design, building three or four prototypes and testing them in the tunnel. But more people had to be hired as related issues wormed their way onto the agenda: vibration, noise, cost, height, wind shear, gyroscopic precession, cyclic stress, roof strength, materials, gearing, efficiency, phasing with the grid, planning permissions. What had seemed a simple wheeze had turned into a monster that was eating up all the attention and resources of the half-built Centre. And it was too late to turn back.

Beard preferred to go around alone to witness guiltily the consequences of his casual proposal. By the early summer of 2000 the post-docs each had a small cubicle of their own. Breaking up the group had helped, as had the nameplates on the door, but Beard put it down mostly to his own perceptiveness, the way each of the young men, after seven or eight months, was drifting into focus. He had made a mere half-dozen trips from Reading station in the Prius when, looking up from a speech he was to give that night in Oxford, he realised that, of course, the same driver had picked him up each time. He was one of the two who actually had a ponytail, a tall, thin-faced lad with a mouth overstuffed with large teeth and goofy smile. He came from outside Swaffham in Norfolk, Beard learned in this, his first focused conversation, and had been at Imperial, then Cambridge, then two years at Caltech in Pasadena, and none of these fabled places had diluted the pure inflections of his rural accent and its innocent swerves and dips and persistent rising line, suggestive to Beard of hedgerows and hayricks. His name was Tom Aldous. He told the Chief in that first chat that he had applied to work at the Centre because he thought the planet was in danger, and that his background in particle physics might be of some use, and that when he saw that Beard himself was going to lead the team, Beard of the Beard–Einstein Conflation, he, Tom Aldous, excitedly assumed that the Centre would have as its prime concern solar energy, particularly artificial photosynthesis and what he called nano-solar, about which he was convinced . . .

'Solar energy?' Beard said mildly. He knew perfectly well what was meant, but still, the term had a dubious halo of meaning, an invocation of New Age Druids in robes dancing round Stonehenge at Midsummer's dusk. He also distrusted anyone who routinely referred to 'the planet' as proof of thinking big.

'Yes!' Aldous smiled with his many teeth into the rear-view mirror. It would not have occurred to him that the Chief was not an expert in the field. 'It's all out there, waiting for us to understand how to use it, and when we do, we'll be amazed we ever thought of burning coal and oil and the like.'

Beard was intrigued by the way Aldous said 'loike'. It seemed to mock what he was trying to say. They were going along a four-lane ring road with flowering hawthorns in the central reservation uselessly casting their scent at the passing traffic. The previous night, with no expectation of sleep, he had lain on his bed in his dressing gown reading while she stayed out all night. It was an unpublished bundle of letters to various colleagues from Paul Dirac, a man entirely claimed by science, bereft of small talk and other human skills. At six forty-five, Beard had set down the typescript and had gone to the bathroom to shave. Sunlight was already sloping through the front-garden birch and patterning the marble floor beneath his toes. What a waste, a failure of good governance, to have the sun so high so early in the day. He could not bear to count, he thought as he took his razor to the new sprouting hair between his eyebrows to give himself a younger look, all the hours of daylight he had ever missed in summer. But what could he have done, what was there for any young man at seven in the morning at any time of year, beyond sleep or getting to work? Now his sleep deficit stretched back weeks.

'Do you think we could ever get by,' he asked, stifling a yawn, 'without coal and oil and gas?'

Aldous was taking them at a clip around a giant roundabout as big and busy as a racing circuit, that slung them centrifugally out upon a descending slip road and down onto the motorway, into the redoubled roar of onrushing vehicles, and trucks the size of five terraced houses whining in file towards Bristol at eighty-five miles per hour, and everyone else lining up to shoot past. Exactly so—how long could this go on? Beard, weak and tender from sleeplessness, felt belittled. The M4 demonstrated a passion for existence which he could no longer match. He was for the B-road, a cart track, a footpath. Shrinking inside his Harris tweed jacket, he listened to Tom Aldous, who spoke with the lilting confidence of a prize pupil providing the answers he thinks he knows his teacher wants.

'Coal and then oil have made us, but now we know, burning the stuff will ruin us. We need a different fuel or we fail, we sink. It's about another industrial revolution. And there's no way round it, the future is electricity and hydrogen, the only two energy carriers we know that are clean at the point of use.'

'So, more nuclear power.'

The boy took his eyes off the road to lock with Beard's in the mirror—but for too long, and the older man, tensing on the back seat, looked away to encourage the driver's gaze back on the mayhem outside.

'Dirty, dangerous, expensive. But you know, we've already got a nuclear power station up and running with a great safety record making clean energy converting hydrogen to helium at no cost, nicely situated ninety-three million miles away. You know what I always think, Professor Beard? If an alien arrived on earth and saw all this sunlight, he'd be amazed to hear that we think we've got an energy problem. Photovoltaics! I read Einstein on it, I read you. The Conflation is brilliant. And God's greatest gift to us is surely this, that a photon striking a semiconductor releases an electron. The laws of physics are so benign, so generous. And get this. There's a guy in a forest in the rain and he's dying of thirst. He has an axe and he starts cutting down the trees to drink the sap. A mouthful in each tree. All around him is a wasteland, no wildlife, and he knows that thanks to him the forest is disappearing fast. So why doesn't he just open his mouth and drink the rain?

Because he's brilliant at chopping down trees, he's always done things this way, and he thinks that people who advocate rain-drinking are weird. That rain is our sunlight, Professor Beard. It drenches our planet, drives our climate and its life. A sweet rain of photons, and all we have to do is hold out our cups! D'you know, I read this guy saying somewhere that less than an hour's worth of all the sunlight falling on the earth would satisfy the whole world's needs for a year.'

Unimpressed, Beard said, 'And what was this guy taking as his measure of solar irradiance?'

'One quarter of the solar constant.'

'Too optimistic. You'd need to halve that again.'

'My point stands, Professor Beard. Solar arrays on a tiny fraction of the world's deserts would give us all the power we need.'

The Norfolk lad's bucolic tone, so at odds with what he was saying, was beginning to aggravate Beard's raw condition. He said sullenly, 'If you could distribute it.'

'Yes. New DC lines! That's just money and effort. Worth it for the planet! For our future, Professor Beard!'

Beard snapped the pages of his speech to indicate that the conversation was at a close. The essence of a crank was, firstly, to believe that all the world's problems could be reduced to one, and be solved. And secondly, to go on about it non-stop.

But Tom Aldous was not done with him yet. As they arrived at the Centre and the gates were raised, he said, as though there had been no break in the discussion, 'That's why, I mean, no disrespect, that's why I think we're wasting our time with this micro wind-power stuff. The technology's already good enough. The government just needs to make it attractive to people—it's stroke-of-the-pen stuff, the market will do the rest. There's so much money to be made. But solar—cutting-edge artificial photosynthesis—there's great basic research to do on the nanotechnology. Professor, it could be us!'

Aldous was holding open the door and Beard was climbing wearily out. He said, 'Thank you for your thoughts. But really, you should learn to keep your eyes on the road.' And he turned away to shake Braby's hand.

On his weekly round, therefore, he hoped to avoid running into Aldous alone, for the young man was always trying to convince him of photovoltaics, or his quantum explanation of photovoltaics, or to oppress him generally with friendliness and enthusiasm, and seemed oblivious to Beard's surliness whenever he repeated the case for dropping WUDU. Of course it ought to be abandoned, when it was devouring nearly all the budget and growing in complication as it diminished in interest. But it had been Beard's idea, and reversing it would be a personal disaster. So he was coming to dislike this young man, his big-boned goofy face and flaring nostrils, his ponytail, his wrist bracelet of grubby red and green string intertwined, his holier-than-thou diet of salad and yoghurt in the canteen, his habit of bringing his tray over unasked and sitting as close as possible to the Chief, who could only be depressed to learn that Aldous had boxed for Norfolk in the county championships, had rowed for his college at Cambridge, had come seventh in a San Francisco marathon. There were novels Aldous wanted him to read—novels!—and developments in contemporary music he thought Beard should be aware of, and movies that were of particular relevance, documentaries about climate change which Aldous had seen at least twice but would happily see again if there was a chance of making the Chief sit through them too. Aldous had a mind that was designed, through the medium of a Norfolk accent, to offer tireless advice, make recommendations, urge changes, or express enthusiasm for some journey or holiday or book or vitamin, which itself was a form of exhortation. Nothing eroded Beard's goodwill more than to hear again that he must spend a month in the Vale of Swat.

In the building where once brick dust and fibreglass insulation had been tested for non-beneficial effects, he wandered between labs and listened to progress reports from engineers, designers and mysteriously termed energy consultants, who were responsible for a long document called 'Discovering Micro Wind 4.2', of which he could not bring himself to read even the first paragraph. During that summer so many were taken on by the Department of Human Resources, which had just been taken on itself, that each week he was obliged to explain who he was to half a dozen strangers. There were very few who were not busy with WUDU, and as he went about, Beard became more downhearted. For all the toil, nothing was ready for testing at Farnborough, no one had really addressed the turbulence problem, and no one was thinking much about what might happen when the wind did not blow because no one had the first idea about storing electricity cheaply and efficiently. That would have been a radical project, designing a powerful new battery for domestic supply, but it was too late to suggest it now, with everyone committed to WUDU, and besides, battery research was what Tom Aldous kept suggesting. Far better to build a boutique nuclear reactor on the Dorset Jurassic Coast than to wreck a million roofs with the shearing and vibration, the backward force and twist and torque of some worthless gadget for which the wind was rarely strong enough to motivate a useful current.

How could it be, Beard wondered with a touch of self-pity as he left one office and went glumly towards the next, that a chance remark of his had sent everyone rushing on this pointless quest? The answer was simple. In response to his proposal, there had been memoranda, detailed proposals one hundred and ninety-seven pages long, budget outlines and spreadsheets, and he had initialled his approval on each without reading them. And why was that? Because Patrice was starting her affair with Tarpin and he was not able to think of anything else.

He was going back along the corridor, passing Braby's office on his way to talk to a materials specialist, and there was Braby himself, waiting for him just inside his door, and waving him in excitedly. Behind him, taping a drawing to a whiteboard, was one of the two ponytails called Mike.

'I think we've got something,' Braby said as he closed the door behind Beard. 'Mike's just brought it over.'

'Don't get the wrong idea, Professor Beard,'

Mike said. 'I didn't draw this. I found it.'

Braby took hold of Beard's sleeve and tugged him to the board.

'Just look at it. I need your opinion.'

On a large sheet there was one formally executed drawing surrounded by half a dozen sketches—doodles with a solid but wavering line of the kind one might see in Leonardo's notebooks. Watched intently by the other two, Beard was staring at the centrepiece, a thick column containing a mess of lines and cutaways that resolved at last into a quadruple helix making one complete turn, and at the base, in less detail, a boxy representation of a generator. One of the doodles showed a roofline, with a TV aerial and the helix set on a short vertical pole strapped to the side of a chimney—not a good mounting at all. For two minutes he stared in silence.

'Well?' Braby said.

'Well,' Beard muttered. 'It's something.'

Braby laughed. 'I *thought* it was. I don't know how it works, but I just knew it was.'

'It's a variant on the Darrieus machine, the old egg beater.' In the long-ago days when he was happily, or less obsessively, married, Beard had spent an afternoon reading up on the history of wind turbines. At that stage he had thought the physics was relatively simple. 'But what's different here is the blades are canted into a helix with a twist of sixty degrees. And there are four of them to spread the torque and perhaps help it self-start. Probably do well out of an upward-tilting airflow. Might be good on a roof, you never know. So, who came up with this?'

But he already knew the answer and his

weariness redoubled. To listen to the Swan of Swaffham celebrate a breakthrough, the dawn of a new era in turbine design, would be more than he could bear today. It would have to be next week, for what he wanted at that moment was to sit somewhere quiet and think about Patrice, excite himself to no purpose. That was how bad it was.

Mike scratched at the base of his ponytail, which showed traces, like blanket stitching, of mutinous grey. 'It was on Tom's desk. We guessed he must have left it out for us to see. Then we got excited, couldn't find him anywhere. We made a copy for the engineers and they already like it.'

Jock Braby did an agitated turn about his office, returned to his desk and snatched his jacket off the back of a chair. The snob in Beard made him want to take the civil servant aside to tell him that it was not done, not since the Bletchley era, or at least, since Beard's own undergraduate days, to have a row of ballpoints in one's jacket top pocket. But he only ever thought his advice, he never gave it.

In a state of muted excitement, Braby was dignified, stooping from a height towards his companions and speaking in a measured, husky tone, as though at a sword's touch he had just straightened the knee from a royal cushion. 'I'm going to talk to Aldous, then I'm going to take him with me to Design. We need proper drawings. They can sit down with him and get to work, and meanwhile, Mike, you and the other boys can do the maths, you know, Brecht's Law and so on.'

'Betz's Law.'

'Quite so.' And he was gone.

When Beard was done with his rounds, he settled alone with a few chocolate biscuits on a plate and a mug of stewed coffee from an urn in the deserted common room, behind the canteen, for a long time the only comfortable place in the Centre, and let his thoughts return to the object of his obsession, fixing, with a near-pleasant heaviness in his limbs, on certain details he had lately neglected. But first he had to heave himself out of his chair and cross the room to turn off the murmuring television, forever tuned to a news channel. Bush v Gore, absorbing the precious attention of the disenfranchised majority of the world's population. He settled down again and took a grip on his plate.

Patrice was by far the most beautiful of all his wives, or rather, she was in her angular fair-haired way, so it seemed to him now, the only beautiful wife he had ever had. The other four had missed beauty by millimetres—a nose too thin, a mouth too wide, a minimally defective or recessive chin or forehead—and they had appealed, these lesser wives, only from a particular perspective, or by an effort of will or imagination, or through self-deceiving desire. Certain details then, concerning Patrice. For example, the narrowness of her buttocks. A single large hand could span them. The creamy tautness of her skin between protruding points of pelvic bone. The startling polymorphism that had formed her fine, straw-blonde pubic hair. Would he ever see any of these treasures again? And now, unsensual as it was, he had to consider the bruise beneath her eye. She would not talk to him, and he might never know the truth. He could deal only in probabilities. Suppose his plan had worked, that the woman in his room, whose footfalls he had drummed with his palms on the stairs, had not enraged but endeared and bound Patrice to him, made her anxious at what she thought she was about to lose, prompted her to tell Tarpin that the affair was over, that she was returning to her husband—and provoked his fury. In that case, her blackened cheekbone signalled that she was almost his, Beard's, again. Too much wish-fulfilment in that. What then?

Mechanically, he conveyed biscuits from plate to mouth. Perhaps the entire entanglement was going to take an improbable course. Most things were improbable. There were bruised and broken women who could not stay away from their violent men. Organisers of women's refuges often lamented this quirk of human nature. If she was addicted to her fate there would be more blows to the face. His beautiful Patrice. Unbearable. Unthinkable. What *then*? She could be sickened as much by Michael's sympathy as by Rodney's violence, and want to be shot of them both. Or, he could go into his bedroom one night and discover her already there, waiting for him, naked on the marital bed, on her back as of old, legs parted, and he was going towards her, murmuring her name, and now he too was naked. It was going to be easy, and when he reached her side he cupped her left . . . But he was no longer alone, and he did not have to look up to know whose shape was in the doorway.

Without pouring himself a coffee—he allowed himself no stimulants and thought Beard should do the same—Aldous sat down beside the Chief and, skipping preliminaries, said, 'I seriously urge you to read the piece on thin-film solar in next week's *Nature*.'

Some of the blood supply that should have been in Beard's brain was still in his penis, though draining quickly, otherwise he might have had the presence of mind to tell Aldous to go away.

Instead, he said, 'Braby's looking for you.'

'That's what I heard. You've all seen my turbine drawing.'

'He's probably in his office now.'

In a show of professional exhaustion, Aldous removed his baseball cap, leaned back in the armchair and closed his eyes. 'I should have destroyed it.'

'It has some promise,' Beard said, much against his will. He distrusted anyone off a baseball field in a baseball cap, whichever way round it was worn.

'That's the point. Actually, it's revolutionary. Talk about smooth torque! Optimal angle of attack for any direction of wind flow. Turbulence problem solved! Don't get me wrong, Professor Beard, it's brilliant. But d'you know, if the Centre takes it up, that'll be three wasted years of development, doing work that a commercial firm could be doing with a view to making money. And it's not important enough, micro wind is not going to solve the problem, Professor. The wind doesn't blow hard enough in most towns. We need a new energy source for the whole of civilisation. There really isn't much time. We should be doing the basics on solar, before the Germans and Japanese run away with it, before the Americans wake up. I've got some ideas. Even with our crappy climate, there's infrared. But why am I telling this to you, of all people? We need to take another look at photosynthesis, see what we can learn. I've got some great ideas there too. I'm putting together a file for you. And now I've just seen Mr Braby heading towards Design with my stupid drawing in his hand. Oh Christ!'

He clamped a hand over his closed eyes in another show—this time, of undeserved suffering stoically endured.

'I'm a simple man, Professor Beard. I just want to do what's right by the planet.'

'I see,' Beard said, suddenly unable to face the final biscuit as it appeared in his grasp. He put it back on the plate and with some effort pushed himself out of his chair. 'I need to be getting back now. You'll need to drive me to the station.'

'No point,' Aldous said, and was out of his chair and crossing the room in three strides to the TV set, where he changed stations and paused, waiting for one item to give way to another, then turned up the volume. It was as if he had conjured the story for his own purposes, driven an elderly couple to destitution and despair and persuaded them to throw themselves hand in hand in front of the London to Oxford train. The local news report showed nothing more gory than the lines of frustrated passengers at Reading station being turned away and others waiting for special coaches that had failed to turn up.

The young man was guiding Beard towards the door, as one might a mental patient in need of a bath. 'I live not far from Belsize Park and I'm going home now. It's not a Prius, but it'll get you to your door.'

He did not know how Aldous knew where he lived, but there was no point asking. And because Beard now intended to go home, back to the headquarters of his misery, he had no interest in sending Aldous to see Jock Braby.

Within minutes the Chief was sitting in the front

of a rusty Ford Escort, pretending to listen to an insider's account of what he might expect to find in next year's International Panel on Climate Change report. Now the driver's line of gaze had to deviate a whole ninety degrees from the road to engage with his passenger, sometimes for seconds on end, during which time, by Beard's calculation, they had travelled several hundred metres. You don't have to look at me to talk to me, he wanted to say, as he watched the traffic ahead, trying to predict the moment when he might seize the wheel. But even Beard found it difficult to criticise a man who was giving him a lift, his host in effect. Rather die or spend a life as a morose quadriplegic than be impolite.

After outlining what he expected to read next year in the third IPCC report, Aldous told Beard—and was the fiftieth person to do so in the past twelve months—that the last ten years of the twentieth century had been the warmest ten, or was it nine, on record. Then he was musing on climate sensitivity, the temperature rise associated with a doubling of CO_2 above pre-industrial levels. As they entered London proper, it was radiative forcing, and after that the familiar litany of shrinking glaciers, encroaching deserts, dissolving coral reefs, disrupted ocean currents, rising sea levels, disappearing this and that, on and on, while Beard sank into a gloom of in-attention, not because the *planet* was in peril—that moronic word again—but because someone was telling him it was with such enthusiasm. This was what he disliked about political people—injustice and calamity animated them, it was their milk, their lifeblood, it *pleasured* them.

So climate change was consuming Tom Aldous. Did he have other subjects? Yes, he did. He was concerned about the emissions from his car and had found an engineer in Dagenham who was going to help him convert it to run on electricity. The drive train was good, the problem was the battery—he would need to recharge it every thirty miles. He would just about make it into work if he travelled no faster than eighteen mph. Finally, Beard forced Aldous into the human arena by asking him where he lived. In a studio flat at the bottom of his uncle's garden in Hampstead. Each weekend he drove to Swaffham to visit his father, who was ill with a lung infection. The mother was long dead.

The story of the mother was about to begin as they pulled up outside the house. Beard was interrupting to speak his thanks, keen to bring the encounter to an end, but Aldous was out of the car and hurrying round to open the passenger's door and help him out.

'I can manage, I can manage,' Beard said testily, but with the recent weight-gain, he almost could not, the wretched car was so low-slung. Aldous accompanied him up the path, again in psychiatric-nurse style, and when they were at the front door and Beard was reaching for his key, asked if he might use the lavatory. How to refuse? Just as they stepped into the house he remembered that it was Patrice's afternoon off, and there she was, at the head of the stairs, in rakish blue eyepatch, tight jeans, pale green cashmere sweater, Turkish slippers, coming down to meet them with pleasant smiles and the offer of coffee as soon as her husband had made the introductions.

For twenty minutes they sat at the kitchen table, and she was kind, she cocked her head sweetly as she listened to the story of Tom Aldous's mother and asked sympathetic questions, and told the story of her own mother, who also died young. Then the conversation lightened, and her eyes met Beard's whenever she laughed, she included him, she listened with a half-smile when he spoke, appeared amused when he made a joke, and at one point touched his hand to interrupt him. Tom Aldous was suddenly blessed with expressiveness and humour, and made them laugh with an account of his father, a formidable history teacher, now a cantankerous invalid, who fed his hospital lunch to a ravenous red kite. Aldous kept turning away and grinning, and self-consciously running his hand up his neck to touch his ponytail. At no point did he remember that the planet was in peril.

And so the married couple harmoniously entertained the merry young man, and by the time he stood to leave it was clear that something wondrous had happened, there had been a fundamental shift in Patrice's attitude towards her husband. After seeing Aldous to his car, Beard, not daring to believe that his plan, summoning a woman on the stairs with his bare hands, had actually worked, hurried back into the house to learn more. But the kitchen was deserted, the cups with their dregs were still in place on the table, the house was quiet again. Patrice had retreated to her room, and when he went up and tapped on her door she told him plainly to go away. She had only wished to torment him with a glimpse of the life they once had. It was her absence she wanted him to savour.

He did not catch sight of her until the following evening, as she left the house, leaving behind a trail of unfamiliar scent.

* * *

The weeks passed and little changed. The autumn term began at Patrice's primary school. In the early evenings she marked work and prepared classes, and three or four times a week left the house around seven or eight to be at Tarpin's. When the clocks went back in late October and she went up the garden path in darkness, her absence was all the more complete. Nothing came of her intention to have her lover round to dinner, at least, not while Beard was in the house. Occasional meetings took him out of town for the night, and when he returned he saw no sign of Tarpin's presence, unless it was in the deeper sheen of the oak dining-room table or the neatness of the kitchen, with every pot and pan unusually stowed.

But in early November he went into the walk-in larder at the rear of the house, near the back door, in search of a light bulb. It was a cold and windowless room with brick-and-stone shelves where various household hardware and junk and unwanted presents had spilled into the space intended for provisions. On the far wall was a single ventilation slot which showed pinpricks of daylight, and directly underneath, on the floor, was a dirty canvas bag. He stood over it, letting his outrage grow, and then, noticing that the top was undone, parted it with his foot. He saw tools—different-sized hammers, bolsters and heavy-duty screwdrivers and, lying right on top, a chocolate-bar wrapper, a brown apple core, a comb and, to his disgust, a crumpled used paper tissue. The bag could not have been left behind when Tarpin was working on the bathroom, for that was many months back and Beard knew he would have seen it. It was clear enough. While he was in Paris or Edinburgh, the builder had come straight from work to see Patrice, had forgotten his tools the next morning, or did not need them, and she had stowed them in here. He wanted to throw them out immediately, but the handles of the bag were black and greasy, and Beard felt revulsion at touching anything of Tarpin's. He found the bulb and went into the kitchen to pour himself a scotch. It was three in the afternoon.

Early the next day, a cold Sunday, he found Rodney Tarpin's address on an invoice and, after deciding not to shave and drinking three cups of strong coffee, and pulling on a pair of old leather boots that added an inch to his height and a thick woollen shirt that put muscle on his upper arms, he drove towards Cricklewood. On the radio, exclusively American affairs. Commentators were still picking over last month's bombing of the warship USS *Cole* by a group called al-Qaeda, but the main item was the same old thing, it had run all summer and autumn and was wearing on his patience. Bush versus Gore. Beard was not an American citizen, he had no vote in this fight, and still was obliged by the news service, for which he was compelled to pay a fee, to attend to every bland development. He was aggressively apolitical—to the fingertips, he liked to say. He disliked the overheated non-arguments, the efforts each side made to misunderstand and misrepresent the other, the amnesia that spooled behind each 'issue' as it arose. To Beard, the United States was the fascinating entity that owned three quarters of the world's science. The rest was froth and, in this case, a struggle within an elite—the privileged son of a former president jostling with the high-born son of a senator. With the polls long closed, it seemed, Gore had phoned Bush to retract his concession of defeat, Florida was too close to call, there would be an automatic recount—'Circumstances have changed since I first called you' was the understatement Al Gore had used.

In office, both men would be bound by the same constraints, both pinned down by the same facts, by advisors from the same graduate colleges, schooled in like-minded orthodoxies—Beard had little interest in the detail. It could make no significant difference to the world at large, was his considered opinion as he rolled through Swiss Cottage, if Bush rather than Gore, Tweedledum rather than Tweedledee, was president for the first four or eight years of the twenty-first century.

The previous afternoon and evening with the scotch had bequeathed a reckless clarity, as well as a pleasant sensation of invincibility. Now he saw that he had been taking matters too seriously. Unfaithful wife? Then get another! Cricklewood had a hung-over, pacified look with few pedestrians about, and the Sunday-morning tranquillity reminded him that his mission was simply to appease his curiosity. He had a right to know where Patrice spent half her week and how his adversary lived. A mile further on, through a sequence of side turns, Tarpin's road turned out to be a four-lane urban motorway a mile long, connecting two arterial routes, a provisional, accidental place where the houses, pre-war semis, had an embattled, windswept look. He parked in a lay-by right outside the drive and stared at the place he had seen in the photograph, at the slats of dark-stained pine bolted to the front elevations to create a sixteenth-century look, at the motor boat slumped uncomfortably on its trailer—it could have been a rowing boat hiding under the wind-shredded plastic cover—at the coach lamp on a black post by the front door, which was in the Georgian style, and, a bold recent addition, lying on its side on the concrete, surrounded by neatly weeded beds, a red phone box. Between the near-black timbers, the house was painted brilliant white, the floral curtains behind the leaded panes were trimly ruched and drawn open.

Beard had no strong views on interior or exterior design, no prejudices against garden coach lamps and the like, and the attempt to give a nineteen-thirties suburban house an Elizabethan appearance seemed to him innocently patriotic. If he had not loathed Rodney Tarpin, he would have thought that the place suggested decency, hard work, simple-minded optimism. He knew from conversations way back that Mrs Tarpin had left last year with the three children and was living with a Welsh quantity surveyor on the Costa Brava, so there was some pathos too in the way Rodney was keeping the place up. But this was where Patrice came regularly to be fucked, and every detail, even the little wishing well and the posse of dwarfs clustered by its handle, seemed hostile. He hated them in return. Was Tarpin going to erect the phone box in Patrice's honour? He could hear her pretending to like it. *Darling, that's so original, so creative* . . . Enough! He got out of the car.

Because his wife had been up this way so many times before him, and because he had once been Tarpin's employer, Beard felt entitled and at ease as he went up the drive. From one of the black gloss-painted down-pipes came the tinkle of falling water, and from the drain at its base steam rose into the November air. The master of the house was at his ablutions, rinsing from his body the DNA of Mrs Beard. The front door with its Palladian portico had an unused look, so Beard followed a narrow concrete path squeezed between the house and a wooden boundary fence that led to a side door and continued through an open gate into the back garden. He remembered Tarpin boasting of a hot tub and he wanted to see. She may or may not have been in it, but he was in the mood to be thorough, he needed to know everything.

A treeless patch of unmown lawn was separated on three sides from the neighbours by a chain-link fence just beyond which a pylon stood astride the cluttered land that lay between the houses, and he could hear the homely crackle of the power lines. Electrons—so durable, so fundamental. He had spent much of his youth thinking about them. At the age of twenty-one he had read in wonder the Dirac Equation of 1928 in its full form, predicting the spin of an electron. A thing of pure beauty, that equation, one of the greatest intellectual feats ever performed, correctly demanding of nature the existence of antiparticles and placing before the young reader the wide horizons of the 'Dirac sea'.

That was when he was a scientist, and now he was a bureaucrat and never thought about electrons. In the mid nineties he had stood with a small crowd in Westminster Abbey while Stephen Hawking delivered a speech in front of the memorial carved in stone, the exquisitely succinct form of the equation—$i\gamma.\delta\psi = m\psi$—and Beard had, for the final time, felt a stirring of the old excitement. All gone now.

Closer to the house was a square of hard standing where a rusting clothes tree stood, and bits of a fridge, and stacked white plastic garden furniture, and there it was, right by the stack, a large hardwood box, eight feet by eight, with padlocked lid supporting a coil of black hosepipe. He was relieved that this tub was not the Californian dream he had unconsciously assumed—no sequoias, no cicadas, no Sierra Nevada. But when he walked back towards the side door he remained unhappy, for now it was confirmed—it could only be the sex. What else would bring her to this dingy patch? But then, in his condition, was it not unhappiness that he was looking for?

At that thought he heard a sound above him and, looking up, saw on the first floor a steamed-up steel-framed window swing open, then Rodney Tarpin's pink, wet face.

'Oi!'

Abruptly, the face disappeared, and the window remained open, allowing shower steam to billow out, and from inside the house came a muffled sound of bare feet pounding at speed down carpeted stairs. As Beard waited by the side door, arms folded against his chest, he had no plan, he had no idea what he wanted to say. He had spent too much time brooding, waiting, and now he wanted something to happen. It hardly mattered what it was.

Two bolts were drawn back, the aluminium handle shot down, the door flew inwards and his wife's lover stood before him on the threshold.

Beard thought it important to speak first. 'Mr Tarpin. Good morning.'

'What the fuck do you want?' The stress in his query was on the 'you'. He wore a not very large red towel tucked around his considerable waist. Water droplets trickled from his head onto his shoulders and meandered down through his chest hair in the zigzag movements of a pinball.

'I thought I'd come and have a look round.'

'Oh yeah? So you just walk in here.'

'My wife does.'

Tarpin seemed put out at the directness of this reference, as though he thought it unfair, or going a little too far. Still faintly steaming, he stepped out onto the path, apparently oblivious to the cold—two degrees centigrade, according to the digital display in the car. Beard was standing seven or eight feet back, arms still crossed, five feet six in his boots, and did not give way when Tarpin planted himself right in front of him. Even barefoot, he was a big fellow, certainly strong above the waist, but thin-shanked below it—a builder's build—and also flabby across the chest, recent fat smeared over muscle, with a beer and junk-food gut whose lateral extension far exceeded Beard's own. That towel was hanging by a thread. What was Patrice doing with such a man if not seeking the perfection, the ideal, of her husband's form? Tarpin's face was a curiosity. It had a ratty look, not entirely without charm, but it was too small for the head. A small man's whiskery, inquisitive features had been sunk or projected onto a space they could not fill. Tarpin peeped out from his own skull as though he was wearing an outsized chador. Since Beard had last seen him, the builder had lost a tooth, an upper incisor. Beard was disappointed not to see a tattoo, a snake or motorbike or hymn to his mum. But the physicist, as he fleetingly acknowledged, was an ageing bourgeois in the grip of stereotypical thinking. Tarpin was too old for a body piercing, but sitting right on the skyline of his shoulder, protruding a good half-inch, was a growth of twisted skin, a tag, that resembled a miniature human ear, or a sailor's minuscule parrot. A few turns of tightly tied dental floss and it would be gone in a week, but perhaps women were touched by such a flaw, by such vulnerability in so large a man with his own business and three employees. Patrice's tongue would surely have explored its tiny folds.

Tarpin said, 'What I do with your wife is my business,' and he laughed at his own joke. 'And you can fuck off out of it.'

Beard was stalled for a moment, for it was not a bad line, and in this hiatus it occurred to him that what he wanted, no, *intended* to do, any second now, was to kick Tarpin's bare shin very hard, hard enough to break a bone. The prospect thrilled him and made his heart beat faster. He could not remember if it was these boots or some others thrown out long ago that had the steel tips. It did not matter. How odd, that the man he had once irrationally half-despised as an intruder into his domestic peace, with his drills, tuneless whistling and unbounded dust-creation, and puerile station jabbering on a tinny radio all afternoon, this hireling was now his adversary in equal combat. Only Beard would have considered it equal. Over many years, his colleagues had noted, and sometimes despaired, that in confrontations—theoretical physics naturally had its share—Beard possessed the gift, or curse, of recklessness.

'You hit my wife,' he said, his voice constricted by his racing pulse.

He had already glanced down and seen the angled plane of Tarpin's shin, white, flecked with sparse black hairs like an ill-plucked turkey. And now Beard, something of a sportsman in his day, despite his height, was shifting his weight onto his left foot. He would remember to spread his arms for balance, and if there was time enough he might half turn and crush a toe beneath his heel.

It did not occur to him how obvious it was that he was about to attack. His rounded chest heaved plainly, his thin arms were raised and tensed, and his face was strained, lost in the solipsism of an exciting plan. It was likely that Tarpin had been in many scraps as an adult. Before Beard could duck, Tarpin had drawn back his arm and lashed the older man's right cheek and ear with an open-handed smack. Beard's consciousness exploded behind his eyes, and for seconds afterwards the world was a humming white blank. When it seeped back, Tarpin was still there, clutching at his towel, which had loosened with the movement.

'The next one'll hurt,' he said.

This was the kind of treatment old-fashioned

movie heroes used on the woman they loved, to calm them. The builder regarded Beard as unworthy of a proper punch. But clearly, more was on the way. Fortunately, at that moment there came from next door the sound of children's voices approaching up the path, and whispered exclamations and suppressed giggles at the sight of their near-naked tubby neighbour. Then three shy faces at different heights and three pairs of wide brown eyes peered over the fence. Tarpin hurried into the house. He might have gone to fetch a larger towel, or a coat, and it seemed to Beard a good moment to be on his way. But he had his pride and was careful not to appear in a hurry. As he walked down the drive, past the boat slewed in its cradle and the recumbent phone box, he felt his face stinging and burning in the cold—that slap really *hurt*—and there was a continuous sound in his ear, an electronic whine, and by the time he reached his car he was giddy and half deaf. As he started the engine he looked across at the house and, sure enough, Tarpin in tracksuit and trainers with flailing laces was coming towards him with a firm stride. Beard saw no good reason to linger in Cricklewood.

* * *

In the remaining three weeks of that year, everything began to change. There arrived an invitation to the North Pole—at least, that was how he described it to himself and everyone else. In fact, the destination was well below the eightieth parallel, and he would be staying on a 'well-appointed, toastily-heated vessel of richly-carpeted oak-panelled corridors with tasselled wall lamps', so a brochure promised, on a ship that would be placidly frozen into a semi-remote fjord, a long snowmobile ride north of Longyearbyen on the island of Spitsbergen. The three hardships would be the size of his cabin, limited email opportunities, and a wine list confined to a North African *vin de pays*. The party would comprise twenty artists and scientists concerned with climate change, and conveniently, just ten miles away, was a dramatically retreating glacier whose sheer blue cliffs regularly calved mansion-sized blocks of ice onto the shore of the fjord. An Italian chef of 'international renown' would be in attendance, and predatory polar bears would be shot if necessary by a guide with a high-calibre rifle. There were no lecturing duties—Beard's presence would be sufficient—and the foundation would bear all his expenses, while the guilty discharge of carbon dioxide from twenty return flights and snowmobile rides and sixty hot meals a day served in polar conditions would be offset by planting three thousand trees in Venezuela as soon as a site could be identified and local officials bribed.

Word soon got round the Centre that he was going to the North Pole to 'see global warming for himself', and some said he would be towed by dogs and others that he would be pulling his own sledge. Even Beard was embarrassed, and let it be known that it was 'unlikely' that he would get all the way to the Pole, and a good part of his time would be 'in camp'. Jock Braby was amazed by Beard's commitment to the cause and offered to arrange a send-off party in the common room.

In the same week as the North Pole summons he

began an affair with a not-so-young accountant he had met on a train and asked out to dinner. She was pleasantly dull, worked for a fertiliser corporation, and it was all over in three weeks. Crucially, however, the edge of his obsession with his wife was blunted—minimally, and not all the time, but he knew he had crossed a line. It saddened him, to know that he would soon stop desiring her altogether, for it gave him a view of the obvious truth, that it was already over and that the comfortable house and their possessions would have to be divvied up, and after a year or two he might never see her again. Visiting Tarpin had also helped initiate his disaffection. How could he continue to love a woman who wanted a man like that? Why punish herself so thoroughly just to insult her husband?

What else did he not know about her? One answer came just before Christmas, in a long-delayed conversation that became an understated row of cold finality. She had known for half a year that his mathematician from Humboldt, Suzanne Reuben, was barely a tenth of the story. Patrice had most of the rest of the truth and, pacing and despoiling the sitting-room floorboards in her stilettos, enumerated tersely the names, places and approximate dates, a dossier memorised with an obsessiveness that matched his own. The cheerfulness she had shown around the house, she said, was to conceal her wretchedness, the affair with Tarpin was supposed to save her from humiliation. She demanded to know how Beard was going to explain away eleven affairs in five years. He was about to remind her of his mother, who ran up a higher score, when Patrice left the room. She had come to talk, not to listen. Here it was at last, the confrontation he had been wanting all these months. Now he could not think why. He lay on the sofa, legs propped on the glass coffee table, closed his eyes and felt the first longings for the cold pure air of the treeless Arctic.

In late February he arranged to leave from the Centre for Heathrow, and so the farewell party in the communal room took place while his taxi stood outside, and his bag stuffed with his old skiing clothes waited by the door. Sixty-one people were now employed full-time, and most of them crowded in to hear Jock Braby's speech, for this was more than a send-off, it was a celebration of the shining steel object mounted on two crates in the middle of the room, a prototype designed and constructed in record time, ready to be tested in the Farnborough wind tunnels, Tom Aldous's quadruple-helix wind turbine. Many noted how it resembled in more intricate form Crick and Watson's model without the base pairs, and some tried to remember and adapt Rosalind Franklin's famous remark that it was too beautiful not to be true, or, in this case, not to work. In his speech, Braby reminded the team that it was too early for congratulations, there was far more work to be done, but he wanted everyone to see just how far the project had progressed, and how revolutionary it would be. With uncustomary lyricism, he summoned an image of a townscape, as seen from a nearby hill, and five thousand roofs glittering in the setting sun with the gyrations of their silver turbines, far more beautiful, he thought, than the TV aerials that had transformed the urban prospect in the nineteen fifties.

Throughout, Tom Aldous kept himself well to the back of the crowd and appeared to be avoiding Beard, which was fine since both men knew the project was doomed and collusion in the fact would have been in poor taste when everyone was so happy. Braby now turned to Beard and wished him well on an eight-week journey he knew would have its hazards and hardships. He reminded the team that the climate models had predicted that the earliest and most radical signs of planetary warming would be observed in the Arctic, and said how proud he was that it was the Centre's own Chief—many fond chuckles at that word—who was going to brave the harshest conditions in order to see for himself.

Then Beard stepped forward to say a few words. He had no idea how Braby had got hold of the idea that he was going away for eight weeks. His trip was for six nights, but it was hardly appropriate to contradict a colleague in public. Nor did he mention the toasty ship and the tasselled lamps, but instead confessed to being proud and excited to be associated with an institution that was bound for 'great things'—he would not allow himself to be more specific—and predicted that one day their Centre would outstrip its American rival in Golden, Colorado. A toast, a round of applause, a quick succession of handshakes and backslaps, and Beard was moving towards his taxi, with Jock Braby himself carrying his suitcase, and as the car pulled away the ponytails whooped and pounded on the roof, but Aldous was not among them.

* * *

For all the hours he spent on journeys, he was not a well-adapted traveller, not because he was chaotic or fearful, but because long journeys always brought him up against a certain mental deficiency, an emptiness, a restless boredom that was, he thought, as he buckled himself into his seat, the expression of his true state, habitually obscured by the daily round or by sleep. He was not able to read seriously on an airplane. Even on firm ground he never read full-length books all the way through. He was one of those travellers who stare out the window, regardless of the view, or at the seat in front of him, or flip backwards through an in-flight magazine. At best he read popular science magazines like the *Scientific American* he had now, to keep himself up to date, in layman's terms, with physics generally. But even then his concentration was marred, for a lifetime's habit made him inconveniently watchful for his own name. He saw it as if in bold. It could leap out at him from an unread double page of small print, and sometimes he could sense it coming before the page-turn. Another distraction was an overdeveloped awareness of the precise location in the aisle of the drinks trolley, of that muffled clinking sound and its asymptotic approach. And with or without a drink, he was prone at altitude to meandering sexual fantasies or memories, or a mix of both.

But with the cheers of his colleagues still resonating, Beard was doing his best, as his plane set its northward course, to be serious and settle down to read in his magazine a luridly illustrated article about photons and antimatter, and sure enough, within five minutes experienced that cool little leap of the heart when he saw in parenthesis the entire cue—the Beard–Einstein Conflation. Not the Bose–Einstein Condensate, not the Einstein–Podolsky–Rosen Paradox, not pure Einstein, but the genuine article, and in his simple joy he longed all the harder for the trolley, still two and a half metres distant. He was well aware of the singularity by which the tiny vehicle of his talent, a child's tricycle say, had hitched a ride behind the juggernaut of a world-historical genius. Einstein had upended mankind's understanding of light, gravity, space, time, matter and energy, founded modern cosmology, spoken out on democracy, on God or his absence, argued for the Bomb, then against it, played the violin, sailed boats, had children, given his Prize money to his first wife, invented a fridge. Beard had nothing beyond his Conflation, or his half of it. Like a shipwrecked man, he had clung to this single plank, and counted himself privileged. How had it come about? Perhaps it was true that the Committee, angrily divided between three front-runners, had settled for its fourth choice. However Beard's name had slipped through, it was generally felt that it was the turn of British physics anyway, though, in certain senior common rooms, some muttered that the Committee in its compromise had confused Michael Beard with Sir Michael Bird, the gifted amateur pianist who worked on neutron spectroscopy.

Those ungenerous rumours aside, what a brief state of grace, those blessed months of frenetic calculation and revision in the old rectory on the South Downs, trapped in a soundscape formed by the complaints of his first wife, Maisie, and the incessant wailing of the lodgers' identical babies. What a feat of concentration! So long ago, so hard to recall the driven kind of person he once was or the actual texture of those days. It sometimes seemed to Beard that he had coasted all his life on an obscure young man's work, a far cleverer and more devoted theoretical physicist than he could ever hope to be. He had to acknowledge the fact—that twenty-one-year-old physicist was a genius. But where was he now? Was he really the same Michael Beard whose paper caused Richard Feynman to explode with excitement and interrupt the proceedings of the 1972 Solvay Conference? Did anyone still remember or care about that famous Solvay 'magic moment'? As for those shrieking twins, he had seen for himself last year, at the wedding of one or the other, that they were now overweight coves in their thirties, a dentist and a hedge-fund manager, identically pompous. As old as the Conflation.

After drinks and lunch and more drinks, he allowed the magazine to slide from his lap and, gazing at the button that held in place the headrest cover of the seat in front (he did not have a window seat), fell into familiar reveries and took it as a sign of burgeoning mental health that Patrice was not his sole topic. He had been sent biographical notes and pictures of his fellow guests on the frozen fjord and been struck by the smile of a certain conceptual artist whose name, Stella Polkinghorne, was familiar, even to him. Her most recent media storm involved an accusation of an infringement of copyright that had never come to court. She had constructed for the Tate Modern a scaled-up Monopoly set on a playing field in

Catford, each side of the painted board a hundred metres long, a space one could stroll about in, with near-life-sized houses on Park Lane and the Old Kent Road, accommodation one could enter to observe an unequal distribution of wealth. In the empty homes of the Mayfair rich, tapestries, woodcuts by Dürer and discarded champagne bottles, while down the Old Kent Road, among the East End poor, junk-food wrappers, discarded syringes, a TV playing soaps. The dice were two metres high, the Community Chest cards were lowered in place by crane, the dog-eared banknotes made of plywood were in tottering 25-metre piles on the grass. In all, an indictment, it was supposed, of a money-obsessed culture. *Do Not Pass Go* was celebrated, reviled, photographed from the air by passengers on their descent into Heathrow. Children liked stampeding across the board in herds and crawling inside the top-hat token. The makers of the game began a legal case, which they dropped in the face of public derision and rising sales. A local-business association on the Old Kent Road also brought a case, or said it would, and nothing was heard.

Polkinghorne's disembodied smile presided over Beard's melancholic reflections on the end of his marriage. He experienced a genial blend of sadness, anger, nostalgia (those early months were bliss), and a warm, self-forgiving sense of failure. And repetition. Five was enough. He would never go through this again, and with that thought came the familiar recognition of his new freedom. When matters were settled, he would buy a small London flat, he would be responsible only for himself, he would guard ferociously his independence and cure himself of this strange lifelong habit of marriage. It was lovers he needed, not wives.

Passively, he let himself be processed through Oslo, then Trondheim. The flight to Longyearbyen was delayed by two and a half hours, during which he sat in a plastic moulded chair and read the *Herald Tribune* with total concentration and no recall. It was three in the morning when his taxi stopped by giant mounds of snow outside his hotel. He had not eaten in hours. Dressed in sweater, anorak and long johns, he lay in bed, hemmed in on three sides by chunky wooden beams, and ate all the salted snacks in the minibar, and then all the sugary snacks, and when he was woken by reception at eight the following morning to be told that everyone was waiting for him downstairs, the wrapper of a Mars bar was still folded in his fist.

His immediate need was to satisfy his thirst, but the water from the tap on his basin was so intensely cold, so fiery on the lips and he drank so deeply that he developed shooting pains in his face and temples that had not receded by the time he descended with his luggage, still dazed from lack of sleep, to the lobby to meet his group—already breakfasted, already boisterous, already zipping themselves into their special-issue snowmobile suits. In the lobby's dim solar-powered light and the press of overdressed bodies he did not catch sight of Stella Polkinghorne. Yes, it came back to him now, the manic larkiness of the English in large groups. From different corners of the crowded space came abrupt shouts of individual laughter and cackles in unison. And it was eight twenty in the morning. Forcing a smile, pretending gamely not to be oppressed, he shook many hands, was told many names and remembered no one because his thoughts were on the coffee he was too late for. How could he start his day? The urn was empty, the breakfast table was being cleared away by a girl who did not speak English, did not even understand the planetary word 'coffee', even when pronounced loudly, and now one of the organisers, a great elk of a man called Jan, was telling him it was too late for coffee and was guiding him towards his very own pile of outer clothing and saying he must hurry, a snowstorm was expected within two hours and the group needed to get going.

The place was emptying, and he was not ready. Someone very old with snow in his beard and a damp, unlit cigarette on his lower lip came in muttering ill-temperedly, snatched Beard's bag, took it out to a sledge hitched to a snowmobile and drove off. Both the waitress and Jan had disappeared, and Beard was the only person in the lobby. This was a long-forgotten experience from his schooldays, not only being late, but feeling ignorant and incompetent and wretched, with everyone else mysteriously in the know, as though in league against him. Fatso Beard, always last, useless at team games. With that memory came added clumsiness and indecision. Although he was dressed in ski clothes of many layers, he was expected to climb inside this extra skin, even to wear his own boots inside another pair. There were inner gloves and giant outer gloves, a heavy balaclava made of carpet underlay to wear over his own, and goggles, and a motorcycle helmet.

He got into the suit—it must have weighed twenty pounds—put on the dusty balaclava, squeezed his head into the helmet, put on the inner and outer gloves, then realised that he would not be able to put on the goggles while wearing the gloves, took off the gloves, clamped on the goggles, put on the inner and outer gloves, then remembered that his own ski goggles and gloves, hip flask and stick of lipsalve on the seat next to him would need to be stowed. He took off the inner and outer gloves, put his stuff in a pocket inside his jacket after much struggling with the zip of the outer suit, put on the inner and outer gloves again and found that in the damp warm air of the lobby, and with his own impatient perspiring, his goggles were fogging up. Hot and tired, an unpleasant combination, he stood suddenly in exasperation, turned and collided with a beam or a column, he couldn't see which, with a massive cracking sound. How fortunate it was that the Nobel laureate was wearing a helmet. No damage to his skull, but there was now a diagonal crack across the left eyepiece of his goggles, an almost straight line that refracted and diffused the low yellow light in the lobby. To remove the helmet, balaclava and goggles and wipe the condensation from them he had to remove all four gloves, and now that his hands were sweating these items were not so easy to dislodge. Once the goggles were off, it was straightforward enough to bring them to the almost-cleared breakfast table and take a crumpled paper napkin, used, but not much used, to polish the lens. Perhaps it was butter, perhaps it was porridge or marmalade that smeared the already scratched plastic, but at least the condensation was off, and it was relatively simple, after replacing the balaclava, to secure the goggles around the helmet and lower it over his head and put on all four gloves and stand, ready at last to face the elements.

His vision was much restricted by the new breakfast coating, otherwise he would have seen the boots earlier lying on their sides under his chair. Off with the gloves then—he was not going to lose his temper—and then, after some fiddling with the laces, he decided he would see better without the goggles. Clear sight confirmed that the boots were far too small, by at least three sizes, and there was some relief in knowing that not all the incompetence was his own. But he was game, and thought he would give it one last try, and that was how Jan, entering the lobby with a blast of icy air, found him, trying to push his foot in its hiking boot into a fur-lined snow shoe.

'My God, you thick or which?'

The giant elk man kneeled before him and with impatient tugs removed his hiking boots, tied the laces together and slung the pair around Beard's neck.

'Now try.'

His feet slid in, Jan secured the laces at speed and stood.

'Come on, man. Let's go!'

Possibly it was his embarrassment that helped fog up the goggles again, but he had a pretty good idea of the direction of the door, and he had the rough outline of Jan's shoulder to guide him.

'You drive a snowmobile before?'

'Of course,' he lied.

'Good good. I want to catch the others.'

'How far is it to the ship?'

'One hundred fifteen kilometres.'

When they stepped out, the wind slapped his face, no less hard than Tarpin had, and with the same stinging aftermath. The condensation inside his goggles froze instantly but for a small patch, through the marmalade veneer of which he could just make out Jan's form retreating along a path cut through the deep snow that wound between the shapes of buildings. After ten minutes they arrived at the edge of the settlement before a vast white plain that stretched away into a mist. It may have been an airfield, for there was an orange windsock nearby straining in the horizontal position. Parked by a ditch were two snowmobiles, noisily pumping out a blue-black mist of their own.

'I follow you,' Jan said. 'Minimum fifty kilometres an hour if we want to arrive before the storm. OK?'

'OK.'

But it was not OK. The wind was strong and they would be driving straight into it. Deep inside his helmet, the tips of his ears were already numb, and so were the tip of his nose and his toes. To see he was obliged to tilt his head and angle his sightline through a diminishing area of semi-clarity, avoiding at the same time the illuminated crack over his left eye. But all this was incidental, blindness and pain he could live with. A more urgent problem was oppressing him as he turned towards his snowmobile. In his hurry and thickheadedness that morning, he had omitted all the usual routines. He had not shaved or washed and, except to drink a pint of freezing water, had not set foot inside the bathroom. Then he had hurried out of the room with his bag. Now it was minus twenty-six, wind force five, they were pressed for time, a storm was looming, Jan was already astride his machine and gunning the engine, and Beard, trapped inside many layers of intractable clothing, needed to urinate.

As best he could, he looked about him. The nearest houses were four hundred metres away, and showed great blank walls with one or two miniature windows—bathroom windows surely. Oh to be there, in a heated tiled room, barefoot in his pyjamas, taking a leisurely piss before crawling back under the duvet for one extra hour. But he could go right here, in the ditch, turn his back to the wind, remove his gloves, grapple bare-fingered with the frozen chunky zip of his one-piece snowmobile suit, grope under his jacket to reach the shoulder buckles of his salopettes and somehow push them down, burrow past sweater, shirt, long silk undershirt, long johns, underpants, to gain at last the moment of the release he dared not think about. No, it was too difficult, it would have to wait, and besides, he felt better as soon as he was sitting down in the saddle of his snowmobile.

It was an underpowered motorbike on skids and easy enough to drive. One twist of the throttle on the right handlebar and the thing slid forward with the shriek of an overworked engine and a puff of stinking black exhaust. Within seconds he was bouncing across the plain, following through the sight holes of his goggles the tracks left by the rest of the group, which were mercifully side-lit by the rising sun. The wind, suddenly a sixty-mile-an-hour gale, cut through his layers, his nostril hairs stiffened into steel pins, his teeth, all his teeth, ached, his face felt peeled raw. By a miracle of osmosis, every breath he exhaled found its way inside his goggles and froze, and within ten minutes he could see nothing at all but blurry crystals and had to stop. Jan pulled alongside. Surprisingly, he was sympathetic.

'This you do.'

He raised a flap of flimsy tin casing and wedged the goggles over the engine. They were on a tongue of land, some three hundred metres wide, that ran between two lakes, or perhaps it was a bay, perhaps the sea was close by. Beard was too cold to ask. The endless snow was orange in the morning sunlight, their track ahead led straight towards a low mountain range many miles off, and hovering over it, or behind it, was a long tube of black cloud. He would have stepped away to relieve himself while they waited, but now the wind was even harsher, and perhaps his need was not really so pressing. It was incredible, he thought, no, it was criminal, that the citizens of Spitsbergen should think it reasonable to go about in this climate on a kind of motorbike, when some kind of humanely enclosed vehicle with a heater, a proper windscreen, a seat with a backrest—a car!—might save a life or two. His moment of indignation briefly diverted him and it was only when he was back in the saddle, wearing his de-iced goggles, and driving once more into a roar of fiery air, that he realised he had arrived at a point when he must make an immediate choice: stop and piss now, or allow his bladder to rupture, which would cause him to die of an internal infection, or drench himself and freeze to death. But he kept going. He guessed there remained a hundred kilometres to cover, he was doing forty kilometres an hour. Two and a half hours. Clearly impossible.

But still he did not stop. He distracted himself by attempting to recall the last occasion he had urinated. Surely it was at Longyearbyen airport, while he waited for his luggage, late at night, the day before yesterday. Thirty-five hours without a piss. Had he simply forgotten? Was he really that busy?

The moment he understood that it was the cold that had confused him and made him add the extra day, he stopped, and in his eagerness half fell off the snowmobile onto the track. He heard Jan's machine bump into the rear of his, but he did not look back as he hurried away. It was a different kind of terrain they were on now. Their route made a shallow S through a gully enclosed on each side by thirty-foot walls of rock and ice. A vestigial sense of propriety drew him to the base of one wall, as though to a urinal, where he stood doubled up, with his back to the wind, and used his teeth to pull off the outer glove on his right hand. He heard Jan call out to him, but could not bear to be spoken to now. Biting at the end of each finger in turn, he worked the glove lining off. Immediately, his hand became numb and slow. It took him more than two minutes to unfasten the zip of his snowmobile suit, and then he found that he needed two hands to get through his jacket to the shoulder releases of his salopettes, so he pulled off the gloves on his left hand with his slow-moving right. Once more, his goggles were misting up and freezing over. But he had to admire his own calm, as he delved and tugged through the layers, as his precious body warmth bled out into the vicious cold and the wind whipped round his back, into the cliff and onto his face. Only in the final seconds, when his clumsy pink hand, as cold as a stranger's, reached into his underpants, did he think he might lose control. But at last, with a joyous shout that was lost to the gale, he directed his stream against the ice wall.

His mistake was to wait a few seconds at the end, as men of his age tended to do, mindful that there might be more. He should have turned his head to hear what Jan had shouted. Or perhaps he could only have avoided the inevitable if he had accepted one of the other invitations, to the Seychelles or Johannesburg or San Diego, or if, as he thought later with some bitterness, climate change, radical warming above the Arctic Circle, was actually taking place and was not a figment of the activist imagination. For when his business was done he discovered that his penis had attached itself to the zip of his snowmobile suit, had frozen in hard along its length, the way only living flesh can do on sub-zero metal. He wasted precious seconds, gazing at his situation in shock. When at last he pulled tentatively, he experienced intense pain. And he was already in pain from the cold.

He remained standing with his legs apart, facing the rock wall. He did not dare do as one might with a sticking plaster, and rip himself away in one stroke. He had read of an American hiking alone in the wilderness who got his arm trapped behind a rock and sawed through his own elbow with a penknife. Beard was not that kind of dedicated person, and after all, an elbow, a forearm, a hand were one of a pair and, to an extent, disposable. As the polar wind raged against the cliff-face and rebounded against his shivering form, he watched in horror as his penis shrank even smaller, and curled tighter against the zip. And not only was it shrinking before his eyes, but it was turning white. Not the white of a blank page, but the sparkling silver of a Christmas bauble.

He was close to panicking, but could not bring himself to call for help. It was additionally difficult not to panic with his head smothered by carpet underlay and a thick helmet and goggles with diminishing visibility. For want of anything else to do, he covered himself with a cupped hand, a hand like a block of ice. He was beginning to feel sluggish, even sleepy, the way people are supposed to be in extreme cold, and his thoughts lurched in slow motion. He saw Jock Braby on TV proclaim an obituary through a forgiving smile. *He went to see global warming for himself*. Nonsense, of course he would survive. But this was it, a life without a penis. How his ex-wives, especially Patrice, would enjoy themselves. But he would tell no one. He would live quietly with his secret. He would live in a monastery, do good works, visit the poor. As he stood dithering, he wondered for the first time in his adult life whether there might be purposeful design in human lives, and entities like Greek gods, imposing ironies, extracting revenge, imposing their rough justice.

But the rationalist in Michael Beard died hard. There was a problem, and he should attempt to solve it. He was reaching lugubriously into the inside pocket of his jacket. In his post-doc years he had worked for a while in low-temperature physics, but even as a schoolboy, as Fatso Beard, bad at games, a swot at science, he knew the basics. Pure ethanol froze at minus one hundred and fourteen degrees, everyone knew that. Brandy at eighty per cent proof would be forty per cent ethanol by volume, giving a freezing point of . . . minus forty-five point six. At last, the hip flask was in his hand, the top came off after only a brief struggle, and generously he poured his libation and within seconds he was free.

When he put it away, his unfortunate cock was as hard as ice, but no longer white. It was also stinging, an excruciating hot-needle pain that slowed his efforts to get dressed. After ten minutes, in one piece at last, he turned and stumbled back onto the track and found his guide waiting.

'Sorry about that. Call of nature.'

Jan caught hold of his elbow. 'You in bad shape, man. Look, you dropped your boots off your neck. We go both on my bike. We gonna pick up your machine later.'

He let himself be guided to Jan's snowmobile and it was there that the calamity finally happened. As he raised a leg to hoist himself onto his place behind the guide, he felt, and even thought he heard, a terrible rending pain in his groin, a cracking and a parting, like a birth, like a glacier calving. He gave a shout, and Jan turned to steady him and settle him in place.

'It's one hour, is all. You'll be OK.'

Something cold and hard had dropped from Beard's groin and fallen down inside the leg of his longjohns and was now lodged just above his kneecap. He put his hand between his legs and there was nothing. He put his hand on his knee and the hideous object, less than two inches long, was stiff like a bone. It did not feel, or it no longer felt, like a part of himself. Jan kick-started the engine and they set off at a crazy speed, careening over ice ridges as hard as concrete, swerving round near-vertical banks like reckless adepts in a velodrome. Why was he not at home in bed? Beard cowered out of the wind behind Jan's broad back. The burning sensation in his groin was spreading, his cock had slipped round and was nestling under the crook of his knee, and they were speeding in the wrong direction, hurtling northwards towards the Pole, deeper into the wilderness, into the frozen dark, when they should have been rushing towards a well-lit emergency room in Longyearbyen. Surely, the intense cold would work to his advantage, keeping the organ alive. But microsurgery? In Longyearbyen, population fifteen hundred? Beard thought he was about to be sick, but instead he slipped his hands through the belt at the back of Jan's jacket and let his head drop onto his protector's spine and fell into a doze, and it was only the sudden silencing of the snowmobile's motor that woke him, and he saw looming above him out of the ice the dark hull of the ship where he would spend the week.

* * *

It turned out that Beard was the only scientist among a committed band of artists. The entire world and all its follies, one of which was to warm up the planet, was to their south, which seemed to be in every direction. Before dinner that night in the mess room, the convenor, Barry Pickett, a benign and wizened fellow, who had rowed across the Atlantic single-handed before he devoted his life to recording the music of nature (the rustling of leaves, the crashing of waves), addressed the gathering of the Eighty Degrees North Seminar.

'We are a social species,' he began, with the kind of biological flourish that Beard generally distrusted, 'and we cannot survive without some basic rules. Up here, in these conditions, they are even more important. The first concerns the boot room.'

It was simple enough. Below the wheelhouse was a cramped, underlit changing room. All coming on board must stop there and remove and hang up their outer layers. On no account was wet, snowy or iced-up clothing to be brought into the living quarters. Prohibited items included helmets, goggles, balaclavas, gloves, boots, wet socks and snowmobile suits. Wet, snowy, icy or dry, they were to remain in the boot room. Penalty for infringement was certain death. There was forgiving laughter from the good-natured artists, pink-faced, sensible folk in chunky sweaters and work shirts. Beard, squashed in a corner with his fifth glass of Libyan *vin de pays*, dosed up on painkillers and in pain, constitutionally hostile to groups, feigned a smile. He did not like to be part of a group, but he did not want the group to know. There were other rules and housekeeping items, and his attention was drifting. From behind Pickett, from the galley on the other side of an oak-veneered wall, came the smell of frying meat and garlic, and the sounds of spoons against saucepans and the hectoring growl of the international chef chivvying an underling. Hard to ignore the kitchen when it was already eight twenty and there had been nothing to eat for hours. Not being able to eat when he chose was one of the freedoms Beard had left behind in the foolish south.

All day the sun had stood barely five degrees above the horizon, and at two thirty, as though giving up on a bad job, it had sunk. Beard witnessed the moment through a porthole by his bunk, where he lay in agony. He saw the flat snowy vastness of the fjord turn blue, then black. How could he have imagined that being indoors eighteen hours a day with twenty others in a cramped space was a portal to liberty? On arrival, as he passed through the mess room on his way to find his quarters, the first thing he had seen, propped in a corner, was an acoustic guitar, surely awaiting its strummer and a tyrannous sing-along. A large section of bookcase was taken up with board games, and ancient packs of cards. He might as well have checked into an old people's home. Monopoly was surely among the games, and here was reason for further regret. Jan had helped him off the snowmobile, half carried him up the gangplank, and shown him into the boot room. Moving slowly, with grunts and moans, Beard had set about removing his outer layers, unzipping his snowmobile suit, terrified of what he was about to discover. In the deep gloom of the place it took a while to find an unoccupied station to hang his stuff on, and as he did, on hook number twenty-eight, he heard a pleasant, deep female voice behind him saying kindly,

'This just dropped out the bottom of your trousers.'

He turned. It was Stella Polkinghorne holding out something thin and grey. It was actually in her hand, between her forefinger and thumb.

'I think it's your lipsalve.'

She said her name, he said his, they shook hands. She said she was deeply honoured to meet a great scientist, and he said that he was a long-time admirer of her work. It was only at this point that they released their hands. It was not exactly a beautiful face, but broad and friendly, with blonde hair straggling out from under a woollen cap. He liked the way her curious gaze met his. A broken front tooth gave her a reckless, humorous look. She said she was looking forward to getting to know him, and he said he felt the same about her, and then she hesitated, apparently not wanting to leave and unable to think of something else to say, and nor could he, distracted as he was by pain.

Then she said, 'I'll see you then,' and she went through into the ship.

All afternoon he lay on his bunk in a haze of foolish schemes and regrets, examining and re-examining the damage to his skin, making plans for his immediate departure, and replaying his encounter. He could send an email urgently recalling himself to England. But he could not face the snowmobile journey back to the airport. A helicopter would have to come from Longyearbyen. How much did they cost? A thousand pounds an hour perhaps. Three hours then, worth every penny, to avoid singing 'Ten Green Bottles'. Looking forward to getting to know him. That could mean anything. No, it meant only one thing. And what luck—he had seen from a schedule on a noticeboard that he was the only guest not sharing a cabin. But he was out of commission, possibly for weeks. He took another look. His injury resembled a scalding, he was swollen and pink, he needed to be alone, he wanted to go home, he should try and sit next to her at dinner tonight. But he would not be here. The helicopter was coming. But it would not fly at night. There were other kinds of sex they could have, or that she could have. What would be the point of that? Perhaps he was getting better. He took another peek.

Finally it had been hunger and the need for a drink that drove him from his cabin. After Pickett's speech, Beard was not able to move out of his corner in time to sit next to Stella Polkinghorne and instead found himself wedged between the bulkhead and a famous ice sculptor from Mallorca called Jesus, an elderly man with a mournful face and curved yellowish-white moustache who smelled richly of cigars, and had a wheezing, honking sound in his voice like a teddy bear's growl. After they had introduced themselves, Beard suggested that such a profession might be difficult to pursue in the Balearics. Jesus explained that back in the old days, the ice houses in the mountains kept the fishmongers of Palma supplied with giant blocks of ice in summer, and this was how his grandfather learned the skills he passed on to his son, who passed them on to his. Jesus had won many ice-carving competitions in cities around the world—a recent triumph was in Riyadh—and his speciality was penguins. He imported whisky when he was not carving, had four sons and five daughters, and had founded twenty years ago a school for blind children outside the port of Andratx. His wife and two of the sons ran his olive and vineyard estate in the Tramuntana, high on the sea cliffs fifteen kilometres south of Pollensa, not so far from the famous Cova de ses Bruixes, the Witches Cave. Beard's pain was lifting, the painkillers had a strong euphoric effect. He had never enjoyed anything quite so good as the steak, French fries, green salad and red wine before him. And Jesus—he had never met anyone with this name, even though he knew it was common in Spain—seemed to him the most interesting man he had met in years.

In reply to the reciprocal question, Beard said he was a theoretical physicist. It always sounded like a lie. The sculptor paused, perhaps to rehearse mentally his English, then asked a surprising question. Señor Beard was to excuse an uneducated man's naïvety and ignorance, but was the strange reality described by quantum mechanics a description of the actual world, or was it simply a system that happened to work? Infected by the Mallorcan's courtly style, Beard complimented him on the question. He could not have phrased it better himself, for there was no better interrogation of quantum theory than this. It was a matter that had dominated years of Einstein's life and led him to insist that the theory was correct but incomplete. Intuitively, he just could not accept that there was no reality without an observer, or that this reality was defined by the observer, as Bohr and the rest seemed to be saying. In Einstein's memorable phrase, there was out there a 'real factual situation'. 'When a mouse observes,' he had once asked, 'does that change the state of the universe?' Quantum mechanics seemed to imply that a measurement of the state of one particle could instantaneously determine the state of another, even if it was far away. But this was 'spiritualistic' in Einstein's view, it was 'spooky action at a distance', for nothing could move faster than the speed of light. Beard the realist was sympathetic to Einstein's extended, failing battle with the brilliant coterie of quantum pioneers, but it had to be faced: the experimental proof suggested that there really could be long-range spooky correlations, and that the texture of reality at the small and large scale really did defy common sense. Einstein was also convinced that the mathematics needed to describe the universe would ultimately be shown to be elegant and relatively simple. But even in his lifetime, two new fundamental forces had been found, and ever since, the view had been complicated by a messy array of new particles and antiparticles, as well as various imaginary dimensions and all kinds of untidy accommodations. But Beard still clung to the hope that as yet more was revealed, a genius would arise to propose an overarching theory binding all in a formulation of astounding beauty. After many years (this was his little joke as he placed a confiding hand on Jesus's frail arm), he had finally given up hopes of being the mortal chosen to find this grail.

He said all this over the rising din of twenty climate-change artists settling down to the wine as the plates were cleared away. Jesus failed or refused to detect the self-irony and pronounced solemnly, turning his sad, drooping face to gaze about the crowded quarters, that it was a mistake to abandon hope at any stage of life. All his best penguins, the ones truest to life and most expressive of pure form, had been carved in the last two years, and recently he had started on polar bears, creatures much threatened by rising temperatures and, at one time, well beyond the reach of his artistic powers. In his humble view, it was important never to lose faith in the possibility of profound inner change. Clearly, a scientist like Señor Beard should strive for this theory, for this beauty, for what was life without the highest ambitions?

How could Beard confide to Jesus that he had done no serious science in years, and that he did not believe in profound inner change? Only slow inner and outer decay. He was returning the conversation to the safer ground of penguin as compared to polar-bear ice carving, but as he did so he felt his spirits sinking back. The painkillers were wearing off, the wine, this same wine, now tasted thin and sharp, the cheerfulness around him was reminding him that his marriage was over. He felt weary, and too cynical for the company. His liveliness in conversation was revealed as a fake, a product of shock, drugs and drink.

He brought the conversation to an end and said goodnight to Jesus and, muttering apologies, squeezed along the packed rows to the aisle. All the conversations he passed through were of art and climate change. At the next table a choreographer, a woman he had not seen before, sleek and beautiful and brimming with goodwill, was describing through a French accent a geometric dance she had planned to take place on the ice. He could not stand it, the optimism was crushing him. Everyone but Beard was worried about global warming and was merry, and he was uniquely morose. He cared only for darkness and silence.

He lay a long while on his bunk in the airless cabin, kept awake by the throbbing in his groin—his heartbeat seemed to have migrated down there—and listening to voices and laughter, and wondering if his misanthropy would last all week. The helicopter idea he now saw was absurd. Coming away from his life in remote Belsize Park to this lifeless wilderness had confronted him with the idiocy of his existence. Patrice, Tarpin, the Centre and all the other pseudo-work he did to mask his irrelevance. What was life without the highest ambitions? The answer was exactly this, another night of unmemorable insomnia.

Two hours later he was on the edge of sleep when there came the sound of the guitar being tuned and he groaned and turned angrily on his side. But it was not strumming and singing he heard through the woodwork, but a tenderly played melody that sounded Spanish, reflective, with a touch of lightness and precision, like something of Mozart's. In the morning he would learn that it was a study by Fernando Sor. Lying in total darkness on his narrow bed he did not doubt that it was Jesus who played, as if to him, and it was to this melancholy air that at last he fell asleep.

*   *   *

It was late in the morning, the sun was up and shining heroically at a slant across the brilliant fjord, while Beard moved effortfully through the dimness of the boot room, trying to find his stuff. He was standing opposite peg number eighteen, on which, the day before, he knew this for a fact, he had hung his snowmobile suit. Directly below the peg was a wire basket where he had stowed his goggles, helmet and smaller items, and below that, under a slatted bench, was the compartment in which he had placed his boots. Even from down here, directly beneath the wheelhouse, he could hear the roar of many snowmobiles—getting them started in the morning was, apparently, an ordeal. A party of six, plus Jan armed with a rifle, was about to set off up the fjord to investigate the glacier. Five and the guide were already out on the ice, stamping their feet and flapping their arms to keep warm, and Beard as always was last. Someone had taken his gear, or some of it. His suit was not on its peg, his wire basket had been shoved along to position nineteen, only his boots—if they were his boots—were in the correct position. His undesirable cracked goggles were lying on the floor.

He took a suit—it was probably his anyway—from peg seventeen. It turned out to be at least two sizes too big, but once it was on he was not inclined to remove it. The boots, however, were a size too small. Among the smaller items in the basket only a glove liner was missing, and he made it up by taking a spare liner from number twenty-three, and promised himself to return it. The crack in his goggles no longer troubled him. He stepped out on deck to ironic applause from the group waiting below on the ice and, wanting to get in the spirit of group life, he made a bow. Even in his hurry, he had time to take in the scene from the top of the shallow ramp of the gangplank. There were many figures scattered on the ice around the ship. The helmets transformed the proportions of their heads, the snowmobile suits swelled their rumps, so that from a distance they resembled infants in a nursery playground. The choreographer and three friends were marking out her geometric dance; two figures were building what looked like a snowman or a statue; a lone person, probably Pickett, was rigging a microphone between two cones of ice; a person with a chainsaw was helping another, surely Jesus, load four ice blocks onto a sledge; someone was kneeling to polish a lens of ice a metre across. Another figure was going about in circles with a red flag and a whistle for the benefit of a movie camera on a tripod.

He had amazed himself by volunteering so soon for another snowmobile ride. Claustrophobia had driven him out, and the tawny light across the fjord as seen from the mess windows, and the fact that it was not permitted to go anywhere without a guide and his gun. He sat astride the last machine and the group set off in single file across the ice in an easterly direction, deeper into the fjord. It should have been fun, to be skimming down a wide corridor of ice and snow, with mountains rising sheer on both sides. But once again, the wind cut through every layer, the cracked goggles fogged up and froze within minutes and Beard could make out no more than a greyish blob of the machine in front. He was directly in the wash of six exhausts. For ten kilometres Jan kept up a wild speed. Where the winds had stripped the snow away, the surface of the fjord was like ridged iron and the snowmobiles rattled and bucked.

Twenty minutes later they were standing in sudden silence a hundred metres from the glacier's terminus, a broken blue wall that stretched for fifteen kilometres across the valley. The impression was of a ruined city, grubby and dissolute, with rubble, broken towers and giant fissures. At minus twenty-eight, it was too cold today, Jan explained, for displays of ice shearing away in the cause of polar warming. They passed an hour taking photographs and walking up and down. Then someone saw a print in the snow. They huddled round it, and stepped back to allow their guide, whose rifle was over his shoulder, to display his expertise. A polar bear's print, of course, and very new. The snow was thin where they stood, and it was not easy to find another impression. Jan used his binoculars to scan the horizon.

'Ah,' he said quietly. 'I think we leave now.'

He pointed and at first they saw nothing. But when it moved, it was clear enough. At a distance of a mile or so, a bear was ambling towards them.

'He's hungry,' Jan said forgivingly. 'Time for skidoos.'

Even with the prospect of being eaten alive, dignity prevailed and they only half ran to the machines. As he reached his, Beard knew what to expect. Everything about this trip had conspired to reduce him. Why would his luck change now? He pushed the button. Nothing. Fine. So let his sinews be stripped from his bones. He tried again, then again. Around him, clouds of blue smoke, and high-pitched roars, the proper expression at last of full-throated panic. Already, half the party was shooting away in the direction of the ship. It was every-man-for-himself. Beard wasted no energy cursing. He pulled out the choke lever, though he knew it was a mistake, for the engine was still warm. He tried again. And again, nothing. He smelled petrol. He had flooded the engine and he deserved to die. Now all the others had gone, along with the guide, whose dereliction of duty Beard resolved to report to Pickett, or the King of Norway. His agitation was steaming up his goggles, and, as usual, the steam froze. Pointless then, to look back, but he did it all the same, and saw frozen steam fringed with a glimpse of the fjord's ice. It was reasonable to assume the bear was still coming, but he had clearly underestimated its speed over the ground, because at that moment his shoulder was struck a heavy blow.

Rather than turn and have his face ripped away, he hunched his shoulders in expectation of the worst. His last thought—that in his carelessly unchanged will he had left everything to Patrice for Tarpin's use—would have been a dismal one, but what he heard was the guide's voice.

'Let me do it.'

The Nobel laureate had been pressing the headlight switch. The machine came to life at first touch.

'Go,' Jan said. 'I'm behind you.'

Despite the danger he was in, Beard glanced back again, hoping to catch sight, for anecdote's sake, of the animal he was about to outpace. In the narrow perimeter of semi-clarity that surrounded the goggle's frozen fog patch there was movement, but it may have been the guide's hand or a corner of his own balaclava. In the account he would give for the rest of his life, the one that became his true memory, a polar bear with open jaws was twenty metres distant and running at him when his snowmobile started forward, not because, or not only because, he was a liar, but because he instinctively knew it was wrong to dishonour a good story.

Racing away across the rackety ice, he gave out a whoop of joy that was lost to the icy hurricane in his face. How liberating to discover in the modern age that he, a city-dweller, an indoors man who lived by the keyboard and screen, could be tracked and ravaged and be an entire meal, a source of nourishment to others.

Perhaps that was the best moment of his week. They were back at their base within minutes, it seemed. Already, at one forty-five, there was a deeper chill in the air, and orange evening light illuminated the few artists who had not yet retreated into the ship. His groin was so tender that he waited until the others had gone inside, then he walked backwards up the gangplank. It hurt less that way. He paused in the entrance of the boot room, waiting for his eyes to adjust to the poor light, and soon it was clear enough—someone had hung all his stuff at Beard's station. In a constructive spirit, he removed the lot, boots and all, to a vacant spot in a corner. When he took off his woollen balaclava, it slipped to the floor with a clunk and seemed to stare up at him in open-mouthed disbelief. What was he doing here? He put his gear away, then he went to the mess room, said a round of hellos to the half-dozen people there, and took a hot drink to his cabin and lay on the bunk.

It was an accident of cartography that placed the South Pole under the North, but he could not dispel the impression that he was near the top of the world and that everybody else, Patrice included, was below him. He had an overview then, and they became a feature of his week, these afternoons in the Arctic dusk, when he reminded himself over the cocoa that his life was about to empty out and that he must begin again, take himself in hand, lose weight, get fit, live in a simple, organised style. And get serious at last about work, though he had no idea what work he could do that was not detached from or eased by his peculiar fame. Must he give forever the same lecture series about his one small contribution, sit on committees, be a Presence? He had no answers, but the musing was comforting and often he fell asleep in the darkness of three o'clock and woke hungry, with renewed appetite for the *vin de pays*.

After his deliverance from the jaws of a polar bear, he did nothing adventurous all week. Bolder types went off with a guide to hike in the mountains, or make a snow cave, or explored on snowmobiles a steep valley that rose through rocky outcrops on the far side of the fjord. Each day he spent two or three hours outside the ship, pottering about with the others. He was taken on as an assistant, holding an end of a piece of string, cutting blocks of ice for Jesus, helping with Pickett's microphones, joining in the dance. This involved being filmed walking in single file at a measured pace behind a dozen others for two hundred yards in a straight line, before making a right-angled turn and walking the same distance before the next turn. It was soothing, he was content to think of nothing and be told what to do. In a warmer climate, with better health, he might have tried his chances with the choreographer, slender Elodie, from Montpellier, especially if she had come away without her husband, a bullet-headed photographer who had once played rugby for France. Stella Polkinghorne also had a husband—the convenor, Barry Pickett.

Beard's life, then, was simplified. Caring little for art or climate change, and even less for art about climate change, he kept his thoughts to himself and was affable, and was surprised to find himself faintly popular. His mind emptied as he went about the ice on his errands. One lunchtime he carried out from the ship cups of tomato soup, which froze as he reached the bottom of the gangplank. They were incorporated into a sculpture. His spirits rose, or ceased to sink. He thought about his fitness again. Only ten or twelve years before, he had played a plausible game of tennis, compensating for his height with a vicious, stabbing little forehand volley at the net. And he had once skied with near competence. Eight years ago he could still touch his toes. Surely, it was not inevitable that he should get heavier by the month until he dropped dead? He arranged to take a daily hike on the fjord, a two-mile circuit around the ship, escorted by Jan carrying a gun. After the second excursion, lying on his bunk in the afternoon with aching legs, he made a mental list of the food he would no longer touch. He was fifteen pounds overweight. Act now, or die early. He swore off all the usual things—dairy produce, red meat, fried food, cakes, salted nuts. And crisps, for which he had a particular weakness. There were other items, but he was asleep before the list was complete. During the last three days of his stay he kept to the new regime.

From the second day, the disorder in the boot

room was noticeable, even to Beard. He suspected that he never wore the same boots on consecutive days. Even though he wrapped his goggles (these ones were undamaged) in his inner balaclava on the third day, they were gone by the fourth, and the balaclava was on the floor, soaking up water. That morning he saw several snowmobile suits, also on the floor. They had a trampled appearance, and he decided, without looking too closely, that none could be his. Pickett admitted to him, while they were out recording the sound of the wind in the ship's rigging, that for two days he had been wearing two left boots. But he was a hardy sort who did not seem to mind. Beard did mind. He was not a communally-spirited person, but there were certain decencies he took for granted—in himself, and therefore in others. He always put his stuff on and below the same peg, number seventeen, and was disappointed to note that others had trouble observing such simple procedures. Gloves were a particular problem, for it was impossible to go outside without them. As a precaution, he stuffed his inside his boots, along with the glove liners. The next day the boots were gone.

He liked the evenings. By the time they started gathering in the mess room before dinner, it had been dark for five hours. There was two hours' drinking before the first course. The wine was from a neglected region of Libya. He generally started on the white, drank the red until he sickened and returned to the white, and there was generally enough time to switch back before bedtime. After dinner, there was, of course, only one topic. Mostly, Beard listened. Never before had he encountered idealists in such concentration and he was by turns intrigued, embarrassed, constrained. When Pickett asked him on the third night to talk about his work, he stood up to speak. He described the Centre and the quadruple-helix rooftop wind turbine, plausibly claiming it as his own initiative. It was a revolutionary design, he told the room, and he made a sketch to be passed around. It would cut household bills by eighty-five per cent, a saving that would be the equivalent of building—not quite drunk, he summoned a number—*twenty-three* medium-sized power stations. There were respectful questions, and he answered them judiciously, lucidly. He was among scientific illiterates and could have said anything. There was an impassioned statement of support from Stella Polkinghorne. She said that Beard was the only one here doing something 'real', at which the whole room warmed to him and applauded loudly. He had never cared much what others thought, but now—how lowering—he was touched and could not conceal it, to be, for just a few minutes, the darling of the ship.

Otherwise, he listened and drank. After two or three glasses of the white, the red went down painlessly, like water, at least at first. There were themes—some were canonic and chased each other crazily, others were fugal and ran concurrently, as disappointment did with bitterness: the century had ended and climate change remained a marginal concern, Bush had torn up Clinton's modest proposals, the United States would turn its back on Kyoto, Blair showed no grip on the subject, the long-ago hopes of Rio were lost. Canonically pursuing then overtaking disappointment was alarm. The Gulf Stream would vanish, Europeans would freeze to death in their beds, the Amazon would be a desert, some continents would catch fire, others would drown, and by 2085 the Arctic summer ice would be gone and the polar bears with it. Beard had heard these predictions before and believed none of them. And if he had, he would not have been alarmed. A childless man of a certain age at the end of his fifth marriage could afford a touch of nihilism. The earth could do without Patrice and Michael Beard. And if it shrugged off all the other humans, the biosphere would soldier on, and in a mere ten million years teem with strange new forms, perhaps none of them clever in an apeish way. Then who would regret that no one remembered Shakespeare, Bach, Einstein, or the Beard–Einstein Conflation?

While dark and even greater cold enveloped the ship in the lonely frozen fjord, and the brave yellow gleam from its portholes was the only light, the only sign of life for a hundred miles across the crackling icy wastes, other themes flourished symphonically: what was to be done, what treaties were to be made between the quarrelsome nations, what concessions, what gifts should the rich world self-interestedly make to the poor? In the mess room's humid after-dinner warmth, it seemed to the owners of full stomachs sealed with wine that it was only reason that could prevail against short-term interests and greed, only rationality could draw, by way of warning, the indistinct cartoon of a calamitous future in which all must bake, shiver or drown.

The statehood-and-treaty talk was worldly in

comparison with another leitmotiv that summoned a cooling measure of austere plainsong, a puritanical air from the old conservation days, distrustful of technological fixes, determined that what was required was a different way of life for everyone, a lighter tread on the precious filigree of ecosystems, a near-religious regard for new rules of human fulfilment in order to flourish beyond supermarkets, airports, concrete, traffic, even power stations—a minority view, but heard with guilty respect by all who had steered a stinking snowmobile across the pristine land.

Listening, as he usually did, with Jesus at his side from their corner of the mess room, Beard interjected only once, on the last evening when a gangling novelist called Meredith, appearing to forget there was a physicist present, said that Heisenberg's Uncertainty Principle, which stipulated that the more one knew of a particle's position, the less one knew of its velocity, and vice versa, encapsulated for our time the loss of a 'moral compass', the difficulty of absolute judgements. Beard was peevish in his interruption. It was worthwhile to be correct, he told this crop-haired fellow with rimless glasses. What was at issue was not velocity but momentum, in other words, mass times velocity. At such hair-splitting there were muted groans. Beard said that the principle had no application to the moral sphere. On the contrary, quantum mechanics was a superb predictor of the statistical probability of physical states. The novelist blushed but would not give way. Did he not know who he was talking to? Fine, yes, OK, statistical probability, he insisted, but that was not certainty. And Beard, just finishing his eighth glass of wine and feeling nose and upper lip elevate in contempt for an ignorant trespasser on his field, said loudly that the principle was not incompatible with knowing precisely the state of, say, a photon, so long as one could observe it repeatedly. The analogy in the moral sphere might be to re-examine a moral problem a number of times before arriving at a conclusion. But this was the point—Heisenberg's Principle would only have application if the sum of right plus wrong divided by the square root of two had any meaning.

The silence in the room was not so much stunned as embarrassed. Meredith stared helplessly as Beard brought his fist down hard on the table. 'So come on. Tell me. Let's hear you apply Heisenberg to ethics. Right plus wrong over the square root of two. What the hell does it mean? Nothing!'

Barry Pickett intervened to move the discussion on.

That was an isolated discordant note. What was memorable and surprising came every evening, usually late on, in the bright tones of a marching brass band, or the sound of massed voices in unison, elated in common purpose and obliterating for a while all disappointment, all bitterness. Beard would not have believed it possible that he would be in a room drinking with so many seized by the same particular assumption, that it was art in its highest forms, poetry, sculpture, dance, abstract music, conceptual art, that would lift climate change as a subject, gild it, palpate it, reveal all the horror and lost beauty and awesome threat, and inspire the public to take thought, take action, or demand it of others. He sat in silent wonder. Idealism was so alien to his nature that he could not raise an objection. He was in new territory, among a friendly tribe of exotics. Those sentinel snowmen guarding the foot of the gangplank, the recorded sound of the wind moaning through the rigging, the disc of polished ice that refracted the day-long setting sun, Jesus's penguins, thirty of them, and three polar bears, marching along the ice beyond the ship's bow, the harsh, impenetrable fragment of a novel punctuated with expletives that Meredith read, or shouted, aloud one evening—all these demonstrations, like prayers, like totem-pole dances, were fashioned to deflect the course of a catastrophe.

Such was the music and magic of ship-bound climate-change talk. Meanwhile, on the other side of the wall he had learned to call a bulkhead, the boot room continued to deteriorate. By midweek four helmets were missing along with three of the heavy snowmobile suits and many smaller items. It was no longer possible for more than two thirds of the company to be outside at the same time. To go out was to steal. The state of the boot room, the gathering entropy, became a subject of Barry Pickett's evening announcements. And Beard, oblivious to his own vital role, his generous assistance in setting the initial conditions, could not help reflecting expansively on this post-lapsarian state. Four days ago the room had started out in orderly condition, with all gear hanging on or stowed below the numbered pegs. Finite resources, equally shared, in the golden age of not so long ago. Now it was a ruin. Even harder to impose order once the room was strewn with backpacks and stuff-bags and supermarket plastic bags half filled with extra gloves and scarves and chocolate bars. No one, he thought, admiring his own generosity, had behaved badly, everyone, in the immediate circumstances, wanting to get out on the ice, had been entirely rational in 'discovering' their missing balaclava or glove in an unexpected spot. It was perverse or cynical of him to take pleasure in the thought, but he could not help himself. How were they to save the earth—assuming it needed saving, which he doubted—when it was so much larger than the boot room?

On the last morning they ate their breakfast to the din of the entire snowmobile fleet warming up outside. They went out onto the ice, many of them missing pieces of their equipment. Beard was without a helmet. While he waited for the signal to leave, he warmed his goggles on the engine, and wound a scarf round his head. The low orange sun was unhindered, there would be a useful tailwind, and it looked like the journey back to Longyearbyen might even be pleasant, if one were fully clothed. There was a shout from the deck. Between them, Barry Pickett and one of the crew were manhandling down the gangplank a huge plastic and fibre sack of the sort that builders use to store sand in. Lost property. They gathered around the treasure and poked about in it. Beard found a helmet that fitted and knew it must be his. No one was ashamed, or even faintly embarrassed. Here was their stuff. Where had it been hiding all this time?

They said their goodbyes to the crew, and set off in loud and poisonous single file across the fjord towards Longyearbyen, keeping to a stately twenty-five kilometres per hour to avoid the cutting headwind. Hunched low over his machine, trying to draw a little of its heat onto his face, Beard found himself in a mellow state—an unfamiliar cast of mind for the morning. He was not even hung-over. On the frozen shores of the fjord they slowed to walking pace to navigate deep ruts, trenches, in the ice. He could not remember them from the outward journey. But of course, he had been asleep behind Jan's back. Then they were on a long straight snowy track, passing a hut where, the guides had told them, a great eccentric once lived a lonely life.

If, Beard thought, he ever travelled by spaceship to another galaxy, he would soon be fatally homesick for these, his brothers and sisters up ahead of him, for everyone, ex-wives included. He was suffused with the pleasant illusion of liking people. Entirely forgivable, all of them. And somewhat co-operative, somewhat selfish, sometimes cruel, above all, funny. The snowmobiles were passing through the narrow, high-sided gully, scene of his shame, a moment best buried. He preferred to recall his cool escape from a murderous bear. But yes, he felt unusually warm towards humankind. He even thought that it could warm to him. Everyone, all of us, individually facing oblivion, as a matter of course, and no one complaining much. As a species, not the best imaginable, but certainly the best, no, the most interesting there was. But what about the general disgrace that was the boot room? Evidently, a matter of human nature. And how were we ever going to learn about that? Science of course was fine, and who knew, art was too, but perhaps self-knowledge was beside the point. Boot rooms needed good systems so that flawed creatures could use them properly. Leave nothing, Beard decided, to science or art, or idealism. Only good laws would save the boot room. And citizens who respected the law.

These fondly forgiving and self-forgiving thoughts sustained him until they reached the hotel for lunch. How long ago, it seemed, since they had been there. They handed over their snowmobile suits and the rest, said their goodbyes to Jan, and within the hour they were on their plane to Trondheim. Beard was booked with a different airline for the onward flight to Oslo. The others had four hours to wait. In the confines of the small airport, they seemed reluctant to leave each other's company. They took over the bar and soon started up their music again, the songs, the laments of global calamity, over lunchtime beers and hotdogs. This was where Beard went to find them to say goodbye. He passed twenty minutes in email swaps and embraces. Stella Polkinghorne kissed him on the lips, Jesus gave him his business card. There was a loud hurrah as Beard was leaving the bar. In all, he was reminded that by way of running undemanding errands on the ice and pretending to care about wind turbines, he had attained a degree of unfamiliar popularity. Even the spindly novelist had clasped him to his narrow chest. Beard was still smiling to himself thirty minutes later as his twin-propeller plane bounced down the freezing runway and banked southwards to return him to the mess he had almost managed to forget.

* * *

He stayed overnight in Oslo, changed his reservation to a 6 a.m. flight and was three hours early into Heathrow. As his plane made its approach over Windsor Park it was raining heavily, the dawn sky was greenish-black, all headlights were on along the feed-in roads. Outside the terminal building, in the airport taxi queue, he learned there was a traffic pile-up and ten-mile tailback on the M4, so he went back inside, descended the levels and took the train to Paddington and a cab from there. By the time he arrived outside his house the rain had stopped and was dripping heavily from the blackened branches of the pavement rowan trees. As his taxi pulled away, he stood by his garden gate with his luggage and looked about him, marvelling that among such densely crowded buildings at ten on a weekday morning, there was no one to be seen, not even the sound of a voice or a radio. Belsize Park appeared as empty of life as the Arctic. And there was his home, his very own box of miseries, neat, early Victorian, of grey London brick, with stone mullions on the downstairs windows, and standing on its own patch of wintry garden with its one bare birch and, to the side, an ancient apple tree. Not many London houses had a hundred feet of front garden, and a path of flaking brick in herringbone pattern making a shallow curve to the front door, and mossy brick walls marking the boundaries. Architecturally, it was superior to all his other marital homes, and now it would have to be sold, the contents dispersed, its two owners likewise, not because they habitually disliked each other, though she might loathe him now, but because he had had eleven affairs in five years and she had only one.

An uneven score, and they must live and suffer by unspoken rules.

The front gate made its usual squeak, more of a valedictory quacking sound, as he pushed it open. He was sad, but he was no longer in anguish. That pleasant woman on the train whose name he could no longer recall, the visit to Tarpin's, his chaste interlude on the eightieth parallel (he was almost completely healed) were new layers of a protective coating. However minimally, he was a different man. He was full of regrets, he was sorry that he did not know the trick of making Patrice love him, but he was resigned. He was going indoors to make a start on dismantling the stage set of his marriage. His intention was to begin packing that day. During the dark afternoons on the frozen-in ship, he had had time to reflect, and planned to take only personal belongings. She could have the rest, the sofas, rugs, paintings, knives and forks, and if she could persuade her father, a merchant banker, to buy out his half-share, she could have the house as well. Beard would make the disengagement as painless and efficient as he could. For all he cared, she could set up with Tarpin. No shortage of space on the tussocky front lawn for a boat, lamp post and phone box.

The wheels of his luggage made a plaintive ticking against the path. His last homecoming. He was relieved that he was early, that Patrice would not be at home to fail to greet him, to ignore his return, for this was Friday, a full teaching day, when scores of cross-legged children sang in dissonant unison to her piano in the afternoon. Such details of her existence he would soon forget, or be denied.

Arriving at the front door, and bending with effort against the newly thickened cordon of fat around his waist to rummage in his briefcase for his key, he noticed a change. The cream-painted wire basket that held milk bottles and had a dial and red arrow for indicating to the milkman the day's requirement was not in its usual place. It had been moved, or kicked, more than a foot to the right, leaving exposed a blurred rectangular mark framed in grit on the stone doorstep. Now the basket stood askew at a diagonal, showing its communicative face to the wall. He did not rearrange it. What was the point? Soon he would move into a new place—he had in mind a small, white-walled flat stripped bare of clutter, his domestic Spitsbergen, from where he would devise a new future for himself, lose weight, become agile, and steely with fresh purpose, whose nature was still unclear.

He found his key, opened the front door and, as he pulled his luggage into the hall, was aware of another difference, a slight rearrangement of the air. It was damp, or warm, or both, and scented in an unfamiliar way. More obviously, there was water on the parquet floor, a trail of outrageous wet footprints, or foot-sized puddles, leading from the bottom of the stairs towards the sitting room. Someone—Tarpin, surely, that constant creature of the bathroom—had stepped carelessly from the shower, and was treating the place like his own.

Recklessly, with no other thought than to throw the intruder out, Beard strode along the water trail and entered the room. It could not have been clearer, for there he was on the sofa, with dripping hair, wearing a dressing gown, Beard's dressing gown in black silk with a paisley pattern, a Valentine's gift from Patrice, and he was sitting upright, startled, the newspaper unfolded in his lap. But he was not Tarpin—this was the difficult adjustment, and it took Beard seconds to realign. The man on the sofa was Aldous, Tom Aldous, the post-doc, the Swan of Swaffham, the tip of whose ponytail released a droplet, which fell onto a cushion as the two men stared at each other in silence.

Beard's processes of accommodation were hindered by irrelevant questions and answers. Would he ever want to wear that dressing gown again? He thought not. What were the odds against his meeting both of Patrice's lovers in a sodden state? Extremely long. Naturally, the silence appeared to last many more seconds than it did, and it was broken at last by Aldous with a titter, a nervous whinnying sound he tried to hide behind his hand. His worst fear had been realised. There may have been a very brief moment when he thought that Beard's form in the doorway was an apparition, the paranoid consequence of an overproductive mind. Now he knew it was not. He may, in this short interlude, before either man spoke, have seen before him another more persuasive apparition—his career prospects in shreds. Theoretical physics was a village, and on its green, by the village pump, Beard still had influence. Did Aldous, the Centre's homegrown genius, think he could talk his way out of this? The hand he had used to smother his giggle reached out towards the low glass table that stood in front of the sofa. By a pile of magazines was a coffee cup—tall, in thin white porcelain, one in a set of six bought by Patrice at Henri Bendel's in New York. Aldous raised it to his lips. If the purpose was to demonstrate that he was untroubled or guiltless, the gesture was undermined by the newspaper sliding from his lap onto the floor into a face-down heap. With his eyes still on the master of the house, he took an insolent sip. Beard took a step closer.

'Put that down, man. And *stand* up.'

It was as well that Aldous obeyed, for Beard, seven or eight inches shorter, thirty years older and weak about the arms had no physical means of imposing his will. He had only the rectitude, outrage and whatever authority a cuckold could command. Hands on hips, back straight to attain his entire five feet five, he watched as Aldous struggled to his feet and hastily retied the cord of the dressing gown under which, it was briefly clear, he was naked.

'So, Mr Aldous.'

'Look,' Aldous said with a placating, downward movement of his palms, 'we can talk about this. Professor Beard, can I call you Michael?'

'No.'

'You see, we shouldn't let ourselves be forced into roles that others have written for us when . . .'

Beard took another step forward. He did not believe for a moment that there would be violence, but he did not mind giving the impression that he thought there would be. 'What are you doing in my house?'

The rural Norfolk accent, it seemed then, was well adapted to a special kind of pleading. In such tones the tenantry might once have begged their manorial lord for lower rents in hard times. 'I was going to finish this coffee, see, get dressed, tidy up and leave. I was going to double-lock the door from the outside like I was told and put the key through the letterbox. If you hadn't come back early there wouldn't have . . .'

'I said, what are you doing in my house?'

Using his palms again in a gesture of empty-handed frankness, Aldous said, 'I had dinner with Patrice and I stayed the night. Look, Professor Beard, may I be frank?'

He paused, as if he really did expect an answer. When he did not get one, he continued, 'We both value rationality. We've made careers out of it. So let's not be swept up into responses that are no longer appropriate to the situation. We both know that your marriage is over. Technically, you and Patrice are man and wife, but you're not even on speaking terms and haven't been for ages, and here you are, getting ready to play the injured party, the furious husband catching his wife's lover red-handed, when in fact you're probably thinking of moving out anyway. That's Patrice's impression, and it's certainly her wish.'

Beard waited for more.

'What I mean to say, Professor Beard—I wish you'd let me call you Michael—is that we could skip all the anger and heartache, we could be efficient about this, and we could even be friends.'

'I see.' The question he then put to Aldous came without forethought, and as he asked it, he thought it might perform useful mischief, or at the very least give him a moment to think. 'And what about Rodney Tarpin? What's happened to him?'

Aldous gave a good impression of a man pretending to be unfazed. Slowly, he retied once more the belt of Beard's dressing gown. 'I'm not afraid of Tarpin. And I've recorded two of his phone calls, and a postcard he wrote is now with the police. The man's a maniac, but at least he doesn't hide it.'

Beard said, 'He hit Patrice.'

'That was grotesque,' the young man cried out, seeing a common cause to bind the professor to him. 'How could this guy do a thing like that to such a beautiful woman?'

'And he attacked me. Hit me in the face.'

'He should be in prison.'

'At least now he'll be on your case, not mine. Are the police offering you protection?'

'Well, you know, they said they're rather busy at the moment.'

The urge to punish gave Beard a warm glow that was not unlike love. He said, 'I suppose he intends to kill you. I'd carry a knife if I were you, not that I care either way what happens to you.'

Despite Beard's efforts, Aldous did not appear intimidated by Tarpin. He said simply, 'He doesn't frighten me, Professor Beard.'

'And I suppose Patrice would have told him where you work—I mean, where you used to work.'

Instantly, the young man's cool drained away. He was the supplicant once more, a man with his job on the line.

'Oh now look, Professor Beard. You're taking this too far. Let's go back to the central point. Rationality . . .'

'Deeply irrational,' Beard said, 'to make love to the boss's wife.'

'Honestly, it goes deeper than that. I've been

stupid, I know I've got a lot to learn. But I'm talking about, about a substratum of powerful logic ...'

Beard laughed out loud. Substratum! This was like watching a chess player fight his way out of an approaching checkmate. He could remember no particular occasion, but he knew he had been in such situations himself, probably in front of an outraged wife, just when she had blown his last excuse and then, brilliantly, on a surge, he had produced a sleight of mind, a knight's move in the eleventh dimension, a dazzling projection upwards from the flat-world of the conventional game. Yes, he liked a substratum of powerful logic. He listened.

Aldous spoke breathlessly. 'Three weeks ago I overheard you saying to one of our group that you believed that apart from general relativity, the Dirac Equation was the most beautiful artefact our civilisation had ever produced. I disagree. You do yourself a disservice. There's nothing like the Conflation, nothing like this elaboration of the photovoltaics—nothing more elegant, nothing truer, Professor Beard. Everyone everywhere reveres it. But no one has thought it through from the angle of applied science, and the crisis in climate change. And I have, I've seen the potential of your work in relation to photosynthesis. The fact is, no one understands in detail how plants work, though they pretend they do. No one really understands how photons are converted to chemical energy so efficiently. Classical physics can't explain it. This talk of electron transfer is nonsense, it doesn't add up. How your average leaf transfers energy from one molecular system to another is nothing short of a miracle. But this is the point—the Conflation opens it right up. Quantum coherence is key to the efficiency, you see, with the system sampling all the energy pathways all at once. And the way nanotechnology is heading, we could copy this with the right materials, and then crack water cheaply, and store hydrogen on a domestic or industrial scale. Beautiful! But I'm nothing, I'm no one. I want to show you my ideas, and when you've looked at them, I know you'll go for it. People will listen to you. Quantum coherence in photosynthesis is nothing new, but now we know where to look and what to look at. You could steer this research, you could get a prototype funded. It's too important to let go, it's our future, the whole world's future that's at stake, and that's why we can't afford to be enemies.'

Beard had heard rather too much recently of this whole-world talk. He had never been well disposed to biology enlisting quantum mechanics to its cause. And he had an irrational prejudice against physicists who defected to biology, Schroedinger, Crick and the like, who believed that their brilliant reductionism would carry all before them. In fact, greenery in general—gardening, country rambles, protest movements, photosynthesis, salads—was not to his taste.

'How long have you been fucking my wife?'

Aldous sighed, and seemed about to object. Then his shoulders sagged and he resigned himself. 'About a month after I first met her.'

'After I introduced you.'

'That's it, Professor. You were away for the night, Birmingham or Manchester. I called in on my way home to see if there was anything Patrice needed . . .'

'And there was.'

Again, the wheedling of the rural tenant. 'Honest, Professor Beard. I had no designs on your wife. She's way out of my league. I don't even have a league. She invited me in, then she asked me to stay to dinner—and that was how it began. Later on she told me how it was all over between you, and I sort of persuaded myself that you um . . .'

'Wouldn't mind?'

He knew it already, but it angered Beard, or worse, it pained him, to hear for the second time from Patrice by way of Aldous that she thought the marriage was over. Since the late summer of last year, she had been seeing Aldous, not Tarpin. Or possibly both. The goofy post-doc turned up on her doorstep one August evening and she grabbed another chance to punish her husband.

'Has anyone ever told you how naïve you are, Aldous?'

The young man seized on the word with joy. 'I *am* naïve, Professor Beard! I do science and nothing else. I'm naïve because I don't meet people, I don't go out. I go home and work in the studio in my uncle's garden, often through till dawn. That's how I've always been. But my work is at your disposal. I've been making a file for you. For you and no one else. Please say you'll read it. This is so important.'

Until then the two men had faced each other over a distance of several feet, Aldous standing close to the sofa, with arms clasped in front of him, as if to defend himself against a possible fate or to prevent Beard's dressing gown from swinging open. Beard began to back away. He was tired of listening to Aldous, he wanted to be alone.

He said, 'Now you can leave. I'll be at the Centre tomorrow and I'll see you in Jock Braby's office at eleven.'

As Beard crossed the room, Aldous was pleading, almost shouting. 'No one will ever hire me again. You know that, don't you? This is too important for private revenge.'

As he reached the sitting-room door, Beard turned and said, 'Before you go, clear up the mess in the hall.'

'Professor Beard!'

Aldous was starting to run at him, arms outstretched, his head shaking in denial, his lips stretched across his huge teeth, and it was probably his intention to throw himself at Beard's knees and beg for mercy. He certainly would have had it, for Beard had no wish to set his domestic humiliation before Braby, and therefore the whole Centre. The Chief betrayed, made an ass of by one of the ponytails. But Aldous never reached Beard, he barely made it two metres into his run. The polar-bear rug on the polished floor was waiting for him. It came alive. As his right foot landed on the bear's back, it leaped forward, with its open mouth and yellow teeth bucking into the air. Aldous's legs flew up before him and there was a moment when his considerable length was parallel to the ground, and then his legs rose even further and, though his arms flailed instinctively downwards to break his fall, it was the back of his head that made first contact, not with the floor, not with the edge of the glass table, but with its rounded corner, bluntly penetrating the nape of his neck.

A deep, smothering silence settled on the room, and several seconds passed.

'No, no, please no,' Beard muttered as he crossed the room.

Aldous lay at full stretch on the floorboards, as though laid out by an undertaker, with only minimal space between arms and torso, eyes wide open, lips parted, the dressing gown covering him decently. Beard kneeled down by the young man's shoulder. No breathing, no pulse. There was a halo of blood under his head about nine inches across, and for some reason it did not grow larger. Then Beard saw that blood was seeping away, no, cascading down the gaps between the boards. Blood loss alone would have finished Aldous.

'Oh fuck . . . oh fuck . . .' Beard whispered to himself over and over. Something impossible had happened and he was willing it away, undoing it, reversing it, simply because it could not be. It was too improbable. But with each second the new reality advanced on him, pushed his efforts aside and settled into place. It was true. He also thought of what he should have been doing, of heart massage, of mouth-to-mouth. Like all laboratory workers, he was required to learn these techniques. But something quite still, possessing authority, not so much a voice as a presence lying safely beyond his distress, suggested that he should not touch the body.

He got up and went to the telephone. He was shivering. The stillness of Belsize Park intensified as his hand hesitated above the receiver. The same reasonable presence proposed that he think carefully before dialling. He was not a naturally indecisive man. What was wrong with him? His hand felt dead. It took him some moments to catch up with his own good sense and read the situation as others might. Here was how it looked: a man returns from abroad to find his wife's lover in the house. A confrontation follows. Twenty minutes later the lover is dead from a blow to the back of the head. He slipped, I tell you, he slipped on the rug as he ran across the room towards me. *Oh yes? And why was he running, Mr Beard?* To throw his arms around my knees and plead with me not to have him sacked, to beg me to join with him to save the world from climate change. There would be sceptics. *For the last time, Mr Beard, did you not smear blood on the corner of the table? And what have you done with the murder weapon, Mr Beard?* Innocence would come at a high cost. It would have to be earned, fought for. Media interest would be lacerating. Sex, betrayal, violence, a beautiful woman, an eminent scientist, a dead lover—perfect. Patrice, sincerely or maliciously, would be his chief accuser. Two years thinking of nothing else. Nobel laureate, balding boffin, government appointee, in the dock, fighting to stay out of jail.

At the thought he felt weak in his legs, in the tendons behind his knees, but he did not sit down. It was clear. Only those who loved him would believe him. And no one loved him. He should have had children, grown-up daughters, indignant on his behalf, busy in his defence. He walked across the room towards the hall and then came back. He did not know what to do. Then he did. He went out of the sitting room into the hall, stepped carefully over the trail of puddles and walked into the kitchen, to the drawer where tinfoil and clingfilm and greaseproof rolls were kept. Also in that drawer was a carton of transparent disposable gloves.

He drew on a pair. Nothing criminal in that, but once his hands were encased, he felt invisibility, invincibility steal over him, over his entire body. A mental state, to be sure, but what other states did he have? He did not have a plan, he simply enacted one. His body had a plan. And he walked it through, as though experimentally, believing at every stage he could undo it, go back to the beginning, with nothing lost or compromised. Everything he was doing now merely served a precautionary principle. He might return to the phone, he might summon the emergency services. But just in case he did not, he needed to be prepared. In his light-headed way, he was thinking clearly. He went through the kitchen towards the back door, and walked into the windowless vault where the light bulbs and household junk were kept. It was in exactly the same place, against the wall, the dirty canvas tool bag. He turned over the contents and found a hammer, one of several, with a narrow head that seemed about right. While rummaging, he saw other items he thought he might use. The comb, the used tissue, the withered apple core. He arranged the bag to make it look undisturbed, took the four items into the kitchen and put them in a plastic carrier bag. He took a few sheets of kitchen towel and soaked some of them in water, and was about to return to the sitting room when he changed his mind. He went back into the vault and fetched the tool bag and carried it into the hall and set it down by the front door.

Tom Aldous did not look different, but the rug's frozen laugh appeared sinister to Beard as he kneeled down beside the body. The bear's hard, glassy eyes each captured a warped parallelogram of the sitting-room windows and looked murderous. It was the dead polar bears you had to watch. He set out the four items from the carrier bag in a neat row, staring at the fragment of dried-out apple core, wondering how it might help him. But he could think of no possible use for it and returned it to the bag. As he took the hammer in his hands he understood that his calculations about the precautionary principle, about returning to the beginning, to the phone, were all wrong. What he was about to do could not be undone. He would be putting his innocence behind him. He dipped the head of the hammer in the puddle of blood, smeared the handle, and set it aside to dry. Next, he took the used paper tissue and bloodied that too, and pushed it under the sofa, well out of sight. The comb was trickier, just as he had anticipated. He pulled away some hair from between the teeth and managed to place some between Aldous's fingers. Hairs attached themselves to the gloves, but Beard was not concerned. The hammer head was now half-dry and easily took a hair, as did the handle. He put another single hair on the arm of a chair. Then he used the kitchen towel to wipe down and dry thoroughly the edge and corner of the glass coffee table, though there was no blood there visible to the naked eye.

He stood at last and paused, wondering if there were a simple mistake he was making. Not so far. He put the hammer and the comb and kitchen towel in the bag and went to the front door. Still wearing the gloves, he walked unhurriedly down the garden path and stopped by the gate to look around. There was no one about. He took out the hammer and tossed it into the shrubbery by the front wall, and then went back into the house, removed the gloves and put them in with the apple core, comb and kitchen roll, then folded the bag carefully, so its bloodstained handles were not exposed, and shoved it into an outer zip compartment of his suitcase.

As far as he could tell, there was no blood on his person, his clothes or his shoes. He took his luggage and the tool bag and stepped outside, pulling the front door closed with his foot. The unending gentrification of Belsize Park ensured that he found a skip within a few hundred yards. He dumped the tool bag. Within several minutes he was on Haverstock Hill getting into a cab bound for Portland Place.

He assumed that his state of affectless calm was due to shock and would wear off soon. Before it did he hoped to bump into someone who would recognise him. The taxi dropped him outside the Institute of Physics—he had once been a vice-president—and before going in he found a litter bin and disposed of the plastic bag. Inside the Institute, it was more or less as he had hoped. He had some minor business there and got into conversation with one of the administrators, who knew who he was. Beard mentioned that he had been in Spitsbergen, and then, casually, that he had come straight from Heathrow by cab and had been caught up in a traffic jam. The administrator commiserated. He agreed to keep an eye on the suitcase while Beard went to the British Library.

In the cab to the Euston Road his legs, independently of the rest of his body, began to shake. But he crossed the Library's forecourt like any other scholar, penetrated the building and found a carrel. He called up some papers—historical material relating to a lecture he was due to give—and sweated it out for several hours, waiting for the time, around four fifteen, when he would feel his phone vibrate in his pocket.

Hunched over his documents, he read nothing, but he forced himself to write out some notes. It amazed him, what had happened. Each time he thought about it, it was as if for the first time. He marvelled at what he had done and how he had acted so calmly, without reflection, behaved like a murderer covering his tracks, while obliterating the truth that could have saved him. He was now in deep, the sole witness of his own innocence. In effect, he had panicked, even while he had felt clear-headed. What did he know of forensics? It was at least possible that today's fresh fingerprints, the ones that were his, were notably different from the ones he had left around the house the weeks and months before. In which case, they would be able to tell that he had been in the house that morning and he would become a suspect.

What other mistakes had he made, what unseen neighbours had observed from a window his arrival or departure? Or seen him throw something into the skip? Was he right to have brought the tool bag away with him? When he was kneeling over Aldous a torrent of his own skin flakes and hair and other microscopic compounds might have poured over the boy, over the dressing gown. But it was his own dressing gown, already filled with the organic traces of his own existence. Not so bad then. If the house was filled with his marks, they were his cover. But only if a fingerprint could not be dated. Somewhere in this building, in the stacks, were a thousand books that could tell him, and he dared not call one up. It would make no difference now if he did.

At three fifty he stood stiff-kneed from his carrel and went to wait in the Library's café for the call he knew must come. He spent the time preparing himself by trying to remember what it was he was not supposed to know: that Aldous was in the house, that he was Patrice's lover, that he was dead. There might have been a fourth detail he needed to appear ignorant of, and he was too fretful to recall it. There may even have been a fifth. It was not so easy to concentrate, for the venerable Library and its environs were not quite as hushed and serious as they once were. There were scores of kids, undergraduates, in the café. Their coats and backpacks were piled up in the spaces between the tables, and they wandered the public spaces, the wide staircases, laughing and talking at a relaxed, normal pitch. Perhaps this was some form of open day for schools. The atmosphere was of a student-union building in a modern university—a bar, a pinball machine, table football would not have been out of place. It suited Beard well to feel obscure among the crowds, but he almost missed the call when it came, an hour late by his calculation, and he still had not remembered the fourth and fifth things he should pretend not to know. He had to trust himself and assume they did not exist.

Patrice said, 'Where are you?' Her voice was flat,

and despite everything, he could not restrain a certain foolish hope: at last, she cared about his whereabouts.

He told her, and then he said, 'What's up?'

'The police are here. You've got to come home.'

He said, 'Patrice, what's going on?'

She had put her hand over the receiver. He heard the murmur of a man's voice, and then she said, 'Just come back now.'

'Have we had a break-in?'

There were more voices around her. Dozens of people were in the house. She was starting to repeat herself in the same toneless voice when she gave out a sudden cry as if stabbed in the arm, and half shouted, half wailed, 'It's Rodney, he's killed someone . . .' and a man's voice cut in over her saying, 'Mrs Beard . . .' and then the line went dead.

Beard went back to his carrel to gather up the notes he had taken the trouble to write out, then he hurried across the Library court, past Paolozzi's *Newton*, and it was only when he was on the street, raising his arm for a taxi, that he remembered what he had decided hours before: it would look better to arrive home with his suitcase. He had the taxi wait in Portland Place while he went into the Institute to thank the administrator. On the way to Belsize Park, Beard wondered whether this—not dashing straight home, but making the detour to collect his luggage—was one of those items, that fourth or fifth thing he was supposed to remember. He could not think it through.

* * *

He was interviewed at length on four occasions, and his last account did not waver from the first. Under the sustained pressure of police interrogation, honesty is a fine, unassailable thing, and as a man of science, Beard had an automatic respect for internal consistency. The truth was impregnable. No need to remember what he had said last time when he could return to the source. So yes, his early flight from Oslo brought him into Heathrow at eight. He went straight to the taxi line, and then—this was his only fiction, the rest was mere omission—he was caught up in a long delay on the M4 and did not get to Portland Place until the mid morning. But he had taken many taxis from Heathrow before, and had been in many traffic jams, and memory was wax-soft, and soon his construction formed itself in his mind like any genuine recollection, both vague and certain. He really felt he had lost an hour in the traffic. What did he do during that long taxi journey? He read a paper for peer review. Total concentration. He did not look up to see the pile-up in the middle or fast lanes, or wherever it was. The rest was hard truth—his business at the Institute, his day's work at the Library, interrupted at last by Patrice's call when he happened to be taking a break. With painful honesty he acknowledged that he knew about and had been upset by his wife's affair with Mr Tarpin. But he, Beard, had had many affairs himself, and that, regrettably, was the kind of marriage they had, and probably it was coming to an end. He did not stray from the truth as he described Patrice's black eye, his Sunday-morning visit to Cricklewood, the confrontation and the slap in the face, and how he, unused to violence, had hurried away for his own safety. Though it embarrassed him, he gave the detective inspector a thorough description of the afternoon he introduced Tom Aldous to his wife, and no, he did not notice anything pass between them, and no, he never suspected that while he, Beard, was in the Arctic, and, who knew, perhaps months before, Patrice was making love to Aldous. And yes, of course he knew the boy, a brilliant young scientist who often picked him up from Reading station. No, not obviously likeable. Too self-obsessed, too narrow, too awkward in company. But many people were like that in his field.

Despite all this truth-telling, the interviews were stressful, and the very first terrified him, for he could not be sure that someone had not seen him arriving at the house at ten and leaving forty-five minutes later. But terror was easily translated into an appearance of understandable stress. Matters eased during the remaining three sessions, all of which occurred after Tarpin's arrest, but still, a fair degree of concentration was required. One week into the affair, Beard read in a newspaper—the predictable storm was raging, photographers were by the garden gate all day and much of the night—that no one had seen Tarpin on the morning of Aldous's death. The heavy rain caused the builder to stay alone at home, depriving him of workmates and an alibi. That at least was refreshing. And so were the leaks from the police station to the press about Tarpin's threatening postcard to Aldous, and the two phone calls that the young man had so wisely recorded. Beard's final two interviews were mostly formalities, a tidying up of loose ends, so he was smilingly assured. It seemed clear enough, the police had their man. Beard signed his statement with a flourish.

Out at the Centre, however, Jock Braby was not so pleased. Beard went out to talk to him on the eighth day, straight after his third interview. He decided to drive because he preferred not to be followed onto the Reading train by the press. He was the object of great interest, having been cast as the hapless victim, the unworldly fool and dreamer with a fast wife beyond his control. There was a gaggle of photographers and reporters by the Centre's barrier gates, and the security guards in their peaked caps, deeply impressed and sympathetic, lined up to give Beard their smartest salute as he drove through.

The two men drank tea in Braby's office and Beard told him the whole story, down to the last detail, just as he had told it to the police.

Braby frowned, and frowned deeper, and gestured through his wall in the approximate direction of the main gates. 'This isn't good,' he said more than twice, and began a long, opaque speech with hesitations and fumbling repetitions, and allusions to 'funding' and 'reputation', to 'standing back' and being 'helpful', and it became clear, or less unclear, after ten minutes that what he seemed to want was for Beard to resign, and only after two references to 'the domestic front' was it apparent that Mrs Braby was being invoked and that what was at stake was the knighthood and a degree of hearthside tranquillity. The man was, in theory, his junior and he was asking Beard to step down! Must it be assumed to be his fault, when one of his wife's lovers killed another? But he kept his indignation well hidden and pretended to misunderstand.

'Jock, whatever they're whispering around the Cabinet Office at the moment, you'd be a bloody fool to resign. I'll put in a good word. Keep your head down for a month or two and it will all go quiet again, you'll see.'

In the circumstances, there was nothing for Braby to do but change the subject. They talked about Aldous, and found common ground in their dislike of him, while acknowledging the loss to the Centre. The police had gone through his cubicle and found nothing of interest relating to the case. A few personal effects had already been dispatched to the distraught father in Norfolk.

Braby said, 'Michael, there was a file marked strictly for your eyes only. I had a good look. A lot of inorganic chemistry, and maths, ramblings, I'd say, and probably done in company time.' He handed across a heavy folder. Beard took it, then stood to indicate the conversation was at an end. He was, after all, still the Chief.

Braby walked him along the corridor a little way. 'I suppose we can honour his memory by developing his micro wind-turbine thingy. We're all deeply committed.'

'Oh yes, that,' Beard said. 'Of course. It will be his monument.'

They shook hands and parted.

And what of the marriage? After the body had been taken away, the forensic team withdrawn, the house declared no longer a crime scene, the press gone from the garden gate, at least until Tarpin's trial, and some workmen hired by Beard came in with sander and polisher to remove all traces of the deep floorboard stain in the sitting room, Michael and Patrice returned from their respective lodgings to the marital home in order to empty it of their belongings and put it up for sale and go their separate ways. These were gusty, sunlit days in March, with winds so strong that the unmown grass was flattened silver sides up, and last year's unswept leaves were piled in drifts against the mossy garden walls. It was weather of a bracing, purifying sort, for Beard at least.

True to his plan, and to Patrice's satisfaction, he renounced any claim to the contents of the house—the list was oppressively long—and took only his books, clothes and a few personal belongings. Not only was he going to shed weight, and become trim and fit, he was intent on a slimmed-down life in the plain apartment he had yet to find. A simplifying factor was, of course, the fading of his love for, or obsession with, his wife. In one of their rare exchanges, he told her that her love life had brought nothing but destruction, and grief to an ailing father in Swaffham, and deprived the country of one of its most promising scientists. It amazed Beard how convinced he himself now was by the narrative everyone believed, and how easily he could summon the appropriate memories and emotions. Was it not true that if Patrice had not had an affair with Tom Aldous, he would still be alive today? And was it not also true that Tarpin would probably have wanted Aldous dead? There was no pretence on Beard's part, he was genuinely aggrieved by what Tarpin had done, and it was right to hold Patrice to account. She owed her husband an apology.

Typically, she did not see it that way. She was in deep mourning for what she now believed was the love of her life. Her apologies were due only to the man who could not hear them. She was miserable with guilt at bringing Tarpin into Aldous's life, for failing to protect the younger man, for not taking the threats more seriously. In addition, the burdens of packing and storage were all hers, since she wanted the stuff, which happened to include the rug and coffee table that had murdered her lover. She moved about the house in silent sorrow, working through her lists with numb efficiency. Her husband was at best an irrelevance, though he suspected that she hated him now for indefinable reasons, or for no good reason at all. Her silence, he decided, was preferable to the lethal cheerfulness with which she had wanted to annihilate him during her Tarpin days.

He was not inclined to help her sort through the goods that were now hers, but he made himself useful in other ways. Since there was nothing legally at issue between them, he suggested they share a lawyer. He knew a good one. Beard also knew the right agent to sell their house. He was well practised in these kinds of arrangements. He moved out first, to a rented basement flat in Dorset Square, on the north side of the Marylebone Road, and it was there, three months later, sprawled on a stained floral sofa that smelled like a dog, that he began to read the folder marked 'Strictly for the eyes of Professor M. Beard'. It was turgid stuff, organic as well as inorganic chemistry, interwoven with some quantum informational concepts and certain more obscure subsections of the Conflation. These elements edged towards a theoretical description of the energy exchange in photosynthesis. Presumably, the intention, at some point further into the file, was to suggest how the process might be imitated and adapted somehow, but Beard's attention began to flag, first because the material was impenetrable, second because he needed to buy a flat, and then, five months to the day after Tom Aldous's death, the trial of Rodney Tarpin began.

He did not stand a chance, and he seemed to know it. In a tone of near regret, the prosecution laid the matter out: Tarpin's obvious motive, the phoned and written threats, the proven violence, his hair on the murder weapon tossed in the laurels and his hair in the dead man's grip, the tissue containing his dried nasal mucus and Aldous's blood, the lack of an alibi. When Beard's turn came, he spoke to the point. Was he not a citizen who respected the law? He gave a thorough account of his movements on the morning in question, then of his wife's black eye, of his visit to the accused's house and the blow to the face he had received. The case against Tarpin was bad enough, but it was Patrice, also appearing for the prosecution, who sank him. At the witness stand she was described by the press as beautiful and deadly, rigid with contempt for the man who had killed her lover. As a witness, Beard was not permitted to be in court to hear his wife's testimony, and could only read the press reports. He had never known her talk so well, so clearly and to such effect. She mesmerised court and country with her account of Tarpin's possessiveness and brutality, his jealous rages. He was an obsessive, she said, a deranged fantasist who had urged her to kill Aldous in his sleep if she ever saw the chance. He refused to let her go, and what she had thought would be a brief and casual affair became a nightmare lasting months. She was terrified of his violence but did not dare refuse him sex. He slapped her when they made love.

'Do you not enjoy that, Mrs Beard?' she was asked by Tarpin's dapper counsel during cross-examination.

'No,' she said crisply. 'Do you?' There was laughter in the public gallery.

Her most quoted, celebrated remark must have been practised in front of the mirror. 'When he killed my Tommy, the nation lost a genius,' she said. 'And I lost the only man I ever loved.'

The jury was out for only three hours and no one, not even Tarpin, could have been surprised by the verdict.

It was during the six days that separated the jury foreman's announcement and the judge's sentencing that Beard took up Aldous's file again. It was the least he could do, to honour the dead, and he was agitated, he needed distraction. Second time around, he understood more, and began to be interested, even a little excited. The task Aldous had set himself was to discover then copy the ways of plants, perfected by evolution during three billion years of trial and error. Deploying techniques and materials still only talked of in nanotechnology, the idea was to exploit direct energy from sunlight to split water into hydrogen and oxygen using special light-sensitive dyes in place of chlorophyll and catalysts containing manganese and calcium. The stored gases would be taken up by a fuel cell to generate electricity. Another idea, also taken from the lives of plants, was to combine carbon dioxide from the atmosphere with sunlight and water to make an all-purpose liquid fuel. It was brilliant or insane—he was not sure. Marking each of his pages with last year's date, he began some notes of his own, and then stopped because the next day, a Tuesday, the court sat, and the accused stood to hear his fate. Tarpin listened to the judge with the same intent and dreamy detachment with which he had followed all the proceedings and had protested, all too feebly, his innocence. According to the press reports, he kept looking in Patrice's direction (Beard could imagine that inquisitive, rodent look), but she kept her face turned from him.

On the steps outside the court, she told the press and TV cameras that the sentence was not long enough, given the damage he had done. During the following week, some commentators agreed with her, while others thought it too severe for what the French might have called a crime of passion. However, watching the news that night in his socks, lying on the stinking sofa, amid the novel squalor of his bachelor apartment, with Aldous's pages spread across his lap, Beard considered sixteen years was just about right.

Part Two

2005

He was running out of time. Everyone was, it was the general condition, but Michael Beard, bloated by an unwanted lunch, shifting under his seat belt, could think only of the diminishing hours of his day, and of what he stood to lose. It was two thirty and his plane, already one hour late, still lumbered oafishly clockwise in a stack above south London. Too troubled to continue reading, gnawing ineffectually from time to time and from an awkward angle on a tender spike of cuticle in the corner of his thumbnail, a whitlow in the making, he watched his familiar corner of England rotate below him. What else could he do? This was not the time for lofty retrospection or overviews, just when he should have been rushing down streets, along corridors, but much of his past and many of his preoccupations were down there, three thousand metres below the expensive seat that others, as usual, had paid for.

Here was a commonplace sight that would have astounded Newton or Dickens. He was gazing east, through a great rim of ginger grime—it could have been detached from an unwashed bathtub and suspended in the air. He was looking past the City, down the bulging, widening Thames, past oil and gas storage tanks towards the brown flatlands of Kent and Essex and the scene of his childhood, and the outsized hospital where his mother died, not long after she told him of her secret life, and beyond, the open jaw of the tidal estuary, and the North Sea, an unwrinkled nursery blue in the February sunshine. Then his gaze was rotated southwards through a silvery haze over the Weald of Sussex towards the soft line of the South Downs, whose gentle folds once cradled his raucous first marriage, a synaesthesia of misguided love, infant excrement and wailing of their lodgers' twins, and the heady quantum calculations that led, fifteen years and two divorces later, to his prize. His Prize, that had half blessed, half ruined his life. Beyond those hills was the English Channel, trimmed with frills of pinkish cloud that obscured the coast of France.

Now a fresh tilt of the aircraft's wings turned him into the sunlight and a view of west London and, just below the trembling engine slung beneath the wing, his improbable destination, the microscopic airport, and around it, the arterial feeds, and traffic pulsing down them like corpuscles, M4, M25, M40, the charmless designations of a hard-headed age. Benignly, the glare from the west softened a little the industrial squalor. He saw the Thames Valley, a pallid winter green, looping between the Berkshire Downs and the Chiltern Hills. Beyond, lost to view, was Oxford and the laboratory-toiling of his undergraduate years, and the finely calculated courting of his first wife, Maisie. And now here it came again, for the sixth time, the colossal disc of London itself, turning like an intricately slotted space station in majestic self-sufficiency. As unplanned as a giant termite nest, as a rain forest, and a thing of beauty, gathering itself to great human intensity at the centre, along the rediscovered river between Westminster and Tower Bridge, dense with confident, playful architecture, new toys. Briefly, he thought he saw the plane's shadow flitting like a free spirit across St James's and over the rooftops, but this was impossible at such a height. He knew about light. Among those millions of roofs, four had sheltered his second, third, fourth and fifth marriages. These alliances had defined his life, and they were all, no point denying it, calamities.

These days, whenever he came in over a big city he felt the same unease and fascination. The giant concrete wounds dressed with steel, these catheters of ceaseless traffic filing to and from the horizon—the remains of the natural world could only shrink before them. The pressure of numbers, the abundance of inventions, the blind forces of desires and needs looked unstoppable and were generating a heat, a modern kind of heat that had become, by clever shifts, his subject, his profession. The hot breath of civilisation. He felt it, everyone was feeling it, on the neck, in the face. Beard, gazing down from his wondrous, and wondrously dirty, machine, believed in his better moments that he had the answer to the problem. At last, he had a mission, it was consuming him, and he was running out of time.

Even as his Essex childhood swung back into view—he was so late!—he could trace the route he should have been making among miniaturised streets as neatly etched by winter sun as a printed circuit. He thought he could see the very building in the Strand he was supposed to be in now. Then it was gone. And there were two other roofs, tipping away from him unseen to the north-west. One sheltered his icy, neglected, chaotic Marylebone apartment. His mind's eye permitted him to see in a darkened room the half-eaten meal he had abandoned three months ago with a half-forgotten friend for some night errand. He had not been back and had not seen her since. The place was a midden. In the bedroom next door, in the unheated air, he saw the sensual disorder of the bed, the pillows on the floor, the orange standby lights of the hi-fi still glowing, and scattered about the place, the books and journals he was reading at the time (he struggled to remember them), and that day's newspapers, a champagne bottle and, in two glasses, the evaporated tidemarks of the inch or two they had failed in their hurry to finish. Over these, over the plates in the dining room, the pans in the kitchen, on the garbage in the pail and spread across the chopping board, and even on the coffee grounds in the dried-out filter paper, there would be vigorous, differently hued fungal growths in creamy whites and soft greyish-greens, a blossoming on the abandoned cheese, the carrots, the hardened gravy. Airborne spores, a parallel civilisation, invisible and mute, successful living entities. Yes, they would have long settled to their specialised feasts, and when the fuel ran out, they would dry to a smear of charcoal dust.

The other roof sheltered Melissa Browne, his somewhat neglected love, and it was under this second that he intended to spend the night. She was so kind to him, so soft, so patient, so pretty, the only viable love in his life. Like many women, she thought he was a brilliant scientist, a genius in need of rescuing. But he was such a careless, faithless, disorganised friend, too elusive, too stonily intent on never marrying again. He hadn't phoned. She was cooking dinner. He didn't deserve her. Guilt and a fresh surge of impatience, a vile brew, made him groan. Did he actually make a sound above the engine's note? And here were the South Downs again to remind him he must never yield, he must never change his mind. His frame could not withstand a sixth marriage.

Whichever direction his gaze fell, this was home, his native corner of the planet. The fields and hedgerows, once tended by medieval peasants or eighteenth-century labourers, still visibly patterned the land in irregular quadrilaterals, and every brook, fence and pigsty, virtually every tree, was known and probably named in the Domesday Book after all-conquering William in 1085 conferred with his advisors and sent his men all over England. And ever since, named again with greater refinement, owned, used, costed, traded, mortgaged; mature like a thick-crusted Stilton, as richly stuffed with varied humanity as Babel, as historical as the Nile Delta, teeming like a charnel house with ghosts, in public discourse as dissonant as a rookery in full throat. One day this brash and ancient kingdom might yield to the force of multiple cravings, to the dreamy temptations of a giant metropolis, a Mexico City, São Paulo and Los Angeles combined, to effloresce from London to the Medway to Southampton to Oxford, back to London, a modern form of quadrilateral, burying all previous hedges and trees. Who knew, perhaps it would be a triumph of racial harmony and brilliant buildings, a world city, the most admired world city in the world.

How, wondered Beard as his plane at last quitted the stack on a banking hairpin tangent and lined itself up north of the Thames to begin its descent, how could we ever begin to restrain ourselves? We appeared, at this height, like a spreading lichen, a ravaging bloom of algae, a mould enveloping a soft fruit—we were such a wild success. Up there with the spores!

*   *   *

Half an hour later, the Berlin flight was docked and he was fourth man off, towing his carry-on luggage, walking stiffly at speed, with unmanful little skips and hops (his knees, his body, indeed his mind, were no longer capable of simple running), down the sealed capillaries, the carpeted steel tubes that fed him through the airport's innards towards the immigration hall. Far quicker to pound alongside the hundred-metre moving walkway than squeeze by the dreamy, motionless voyagers and their luggage blocking the runs. At least a dozen young men off his plane, hurrying more effectively, overtook him along this stretch, lean, crop-headed business types, raincoats flapping over their forearms, unhindered by their weighty shoulder bags, talking easily as they flew by. An avenue of ads for banking and office services, weakly humorous, effortfully eye-catching—clearly, advertising was an industry for third-raters—increased his irritation in the unventilated, overlit corridors. He knew it too well, the special kind of mental suffocation that came from contact with aggressive low intelligence. Now, planetary stupidity was his business. And by failing to be punctual, he was being stupid too. At best, he would be seventy-five minutes late. Being late was a special kind of modern suffering, with blended elements of rising tension, self-blame, self-pity, misanthropy and a yearning for what could not be had outside theoretical physics—time reversal.

And commanding yourself to be stoical did not get you there any sooner.

For an unnaturally large fee, he was to address an energy conference attended by institutional investors, pension-fund managers, solid types who would not easily be persuaded that the world, their world, was in danger and that they should align their investment patterns accordingly. Through inertia, blind professional custom, they were bound to their old familiars, oil, gas, coal, forestry. He was to persuade them that what they currently made profitable would one day destroy them. On these occasions it was necessary to speak in general terms, of course, but if Beard, already the owner of a dozen patents, could shift them, even by the smallest of fractions, his own company must benefit. They were waiting for him in the Savoy, in two connecting suites facing out over the river, and though they had received advance apologies for his lateness, soon they were bound to melt away to their next meetings, and this frail miracle of appointment-diary co-ordination, four months in the conjuring, would give way to even greater scepticism and fatal withdrawal. Another reason to be in London was to sign the option tomorrow at the US Embassy on a four-hundred-acre site in the south-western scrub desert of New Mexico, a sand-grain speck in the baking vastness. And when the investors were happy, the funds were in, the tax breaks settled, the construction on a scaled-up prototype would begin. Thinking about it made him dizzy with impatience.

Ten minutes of hurry, then Beard, breathless, sweating under his coat, was standing stalled in immigration, buried in a line ten men deep, hundreds long, inching forward among supplicants waiting to be granted entry to their own country. Long minutes passed, and he could feel himself becoming less reasonable. There came to him an image of precious fluid—blood, milk, wine—draining from a tank. He could not restrain a growing sense of thwarted entitlement: someone should have been there to bring him to the front, ahead of the ordinary crowd, to waive the formalities, conduct him to a limo. Did no one here know who he was? Wasn't he a VIP after all? Yes, he was, just like everyone else. At moments like this, his misanthropy sensitised him to the people packed tight around him, no longer fellow travellers, but adversaries, competitors in a slow race. And he could not help himself, he was on the lookout for one of those cheats who edge up on the periphery of vision, moving while pretending not to, cutting in with a sly shuffle, a subtle turn of the shoulder. Burdening others by stealing time.

He had reached the place where the amorphous overlapping ten queues narrowed down to three in order to line up for the immigration desks. And here he came, a gaunt parchment-faced fellow in a loden coat (Beard had always despised the style), sliding in from the left, trying to use his height to squirm ahead, angling his oversized briefcase at knee height to use as a wedge. Abruptly, driven by shameless rectitude, Beard stepped forward to deny the man space, and felt the briefcase bang against his knee. At that moment Beard turned and sought out his gaze and said politely, though his heart beat a little harder, 'Terribly sorry.'

A rebuke poorly disguised as an apology, pretending manners to a man he would rather at that moment kill. It was good to be back in England.

But looking into the man's face revealed just how ancient a cheat this was. Eighty-five at least, with sepia liver spots from papery forehead to puckered throat, and an air of slack-jawed vacancy, and pendulous lower lip faintly trembling and wet. Of course, the old had to get ahead. They had less time. They were almost dead. Their hurry was greater than his, and forgiveness, even an apology, was in order. But the old man had faded away, fallen back somewhere behind, out of sight, in disgrace. Too late to offer him a favourable place in the queue.

And so it was that Beard, heartless scourge of the frail, appeared before an official somewhat chastened, loathing himself a little and therefore not so surprised that his photograph or his height, his date of birth or his next of kin should be the cause of suspicion and a degree of expert frowning. The official snapped the pages of his passport in rapid sequence, glanced at Beard, flipped them back, then, following a moment's consideration, set the document face down on a scanner. She was in her late twenties, possibly less than half his age. Parents' country of origin he guessed to be Ethiopia. If she slid off her high stool now, stepped down from her station and kicked off her high heels, she would still stand six inches taller than him.

He was rotund, slow-moving, pinkly hot—and late. She was sleekly attuned to her current task, guarding the portals of her nation against undesirables. He watched her as she stared at his details on her screen, as her right hand, faintly purplish about the palm, fluttered insouciantly across her keyboard in pursuit of some other angle on him, a deeper perspective, he suddenly hoped. From the high internal scaffolding of the immigration hall a silence appeared to descend like thickening snow, a delicious chill, and all sense of hurry left him. This fine-textured, light-absorbent, light-loving skin, these high-pitched cheekbones (he saw only one) with a delicate dip and sculpted curve, these brown eyes resting gravely on his case, this happy marriage, as he saw it, of intelligence and grace. Millennia ago, under cool canopies in some secret desert redoubt, the genes of a gazelle had entered the local human pool. Such a fantasy of miscegenation could be a form of racism or simple adoration, but either way he was in no mood to banish it. It lingered as he gazed at the black left hand and wrist, long and narrow like a salad tosser, resting inert by the foxed covers of his upturned passport.

He remained a bold fool in these matters—habits long fixed, not a crumb wiser than his twenty-five-year-old self, no prospects of improvement, so all his past wives agreed—and in the moments before she spoke he indulged the familiar notion of asking if the immigration officer was free for dinner. He asked many women, total strangers, to dinner, and not everyone said no. His involvement with Patrice had begun over such a feast, and set in train such disgraceful events, that even now, ten years on, he still remembered what he ordered. It predicted all that was to come, it was a curse: a skate with capers and burned butter, an over-salted salad of wild rocket, a yeasty Pinot Grigio, surely corked, and he too fatally entranced to call the sommelier across.

The young woman met his eye and said, 'You've travelled a lot in the Middle East.'

Her 'lot' was glottal, the statement intoned as a question. What linguists called uptalk, so he had recently learned. Lately he had become something of a language snob, an inverted language snob, whose age and limited connections prevented him from understanding much about accent and status in England these days. The year before, he had begun an affair with a London waitress whom he took to be the lively feral creature of some forsaken housing estate. But it turned out she had grown up in the Surrey Hills in a Lutyens house hidden among high laurels, and her father was an ennobled mathematician, a fellow member of the Royal Society. Beard had fled. Now here he was again, thrilling to his own idea of something demotic, or racy.

He said neutrally. 'Yes. that's right.'

'Libya. Egypt, Sudan. And the rest. Business is it?'

He nodded.

'And what is that?'

He had been asked many times at desks like this. He said, 'Energy consultant.'

'Is that oil?'

Again, the hint of the elided glottal tugged at something unwholesome in him.

'No. Solar.'

'CSP is it?'

Not quite right, but he nodded. She *knew*. In a dazed moment of virtuous hope and carnal self-interest, his imagination leap-frogged past dinner to the time when she had served out her notice with the immigration service and, smoothly competent, was travelling by his side, working with and for him, living for and with him and his vision of a world cleansed and cooled and energised by photovoltaics, by concentrated solar power, above all by his own artificial photosynthesis, and by systems centralised or distributed and grid-tied. He would teach her all he knew about thin film, heliostats, feed-in tariffs. She would be efficient in hours; out of them, generous, athletic, with low tastes.

He was starting to say conversationally, 'So you take an interest in . . .' as she spoke over him.

'Thank you, Mr Beard.' She was offering him his passport with her right hand, reaching over her neglected left where it lay unmoving on the desk. Of course! Unusable, wasted, withered. His ridiculous fantasy surged further, swelling into protective, nurturing affection for her congenitally useless left arm. She would eat dinner with a fork in her right hand; naturally, he would do the same.

His invitation was on his lips as her gaze slipped from his face towards the head of the queue behind, her smile fading as she called, 'Next.'

This was the weakness he had to live with, his own withered arm, the mental playlets, wholly infantile, that generally led nowhere, occasionally brought him trouble and only very rarely joy. But similar daydreams—manic moments, brief neural bursts, compacted but cloudy episodes that braided the actual with the unreal, and threaded gaudy beads of the impossible, the outrageous and contradictory along thought-lines of indeterminate logic—had long ago brought him to formulate his Conflation. The poetic, the scientific, the erotic—

why should the imagination care which master it served?

He hurried across baggage reclaim, past the creaking carousels and bored crowds beneath the information screens, through deserted customs, past the sinister one-way glass and the stainless-steel examination tables like bare mortuary slabs, then out along the lines of dead-eyed drivers and their boards—Kuwait Balloon Adventures, Bishop Dolan, Ted of Mr Kipling—and crossed the departure hall, fully aware that he was not quite making a direct line to the stairs that led down to his train, nor was he quite aiming for the down-at-heel airport shop that sold newspapers, luggage straps and related clutter. Was he going to be weak and go in there as he always did? He thought not. But his route was bending that way. He was a public intellectual of a sort, he needed to be informed, and it was natural that he should buy a newspaper, however pressed for time. At moments of important decision-making, the mind could be considered as a parliament, a debating chamber. Different factions contended, short- and long-term interests were entrenched in mutual loathing. Not only were motions tabled and opposed, certain proposals were aired in order to mask others. Sessions could be devious as well as stormy.

He knew this shop too well, and it seemed he was walking directly towards it now. He was simply going in to take a look, test his will, buy a newspaper and nothing besides. If only it were pornography that he was trying to resist, then failure could do him no harm. But pictures of girls or parts of girls no longer stirred him much. His problem was even more banal than top-rack glossies. Now he was at the counter, sorting the pound coins from euros in his hand, with four newspapers under his arm, not one, as if excess in one endeavour might immunise him in another, and as he handed them across for their bar codes to be scanned, he saw at the edge of vision, in the array beneath the till, the gleam of the thing he wanted, the thing he did not want to want, a dozen of them in a line, and without deciding to he was taking one—so light!—and adding it to his pile, partly obliterating a picture of the prime minister waving from the doorway of a church.

It was a plastic foil bag of finely sliced potatoes boiled in oil and dusted in salt, industrialised powdered foodstuffs, preservatives, enhancers, hydrolysing and raising agents, acidity regulators and colouring. Salt and vinegar flavoured crisps. He was still stuffed from his lunch, but this particular chemical feast could not be found in Paris, Berlin or Tokyo and he longed for it now, the actinic sting of these thirty grams—a drug dealer's measure. One last jolt to the system, then he would never touch the junk again. He thought there was every chance of resisting it until he was on the Paddington train. He stuffed the bag in the pocket of his jacket, took up his burden of papers and his wheeled luggage and continued across the concourse. He was thirty-five pounds overweight. About his future lightness he had made many general resolutions and virtuous promises, often after dinner with a glass in his hand, and all parliamentary heads nodding in assent. What defeated him was always the present, the moment of vivid confrontation with the affirming tidbit, the extra course, the meal he did not really need, when the short-term faction carried the day.

The flight from Berlin was a typical failure. At the start, as he lowered his broad rear into his seat, barely two hours after a meaty Germanic breakfast, he was forming his resolutions: no drinks but water, no snacks, a green-leaf salad, a portion of fish, no pudding, and at the same time, at the approach of a silver tray and the murmured invitation of a female voice, his hand was closing round the stem of his runway champagne. A half-hour later he was ripping open the sachet of a salt-studded, beef-glazed, toasted corn-type sticklet snack that came with his jumbo gin and tonic. Then there was spread before him a white tablecloth, the sight of which fired some neuronal starter gun for his stomach juices. The gin melted his remaining resolve. He chose the starter he had decided against: quails' legs wrapped in bacon on a bed of creamed garlic. Then, cubes of pork belly mounted on a hill-fort of buttered rice. The word '*pavé*' was another of those starter guns: a paving slab of chocolate sponge encased in chocolate under a chocolate sauce; goat's cheese, cow's cheese in a nest of white grapes, three rolls, a chocolate mint, three glasses of Burgundy, and finally, as though it would absolve him of all else, he forced himself back through the menu to confront the oil-sodden salad that came with the quail. When his tray was removed, only the grapes remained.

*   *   *

He bought his ticket and settled himself at a table on the half-empty train. Sitting opposite was one of those young men in their thirties with shaved head, chubby face and gymnasium-thickened neck who were, to Beard's undiscerning eye, impossible to tell apart. This man, however, was distinguished by piercings in his ears. For some unacknowledged seconds there was an under-the-table negotiation, a polite ballet, for leg space. Then the younger man proceeded with the message he was tapping into his phone, and Beard, scanning the front pages, experienced the familiar mental narrowing of homecoming. These were surely the very papers he had read before he left, weeks before. Here were the same headlines, over the same photograph, asking the same question. When would Blair go? Tomorrow? Straight after the next election, assuming he won? A year in, or two, or after a whole fourth term? Was this not exactly the same number of Shia citizens in Baghdad, slaughtered by al-Qaeda as they queued to buy bread? That story apart (Beard was riffling through his pile), the tsunami had taken over a quarter of a million lives, which had raised for some, just as it had last month, the question of God's existence. Elsewhere, the country was, as ever, pronounced to be in ruins, its governance, finances, health service, justice and education systems, military, transport infrastructure and public morals in a state of terminal inanition. From habit, he looked out for climate-change articles. Nothing today. Solar? Nothing—but there would be soon.

He set the papers down on the seat beside him and attended to his palmtop, scrolling through the fifteen messages it had absorbed since his departure from Berlin Tegel. Fourteen related to his project. His American partner, Toby Hammer, confirmed that the documents were at Grosvenor Square. The ranch owner wanted his option money transferred to an account in El Paso and not the one in Alamogordo. The local Chamber of Commerce politely requested a 'cleaner' estimate of the number of jobs the installation would provide for the citizens of Lordsburg. Whenever he saw the name of that small town, his mood improved. He wanted to be there now, on its northern edge, gazing over the dazzling immensity towards the spot, out along the straight road to Silver City, where their work would begin. Lordsburg Holiday Inn wanted him to know that his booking next month was confirmed, in the usual room, and at a lower rate for a faithful customer. For the third time that month, a note from Jock Braby, wanting to meet. He would have heard the rumours of good results at Imperial and now he would be wanting some share of the success. And this, from the man who had arranged Beard's sacking from the Centre. An afterthought from Toby Hammer. He had found a cheap source of iron filings. Only one personal message: *Don't forget dinner at 8. Main course is you. I love you, Melissa.*

I love you. She had written and said this many times, but he had never said it back to her, not even in moments of abandon. And not because he thought he did not love her. He was never quite sure on that count. Long ago he had learned never to declare love to anyone. With Melissa he dreaded the question these three words of supernatural torque must raise. Would he commit to her for the rest of his life and father her child?

She longed for the baby that circumstances had denied her. But his entire case history convinced him that if he went along with the plan, he was bound to bring disappointment to this artless, pretty young woman, who was eighteen years younger than him. She was at that age when a childless woman should be in a hurry. If he would not step up to perform his duties, he should bow out. She surely would need a period of adjustment, and then time to find a replacement. But she did not want him to go, and he could not bring himself to leave. And yet—to be an inadequate husband all over again, for the sixth time, to be father of an infant at sixty. Ridiculous regression!

It was agony to discuss the matter with her. The last occasion, in a restaurant in Piccadilly, she was wet-eyed when she said that she would rather not have a child than lose him. Unbearable. The stuff of agony-aunt columns. He could not believe her. If he really loved her, he thought, he should free her and leave her now. But he liked her and was weak. How could he refuse this improbable gift? Who else as young would take on so tenderly a man as faintly absurd, short, tubby, ageing, as scalded by public disgrace, corrupted by a whiff of failure, consumed by his cranky affair with sunbeams?

So he made the poorest choice of all. Barely a choice, more a kind of instinctual funk. Without quite cutting loose, he had kept his distance—he was working abroad anyway. He had seen other women, and all the while half hoped for and wholly dreaded the call she would make to tell him of the eager, talented buck prowling at the peripheries of her existence, about to make, or having just made, an entrance. And then, if he was weak enough, he would hurry back to defend what he would suddenly decide was his, and she would be grateful, the buck would be dispatched (the buck stops here!), the mess would remain, and he would be one step nearer the wrong decision.

He put away the palmtop, leaned back in his seat and half closed his eyes. Right before him on the table, shimmering through his barely parted lashes, were the salt and vinegar crisps, and just beyond the packet was a plastic bottle of mineral water belonging to the young man. Beard wondered whether he should be looking over the notes for his speech, but general travel fatigue as well as the lunchtime drinks had rendered him, for the moment, inert, and he believed he knew the material well enough, and on a card in his top pocket were various useful quotes. As for the snack, he wanted it less than he did, but he still wanted it. Certain of those industrial compounds might stir his metabolism into wakefulness. It was his palate, rather than his stomach, that was looking forward to the acidic tang of the dust coating each brittle slice. He had shown decent restraint—the train had been moving for several minutes now—and there was no good reason to hold back.

He pulled himself up in his seat and leaned forward, elbows on the table, hands propping his chin for several reflective seconds, gaze fixed on the gaudy wrapper, silver, red and blue, with cartoon animals cavorting below a Union Jack. So childish of him, this infatuation, so weak, so harmful, a microcosm of all past errors and folly, of that impatient way he had of having to have what he wanted instantly. He took the bag in both hands and pulled its neck apart, discharging a clammy fragrance of frying fat and vinegar. It was an artful laboratory simulation of the corner fish and chip shop, an enactment of fond memories and desire and nationhood. That flag was a considered choice. He lifted clear a single crisp between forefinger and thumb, replaced the bag on the table, and sat back. He was a man to take his pleasures seriously. The trick was to set the fragment on the centre of the tongue and, after a moment's spreading sensation, push the potato up hard to shatter against the roof of the mouth. His theory was that the rigid irregular surface caused tiny abrasions in the soft flesh into which salt and chemicals poured, creating a mild and distinctive pleasure-pain.

Like a master of wine at a grand tasting, he had closed his eyes. When he opened them he was staring into the level grey-blue gaze of the man opposite. Feeling only slightly ashamed, Beard made a gesture of impatience and looked away. He knew how he must have appeared, a plump fool of a certain age communing intensely with a morsel of junk food. He had been behaving as though alone. So what? As long as he harmed or offended no one, that was his right. He no longer cared much what others thought of him. There were few benefits in growing older, and this was one. In a simple assertion of selfhood, rather than to satisfy his contemptible needs, he put out a hand to take another crisp, and as he did so, met again the other man's stare. It was narrow, hard, unblinking, expressive of little beyond a ferocious curiosity. It occurred to Beard that he might be sitting across from a psychopath. So be it. He could be a bit of one himself. The salty residue from the first round gave him the impression that he was bleeding from the gums. He slumped back in his seat, opened his mouth and repeated the experience, although this time he kept his eyes open. Inevitably, the second crisp was less piquant, less surprising, less penetrating than the first, and it was precisely this shortfall, this sensual disappointment, that prompted the need, familiar to drug addicts, to increase the dose. He would eat two crisps at once.

It was at this moment, as he glanced up, that he witnessed his fellow passenger sitting forward, gaze still eerily fixed, elbows on the table, perhaps in conscious parody. Then, letting one forearm drop, crane-like down onto the bag, the man stole a crisp, probably the largest in the packet, held it in front of his face for a second or two, then ate it, not with Beard's fastidiousness, but with an insolent chewing motion, with lips parted so that one could glimpse it turning to paste on his tongue. The man did not even blink, his stare was so intense. And the act was so flagrant, so unorthodox, that even Beard, who was quite capable of unconventional thought—how else had he won his Prize?—could only sit in frozen shock and try, for dignity's sake, by remaining expressionless, to betray no sign of emotion.

The two men were locked into each other's gaze, and now Beard was determined not to look away. No question, the man's behaviour was aggressive, the act was naked theft, however trivial the goods. And if it came to physical struggle, Beard did not doubt that he would be on the floor in seconds, with broken arms or head. But there was also a possibility of another element, of something playful behind this steeliness and mockery of an older man's ridiculous pleasure in junk food. Or a tease, in the old-fashioned situationist mode, of a stuffy bourgeois. Or worse, the fellow believed that Beard was gay, and this was a come-on, a kind of modern opening known only to certain subgroups for whom his purple silk tie, as a hypothesis, was an accidental signal, an open invitation to seduction. Wasn't an earring in one ear or the other, he had forgotten which, once a significant marker of sexual orientation? This man had two earrings in each ear. The physicist knew much about light, but about forms of public expression in contemporary culture he was in the dark. Finally, returning to his initial surmise, Beard continued to wonder if his fellow passenger was a psychiatric case on an unlicensed drug holiday from the lithium, in which case it was a bad idea to continue to stare into his eyes. At this, Beard looked away and did the only thing that came to mind. He took another crisp.

What did he expect? As soon as this crisp was on Beard's tongue, the man's hand dropped again, and this time he took two, just as Beard himself had intended, and ate them in the same jaunty, vulgar manner. It would surely not be a good move to snatch the bag away from the table—too physical, too abrupt. Dangerous, to be breaking new ground, inviting a scuffle. Would anyone save him if it came to that? Beard glanced around the compartment. Passengers were reading, or staring numb-faced into space, or out the window at the wintry west-London suburbs, oblivious to the drama. What interest was there in two men silently sharing a snack? It was paradoxical, but as Beard saw it, there was more sense in continuing what had already begun. It did not occur to him to avoid confrontation with a stronger man by giving way and letting him have the bag to himself. Beard would not be bullied. He may have been short and overweight, but he had a developed sense of justice and always stood his ground. He was capable of being reckless. There had been some ruinous consequences. He took another slice of fried potato. His opponent, his stare still fixed on Beard, did the same. Then again, and again, for two further rounds, their hands came down on the bag, in steady, deliberate rather than rapid succession, and never quite touched. When there were only two crisps left, the young man retrieved the bag and, in a parody of politeness, offered them to Beard. The only response to this, the final insult, was to turn away.

It was an outrage. The train was beginning to slow, people were reaching for their coats, a computerised voice reminded passengers not to leave the train without their luggage. In a move that secured his triumph, the young man balled up in his fist the plastic bag and stuffed it into the waste bin under the table. Diligently, he used a hand to wipe the table clear of crumbs and grains of salt. Beard's humiliation was complete. This was how it was to grow older, to be pushed around by the young, the strong, and have no redress. With a warming touch of self-pity, he sensed that every injustice, every historical oppression, unwarranted invasion, chaotic warlordism, every tyrannical break with the rule of law was compacted in this moment, and he was bound by self-respect and his duty to underdogs everywhere to make a show of resistance. Otherwise, he could never live with himself. He lunged forward, seized his opponent's bottle of water, snapped off its top and drank deeply—he was thirsty anyway—drank it down to the bottom, every last drop of its twenty-five centilitres. He tossed the bottle on the table with a defiant, come-and-get-me look. The blue bottle cap rolled onto the floor.

The young man thought for a moment, then stood and stepped into the aisle, revealing his full height, somewhere around six two. Beard, already beginning to regret his defiance, remained in his seat, determined not to cringe. The man reached up, and with one smooth movement of his overdeveloped arm, he swung Beard's luggage to the floor, setting it down gently by its owner. If this was an act of contrition, Beard was not moved, and he returned a snarling look of contempt. His adversary hesitated a moment, gazing down at the older man with an expression of sorrow or pity, and then he turned and loped away down the compartment.

Beard let him get well clear before he stood. He never wanted to see the fellow again. A full minute passed before he stepped out onto the platform. Trembling a little now, with anger or shock, or a little of both, he had some difficulty getting himself into his coat—its belt was tangled around a sleeve. His shoelace was loose. As he kneeled to retie it with fingers not yet fully obedient, he remembered his heap of newspapers and decided to leave them where they were. At last, more or less composed, he made his way along the platform towards the ticket barrier. This was the moment that would remain with him, and come to stand for every recalculation he would ever make about his past, every revised or improved perspective he would ever gain on his own history, his own stupidity and other people's motives. He had stopped twenty feet short of the barrier. He set his wheeled luggage on end and reached under his coat into his jacket pocket for his ticket. There was something else in there, something plastic, bulky, lightweight, crunchy. There came to him a confused childhood memory of a magic trick at a village fete, when some master of the art had pulled from ten-year-old Michael Beard's ear an egg, or rabbit or chicken, something physically impossible, just like this: his crisps, the ones he had already eaten. He pulled the bag clear and, stupefied, stared at it, the Union Jack, the dancing cartoon animals, willing them to melt away. And that other bag? What a cascade of recalibration of every instant, every impulse, of the nature of the man he never wanted to see again, and of how he, Beard, must have seemed—a vicious madman.

He was so entirely in the wrong that for the moment it felt like liberation, strangely like joy. There could be no excuses, he had no defence. He also felt a mirthless impulse to laugh. His error was so unambiguous, so unsullied, he stood so completely revealed to himself, a naked fool, that he felt purified and redeemed, like a penitent, like an elated medieval flagellant with a newly flayed back. That poor fellow whose food and drink you devoured, who offered you his last morsels, fetched down your luggage, was a friend to man. No, no, that was not for now, the agony of retrospection must be postponed.

Despite the need to hurry to his appointment, he remained on the busy platform a good while, below the distant glass roof and its clattering echoes, while passengers stepped around him, and he held the bag of crisps against his chest, feeling himself, quite mistakenly, intensely illuminated.

* * *

In the taxi from Paddington to the Savoy he reminded himself to be careful, for he was feeling accident-prone and was about to speak in public, and afterwards, in the conference interval, was contractually bound to mingle, and might well confront journalists, men and women whose outward appearance of humanity and intelligence masked cold-hearted predation. They knew from past successes that he could be coaxed into indiscretion, or an expansive hypothesis—wasn't free-thinking his duty?—which would appear crazed or dim-witted in print, once stripped of all conditionals, all hedging, all playfulness. A speculative remark had already cost him the headline 'Nobel Prof: End Is Nigh'.

His own end—it seemed like that at the time—came only last year, and the curious thing was that people had already started to forget. This amounted to a kind of forgiveness. It was generally known there had been a fuss, a stirring of the news currents around Michael Beard, but the details were blurring. He had been proved wrong about something, or was he in the right all along? Did he assault someone, or was he the victim? Didn't that someone get arrested? Back then, as the storm broke, a colleague, an eminence in computer modelling, told him that the picture of the Nobel prizewinner being led handcuffed through a jeering crowd was carried in four hundred and eighty-three newspapers. This fact remained with Beard, his humiliation had been planetary, but it seemed to have remained with no one else. New material had befuddled the public memory, fresh scandals, sporting events, confessions, war, celebrity gossip and the tsunami had wiped clean his slate. A twelve-month torrent, swelling steadily, had carried him to safer ground.

Even his own recollection of the events, their precise emotional tone, was beginning to fragment. To be the focus of press attention was to experience a form of vertigo and bewilderment. Mercifully, his own particular memory stain was fading to an indistinct watermark. But certain details remained sharp, kept alive by the retelling. He believed that anecdotes were a blight on conversation, and yet still he went on telling them. He often related how it was not the case that the feel of handcuffs on the skin was of cold steel, as one reads in detective novels. Those placed on him had been warmed by a long morning inside the armless gabardine jacket of the arresting policewoman. It was the intimate snugness of the fit around his wrists, the feel of transferred body warmth, that was sinister. Likewise, the cliché was that whenever you read a press story on any subject of which you had personal knowledge, there was at least one salient fact wrong. But that was not his experience. He marvelled at the unearthing of a quantity of accurate facts about himself. The distortion was in the way in which they were juxtaposed, wrought into fresh implication, millimetres beyond the reach of a libel lawyer. And he was impressed too by the research, by how these restless newspaper types had, in a matter of a day or two, penetrated deep into the obscure quarters, into the slums of an overcrowded personal life, drawing in one instance a bounty of malice from his third wife's older brother, a near-mute recluse who had always loathed Beard and who lived without a telephone by a dirt track along a deserted north-westerly peninsula on Bruny Island off the coast of Tasmania.

The press upended Beard's life as one might a wastepaper basket. A couple of shakes, and there tipped into view all kinds of half-forgotten scraps. In other circumstances it might have been a service worth paying for. Independently of each other, his ex-wives, good old Maisie, Ruth, Eleanor, Karen and Patrice, refused to talk to the press. That touched him deeply. Of the past lovers, most were loyal, and only a rump spoke up: one lab assistant, one office administrator. There were also two scientists, failures, nobodies, both of them. Intriguingly, there were also some impostors. The Last Trump sounded, and from their graves and catacombs this pint-sized crowd of ex-lovers and pretenders crawled towards the light, to stand before their Maker, a journalist with a chequebook, and denounce Beard as a woman-hater, an exploiter, a louse.

But being silent or loyal got no one off the hook. The coverage was total. Until the attention of the press was distracted by a football scandal, he was its plaything. One front page rendered him in cartoon form as a leering goat, beckoning with limp hoof as it lounged against the caption: 'See

Inside: Beard's Women'. Even as he opened the paper with sickening heart and scanned a gallery of faces, which included colleagues, old friends, the wives, Melissa, something in him stirred and an inner voice, steely, beyond humiliation, murmured that he had not done so badly in three or four decades, that all these women had the gleam of quality, of high self-possession. As for the impostors, the chancers, there were actually three, all not quite beautiful. But how could he not be interested in the fictitious nights they spent with him? He was flattered.

In all, however, it was a miserable time. It had started out innocently enough, with a mouse-click of assent to an invitation to be the titular head of a government scheme to promote physics in schools and universities, to entice more graduates, more teachers, into the profession, to glory in past achievements and make intellectual heroes out of physicists. When the invitation came, he was busier than he had ever been in his life and he could so easily have refused. He had an artificial-photosynthesis project at Imperial College, with fifteen people working for him. He was still at the Centre, though mostly for the purpose of drawing his fee. And it was important, he felt, to keep his new work out of Jock Braby's reach. Beard had started his company, he was acquiring patents on catalysts and other processes, and he had found Toby Hammer, a wiry ex-drunk, a fixer and go-between, who knew his way round campus bureaucracies and state legislatures and the homes of venture capitalists. Beard and Hammer had been looking for a solar-rich site, first in the Libyan Sahara, then in Egypt, then Arizona and

Nevada, and finally, as a decent compromise, in New Mexico. Now Beard was alive with purpose and was shedding many of his old sinecures. But this request came through the Institute of Physics and was difficult to refuse.

And so he sat for the first time with his committee in a seminar room in Imperial College. His colleagues were three professors of physics from Newcastle, Manchester and Cambridge, two secondary-school teachers from Edinburgh and London, two headmasters from Belfast and Cardiff, and a professor of science studies from Oxford. Beard asked the members to introduce themselves in turn and explain a little about their background and their work. This was a mistake. The physics professors went on too long. They were impressed by their own work and they were instinctively competitive. If the first was going to speak in great detail, then so were the second and the third.

It was not old habits alone that made Beard impatient to hear from the professor of science studies, for the subject itself was a novelty to him. She was the last to speak, and introduced herself as Nancy Temple. Her face was round, not exactly pretty, but pleasant and open, and its pink blush had a childlike, well-defined edge curving down from cheekbone to jawline. He thought it could do no harm to ask her out to dinner. She began by noting that she was the only woman in the room, and that the committee reflected one of the very problems it might want to address. Round the table, everyone, including Beard, who had invited all of those present except Nancy Temple, murmured his emphatic assent. Her voice had the hypnotic sing-song inflections of Ulster. She confirmed that she had grown up in a middle-class suburb of Belfast and attended Queen's University, where she studied social anthropology.

She said she could best explain her field by outlining a recent project, a four-month in-depth study of a genetics lab in Glasgow as it set out to isolate and describe a lion's gene, Trim-5, and its function. Her purpose was to demonstrate that this gene, or any gene, was, in the strongest sense, socially constructed. Without the various 'entexting' tools the scientists used—the single-photon luminometer, the flow cytometer, immuno-fluorescence, and so on—the gene could not be said to exist. These tools were expensive to own, expensive to learn to use, and were therefore replete with social meaning. The gene was not an objective entity, merely waiting to be revealed by scientists. It was entirely manufactured by their hypotheses, their creativity, and by their instrumentation, without which it could not be detected. And when it was finally expressed in terms of its so-called base pairs and its probable role, that description, that text, only had meaning, and only derived its reality, from within the limited network of geneticists who might read about it. Outside those networks, Trim-5 did not exist.

During this presentation, Beard and the physicists from universities and schools listened in some embarrassment. Politely, they avoided exchanging glances. They tended to take the conventional view, that the world existed independently, in all its mystery, awaiting description and explanation, though that did not prevent the observer leaving thumbprints all over the field of observation. Beard had heard rumours that strange ideas were commonplace among the liberal-arts departments. It was said that humanities students were routinely taught that science was just one more belief system, no more or less truthful than religion or astrology. He had always thought that this must be a slur against his colleagues on the arts side. The results surely spoke for themselves. Who was going to submit to a vaccine designed by a priest?

When Nancy Temple came to the end of her speech, Newcastle and Cambridge spoke up simultaneously, more in wonder than in anger. 'Where does that leave Huntington's, for example?' one said as the other was asking, 'Do you honestly believe that what you don't know about doesn't exist?'

Beard, chivalrous to the hilt, thought it his duty to protect her and was about to step in, but Professor Temple was replying in a tolerant manner.

'Huntington's is also culturally inscribed. It was once a narrative about divine punishment or demonic possession. Now it's the story of a faulty gene, and one day it will likely transmute into something else. As for the genes we know nothing about, well, obviously, I have nothing to say. Of the genes that have been described, clearly they can only come to us mediated by culture.'

It was her calmness that provoked the uproar, and this time the chairman intervened firmly—he was an old hand at this game—to remind the committee that time was limited and guide its attention towards item two on the agenda. The brief was to convene twelve times in thirteen months and then make recommendations. Now was the time to pencil in some provisional dates.

Later that afternoon, the committee arranged itself behind a long table in a room at the Royal Society for the press launch of what had been named by a government public-relations department as Physics UK. It had its own logo displayed on an easel, a flighty monogram of the letters E, M and C squared impaled upon an 'equals' sign, to resemble an asymmetric garden shrub. Beard introduced his colleagues, made some opening remarks and invited questions from the journalists, who, slumped over their recorders and notebooks, seemed depressed by the seriousness of their assignment, its scandalous lack of controversy. Who was going to take a brave stand against more physicists? The questions were dull, the answers diligent. The whole project was lamentably worthy. Why do the government the favour of writing it up at length?

Then a woman from a mid-market tabloid asked a question, also routine, something of an old chestnut, and Beard replied, as he thought, blandly. It was true, women were under-represented in physics and always had been. The problem had often been discussed, and (he was mindful of Professor Temple as he said it) certainly his committee would be looking at it again to see if there were new ways of encouraging more girls into the subject. He believed there were no longer any institutional barriers or prejudices. There were other branches of science where women were well represented, and some where they predominated. And then, because he was boring himself, he added that it might have to be accepted one day that a ceiling had been reached. Although there were many gifted women physicists, it was at least conceivable that they would always remain in a minority, albeit a substantial one, in this particular field. There might always be more men than women who *wanted* to work in physics. There was a consensus in cognitive psychology, based on a wide range of experimental work, that in statistical terms the brains of men and women were significantly different. This was emphatically not a question of gender superiority, nor was it a matter of social conditioning, though of course it played a reinforcing role. These were widely observed innate differences in cognitive ability. In studies and metastudies, women were shown to have, on average, greater language skills, better visual memory, clearer emotional judgement and superior mathematical calculation. Men scored higher in mathematical problem-solving and abstract reasoning, and in visual-spatial awareness. Men and women had different priorities in life, different attitudes to risk, to status, to hierarchies. Above all, and this was the really striking difference, amounting to roughly one standard deviation, and the one to have been studied repeatedly: from early in life, girls tended to be more interested in people, boys more in things and abstract rules. And this difference showed in the fields of science they tended to choose: more women in the life sciences and the social sciences, more men in engineering and physics.

Beard noticed that he was losing the room's attention. Phrases like 'standard deviation' generally had this effect on journalists. A few people at the back were talking among themselves.

In the front row, a gentlemanly reporter of a certain age had closed his eyes. Beard pressed on towards his conclusion. There was surely much to be done to get more women into physics and to make them feel welcome there. But in one possible future, it might be a waste of effort to strive for parity when there were other branches of study that women preferred.

The journalist who had asked the question was nodding numbly. Behind her, someone else was starting to ask an unrelated question. The morning would have passed into oblivion like any other had not at that moment the professor of science studies suddenly stood, blushing pink, squared her papers against the table with a loud rap and announced to the room, 'Before I go outside to be sick, and I mean violently sick because of what I've just heard, I wish to announce my resignation from Professor Beard's committee.'

She strode away towards the door, amid a din of voices and of chairs pushed back across the parquet as the journalists leaped to their feet. Professionally engaged at last, delighted, desperate, competitive, they hurried after her.

As the room emptied, Professor Jack Pollard, the quantum-gravity specialist from Newcastle, who had given the Reith Lectures not so long ago and seemed to know everything, said in Beard's ear, 'You've put your foot in it now. She's postmodern, you see, a blank-slater, a strong social constructivist. They all are, you know. Shall we have a coffee?'

At the time, these terms meant little to Beard. He had one thought. This was not the way to tender a resignation. Then an even simpler second thought. He should leave as quickly as possible, even though he knew that Pollard wanted to gossip. In different circumstances, Beard would happily have sat with him in a café for an hour. There was a community, a shifting international group who knew each other jealously, affectionately, possessively, and had, with notable defections and deaths, travelled together since the heroic old days of classical string theory in pursuit of its grail, the unification of the fundamental forces with gravity. They had eventually seen the limitations of strings and embraced superstrings and heterotic string theory to arrive by these threads in the cavernous maternal shelter of M-theory. Each breakthrough had generated a new set of problems, inconsistencies, physical implausibilities. Ten dimensions, then, with a backward glance at the super-gravity men, eleven! Dimensions tightly wrapped on six circles, the rediscovery of Kaluza and Klein from the nineteen twenties, the delightful intricacies of Calabi–Yau manifolds and orbifolds! And the singular drama of the universe in its first one hundreth of a second! Beard had played no creative part, and did not quite have the mathematical reach, but he knew the gossip. And the jokes—the string theorist caught in bed with another woman who exclaimed to his wife, 'Darling, I can explain everything!' What a long hard road it had been, and so it remained—the outer edge of human intellectual grasp interwoven with all-too-human stories. The theorist who neglected his dying wife, and still failed to restate the problem. The obscure post-doc who resolved a set of contradictions in a liberating insight that wrecked his health. The famous convention that shamefully neglected an old eminence. The brown-nosing mediocrity who got the super-grant. The bust-up between two giants who once shared a lab.

Yes, he would have loved a chat, but he sensed a contraction around him, something like gathering darkness or its emotional equivalent. He was in trouble, and he should fade away before he made things worse. He apologised quickly to Pollard and the rest, took his briefcase and walked from the room, across the hall and left by the main entrance. Outside, sunlight and the city's background hum appeared to shrink his concerns. A mountain range might have had the same effect. Perhaps this was a fuss about nothing. As he passed he caught snatches of Nancy Temple's pavement press conference, delivered with lilting reasonableness: '. . . resurgent eugenics . . . sinister claims about human nature . . . neo-liberal attack on collectivity . . .' Nice punchy lines for the tabloids. Some of the journalists crowding around her were using the roof of a parked car as a writing desk, others were already phoning the story in. Perhaps she did not know that the excitement was in part about the government. One of its committees was in trouble. Another Blair failure.

Beard ignored the voices calling out his first name as he crossed the road. Never help feed a press story about yourself. But the next day he wondered if he should have turned back when he read of himself 'scuttling away in shame' under the headline 'Nobel Prof Says No To Lab Chicks'.

At first it seemed that this particular story had no staying power, no legs. After a minor eruption of morning headlines, there was silence for two days.

He thought he had come through. But during that time one tabloid was busy with its research. On Saturday, Beard's 'love life' was revealed and artfully braided with the 'no to girls in white coats' story. On Sunday the other papers picked it up and piled in and he was reinvented as 'the bonking boffin', a 'Nobel love-rat', and a kind of learned satyr—'the prof-goat'. There were references to the Aldous murder case, but Beard's earlier incarnation as the harmless, dreamy cuckold, the innocent fool, the dupe of a flighty wife, was conveniently forgotten. Now he was a loathed figure, seducing women even as he drove them out of science. In the more serious press, he was described as a physicist turned 'genetic determinist', a fanatical sociobiologist whose ideas about gender difference were shown to be indirectly derived from social Darwinism, which in turn had spawned Third Reich race theories. Then, daringly building on this, a journalist, more in the spirit of playful diary-page spite than genuine conviction, suggested that Beard was a neo-Nazi. No one took the charge seriously for a moment, but it became possible for other papers to take up the term even as they dismissed it, carefully bracketing and legalising the insult with quotation marks. Beard became the 'neo-Nazi' Professor.

An article in one left-of-centre paper argued that most important differences between men and women were cultural constructs. In response, Beard wrote a feebly sarcastic letter, a mere six lines, four hours and a score of drafts in the making, protesting that these days men could not get pregnant and that it was all society's fault. It was published, but no one seemed to notice.

A week later, the same paper hosted a debate between Beard and Temple and others on 'Women and Physics' at the ICA. By now he was determined to put the world right about his views. He shared the platform with various academics from the humanities, mostly men, all hostile. For reasons that were not explained, Professor Temple was not there and had sent along a colleague in her place. And where were all the scientists? he kept asking the organisers before the event. No one seemed to know.

The main theatre was sold out. In another room a second crowd watched on monitors. Press coverage had done its trick of creating a hunger. People wanted to see for themselves a modern monster in the flesh and be horrified. There were even gasps when he got to his feet. To a rising swell of scornful moaning, Beard covered the same ground, the same cognitive studies again, but in greater detail. When he mentioned the metastudies reporting that girls' language skills were greater on average than boys', there was a roar of derision and a speaker on the platform rose fearsomely to denounce him for the 'crude objectivism by which he seeks to maintain and advance the social dominance of the white male elite'. The moment the fellow sat down he was rewarded by the kind of cheers that might presage a revolution. Bewildered, Beard did not get the connection. He was completely lost. When, later, he irritably demanded of the meeting if it thought that gravity too was a social construct, he was booed, and a woman in the audience stood to propose in stern, headmistressly tones that he reflect on the 'hegemonic arrogance' of his question. What gave him the right? By what invisible dispensation of power in the current social arrangement did he think that he was entitled to set the question in these terms? He was baffled, he had no answer. 'Hegemonic' was a frequent term of abuse. Another was 'reductionist'. In exasperation, Beard said that without reductionism there could be no science. There was prolonged laughter when someone from the floor shouted, 'Exactly!'

Nancy Temple's replacement was Susan Appelbaum, a visiting academic from Tel Aviv, who lectured in cognitive psychology and was as light as a bird in her red and blue frock, with a twittering voice to match. She was nervous speaking in public and made an awkward start. In the theatre there was suspicion and some confusion. From the point of view of the audience, which seemed to be of one mind in all things, she had points in her favour and points against. As a woman she was a poor hegemon, and being unconfident, poorer still (Beard thought he was getting the hang of this term). Also, after a few minutes, it was clear she was speaking against Beard. On the other hand, she was a Jew, an Israeli and, by association, an oppressor of Palestinians. Perhaps she was a Zionist, perhaps she had served in the army. And once she got under way, the hostility in the room began to grow. This was a postmodern crowd with well-developed antennae for the unacceptable line. Its heart, when not seized by correct utterance from correct quarters, turned cold. The lady from Tel Aviv was forthright about her reactionary position, which included various underlying assumptions she shared with Beard. She was an objectivist, in that she believed the world existed independently of the language that described it, she spoke in praise of reductionist analysis, she was an empiricist and, by her own proud admission, an 'Enlightenment rationalist', which was, Beard sensed from the groaning dissent in the audience, a tad regressive, if not hegemonic after all. There was, she insisted, such a thing as biological sex differences in cognition, but only empirical evidence should shape our view. There was a human nature and it had an evolutionary history. We were not born *tabula rasa*. By the time her introduction was over, she was having difficulty holding the theatre's attention.

Not many listened to Appelbaum as she confronted Beard's arguments. She knew all the same studies, and many more. Some of them she had conducted herself. The literature was clear—there were no significant differences in cognition that gave males an advantage in maths or physics. Divergences between boys and girls, men and women, only emerged in complex tests where subjects were offered more than one route to a solution: men and women chose differently. The people-versus-things distinction was mythology and had distorted some poorly designed but much-cited experiments. On social factors, on the other hand, the studies were eloquent—perceptions and expectations were far stronger signals than objectively measured differences between men and women. This should have pleased her audience, but they didn't catch it, they weren't attending as she described experiments in which babies were assigned random gender names and adults were asked to judge their various activities. Or parents were asked to predict their children's abilities in a given task. Or academics were required to evaluate fictitious male and female candidates with identical qualifications. These, she said, were statistically significant data that showed that perception of gender was a powerful determinant of attitudes. And there were well-studied self-sustaining loops—people applied to departments where there were people 'like them', and where they were likely to have success.

By the time Appelbaum started in on her conclusion, Beard thought he was the only one listening. Statistics were clearly not a postmodern concern, and nor were historical anecdotes. She referred to the life of Fanny Mendelssohn, recognised at the time as a prodigous musical talent, the equal of her brother, Felix. Famously, her father explained to her in a letter that while music would be her brother's profession, for her, music must remain an ornament, for Sundays. A hundred years ago, many 'scientific' reasons were advanced why women could not be doctors. Today, there remained unconscious or unintentional, widely diffused differences in the ways boys and girls, men and women, were understood and judged. From cradle to first job application and beyond, in a sustained arc of development, these cultural factors were shown by empirical investigation to be vastly more significant than biology. It was plain why there were so few women in physics.

She sat down to no applause. But there was general relief that she was finally done. Ten minutes later the meeting broke up. Beard headed straight for the exit, feeling reprieved. Some might have said that he had just taken a good kicking, others that he had triumphed. What did he know? He was a physicist after all, not a cognitive psychologist. But pleasingly, here at the ICA, he was hated no more than he had been at the start. These people were not going to take their lead from an Israeli. That was hardly fine, but there was nothing he could do about it. And *he* was fine, he was still in one piece. As he went along the corridor, the crowd parted for him, no doubt in distaste, and he was at the door onto the Mall in seconds and stepping out into bright sunshine and a reception party, about thirty chanting protestors with placards—No To Eugenics! Nazi Professor Out!—and a dozen press, mostly cameramen, and four members of the Metropolitan Police.

Perhaps matters would have turned out better if Beard had not brought out from the event indoors a mood of jaunty defiance. There were half a dozen older women among the demonstrators. One of them nipped out from behind a policeman, took a tomato from a brown paper bag and threw it at Beard. She was ten feet away and there was no time to dodge. A rotten tomato is an item of urban legend. This one, though soft, looked perfectly edible. It flopped against his lapel and clung there a moment. When it fell he caught it in his open palm, and with a quick, impulsive movement chucked it back, an entirely playful gesture, he tried to explain afterwards, without anger or malice. Why else throw it underarm? The tomato, its skin now ruptured, hit the woman full in the face, just to the right of her nose. With a strange sound, a plaintive musical hoot, the woman, who was about Beard's age and almost as plump, brought her hands up to her face, somehow trapping and smearing the tomato against her features, and at the same time sank to her knees.

In colour, it made a dramatic photograph. Taken from behind Beard, it showed him looming over a woman cowering on the ground, the victim of a gory assault. In Germany it was on the cover of a magazine with the headline 'Protester Felled By "Neo-Nazi" Professor'. In the background, not quite out of focus, was the relevant placard. Another picture, also widely used, taken over the head of the kneeling woman, revealed Beard's heartless smile. He could not help himself, he was genuinely amused. The tomato was so soft, his toss so gentle, the woman's reaction so comically overplayed, a policeman so solicitous in bending over her, another so self-important as he urgently radioed for an ambulance. This was street theatre. A policewoman touched Beard's arm and said tonelessly that she was arresting him for assault. A second policewoman stood close, pressing her shoulder against his to let him know that struggle was useless. The handcuffs, alive with the young woman's body warmth, clicked over his wrists to a good-natured cheer from the demonstrators. A half-dozen photographers walked backwards in front of him as he was led towards a patrol car parked on the Mall. As it pulled away they ran alongside, with a great clatter of shoes, snapping Beard in the criminal gloom of the back seat.

The police car drove past the National Portrait Gallery, up the Charing Cross Road and stopped outside Foyles. The arresting officer, who was sitting with Beard, unlocked the handcuffs as her colleague turned round in the front seat and said, 'You can go now, sir.'

'I thought you were charging me with assault.'

'Just removing you from a scene where there was likely to be a breach of the peace. For your own safety.'

'How considerate of you to think of handcuffing me in front of the press.'

'Kind of you to say so, sir. Only doing our job. But thank you, sir.'

The car door was held open for him, and then he was alone on the pavement, wondering if there was a book he needed to buy. There was not. He went home to his flat and lay brooding in the scum-rimmed bath, gazing through steam clouds at the archipelago of his disrupted selfhood—mountainous paunch, penis tip, unruly toes—scattered in a line across a soapy grey sea. He told himself that things are often not as bad as you think. That was true. But sometimes they are worse: a dying story had been revived.

Over the following week images of the shackled Nobel professor, of the humbled victim kneeling before her persecutor, of his unwholesome grin, digitally multiplied themselves around the world like retroviruses. Out at the Centre, Jock Braby seized his chance and forced Beard's resignation. A lecture series was cancelled in outrage, and at various venues his presence was thought likely to harm the good name of an institution or a fellow visiting dignitary or, at the very least, cause trouble from the students and younger faculty. A kindly civil servant phoned to ask whether he cared to choose between resigning from Physics UK and being sacked. A research centre took the trouble to let him know that the name of Beard, now mud, would cease to appear on its letterhead. In the senior common room of an Oxford college, where he went for solace and coffee, three English-literature dons walked out at the sight of him, heads held high, while their own coffees cooled conspicuously by their abandoned chairs. His phone did not ring much—his friends were silent, or, like his ex-wives, reticent, or baffled. However, Imperial College, delighted with the lab he had set up and the funding he had attracted, stood by him. And he received an affable, comradely letter, bearing the stamp of an Austrian prison, from a neo-Nazi serving time for the murder of a Jewish journalist.

For two weeks he thought of nothing else. To stay away from reading newspapers, as Melissa sweetly proposed, was beyond him. When there was nothing new in the two-kilo wedge of the morning's press, he felt a curious, twisted disappointment at an immediate prospect of emptiness, at having nothing to consume him all day. He had discovered a compulsion to read of this alien, the avatar bearing his name, the goat-monster-seducer, denier of a woman's right to a career in science, eugenicist. He was baffled by how he had ended up stuck with this last label. But after a few blustery walks up and over Primrose Hill among the pushchairs and kite-fliers, he came to a tentative conclusion. The Third Reich had projected a prohibitive shadow more than half a century long over genetics where it touched on human affairs—at least, in the minds of those outside the subject. To suggest the possibility of genetic influence, genetic difference, of an evolutionary past bearing down in some degree on cognition, on men and women, on culture, was to some minds like entering a camp and volunteering to work with Doctor Mengele.

When he tried out this notion on biologist friends they were amused. That was old hat, that was seventies stuff, there was a new consensus now, not only in genetics, but in academic life in general. He was too bitter. Have another drink! But what did they know about journalists or postmodernists? As Beard saw it, the solution was simple. Stick to photons—no resting mass, no charge, no controversy on the human scale. His work in artificial photosynthesis was proceeding well, with a laboratory prototype already using light to split water efficiently into hydrogen and oxygen. Civilisation needed a safe new energy source, and he could be of use. He would be redeemed. Let there be light!

For all that resolve, he thought his disgrace would mark him for years. And then what happened? Nothing. His avatar vanished. Overnight, he was airbrushed from the public prints, a soccer match-fixing story took his place, and the slow-healing amnesia began. For a while he was underemployed, then four months later, he gave six short talks about Einstein for the BBC World Service. A research group in Germany seduced him onto its letterhead. Cambridge saw its chance to steal him from Imperial, then Imperial trumped Cambridge and gave him two more researchers and even more money. UCL wanted a slice of him too, offering as a softener an honorary degree, then Caltech pitched in, and some old friends at MIT wanted to bring him across.

How magnanimous was public life, and how well did the lustre of a Nobel laureate reflect upon an academy and oil the wheels of grant acquisition!

* * *

By the time his taxi had swung round Trafalgar Square and paused to join in a traffic jam along the Strand, he was over an hour and a half late. Five minutes later, he had made no progress. For the past four hours, it suddenly seemed, his thoughts had been cramped by delay and exasperation, until now, sitting in the motionless cab, the confinement became intolerable. He pushed a twenty-pound note through the slot in the driver's screen and climbed out with his luggage and began to tow it towards the Savoy. Walking might make him later still, but acting like a man in a hurry rather than thinking like one was a relief. And barrelling along with his wheeled burden, overtaking and weaving between pedestrians, was the workout he had been promising himself for years. Richly dishevelled, the knot of his purple tie askew, the expensive wool suit in need of a press, the overcoat too warm for the modern English winter, hurrying lopsidedly along, one leg making a decent show of stepping forward, the other stiffly scooting, he bobbed up the Strand like a fat boy on a pogo stick. Inside a minute, he was troubled by a narrow stab of pain in his chest, deep in some neglected lower region of his left lung, among the less frequented alveoli, and he slowed. No meeting was worth dying for. The traffic began to move again, and his own cab, now for hire, shot past him as he shuffled towards the hotel.

In the lobby, two conference organisers were waiting. The younger one took his bag, the other, a very old man in a blazer leaning heavily on a walking stick, with a liver-spotted death mask for a face, pointed at his watch and walked with him up the stairs.

'All is fine,' the fellow croaked through the effort of raising his body weight through the luxurious gravitational field. 'We've rejigged the running order. You're on in five minutes.'

Beard heard this in good heart, for he felt by comparison youthful and unassailable, the motion of his feet across the thick carpet was pleasing and the pain had vanished from his chest.

Another official, younger but more senior, of Indian origin, received him by a set of lofty double doors thrown open to the din of teatime chatter. After the preliminaries—a great honour, a thousand thank yous, much anticipated, about lateness please not to worry—the young man, whose name, Saleel, Beard remembered from email exchanges, ran through the composition of the audience: institutional men and women, a few civil servants, a few academics, no journalists.

But Beard was not fully attentive, for his gaze had shifted from Saleel's face to a view over the young man's dark-suited shoulder of the room and its voluble crowd. Arranged on tables covered in white cloths, framed by high windows and a view of the darkening Thames, were square porcelain dishes densely heaped with plump pillows of crustless sandwiches. Even from where he stood he could make out the fat pink stripes of a smoked-salmon filling. Artfully scattered across the tables were slices of lemons, detached yellow smiles of enticement to which no one in the room was paying much attention. He was not at that moment truly hungry, but he was, in his own term, pre-hungry. That is, he could appreciate how pleasurable it might be, in less than an hour, to lift a few of those items onto a plate and contemplate the river while he ate. And just as easily, he could anticipate the regret he would feel if the dishes were removed too soon, when the afternoon tea break came to an end, which it must do when his talk began. Safer to eat a few now.

Saleel was saying, 'A conservative lot, institutional investors, not scientific, of course, so not too technical would be most heartily appreciated.'

By turning his shoulder into the room, Beard was able to prompt his host, clearly a sensitive and intelligent man, to exclaim as he handed over a white envelope, 'But of course, you need refreshment! And please, your emolument.'

A minute later Beard had the plate and, on it, thick-cut smoked wild salmon speckled with dill and ground black pepper between thin white bread slices, nine heavy quarter segments—a precautionary number, since he did not have to eat them all. But he did, and very quickly, without much satisfaction or even a thought for the river, because a soft-spoken man with a stutter wanted to tell him about his son's physics exam, and then a tall man with a stoop and a jutting ginger beard and large accusing eyes set eerily far apart introduced himself. He was Jeremy Mellon, lecturer in urban studies and folklore. Beard, who was on his sixth piece, felt obliged to ask why

Mellon was here.

'Well, I'm interested in the forms of narrative that climate science has generated. It's an epic story, of course, with a million authors.'

Beard was suspicious. This was the Nancy Temple tendency. People who kept on about narrative tended to have a squiffy view of reality, believing all versions of it to be of equal value. But he did not even have to say, 'How interesting,' for people were setting down their cups and saucers and hurrying to find their seats, and the old fellow with a stick was grimacing at him and once more tapping his watch, and there was only just enough time to bolt down the last three wedges of smoked salmon.

Beard was guided to a purpose-built stage and shown to a moulded orange plastic seat behind a vat of bilious red and yellow tulips. He tried not to look at them. He thought there was a general air of unreality about the gathering. A couple of hundred people sat in ranks, in a shallow arc before him. The pinkness of so many faces looked absurd. Their chatter seemed to resound in an echo chamber. The Savoy was swaying, or undulating gently beneath his feet, as though it had slid into the river and was rocking on the turning tide. He succumbed to a fit of yawning, which he suppressed through tensed nostril wings. He had to face it, he was a little queasy, and it did not help that a heavy-breathing technician with mottled skin and odorous tooth decay or pyorrhoea bent close over his face to attach a radio mic.

While Beard sat cross-kneed, with customary, frozen half-smile, pretending to listen to Saleel's long and too-fulsome introduction, and even more so when at last he stood to bored applause and took his place behind the lectern, gripping tight its edges in both hands, he felt an oily nausea at something monstrous and rotten from the sea, stranded on the tidal mud flats of a stagnant estuary, decaying gaseously in his gut and welling up, contaminating his breath, his words and, suddenly, his thoughts.

'The planet,' he said, surprising himself, 'is sick.'

There was a groan, followed by a susurrus of dismissal from his audience. Pension-fund managers preferred more nuanced terms. But using the word 'sick', rather like vomiting itself, gave Beard some instant relief.

'Curing the patient is a matter of urgency and is going to be expensive—perhaps as much as two per cent of global GDP, and far more if we delay the treatment. I am convinced, and I have come here to tell you, that anyone who wishes to help with the therapy, to be a part of the process and invest in it, is going to make very large sums of money, staggering sums. What's at issue is the creation of another industrial revolution. Here is your opportunity. Coal and then oil have made our civilisation, they have been superb resources, lifting hundreds of millions of us out of the mental prison of rural subsistence. Liberation from the daily grind coupled with our innate curiosity has produced in a mere two hundred years an exponential growth of our knowledge base. The process began in Europe and the United States, has spread in our lifetime to parts of Asia, and now to India and China and South America, with Africa yet to come. All our other problems and conflicts conceal this obvious fact: we barely understand how successful we have been.

'So of course, we should salute our own inventiveness. We are very clever monkeys. But the engine of our industrial revolution has been cheap, accessible energy. We would have got nowhere without it. Look how fantastic it is. A kilogram of gasoline contains roughly thirteen thousand watt hours of energy. Hard to beat. But we want to replace it. So what's next? The best electrical batteries we have store about three hundred watt hours of energy per kilogram. And that's the scale of our problem, thirteen thousand against three hundred. No contest! But unfortunately, we don't have the luxury of choice. We have to replace that gasoline quickly for three compelling reasons. First, and simplest, the oil must run out. No one knows exactly when, but there's a consensus that we'll be at peak production at some point in the next five to fifteen years. After that, production will decline, while the demand for energy will go on rising as the world's population expands and people strive for a better standard of living. Second, many oil-producing areas are politically unstable and we can no longer risk our levels of dependence. Third, and most crucially, burning fossil fuels, putting carbon dioxide and other gases into the atmosphere, is steadily warming the planet, the consequences of which we are only beginning to understand. But the basic science is in. We either slow down, and then stop, or face an economic and human catastrophe on a grand scale within our grandchildren's lifetime.

'And this brings us to the central question, the burning question. How do we slow down and stop while sustaining our civilisation and continuing to bring millions out of poverty? Not by being virtuous, not by going to the bottle bank and turning down the thermostat and buying a smaller car. That merely delays the catastrophe by a year or two. Any delay is useful, but it's not the solution. This matter has to move beyond virtue. Virtue is too passive, too narrow. Virtue can motivate individuals, but for groups, societies, a whole civilisation, it's a weak force. Nations are never virtuous, though they might sometimes think they are. For humanity en masse, greed trumps virtue. So we have to welcome into our solutions the ordinary compulsions of self-interest, and also celebrate novelty, the thrill of invention, the pleasures of ingenuity and co-operation, the satisfaction of profit. Oil and coal are energy carriers, and so, in abstract form, is money. And the answer to that burning question is of course exactly where that money, your money, has to flow—affordable clean energy.

'Imagine if I were standing in front of you two hundred and fifty years ago—you, a collection of country gentlemen and ladies—predicting the coming of the first industrial revolution, and telling you to invest in coal and iron, steam engines, cotton mills and, later, railways. Or a century or so later, with the invention of the internal combustion engine, I foresaw the growing importance of oil and urged you to invest in that. Or a hundred years on, in microprocessors, in personal computers and the internet and the opportunities they offered. So here, ladies and gentlemen, is another such moment. Do not be tempted by the illusion that the world economy and its stock exchanges can exist apart from the world's natural environment.

Our planet earth is a finite entity. You have the data in front of you, you have the choice—the human project must be safely and cleanly fuelled, or it fails, it sinks. You, the market, either rise to this, and get rich along the way, or you sink with all the rest. We are on this rock together, you have nowhere else to go . . .'

He was hearing dismissive whispers from separate quarters of the room, which had begun, he thought, on his words 'warming the planet'. His nausea was rising, that bloated carcass within his own was odiously stirring. While listening to Saleel's introduction he had noticed that the velvet curtain behind him had a gap at its centre—an escape route he might just need. He stopped speaking, inhaled deeply, and made himself stand erect and gaze about the room, trying to identify the dissent. A lifetime of public speaking had taught him the value of the unembarrassed pause. He knew that the solid institutions of the City nurtured a vigorous culture of irrationalist denial, in the face of basic physics and years of good data. The deniers, like people everywhere, wanted business as usual. They feared a threat to shareholder value, they suspected that climate scientists were a self-serving industry, just like themselves. Beard felt towards them all the contempt of the recent convert.

As he drew breath to continue speaking, he experienced a fishy reflux rising from his gorge, like salted anchovies, with a dash of bile. He closed his eyes, swallowed hard, and changed tack.

'I read in yesterday's paper that in just four years' time we'll arrive at the bicentennial of Charles Darwin's birth, and the hundred and fiftieth anniversary of the first edition of *The Origin of Species*. The celebrations are bound to obscure the work of another great Victorian scientist, an Irishman named John Tyndall, who began a serious study of the atmosphere in that same year, 1859. One of his interests was light, which is why I feel a special affinity with him. He was the first to suggest that it was the scattering of light by the atmosphere that made the sky blue, and he was the first to describe and explain the hothouse or greenhouse effect. He built experimental equipment that showed how water vapour, carbon dioxide and other gases prevent the earth's warmth from the sun being radiated back out into space, and so make life possible. Remove this blanket of vapour and gases and, as he famously wrote'—Beard drew a card from the top pocket of his jacket and read—'"You would assuredly destroy every plant capable of being destroyed by a freezing temperature. The warmth of our fields and gardens would pour itself unrequited into space, and the sun would rise upon an island held fast in the iron grip of frost."

'By the beginning of the twentieth century it was known to a few that industrial civilisation was adding carbon dioxide to the atmosphere. In succeeding years it was understood precisely how a molecule of this gas absorbs and contains the longer wavelengths of radiant light and traps heat. The more carbon dioxide, the warmer the planet. In the nineteen sixties an unmanned satellite showed that our neighbour Venus has an atmosphere that is ninety-five per cent carbon dioxide. And it's more than four hundred and sixty degrees at the surface, hot enough to melt zinc.

Without its greenhouse effect, Venus would have roughly the same temperature as the earth. Fifty years ago we were putting thirteen billion metric tons of carbon dioxide into the atmosphere every year. That figure has almost doubled. It's more than twenty-five years since scientists first warned the US government of anthropogenic climate change. In fifteen years there have been three IPCC reports of mounting urgency. Last year a survey of nearly a thousand peer-reviewed papers showed not one dissenting from the majority view. Forget sunspots, forget the Tunguska Meteorite of 1908, ignore the oil-industry lobbies and their think-tank and media clients who pretend, as the tobacco lobby has done, that there are two sides to this, that scientists are divided. The science is relatively simple, one-sided and beyond doubt. Ladies and gentlemen, the question has been discussed and investigated for a hundred and fifty years, for as long as Darwin's *Origin of Species* has been in print, and is as incontestable as the basics of natural selection. We've observed and we know the mechanisms, we've measured and the numbers tell the story, the earth is warming and we know why. There is no scientific controversy, only this plain fact. That may sadden you or frighten you, but it also should position you beyond doubt, free to consider your next move.'

The nausea came in on a fresh wave and threatened to disgrace him. He was sweating coldly, he was aching and weak in his spine. He had to keep talking to distract himself. And he had to talk fast. He was being pursued, he had to run.

'So,' he said, cracking the word through something glutinous in his throat. 'Allow me to make some suggestions. Collectively, according to my enquiries, your various organisations represent around four hundred billion dollars of investments. These are golden days in the global markets and sometimes it seems the party will never end. But you might just have overlooked one sector that is outperforming the rest by doubling every two years. You may have noticed, you may have turned away. Not quite respectable enough, a mere passing fashion, you may have thought, too many of those post-hippie plutocrats from Stanford involved. But also involved are BP, General Electric, Sharp, Mitsubishi. Renewable energy. The revolution has begun. The market will be even more lucrative than coal or oil because the world economy is many times bigger and the rate of change is faster. Colossal fortunes will be made. The sector is seething with vitality, invention—and, above all, growth. It has thousands of unquoted companies positioning themselves with new techniques. Scientists, engineers, designers are pouring into the sector. There are log jams in the patent offices and supply chains. This is an ocean of dreams, of realistic dreams of making hydrogen from algae, aviation fuel from genetically modified microbes, of electricity out of sunlight, wind, tides, waves, cellulose, household waste, of scrubbing carbon dioxide from the air and turning it into a fuel, of imitating the secrets of plant life. An alien landing on our planet and noticing how it was bathed in radiant energy would be amazed to learn that we believe ourselves to have an energy problem, that we ever should have thought of poisoning ourselves by burning fossil fuels or creating plutonium.

‘Imagine we came across a man at the edge of a forest in heavy rainfall. This man is dying of thirst. He has an axe in his hand and he is felling the trees in order to suck sap from the trunks. There are a few mouthfuls in each tree. All around him is devastation, dead trees, no birdsong, and he knows the forest is vanishing. So why doesn’t he tip back his head and drink the rain? Because he cuts trees expertly, because he has always done it this way, because the kind of people who advocate rain-drinking he considers suspicious types.

‘That rain is our sunlight. An energy source drenches our planet, drives its climate and its life. It falls on us in a constant stream, a sweet rain of photons. A single photon striking a semiconductor releases an electron, and so electricity is born, as simple as that, right out of sunbeams. This is photovoltaics. Einstein described it and won a Nobel Prize. If I believed in God, I would say this is his greatest gift to us. Since I don’t, I say how auspicious are the laws of physics! Less than an hour’s worth of all the sunlight falling on the earth would satisfy the whole world’s needs for a year. A fraction of our hot deserts could power our civilisation. No one can own sunlight, no one can privatise or nationalise it. Soon, everyone will harvest it, from rooftops, ships’ sails, from kids’ backpacks. I spoke of poverty at the start—some of the poorest countries in the world are solar rich. We could help them by buying their megawatts. And domestic consumers will love making power out of sunlight and selling it to the grid. It’s primal.

‘There are a dozen proven ways of making electricity out of sunlight, but the ultimate goal is still ahead, and this is close to my heart. I’m talking of artificial photosynthesis, of copying the methods nature took three billion years to perfect. We'll use light directly to make cheap hydrogen and oxygen out of water, and run our turbines night and day, or we'll make fuels out of water, sunlight and carbon dioxide, or we'll build desalination plants that make electricity as well as fresh water. Believe me, this will happen. Solar will expand, and with your help, and with your and your clients' enrichment, it will expand faster. Basic science, the market and our grave situation will determine that this is the future—logic, not idealism, compels it.'

He thought now he was going to be sick. His mind went blank and, fearful of a moment's pause, he spoke of the first thing that came to mind, and lurched into a personal anecdote. Blandly at first, like a man testing a microphone by itemising his breakfast, he summoned for his audience his journey that afternoon from the airport. Before long he was convinced that the story was not such a poor choice after all. He had yet to make real contact with his listeners, he had said nothing droll, and this was England, where people expected to be amused, however faintly, by speeches on public occasions. He was ahead of the nausea now as he described his purchase of newspapers at the airport shop. When he confessed to a weakness for a certain flavour of crisp there was a stirring of muted amusement in the rows of suited figures. Perhaps it was pity.

He was warming to his tale, convinced that it had a useful conclusion that he would discover in the telling. He set it out, the crowded train, the bottle of water on the table and, by it, the lurid packet opened by himself, and the unnerving stare of a large young man. There were appreciative titters as he described the way the adversaries devoured the snack. Beard did not embellish, but he intensified the moment at which he lunged in revenge at the water bottle and drained it in a few gulps and tossed it back on the table. He lingered on the way the man swung the suitcase down from the rack, and on his own furious refusal to engage with him. He spun them out, those seconds on the station platform before the discovery, which he divulged with a quickening of pulse, and a flush of eager pride when his audience chuckled, or even laughed out loud, as he, boldly miming now, held with outstretched arm the second packet before him, like Hamlet with Yorick's skull. Yes, they all seemed to like him a little more.

He hurried towards his conclusion, his excuse for telling this story. Were his points somewhat forced, or had he stumbled upon two important truths? No time to consider.

'What I discovered on Paddington station was, first, that in a grave situation, a crisis, we understand, sometimes too late, that it is not in other people, or in the system, or in the nature of things that the problem lies, but in ourselves, our own follies and unexamined assumptions. And second, there are moments when the acquisition of new information forces us to make a fundamental reinterpretation of our situation. Industrial civilisation is at just such a moment. We pass through a mirror, everything is transformed, the old paradigm makes way for the new.'

But the rhetorical flourish of these final phrases had a desperate air, his voice sounded thin in his ears, his conclusions were hollow after all. Where now? His body knew precisely. He released his grip on the lectern and turned to step somnambulantly through the gap in the curtain into a gloomy space broken by looming columns of what looked like stacked chairs. To the sound of respectable applause, he bent double while his burden, well lubricated by fish oil, slid soundlessly from him. He remained in that position for a few seconds, waiting for more. There was nothing. Then he went out onto the dais to stand, solemnly dabbing at his lips with a handkerchief, while Saleel gave a vote of thanks.

* * *

The pension-fund managers and the rest drifted back to the large reception area where waiters were serving wine. Beard was obliged by the terms of his fee to mingle with his audience for at least half an hour. He stood with a glass of cleansing Chablis as faces above neckties rotated before him. People were well meaning and polite as they told him that his talk was 'interesting', even 'fascinating', but it was obvious that no one's investment strategy was transformed. He learned that earlier in the day an oil analyst had persuaded the room that, with tar sands and deep-sea drilling counted in, there were five decades of known reserves.

A young man of ghastly pallor and brown toothbrush moustache said, 'On top of which, these islands are practically made of coal. If virtue isn't a consideration, why would we risk our customers' money on unproven, non-continuous forms of energy supply?'

And a woman standing next to him, speaking on Beard's behalf, said, 'The Stone Age didn't end because of a shortage of stones.'

He had heard oil sheikh Yamani's feeble line too many times to want to laugh with the rest.

Someone else said, 'There simply isn't enough sun and wind in the UK to drive the economy.'

And another person behind him, invisible to Beard, said, 'So we buy in solar energy from North Africa. Where's your energy security in that?'

He was dealing with these points and accepting a second glass of wine, even though he knew it was time for a scotch, when suddenly the lecturer, Mellon, was there, waiting eagerly with trembling beard for a break in the conversation.

When it came he said, 'I'd love to know where you got that story from.'

'What story?'

'You know. The one about the man on the train.'

'As I said. It happened to me this afternoon.'

'Come now, Professor Beard. We're all grown-ups here.'

The fund managers, sensing that one man was calling another to account, pressed in to hear above the din of voices.

Beard said, 'I've lost you. You'll have to explain.'

'You told it very well, and I can see it suited your purposes.'

'You think I made it up?'

'On the contrary. It's a well-known tale with many variants, much studied in my field. It even has a name—the Unwitting Thief.'

'Really,' Beard said coldly. 'How interesting.'

'Actually, it is. Across the variants are some stable characteristics. For example, the wrongly accused is generally a marginal figure, often threatening—a tinker, an immigrant, a punk, even someone with a disability. Your well-built young man with the earrings fits perfectly. The wrongly accused usually performs an act of kindness for the unwitting thief, and this makes the moment of truth all the more agonising. In your case, he lifts down your luggage. One theory is that the tale of the Unwitting Thief—it's known in the field as UT—expresses anxiety and guilt about our hostility towards minorities. Perhaps it acts in the culture as an unconscious corrective.'

'It must have occurred to you,' Beard said, determined to smile, 'that now and then it actually happens, that people's stories are real. You know, in an age of mass transport, people squashed up together carrying food in identical wrappers.'

'What interests us is the way the tale passes in and out of fashion, goes from lip to lip, falls from view, reappears a few years later in a different form by a process we call communal re-creation. UT was widely known in the States in the early nineteen hundreds. We don't have records of it here until the fifties, and by the early seventies it was everywhere. The writer Douglas Adams put a version of it in a novel in the mid eighties. He always insisted it had actually happened to him on a train—and that's another common feature. By claiming it as personal experience, people localise and authenticate the story—it happened to them, it happened to a friend of theirs—and insulate it from the archetype. They make it original, they claim copyright. UT has appeared in stories by Jeffrey Archer and, I think, by Roald Dahl, it's been told as a true story on the BBC and in the

Guardian. It's the plot of at least two films—*The Lunch Date* and *Boeuf Bourgignon,* and it's also . . .'

'I'm sorry to disappoint you,' Beard said, 'but my experience belongs to me, not the collective bloody unconscious.'

The folklorist had a certain autistic doggedness. 'Yes, what's new about your version is the crisps. I've heard biscuits, apples, cigarettes, whole canteen lunches, never crisps. I might write it up for the *Contemporary Legend Quarterly*, if you don't mind. I'll change your name, of course.'

But Beard had turned aside to touch a waiter's elbow.

The pale pension funder with the little moustache said, 'So these stories go the rounds like dirty jokes.'

'Exactly.'

'Have you heard this story about Bristol Zoo and the car-park attendant. You see, for twenty-four years . . .'

Beard said to the waiter, 'I don't care, as long as it's not a single malt. A triple, straight up, one ice cube, and would you mind bringing it immediately.'

It was six forty-five. There remained only thirteen minutes of contracted mingling. That it would soon be with him, in his hand, his first serious drink of the day, was already reviving his spirits. That, and the prospect of an evening with Melissa. Confident that a waiter in such an establishment would take the trouble to track him down, he walked away from Mellon, who was holding forth on narrative subtypes of blameless theft, and crossed the room to talk to a mild-mannered man in derivatives.

* * *

She was beautiful, she was interesting, she was good (she was truly a good person), so what was wrong with Melissa Browne? It took him more than a year to find out. There was a flaw in her character, like a trapped bubble in a window pane, that warped her view of Michael Beard, and made her believe that he could plausibly fit the part of a good husband and father. He did not understand and could not quite forgive this lapse of judgement. She knew the history, she had some good evidence in front of her, and there was much else she should reasonably suspect, but she remained steadfast in her delusion that she could reclaim him, make him kind, honest, loving and, above all, loyal. Her longing was not, as he thought she saw it, to transform him as he approached his seventh decade, but gently to return him to his natural state, his truest self, the one he failed to lay claim to. This was an unstated ambition. For example, it was not hectoring or denial that would help him lose weight, but lovingly concocted, wholesome, delicious meals, which would ease him back to the shape he had at thirty—his Platonic form. And if her recipes failed, she would have him as he was.

She endured his absences, the silences from abroad, because she was certain he was bound to see the matter her way in the end. Besides, her own life was busy enough. Her patient conviction was touching, and Beard, never a complete cad, felt it like a reproach. During the period of his press bother she had seen him at his worst and was undeterred. She seemed to love him more. With all the passion of a rationalist, she bore him up through the unreasonable storm. But she never brought her reason to bear on her love. If she had, the affair could have been over in minutes. It troubled him to discover that she was one of those women who can only love a man in need of rescue. And she preferred the rescuee to be much older than her. Was he to fall in line then with her sad troupe of past lovers and one ex-husband, elderly dullards, reprobates, losers, louts—exploiters all—whom her kindness had failed to recuperate and who had cheated her out of a child? None of them had banqueted with the King of Sweden, but they were comrades of a sort. Allowing himself to be Melissa's one success would be a proper mark of distinction, but he did not think he was up to the job. He thought he too would cheat her out of a child.

'Why me?' he once asked, when he lay post-coitally supine on her bed. The question seemed ripe, and complimentary in the suggestion that he was not worthy.

'Because,' was her reply, and she moved to sit astride him and brought him on again, her rotund slow-moving Michael, who had long thought that an encore within the half-hour was light years behind him.

She owned a string—if three was a string—of shops across north London selling dance clothes. Professionals from the London companies were her customers, as well as all kinds of amateurs, including young mothers who had tired of yoga classes, and even men as ancient as Beard, inspired to take up tap or tango in one last throw at feeling young. But at the centre of a barely profitable business was an unageing core of tiny dreamers, an inexhaustible *corps de ballet* replenished down the generations—little girls with an old-fashioned yearning to be in tutus, tights, leggings, pumps, twirling before the mirror and the rail, under the stern eye of a flinty ex-prima donna with a heart of gold. The dream of hard work on scuffed boards, of the first night, the first breathless leap onstage before astonished gasps, had survived the electronic age, the girl bands and TV soaps. The resilience of the fantasy gave an impression of genetic compulsion. The smallest tutu in Melissa's stock would fit an infant girl of twelve months. The mothers of these girls remembered their own dreams and sometimes spent hard to live them vicariously.

But dancing in the modern age was precarious. In public consciousness, it surged and fell like a futures market, and Melissa had to be quick in response down the line to distant warehouses. A sudden TV documentary, and during one week four hundred men were in her shops wanting a certain shirt to tango in. A certain movie, a certain musical, a clip on MTV could drive an insatiable, transient need. One lavatory-paper advertisement with a *Swan Lake* theme, and there were more little girls than ever, but clamouring now for rainbow tights, or leggings with a laddered look, or a leotard with an artful tear, just like they wore in the film. And then came lean times when no one danced but dancers and the core of little dreamers, and no one even wanted to look like a dancer, and Melissa could only wait. Useless, she said, to make predictions.

As a hedge against these fluctuations, she widened the appeal of her shops. The eight-year-olds who longed to be ballerinas were a small fraction of their age group, but they shared with their cohort an inexplicable taste for the colour pink. Not just any shade, but a particular soft, candied, babyish pink. All three shops made over part of their window displays to this gentle enticement. Beard visited Melissa at work one Saturday morning and stood in the high-pitched throng to witness the strange power wielded by a narrow band of the electromagnetic spectrum. Who was instructing the girls, how did they know how to behave, how to crave a pink pencil and sharpener, or pink trainers, bed linen, hair grip, satchel, notepaper? Pedantically, he tracked down a paper by an esteemed neuroscientist in Newcastle whose work suggested a gender difference in retinal sensitivity, with females tending to favour the red end of the spectrum. But that hardly explained the Saturday stampede through the shop, or the radical reduction Melissa was able to make in her bank borrowing within the year. In the pink for months! Then, suddenly, colour exhaustion set in and the magic was gone. Overnight, girls did not need pink things. Unwanted stock could not be unloaded in a knockdown sale. It was beyond explanation. There should have been a younger generation of little sisters fresh to pink, but they were not moved. It was not as if another shade took its place. As a sole motivator, colour itself had faded. Pink went to ground, and then, to her credit, at the moment of its resurgence, Melissa was ready.

Despite this liability and daily worries over staff

and suppliers, Dance Studio appeared to Beard a haven of innocent aspiration and pleasures. Once, calling at the Primrose Hill branch to take Melissa to lunch, he waited for her on a stool at the back of the shop and took it all in—Lenochka, the assistant with spiky cropped hair dyed black, lisping Russian-inflected cockney through pierced-tongue jewellery, the piped Tchaikovsky, the scent of sandalwood, a general air of unmockable devotion to children and adults at play. Sitting in the gloom among half-unpacked cardboard boxes he indulged a fantasy (a windowless room sometimes worked on him this way), incrementally erotic, of retiring from the world's ills and gripes and labouring back here, Melissa's partner in all things, cocooned in the stock room, perhaps improving the inventory software or planning special events, with talks and demonstrations, and so placidly tracing the passing years in a swoon of sex and dullness, and one evening, obedient to Melissa's prompting—impossible tawdry dream!—persuading Lenochka to make a threesome on the wide bed in the meticulous flat on Fitzroy Street, and discovering for himself how it felt, a flesh-embedded tongue-jewel's most intimate touch. He surprised himself. He could pass a lifetime right here, dreaming among the unsorted leggings.

That was one haven. The other was Melissa's apartment, a two-minute stroll from the Primrose Hill branch, almost opposite the building where Sylvia Plath once put her head in the oven after setting out bread and milk for her sleeping children. The poet, a daughter of the fifties, was a diligent housewife who kept about her an unpoetically tidy domain, like Melissa's. Beard, on the other hand, was a domestic slob, clean about his person, vain about his clothes, but a dedicated sower of unconscious disorder, for whom the retrieval of his own dropped towel or the closing of a drawer or cupboard door or disposal of a wrapper or apple core would have seemed as purposeful an act as spring cleaning. The lady who once tended his Marylebone flat had walked out without explanation, but he knew why and had not found a replacement. His third wife, Eleanor, once discovered in the pages of a valuable first edition an ancient rasher of his breakfast bacon doubling as a bookmark.

Like many slobs, Beard was appreciative of the order that others created without effort, or any that he noticed. In Melissa's flat, which was spread over two floors, he was particularly happy. She lived such an uncluttered life at home. There were open perspectives untroubled by furniture. The foot-wide beeswaxed floorboards recovered from a Gascony chateau shone with dull perfection. There were no loose objects, all the books were on the shelves in the right order, at least until he visited, and the art on the walls was sparse lithographs, mostly of dancers. There was a single statue, a Henry Moore maquette. Other surfaces justified themselves by their own particular empty dustless gleam. In the bedroom, no clothes were on view, and the bed, unruffled as a millpond, was as big as any he had seen in an American hotel. Melissa's was the sort of place whose ambience Beard could wreck in two minutes by sitting down in it, shrugging off his coat, opening his briefcase and removing his shoes. He never felt at home until he was shoeless. But he was impressed by her apartment, it seemed like the embodiment of mental freedom, and he did his best not to litter it, and was partially successful.

A burglar entering the property, silencing the alarm and taking the trouble to glance about before settling down to work, would never have guessed the nature or even the gender of its owner. The apartment was subdued, cool, masculine in its light browns and battleship greys. Whereas in her shops, as in bed, Melissa was loud, cheerful, generous. She stood only an inch higher than her Michael, was rounded and soft and wide-hipped like a Renoir bather, though not remotely in Beard's plump league. She had black hair that was curly or curled (he would never ask), dark eyes and rich skin colour—nut brown, with a bloom of red across the cheekbones that deepened when she was furious or suddenly happy. She claimed a dash of Tobagan and Venezuelan blood, like Angostura bitters she said, through her great-grandmother. Whatever the truth, she thrived in a heatwave, loathed the cold, defined as under fifteen degrees, and believed she belonged in some other country further south, but it was too late to shift now.

Perhaps she chose the decor in the Fitzroy Street flat to highlight her wardrobe. She wore bold prints (the Tobago inheritance) or deep-hued silks, and had an array of stilettos in reds and greens as well as black, and pastel dancing shoes that never fitted. At home, arranged on a sombre sofa against a neutral wall, she shimmered in her colours, in Beard's eyes, like a new-minted Gauguin in his Marquesas phase.

When he visited, she cooked up a tropical storm. Her well-balanced meals were spicy and much to his taste. Any advantage to his health was easily offset by outsized second helpings. She never served herself much of her own cooking, but she watched him eat from across the table with smouldering satisfaction, telling him that hot spices would burn off his fat and make him an ardent lover, or that she was fattening him up so he could never run away. The latter was closer to the truth. After one of her spreads, feeling neither thinner nor even faintly aroused, he would sit in near silence, sweating in an armchair for half an hour to recover.

How did he ever deserve her? She ran him baths on winter nights and lit candles around the bathroom and squeezed into the oversized roll-top tub with him. She bought him shirts, silk ties, cologne, wine, scotch (she did not drink), underwear and socks. When it was time for him to leave, she booked his flights. In a poor return, he brought back expensive presents from airport duty-free, a modern form of parsimony by way of flagrant convenience and notional tax avoidance, but she did not seem to mind. She loved his physics, the indecipherable sheets of photovoltaic calculation, his 'Arabic', that often spilled across the oak boards, and she made him explain—again—the symbols, the Dirac bras and kets, the tensor products, the Young diagrams. But she too could have been a mathematician. He had seen her complete the morning newspaper sudoku at a speed with which others might fill out a form, hurrying to be done before she rushed to work. She approved of his mission and loyally read climate-change stories in the press. But she told him once that to take the matter seriously would be to think about it all the time. Everything else shrank before it. And so, like everyone she knew, she could not take it seriously, not entirely. Daily life would not permit it. He sometimes quoted this observation in talks.

She talked about her previous lovers with a freedom he could not match. She had never troubled to get seriously involved with a contemporary. Of the various men she described, all were fifteen or twenty years older. The one exception was early on, and he was even more ancient. At the age of twenty she had a year-long affair with a married man, a professional golfer of fifty-six. Now he was seventy-seven, and they still kept in touch. Her preference in partners had a history. She grew up by Clapham Common, in south London, an only child, whose parents divorced when she was eleven. She loved her father and lived with her mother, with whom she often fought. When her mother married the last in a series of 'obnoxious' boyfriends, Melissa went to live with her father across the Common, just as he suffered a stroke. From the age of fourteen she nursed him (intimately, for he was almost completely paralysed) until his death four years later. She told Beard what a therapist friend had told her years ago. Caring for the father she loved at a formative period in her sexual development, then failing to keep him alive, she was guiltily bound in subsequent relationships to the task of finding a replacement, retrieving him from the grave, rescuing him from his misfortune and redeeming her failure.

Beard was equally bound to believe that this was the kind of nonsense that science was invented to protect him from. But he said nothing. So many unexamined assumptions, so many unproven elements! An unconscious that wrote its own craftily concealed stories peppered with inept symbolism? Not a shred of neurological evidence. Repression? Empirically, no such mechanism had been shown to exist. On the contrary, unwanted memories were hard to forget. Sublimation? Likewise, a fairy tale that no serious investigation could sustain. Attending to the toilet needs of her father could just as likely have put her off older men for life, and then there would have been an equally confident Freudian confabulation. Many women who had never nursed a dying father, or had any analogous experience, preferred older men. Why were Melissa's lovers (with one exception) only fifteen or twenty years older, when her father was thirty-seven the day she was born? Could her unconscious, so literal in other regards, not do the simple adding-up?

The truth was simpler. Women knew it in their hearts. Since he was too tactful to say it to her, he was obliged to set it out impartially for himself. Repetition was helpful. Older men were better companions, they were seasoned lovers, they knew the world, they knew themselves. Unlike younger men, they held their emotions in balance. They had read more, seen more, they were warmer, kinder, less boastful, more tolerant, less violent. They were more interesting, they could choose the wine. They had more money. Besides, it irked him to believe that it might not be him she was drawn to, but some symbol of seniority of which he was an acceptable approximation. He was further irked to hear that when she met her first serious love, the errant golfer, he was the same age as her father when he died.

* * *

He took a taxi from the Strand to Primrose Hill and was twenty-five minutes early on Fitzroy Street when he rang her bell. He did not have a key—that was a line he did not wish to cross. When she came to the door, in the moment before they embraced, he sensed that something was not right, or was different. Or she was different. He thought he saw the vestiges of an expression being modified to greet him. Then, they were in each other's arms and the idea was gone. She drew with her out onto the cold stone front step a draught of indoor warmth and beeswax from the apartment and, with it, a scent of spices which mingled with her perfume. One of his presents from some bright airport hell. She exclaimed his name, he hers, they kissed, and held apart to take in the other's face and then embraced again.

As he held her, he felt on his palms the heat of her skin through her red silk blouse. How fogged and monochrome memory was against the living moment. When he was away from her he could only recall in shadow play, or was too busy to attempt to recall, the full vibrancy, the plain and overwhelming fact of her. He forgot the particular touch of her mouth and tongue, her frame, and the way she held herself to dissolve their difference in height when they kissed, the fit of her fingers between his, their degree of springy resistance at the joints, their cool smoothness, length, diameter, the bump of a mole below the knuckle of her left pinkie, and how, when they embraced, his chest was alive to the pressure of her breasts. And this was merely the realm of sensation. How she looked, sounded, tasted—familiar, of course, all of it, but only now that she was here, right in his grasp. Memory, or Beard's memory, was a second-rate device. When he thought of her from Berlin or Rome, it was all relation and generalised desire, it was her nature he considered, herself in abstract, and his own pleasure, not the warm honey smell of her scalp, the surprising taut strength in her arms, how low her voice was pitched when she said his name.

'Michael Beard. Get in the house this minute!'

This old joke summoned a certain kind of crusty old-fashioned parent. He never had cause to say it to her—his stew of a flat was not a place to invite a woman like Melissa Browne. She would not feel comfortable there until she had organised it for him, and that was another line he did not want crossed. She took his bag and he followed her in. When the door was closed they stood in the clean expanse of her sitting room, she put her arms around his neck, he drew her firmly to him and they kissed again. For once, it seemed they might dispense with the obligatory fine-tuning small talk, postpone dinner and go directly to her bedroom. But then, at the sound of a hiss followed by a whip-like crack, a vital prompt from the kitchen, she rushed away with a hiss of her own, a staccato 'shit!', and he made his way to the sofa. He was no longer an ardent young man. He could wait patiently.

By the time she returned five minutes later, his scotch and soda in her hand, he was sprawled on his back reviewing a proposed submission from his Imperial team to *Nature*. The customary detritus of shoes, coat, jacket, tie, open briefcase, papers, open suitcase, spilling clothes and a plastic bag extended across the floor. Tipped so suddenly from the charge of their reunion to the intricacies of molecular plant life, and knowing that, however it happened, he and Melissa would make love within an hour or so, with a meal in prospect too, he felt a rare and settled contentment.

She stood over him, free hand on her hip. 'Make space, Professor.'

He liked her wry, tolerant, lopsided smile. With a grunt, he struggled upright and patted the space beside him and took the glass from her. As she nestled against him, he put the monograph aside and said, 'Just think, your humblest pavement-crack weed has a secret that the best dozen labs in the world are only just beginning to understand.'

He sipped his scotch while her hand lay between his legs. She was caressing him with an abstracted air.

'I've missed you, Michael. Why weeds?'

'I must have told you before. A leaf is a kind of solar panel for splitting water and fixing carbon dioxide. We could imitate it and make hydrogen. I've missed you too.'

Had he? Now that he was kissing her he realised that he should have, for he was excited and happy. But he had not missed anyone, not since the dark summer of 2000, when he pined like a dog for his last, his final, wife. There were people he vaguely looked forward to seeing, but not since that time had he been afflicted by an absence. These days, as soon as he was alone, he read, he drank, he ate, he was on the phone, on the internet, watching TV, travelling to a meeting—or asleep. He was self-sufficient, self-absorbed, his mind a cluster of appetites and dreamy thoughts. Like many clever men who prize objectivity, he was a solipsist at heart, and in his heart was a nugget of ice, which Melissa sensed and intended to melt.

Of course, it was necessary before they made love to have a conversation about their respective lives these past weeks, their states of mind, their day. His fault for not keeping in touch, hers for not holding him to account. So she told him her news. A musical about a working-class lad wanting to be a ballet dancer was keeping turnover above the seasonal average. But few boys came in. It was all down to girls dreaming of such a boy. She told him of the recent death of a respected choreographer who was never quite famous enough for his own taste. At the memorial service, five dancers performed in the narrow aisle of a Soho church, and even the old man's enemies wept.

Michael's arm was around her shoulders, and she was pressed against him, talking into his chest. She looked after her shops, her customers, her staff, her lover, and she wanted someone to take care of her. As he listened, he looked about him—at the brown chaise longue against the wall, the maquette, the eighteenth-century drypoint of dancers in a Utrecht street, a bowl of smooth stones in a copper dish—hoping to identify what it was that appeared to his unobservant eye so subtly altered. Something was out of kilter. He was sure it was not his own possessions. The air itself seemed disordered, the way it does after a smoker has left and his smoke has cleared.

'I love you,' she interrupted her account of the funeral to say, and she bit him playfully on his arm.

He felt tenderly towards her, perhaps as much as he ever had, but one day he might have to disentangle himself, and it would be harder for both of them if he had once said he loved her. But how he would begin to give her up, and when, was beyond him, and he drew her closer to him. What he whispered sounded lame, but it would do.

'You're beautiful, Melissa.'

She went on with her story and he stroked her head and thought that for the first time since he had thrown up behind the velvet curtain, he could imagine himself hungry, perhaps within the half-hour. He was beginning to wonder about the spices in the air. Was it tamarind he could detect, and garlic, limes, ginger, chicken? Her voice was musical and soft, and even, he thought, a little sad. From time to time she drew his head down for a kiss. She was talking about the shops again, drifting into another story, this time about a hole in a ceiling or a floor and something falling through it, about a bad-tempered dachshund left behind by an ancient prima donna with Alzheimer's. And now he too was drifting. He thought he was an average type, no crueller, no better or worse than most. If he was sometimes greedy, selfish, calculating, mendacious, when to be otherwise would embarrass him, then so was everyone else. Human imperfection was a large subject. Consider just a few of the defects. S-shaped backs that easily buckled, breathing and swallowing recklessly sharing a passage, the infectious proximity of sex and excretion, childbirth pure agony, testicles unwieldy and vulnerable, weak eyesight a general affliction, an immune system that could devour its owner. And that was just the body. Among all the yearning rationales for the godhead, the argument from design collapsed with *Homo sapiens*. No god worth his salt could be so careless at the workbench. Beard comfortably shared all of humanity's faults, and here he was, a monster of insincerity, cradling tenderly on his arm a woman he thought he might leave one day soon, listening to her with sensitive expression in the expectation that soon he would have to do some talking himself, when all he wanted was to make love to her without preliminaries, eat the meal she had cooked, drink a bottle of wine and then sleep—without blame, without guilt.

She took his empty glass and stood.

'Food,' she said. 'And I'll get you another.'

But she could not bring herself to leave him, not until she had stood right over him and kissed him again. This kiss was long and deep, and then she clasped him to her, and Beard, still seated, fully aroused, his face part shrouded in the scented gloom of her unbuttoned blouse, his view entirely filled by the division and swell of her breasts, had time to wonder why it oppressed him more than usual, all this talking and listening and cooking before anything properly rewarding could take place. Perhaps he had lost patience with the small print of human contact by spending so much time in loud public places, among worldly professors like himself, each bristling with his personal style of academic grandeur. And when alone, he was mostly among the near-abstraction of cobalt ions, protons, catalysts. And when not alone, in mindless dalliances he preferred not to consider now.

She released him from the embrace and as she straightened she said something, a single phrase he did not hear because at the same time her arms brushed against his ears. Her hands came to rest on his shoulders and he looked up, expecting to exchange a reassuring smile that would neutrally close this particular physical episode and dispatch her to the kitchen, and was surprised to see tears in her eyes, gathering thickly, ready to spill. And oddly, she was smiling, but without humour, as though dismissing or mocking her own feelings. For a superstitious moment he imagined he had upset her with his thoughts, impossibly murmured them aloud, or they had been legibly stamped across his face. But every man was an island, his thoughts were safe. It must be something serious, unconnected with himself. As he stood, he took her hands and they were damp, not only on the palms, but between the fingers, sticky, hot, expressive of a strong emotion it was now his duty—all prospect of pleasure receding—to elicit and understand.

'Melissa,' he said. 'What is it, and what did you just say?'

They kissed again, as tenderly as before. Perhaps it would not be so difficult after all to set the evening on its proper course.

Then she gazed at him in wonder and laughed. 'You idiot. I love you. I said I'm pregnant.'

'Ah . . .'

His mind had softly whited out, the manly equivalent of a neurasthenic faint onto the sofa behind him. Pregnant. He struggled with this ripely swelling word—familiar enough, but for the moment devoid of helpful context, like the face, say, of the local newsagent encountered in an improbable place. Then word, meaning and consequences, biology and fate, clicked into alignment like a steel bolt. His cell door had been open for months, years, and he could have walked free. Too late. While his back was turned one of his own sperm, as brave and cunning as Odysseus, had made the long journey, breached the city wall and buried its identity in her egg. Now he was expected to do the same. In forty years he had talked various women, including two of his wives, into terminations. It was a miracle he had come this far without lapsing into fatherhood. But he would have a tough time persuading Melissa. She was watching him now, lips parted in expectation, waiting for him, for the words, Daddy's first words, that might indicate the course of this new life.

'I'll have that scotch.'

'Come with me.'

He put an arm around her shoulder, and together they stepped over his mess and crossed the boards to her tightly organised kitchen. One large green pot, source of the pervasive aroma, was on the stove on a low heat. Otherwise, apart from a carton of rice, there was no sign of cooking, for the surfaces had been wiped down, all peelings trashed, every implement washed and stowed. A mystery, how someone as rich-bloodedly sensual as Melissa could be so aseptically neat. A baby, with its diurnal tides of entropy, would put her to the test. But this baby must not be, and all that was in question was how long it would take him to convince her of the fact. How could she not see it already, the folly of his shouldering this obligation, and the pathos of it—almost seventy years old and the child not yet ten! Then, the unsuitability of the father's character, his own gifts for entropy, his remorseless preoccupation with work, his recent earnings not even in six figures, his awful past, the risks of transcription error in offering his time-degraded seed to posterity, and her eggs surely feeling the chill of thirty-nine winters. And what of his mission? Would it be an exaggeration to say that the planet could suffer if he were deflected from his course? Perhaps not.

He watched her peer into the green pot and seem satisfied, unscrew the bottle and pour his drink, and take an ice cube from a dispenser. If the arguments he was marshalling were overstated, it was because he feared that the decision might already be out of his hands. She wanted this, she had always wanted this. So they weren't arguments at all, they were pleas. If she loved him she would listen, but she loved him and wanted a child, and was bound to ignore him. The situation was grave, indeed gravid. He took the drink from her and did not knock it back in one, as he would have if he had been alone with this problem, but went at it in rapid sips.

She flashed him a smile and set about her brisk arrangements for the rice, and poured olive oil and lemon juice into a bowl and tipped in rocket leaves from a packet in the fridge. This mound of greenery was surely for herself. Folic acid, phytonutrients, antioxidants, vitamin C. Eating for two. Something had to be done.

She said, 'Do you know, I think for once I'll have a glass of white wine.'

He did not want arrangements for an abortion turning into a celebration of a future birth. Nor did he want his foetal child's neural development compromised by alcohol. He felt so unreasonable, he could not speak. She raised her glass to him, and mutely he raised his. Her measure of wine was no larger than his neat scotch.

'Do you like this skirt?'

This question, her tone suggested, was not a change of subject. It was fine cashmere, charcoal grey, with many folds that swung in a delayed spiral when she turned.

'It's lovely,' he said. 'And so are you. You've never looked better.' Not a good idea to encourage her, but he could not help himself. By way of compensation, he said, 'How pregnant are you?'

'Seven weeks.'

'When did you find out?'

'Day before yesterday.'

'Melissa, tell me. Was it an accident?'

She came over to him and pressed her hand against his cheek. He felt again her radiant body heat. She was the oven, he thought stupidly, in which there was a bun. Their bun.

She whispered finally, 'No.'

'You came off the Pill?'

'The last three times we made love I was off the Pill.'

'You should have told me.'

'You would have resisted me.'

'Yes, I would. You know my feelings about this.'

'And you know mine.'

His glass was already empty. He stepped round her to get to the bottle and helped himself. Now they stood almost the length of the kitchen apart and it was easier for him to say, with an edge of hardness, 'You deceived me then.'

She was coming towards him again. It would be difficult to turn her from this calm, seductive mode. He would have happily settled for a row, with delicacy tossed to the winds. Greater distances traversed. But in this homely stillness, she was coming towards him and he could not help his arousal, and he could see she knew that, which excited him more. From his new angle by her pitiful drinks tray—one amaretto, one near-empty Johnnie Walker, one Baileys—her face was differently lit and he saw that the fine-texturing, high-blooming first-trimester hormones had been working on her skin. Already? He had no idea, but he had never seen her look so pretty or young. When she stopped close in front of him he had to remind himself that he had just, and justly, accused her of deception. He could not allow her to seduce him. She had been dishonest. On the other hand, a measure of sexual release would give him immunity, let him think more clearly and make his life-denying case with more brio.

She said, 'I wasted years thinking I shouldn't have a baby until the right man came along. A lot of idiots and bastards took up my time—my fault as much as theirs. I think you're the right man, but Michael, if you don't think you are, it doesn't matter. I'm going ahead anyway. It'll be sad without you, but not as sad as having nothing. You don't have to decide tonight or next month. You can say no and change your mind later. Perhaps you'll change your mind when you see the baby. That can happen. But one thing I'm sure of—I'm not going to have an argument with you. If you're dead against it, you're free to go. And free to come back.'

'I'll be almost seventy when this child is only ten. What use is that?'

'Fine. Don't get involved. But I think you'd count yourself blessed at seventy to love a ten-year-old and be loved by one.'

Blessed? Where had she got a word like that? He had never heard her use it before.

'And there's another thing.'

She said it mellifluously, she was that sure of her ground. She had smoothed out the crags and precipices of this new landscape and he was wandering through it—completely lost, but not in harm's way, or so she seemed to be suggesting.

'You didn't ask to become a father. I'm not asking for financial support. I've got savings and I've got the shops. If you want to contribute, all the better. If you want to be with us, better still.'

Us. Already this pinhead-sized entity had moved in, it had a social presence. Beard felt both wronged and outmanoeuvred. He was too heavy-footed to articulate whatever general principle Melissa was defying with such efficiency. Did he have no rights? He could not command this child's early annihilation. So what did he want? He attempted a return to basics.

'Whether I stay or go, pay or don't pay, I'll have become the father of your child. Against my will. You didn't ask me because you knew what I would say.'

'If you never see the child and contribute nothing, I don't see how much will have changed for you.'

'That's not for you to say, and besides, you're wrong, dead wrong. Do you really think there's no difference between having a child you never see and having no child? You're forcing choices on me that I never wanted to make.'

He pronounced this with some heat and he believed what he was saying, but it seemed too abstract. His real objections, still without verbal form, lay in a fog.

She must have anticipated his reaction. She seemed untroubled as she turned away from him and began to set the table. When she spoke, she put her hand impersonally on his arm and her voice was conciliatory, even though she was not actually looking at him.

'Try to see it from my side, Michael. In love with you, wanting a baby, not wanting anyone else, seeing you only occasionally and never knowing when, knowing you were seeing other women, and you not making any move to come closer or to leave, and four years drifting by like this. If I did nothing, I'd be at the menopause. And that would be the quiet choice you would have forced on me.'

It sounded a rotten deal. But she had been free to kick him out. He placed his hand over hers where it rested on his arm. A kind of apology.

She lifted the casserole from the stove onto a trivet on the table and gave him a bottle of wine to open. It was a Corbières, a decent one, and he would be drinking it alone. Her two inches of white were barely touched. As he sat down he remembered her present, bath oil and bitter chocolate mints from Berlin Tegel. Exactly the wrong moment to hand them over. A silence settled as she served up the stew. She had neutralised his protest with a list of indictments. He had always assumed she knew about his affairs, but it shocked him, no, it stirred him, to hear her say it so calmly. As he lifted his fork he saw vividly, as though back-projected, brain to retina, a tableau of Melissa and a girl he had known briefly in Milan, kneeling up together, companionably naked on a four-poster against a moraine of sheets and pillows, tenderly expectant, in the low-lit style of a pornographic spread. He even saw the centrefold staples. He blinked this arrangement away and began to eat. But his daydream had tensed the walls of his throat and the first mouthful was difficult to swallow. She had made her reasonable case, and he was struggling, he was in the wrong when he knew he was right, he was in knots even while he suspected that the matter was simple: she had changed the subject.

He let a minute or so pass and then, determined to sound grave rather than querulous, he said, 'The point is, Melissa, there wouldn't really be a choice for me if you went ahead with this. How am I supposed to ignore the existence of my own child? Not possible for me. I guess you were counting on that, and this is what I object to. It's a form of blackmail . . .'

The word hung over them, and he thought that at last they would have the liberating row. But she remained calm, the serene mother-to-be, reflecting while she chewed. She was eating more than usual.

'I wasn't counting on you being unable to ignore our baby. If it's true, I'm happy. I knew you'd be angry, and I don't blame you. I thought of saying it was an accident, but I couldn't live with that.'

Not after she had lived with the contraceptive deceit. But he did not feel like saying that, and nor could he bring himself to say that he saw the future well enough. After a happy interlude, and assuming he did not succumb to marriage, he would become, by degrees, a worthless, unreliable pseudo-husband, and this was what would make a worthless, unreliable father of him. It was what she was choosing, it was her right to choose. This was what women had marched for, birth as well as abortion. Perhaps there was nothing he could do. She was absolving him of responsibility, but this was not how it would unfold, this was not how she would feel when their lives had been transformed, when they repeated the tired, angry scenes, with shouting, the baby wailing, a slamming door, his car starting up with a roar. That was when she would know it was all his fault, whatever she said now, while her unsuspecting brain was soused in optimistic hormones, one of evolution's tricks for getting this child past the first post.

As he refilled his glass he felt the fight, his accusatory sting, give way to light-headed fatalism. He wanted to set the problem aside and direct the evening towards its proper course—by way of amiable conversation with this beautiful, nearly young woman, her generous cooking and the dark wine, towards lovemaking, sleepy embraces, sleep. Was he lazy and sybaritic, or was he affirming a decent appetite for life? He knew the answer. He reached across and put his hand on hers.

'I'm glad you were straight with me. Thank you.'

Keeping his hand in place, he told her that he was sorry for his sharp words, that she was certainly no blackmailer, that he was profoundly happy to be with her again, and that she was right, they must not quarrel. She gazed into his face while he talked as she might a hypnotist's. Her eyes glistened again. She got up and came and kneeled by him and they kissed deeply. By the time she went back to her chair, all seemed well, and they continued with the meal. He put away three portions of chicken and chilli stew while he talked about his work and travels, the conference in Potsdam, the latest from New Mexico, how a team at MIT was working on an artificial photosynthesis process similar to his own, but was eighteen months behind. He talked of design simplicity, of the beauty of no moving parts, of an Oxford team's calculations for the optimal shape of a solar reflector, which was not the parabola he had expected.

He was boring her surely, talking to put distance between himself and the baby, to replace it in her thoughts with his own ideas, his own baby. Sometimes she prompted him with a question, but mostly she was silent, gazing at him with deeply irrational forbearance. She was in love with a bald fat man who seemed to her the essence of seriousness and high purpose, who was the father of her child as well as the father she longed to care for, the father who had not yet fallen in love with his fate, but who, she calmly knew, was bound to yield.

In what he considered layman's terms, he explained the recent excitement—not one electron for every photon, but two, and one day perhaps, even three! As she listened, she adopted the expression he always liked, a wry smile puckered into a pout that barely contained the pressure of a delighted laugh. But nothing he was saying was faintly amusing. She deserved better. So he began to tell her about his adventure on the train, and because he was still feeling bloated and overheated, suggested they move back to the sofa.

When he had told the story at the Savoy, he had drawn directly on his memory of the experience. Now there were three elements—the events as he recalled them, the fresher memory of his first account, and the desire to tell an after-dinner anecdote and make her laugh and like him more and dispel for the moment their one real subject. Everything he now emphasised or modified or added was plausible enough, some of it was true. He plagiarised himself, borrowing turns of phrase, pauses and pacing he had deployed at the lectern. He made his fellow passenger larger and more threatening, he made himself the complete bumbling fool, impulsive, greedy, quick to blame. Towards the end, at the moment when his luggage was lifted down, he exaggerated the young man's patient, saintly quality. With a feel for narrative art, Beard suppressed any detail that might have anticipated and diminished the moment of revelation, when he put a hand in his pocket and found the unopened bag of crisps.

Withholding information worked. At the right moment Melissa shrieked in amazement. She took his head between her hands and shook it and said, 'You idiot, you nincompoop! Oh, I wish I'd been there!' Still laughing, she fetched her wine, that same two inches, and then they kissed, and laughed together, and embraced. She pulled away and said, 'You thug!' and then, wonderingly, 'That poor fellow!'

Recovering at last, she moved closer beside him and said, 'But do you know, something just like that happened to Ivan—you remember Ivan in the shop?'

He did not care to hear about Ivan. He stood with some difficulty and, making a mock chivalrous gesture with open hand and faint bow, guided her towards the bedroom and there, in silence, undressed her. She liked to begin this way, naked while he was fully clothed. He knew nothing of such things but he was certain that in some other century she would have been considered the ideal of feminine beauty, of perfection in a welcoming softness of form. Narrow at the shoulder, swelling to the hip, heavy breasts, two dimples at the base of her spine above generous buttocks. He kissed these dimples now. He was sitting on the edge of the bed, and she turned and lowered herself to sit astride his thighs, arms looped around his neck. She nuzzled and kissed his forehead, he kissed her breasts. But such beauty was not weightless. A fiery pain in his dodgy knee was intensifying, and he thought he had less than a minute before the next move, before a ligament tore from its anchoring in the bone. But she was telling him she loved him, she was whispering *how* she loved him, and he had to wait.

Finally, with a moan that passed for passion, he took her in his arms and lowered her on her back on the bed, and drew back the duvet for her. The bedroom was cooler than he would have liked. He was out of his own clothes with long-practised speed and lying beside her, caressing her in a manner some women found too clinically expert. At these reunions, Melissa was usually impatient to get started, but although she held his cock, ringing it with looped forefinger and thumb, pleasing him immensely with gentle movements, now she seemed to want to talk. Intent on stroking and kissing her and on the enveloping thrill of her touch, he paid little attention at first. Her disconnected words loomed then drifted past him, vivid and random, the way coral-reef fish might appear to a diver. Then he came to and realised that she was talking about being pregnant. Why bring that up now? But of course—what else? For her it was no change of subject at all. Sex, babies, breasts, love, down through the generations an unbroken golden thread. Not a rope to bind his arms and feet, or with which he could hang himself from the nearest beam, just when he thought his life, in its final active stages, was filling with meaning and grand purpose. But he suppressed his impatience, opened his eyes, directed his gaze towards the ceiling, and listened.

'. . . like loving someone you've never met, but that's not it either. We have met, we've always known each other, right from the beginning. Michael, I didn't know it would be like this, that it would start so soon. It's already begun, I'm already in love with her, with him, this tiny person coming towards us from nowhere, curled up inside me in the dark, growing larger every hour, coming to meet us. Sometimes I love it so hard I get an ache in my chest. I'm so lovesick I keep sighing out loud. This is stupid, but isn't it strange and wonderful, how one person can come out of another, like a Russian doll? So strange and ordinary at the same time. I'm so happy. I'm not making sense. I love you, I love this baby inside me and I hope you'll love it too, I think you will, Michael, you will, say you will, say you love this baby . . .'

She had drawn him towards her, and they were making love. Plaintively, she repeated, 'Say you will, please say you will . . .' until it was indecent not to comply, and he said, 'I will,' and he kissed her and thought that perhaps he was not lying because he did not know the future and it was not entirely inconceivable that, in his own way, he might love this child, if it ever existed, and whatever he said now, time and events would scramble, and lovemaking was an enclosed, enchanted world with its own language and rules, its own truth.

She took her pleasures easily, she was a loud, big-hearted lover of the back-clawing school, which was to his taste, but not tonight. As they bucked and turned, and her silky skin turned slick and her cries grew louder in his left ear, he found he could no longer abandon himself completely, and he was troubled, distracted. He wished she had not reminded him of her pregnancy. After many uncountable minutes, the moment was approaching when sexual etiquette required that he time himself, get in step with the shrieking downhill dash to her final orgasm, and he knew he was not ready and might not make it. And so, in those closing seconds, he entered a familiar empty theatre, sat in the stalls and auditioned some women he knew, bringing them onstage in merging sequence at the impossible speed of thought. They appeared in experimental attitudes, in different tableaux that magically involved himself. He summoned and dismissed the girl from Milan, then an Iranian biophysicist, and then Patrice, an old stand-by. But at last he settled on the right choice, the immigration officer with the withered arm. He let her step out coolly from behind her station, and there they stood, fucking against her desk in front of five hundred bored passengers ready with their passports. To Beard, sex in public among indifferent lookers-on was a fantasy of unaccountable appeal, and it worked. He made it just in time.

When he returned from this affair to Melissa's bed, she was kissing his face and saying, 'You're my darling. Thank you. I love you. Michael, I love you. You dear, dear man.'

* * *

He thought it was a police helicopter that disturbed him as it hovered a couple of streets away, but by the time he was fully awake it was receding northwards across the rooftops and it was a neighbour's deep-throated dog making all the noise. His hand was tangled in Melissa's hair, her right leg was crossed over his. He extricated himself, then lay waiting while she murmured in her sleep on a querulous note. When she was settled he slipped out from under the covers. There was never much darkness in a city bedroom and he crossed quickly to the door and went naked along the hallway to the bathroom.

The black slate floor was heated all night and felt good beneath his cold white feet. Let the planet go to hell. Remembering that there were several mirrors—one of them covered an entire wall—he turned the dimmer switch down before he went to the hand basin to drink from the tap. Then he urinated, and afterwards lowered the wooden seat and lid over the bowl. Before he sat, he put on a scarlet dressing gown she had bought him three Christmases ago, and tied it at the waist.

Orgasm sometimes brought on a bout of insomnia. He might have been more comfortable in the sitting room, but to go in there would be a concession to wakefulness, to the next day, the next subchapter of his existence. His mood was sour. He wanted oblivion, and the bathroom was a provisional place, an anteroom to sleep. He did not understand why he felt so rough. He made a tally of the previous day's drinking—just about average—and began to form the familiar resolution, then dismissed it, for he knew he was no match for that late-morning version of himself, for example, en route from Berlin, reclining in the sunlit cabin, a gin and tonic to hand. And what had he been reading on the plane? What other concerns could a rational man have? Three reports in succession. First, an early draft from oil-industry insiders calculating peak oil production in five to eight years. So little time to turn this matter around. Second, also a draft, to be published in the autumn: a quarter of the planet's mammals under threat, a Great Extinction already under way. Third, an academic paper sifting data on Arctic summer ice, proposing 2045 as the disappearance date.

Was he unhappy, reading of this man-made mess? Not at all. He had been content, a frowning serious man at work, not even thinking at that point of the lunch to come, marking significant passages or his professional dissent with pencil underlinings, arrows, balloons, while an oval window framed the azure stratosphere to his left, and ten kilometres below, the treeless north-German plain, flattened and smoothed by centuries of bloody battle, which yielded eventually to treeless Holland and its Mondrian fields. Also to his left, the southern sun, too high for clouds, sent its photon torrent to illuminate and elevate his labours. How could he ever give up gin?

But he was unhappy now at 4 a.m. on his oak and porcelain pedestal, hunched like Blake's *Newton* over his toes, too tired to sleep. This was alcohol's contribution to insomnia—he was parched, exhausted, alert. The usual bundle of congealed anxieties appeared before him in the gloom of the overheated bathroom. They were not all abstract concerns. Some were distinctly embodied: his weight, his heart, which he thought beat too irregularly these days, giddiness when he stood up, pains in his knees, his kidneys, his chest, the smothering tiredness that was always on or near him, a red blotch on the back of his hand that some months ago had turned purplish, the tinnitus that he could hear now, an airy, rushing sound which never left him, the pins-and-needles sensation in his left hand, also constant. He felt his symptoms as crimes. He should see a doctor and make a full confession. But he did not want to hear himself condemned.

Then, the squalid basement flat in Dorset Square, accusing him like an abandoned friend: *when are you coming back?* One oppressive detail was the piles or mounds of unopened mail. There were letters from Tom Aldous's father, who wanted to meet and reminisce about his son. What was Beard supposed to do? This was not the time to take on the burden of an elderly man's distress, of a father still grieving after five years. Then, the precariousness of the project. Would the venture capitalists of Silicon Valley finally open their hearts and bank accounts? Would John P. Hedley the Third, the rancher in New Mexico, change his mind before his proxy and Beard signed the papers in the US Embassy tomorrow? Could he make gases from water even more cheaply, and could he stop them recombining? Must the catalyst be an oxide? If he let his thoughts go towards this problem, he would never sleep. It was easier to think of Melissa's news. Could he have guessed she would be so devious? On this matter, the pregnancy, his three hours' sleep had conferred some certainty. He knew it in his gut, it could not happen, this child could not be, he would not permit it, this homunculus must retreat to the realm of pure thought. That he would talk her round he did not doubt. She cared what he thought of her. That she loved him more than he loved her was the unarguable source of his power.

It was at times like these that he thought of Tom Aldous. Gangling, big-boned, big-toothed Aldous with a head exploding with ideas, not all of them foolish. Poor Tom, long forgotten by the rest of the world. He, Beard, could almost blame himself. He should have hammered to the floor with two-inch nails that ridiculous rug from Patrice's side of the family. He should have opposed her when she insisted on polished boards. He should have objected to that ugly glass table on grounds of safety, not of taste. And though it was hardly his fault that Aldous was in the house when he had no business there, it would have saved his life if Beard had thrown him out right from the start, no mercy, sent him into the cold street in his dressing gown, in Beard's dressing gown, to find his way back to his uncle's place.

But, thought Beard, he must not be too hard on himself. He was the one who was keeping alive the spirit of that young man. Four years ago, in the rented basement flat he now irresponsibly owned, stretched out on the stinking sofa, which was still there, smelling no better, he had seen in ways that no one else could the true value of Tom's work, which in turn was built on Beard's, as his was on Einstein's. And since that time he had sweated, he had done and was still doing the hard work. He was securing the patents, assembling a consortium, he had progressed the lab work, involved some venture capital, and when it all came together, the world would be a better place. All Beard asked, beyond a reasonable return, was sole attribution. For what could precedence or originality mean to the dead? And details of surnames were hardly relevant when the issue was so urgent. In the only sense that mattered, the essence of Aldous would endure.

And what heroic times they had been, the first slow elucidation of the Aldous file, and then, in the evenings, watching from the same supine attitude the TV news, and the latest from the Old Bailey, and seeing his ex-wife-to-be speak up outside the court with trembling clarity and assume the mantle of media darling. As for Tarpin the Builder—that a man guilty of two crimes, fucking Patrice and blacking her eye, should go down for another of which he was innocent never troubled Beard much at all.

No one can predict which of life's vexations insomnia will favour. Even in daylight, in optimal conditions, one rarely exercises a free choice over what to fret about. What needled him now, hours before the winter dawn, as much as health, money, work, an imminent abortion, or an accidental death, was that lecturer, or professor, at the Savoy, Lemon, no, Mellon, with jutting beard and fixed stare, outrageously accusing him of being inauthentic, a fraud, a plagiariser. But Mellon was the real thief, appropriating Beard's genuine experience in order to reduce it to an item of academic interest, a case study in popular delusion, an infectious tidbit doing the rounds like a dirty joke. With the long and easy reach of sleeplessness, he saw his hand close round Mellon's throat and squeeze until he dropped to his knees to make his apology in gasps. Beard could be forceful, but he had never assaulted anyone, not even in childhood. In daydreams, however, he surprised his enemies with astonishing escalations of violence. Now, with a slight acceleration of his pulse, he felt refreshed, more awake than ever. He experienced a resurgence of optimism. His life, after all, had possibilities.

There was, for example, a scheme that fascinated him and he wanted his colleague, Toby Hammer, to take it seriously. Carbon-trading schemes would soon be in place in Europe and one day, perhaps, in the US. The idea was to dump many hundreds of tons of iron filings in the ocean, enriching the waters and encouraging the plankton to bloom. As it grew, it absorbed more carbon dioxide from the air. The precise amount could be calculated in order to claim carbon credits, which could be sold on through the scheme to heavy industry. If a coal-burning company bought enough, it could rightfully claim that its operations were carbon neutral. The idea was to get ahead of the competition before the European markets were fully established. Boats and iron filings needed to be sourced, the proper locations established, and all the legal footwork completed. Toby Hammer needed to get on the job. Some marine biologists, no doubt with secret plans of their own, had heard rumours of his scheme and had been arguing in the press that interfering with the base of the food chain was dangerous. They needed to be blasted out of the water with some sound science. Beard already had two pieces ready for publication, but it was important to hold back until the right moment.

Wrapped in scarlet robes, poised on his throne in the dead of night, he surveyed in princely fashion his recent existence. The iron-filing scheme reminded him of all that was purposeful and decent, and that he must not let himself be dragged down. He would acquire the four hundred acres in New Mexico. They were crossed by ancient power lines on rickety wooden poles, perfectly serviceable, and there was a reliable water source. One day, glass panels angled at the sun, packed with coiled transparent tubes, would cover the grasslands in a shining sea, making hydrogen and oxygen out of light and water for virtually nothing. Compressors would store the hydrogen in massive tanks. Oxygen and hydrogen would recombine to drive the fuel-cell generators. Night and day the plant would supply power to Lordsburg, and illuminate the neon of its tiny strip. Then, as capacity grew, the surrounding settlements would be included—Redrock, Virden, Cotton City and, finally, Silver City. The world would see and come running.

He stirred at last, gathered his dressing gown

around him and made his way through the darkened sitting room, stepping over his own mess to get to the kitchen. There he stood in the gloom before the man-sized fridge, hesitating a moment before pulling on its two-foot-long handle. It opened invitingly with a soft sucking sound, like a kiss. The shelves were subtly lit and diverse, like a glass skyscraper at night, and there was much to consider. Between a radicchio lettuce and a jar of Melissa's homemade jam, in a white bowl covered with silver foil, were the remains of the chicken stew. In the freezer compartment was a half-litre of dark chocolate ice cream. It could thaw while he got started. He took a spoon from a drawer (it would do for both courses) and sat down to his meal, feeling, as he peeled the foil away, already restored.

Part Three

2009

It surprised no one to learn that Michael Beard had been an only child, and he would have been the first to concede that he never quite got the hang of brotherly feeling. His mother, Angela, was an angular beauty who doted on him, and the medium of her love was food. She bottle-fed him with passion, surplus to demand. Some four decades before he won the Nobel Prize for Physics, he came top in the Cold Norton and District Baby Competition, birth-to-six-months class. In those harsh post-war years, ideals of infant beauty resided chiefly in fat, in Churchillian multiple chins, in dreams of an end to rationing and of the reign of plenty to come. Babies were exhibited and judged like prize marrows, and in 1947 four-month-old Michael, bloated and jolly, swept all before him.

However, it was unusual at a village fete for a middle-class woman, a stockbroker's wife, to abandon the cake and chutney stall and enter her child for such a gaudy event. She must have known he was bound to win, just as she later claimed to have always known that he would get a scholarship to Oxford. Once he was on solids, and for the rest of her life, she cooked for him with the same commitment with which she had held the bottle, sending herself in the mid nineteen sixties, despite her illness, on a 'cordon bleu' cookery course so that she might try new meals during his occasional visits home. Her husband, Henry, was a meat-and-two-veg man who despised garlic and the smell of olive oil. Early in the marriage, for reasons that remained private, she withdrew her love from him.

She lived for her son and her legacy was clear: a fat man who restlessly craved the attentions of beautiful women who could cook.

Henry Beard was a lean sort, with drooping moustache and slicked-back brown hair, whose dark suits and brown tweeds seemed a cut too large, especially around the neck. He provided for his miniature family well and, in the fashion of the time, loved his son sternly and with little physical contact. Though he never embraced Michael, and rarely laid an affectionate hand on his shoulder, he supplied all the right kinds of present—Meccano and chemistry sets, build-it-yourself wireless, encyclopedias, model airplanes and books about military history, geology and the lives of great men. He had had a long war, serving as a junior officer in the infantry in Dunkirk, North Africa, Sicily and then, as a lieutenant colonel, in the D-Day landings, where he won a medal. He had arrived at the concentration camp of Belsen a week after it was liberated, and was stationed in Berlin for eight months after the war ended. Like many men of his generation, he did not speak about his experiences and relished the ordinariness of post-war life, its tranquil routines, its tidiness and rising material well-being, and above all its lack of danger, everything that was to appear stifling to those born in the first years of the peace.

In 1952, at the age of forty, when Michael was five years old, Henry Beard gave up his job in a merchant bank in the City and returned to his first love, which was the law. He became a partner in an old firm in nearby Chelmsford and stayed there for the rest of his working life. To celebrate a momentous change and his liberation from the daily commute to Liverpool Street, he bought himself a second-hand Rolls-Royce Silver Cloud. This pale blue machine lasted him thirty-three years, until his death. From the vantage of adulthood and with some retrospective guilt, his son loved him for this grand gesture. But the life of a small-town solicitor, absorbed by matters of conveyancing and probate, settled on Henry Beard even greater tranquillity. At weekends he mostly cared for his roses, or his car, or golf with fellow Rotarians. He stolidly accepted his loveless marriage as the price he must pay for his gains.

It was about this time that Angela Beard began a series of affairs that stretched over eleven years. Young Michael registered no outward hostilities or silent tensions in the home, but then, he was neither observant nor sensitive, and was often in his room after school, building, reading, glueing, and later took up pornography and masturbation full-time, and then girls. Nor at the age of seventeen did he notice that his mother had retreated, exhausted, to the sanctuary of her marriage. He only heard of her adventures when she was dying of breast cancer in her early fifties. She seemed to want his forgiveness for ruining his childhood. By then he was nearing the end of his second year at Oxford and his head was full of maths and girlfriends, physics and drinking, and at first he could not take in what she was telling him. She lay propped up on pillows in her private room on the nineteenth floor of a tower-block hospital with views towards the industrialised salt marshes by Canvey Island and the south shore of the Thames. He was grown-up enough to know that it would have insulted her to say that he had noticed nothing. Or that she was apologising to the wrong person. Or that he could not imagine anyone over thirty having sex. He held her hand and squeezed it to signal his warm feelings and said there was nothing to forgive.

It was only after he had driven home, and had drunk three nightcap scotches with his father, then gone to his old room and lain on the bed fully dressed and considered what she had told him, that he grasped the extent of her achievement. Seventeen lovers in eleven years. Lieutenant Colonel Beard had had all the excitement and danger he could stand by the age of thirty-three. Angela had to have hers. Her lovers were her desert campaign against Rommel, her D-Day and her Berlin. Without them, she had told Michael from her hospital pillows, she would have hated herself and gone mad. But she hated herself anyway for what she thought she had done to her only child. He went back to the hospital the next day, and while she sweatily clung to his hand, told her that his childhood had been the happiest and most secure imaginable, that he had never felt neglected or doubted her love or eaten so well and that he was proud of what he called her appetite for life and hoped to inherit it. It was the first time he had given a speech. These half- and quarter-truths were the best words he had ever spoken. Six weeks later she was dead. Naturally, her love life was a closed subject between father and son, but for years afterwards Michael could not drive through Chelmsford or the surrounding villages without wondering whether this or that old fellow tottering along the pavement or slumped near a bus stop was one of the seventeen.

By the standards of the day, he was a precocious lad when he arrived at Oxford. He had already made love to two girls, he owned a car, a split-screen Morris Minor which he kept in a lock-up off the Cowley Road, and he had an allowance from his father that was far in excess of what other grammar-school boys received. He was clever, sociable, opinionated, unimpressed by, and even a little scornful of, boys from famous schools. He was one of those types, infuriating and indispensable, who was at the front of every queue, had tickets to key events in London, within days knew strategically important people and all kinds of shortcuts, social as well as topographic. He looked much older than eighteen, and was hard-working, organised, tidy, and actually owned and used a desk diary. People sought him out because he could repair radios and record players and kept a soldering iron in his room. For these services, of course, he never asked for money, but he had the knack of calling in favours.

Within weeks of settling in, he had a girlfriend, a 'bad' girl from Oxford High called Susan Doty. Other boys studying maths and physics tended to be closed, mousey types. Outside lab work and tutorials, Michael kept well clear of them, and he also avoided the arty sort of people—they intimidated him with literary references he did not understand. He preferred instead the engineers, who gave him access to the workshops, and the geographers, zoologists and anthropologists, especially the ones who had already done fieldwork in strange places. Beard knew many people but had no close friends. He was never exactly popular, but he was well known, talked about, useful to people and faintly despised.

At the end of his second year, while he was trying to accustom himself to the idea that his mother would soon die, Beard overheard someone in a pub refer to a student at Lady Margaret Hall called Maisie Farmer as a 'dirty girl'. The phrase was used approvingly, as though it were a well-established category of some clinical accuracy. Her bucolic name in this connection intrigued him. He thought of a generous strapping lass, manure-streaked, astride a tractor, and then did not think about her again. The term ended, he went home, his mother died and the summer was lost to grief and boredom, and numbing, inarticulate silences at home with his father. They had never discussed feelings, and had no language for them now. When he saw from the house his father at the bottom of the garden, examining the roses too closely, he was embarrassed, no, horrified, to realise from the tremors along his shoulders that he was weeping. It did not occur to Michael to go out to him. Knowing about his mother's lovers, and not knowing whether his father knew (he guessed he did not), was another impossible obstacle.

He returned to Oxford in September and took a third-floor room in Park Town, a down-at-heel mid-Victorian crescent arranged around a central garden. His walk to the physics buildings each day took him past the front gates of the dirty girl's college by the narrow passageway to University Parks. One morning, on impulse, he wandered in and established at the porter's lodge that a student with the name of Maisie Farmer indeed existed. He discovered later in the same week that she was in her third year, doing English, but he did not let that put him off. For a day or two he wondered about her, and then work and other matters took over and he forgot all about her again, and it was not until late October that a friend introduced him to her and another girl outside the Museum of Natural History.

She was not as he had imagined and at first he was disappointed. She was small, almost frail, intensely pretty, with dark eyes and scant eyebrows and a musical voice with a surprising accent, a hint of cockney, which was unusual in a woman at university in those days. When, in answer to her question, he told her what his subject was, her face went blank and soon she walked on with her friend. He bumped into her alone two days later and asked her to come for a drink and she said no, and said it immediately, before he had quite finished his sentence. It was a measure of Beard's self-confidence that he was surprised. But what did she see in front of her? A stout fellow with an accountant's look and an earnest manner, wearing a tie (in 1967!), with short hair side-parted and, the damning detail, a pen clipped into the breast pocket of his jacket. And he was studying science, a non-subject for fools. She said goodbye politely enough and went on her way, but Beard walked after her and asked if she was free the next day, or the day after that, or at the weekend. No, no, and no. Then he said brightly, 'How about ever?' and she laughed pleasantly, genuinely amused by his persistence, and seemed on the point of changing her mind. But she said, 'There's always never. Can you make never?' to which he replied, 'I'm not free,' and she laughed again and made a sweet little mock punch to his lapel with a child's-sized fist and walked off, leaving him with the impression that he still had a chance, that she had a sense of humour, that he might wear her down.

He did. He researched her. Someone told him she had a special interest in John Milton. It did not take long to discover the century to which this man belonged. A third-year literature student in his college who owed him a favour (procuring tickets to a Cream concert) gave him an hour on Milton, what to read, what to think. He read *Comus* and was astounded by its silliness. He read through *Lycidas*, *Samson Agonistes* and *Il Penseroso*—stilted and rather prissy in parts, he thought. He fared better with *Paradise Lost* and, like many before him, preferred Satan's party to God's. He, Beard that is, memorised passages that appeared to him intelligent and especially sonorous. He read a biography, and four essays he had been told were pivotal. The reading took him one long week. He came close to being thrown out of an antiquarian bookshop in the Turl when he casually asked for a first edition of *Paradise Lost*. He tracked down a kindly tutor who knew about buying old books and confided to him that he wanted to impress a girl with a certain kind of present, and was directed to a bookshop in Covent Garden where he spent half a term's money on an eighteenth-century edition of *Areopagitica*. When he speed-read it on the train back to Oxford, one of the pages cracked in two. He repaired it with Sellotape.

Then, naturally enough, he bumped into her again, this time by the gates of her college, where he had been waiting for two and a half hours. He asked if he could at least walk with her across the Parks. She didn't say no. She was wearing an army-surplus greatcoat over a yellow cardigan and black pleated skirt and patent-leather shoes with strange silver buckles. She was even more beautiful than he had thought. As they went along he politely enquired about her work and she explained, as though to a village idiot, that she was writing about Milton, a well-known English poet of the seventeenth century. He asked her to be more precise about her essay. She was. He ventured an informed opinion. Surprised, she spoke at greater length. To elucidate some point of hers, he quoted the lines 'from morn / To noon he fell', and she breathily completed them, 'from noon to dewy eve'. Making sure to keep his tone tentative, he spoke of Milton's childhood, and then of the Civil War. There were things she did not know and was interested to learn. She knew little of the poet's life, and, amazingly, it seemed that it was not part of her studies, to consider the circumstances of his times. Beard steered her back onto familiar ground. They quoted more of their favourite lines. He asked her which scholars she had read. He had read some of them too, and gently proved it. He had glanced over a bibliography, and his conversation far outran his reading. She disliked *Comus* even more than he did, so he ventured a mild defence and allowed himself to be demolished.

Then he spoke of *Areopagitica* and its relevance to modern politics. At this she stopped on the path and asked significantly what a scientist was doing knowing so much about Milton, and he thought he had been rumbled. He pretended to be just a little insulted. All knowledge interested him, he said, the demarcations between subjects were mere conveniences, or historical accidents, or the inertia of tradition. To illustrate his point, he drew on scraps he had picked up from his anthropologist and zoologist friends. With a first touch of warmth in her voice, she began to ask him questions about himself, though she did not care to hear about physics. And where was he from? Essex, he said. But so was she! From Chingford! That was his lucky break and he seized his chance. He asked her to dinner. She said yes.

He was to count that misty, sunny November afternoon, along the Cherwell river by the Rainbow Bridge, as the point at which the first of his marriages began. Three days later he took her to dinner at the Randolph Hotel, and by then had completed another whole day of Milton. It was already clear that his own special study would be light, and he was naturally drawn to the poem of that name, and learned its last dozen lines by heart, and over the second bottle of wine talked to her of its pathos, a blind man lamenting what he would never see, then celebrating the redeeming power of the imagination. Over the starched tablecloth, wine glass in hand, he recited it to her, ending '. . . thou Celestial light / Shine inward, and the mind through all her powers / Irradiate, there plant eyes, all mist from thence / Purge and disperse, that I may see and tell / Of things invisible to mortal sight'. At these lines he saw the tears well in Maisie's eyes, and reached under his chair to produce his gift, *Areopagitica*, bound in calf leather in 1738. She was stunned. A week later, illicitly in her room, to the sound of *Sergeant Pepper* playing on the Dansette record player he had repaired for her that afternoon with smoking soldering iron, they were lovers at last. The term 'dirty girl', with its suggestion that she was general property, was now obnoxious to him. Still, she was far bolder and wilder, more experimental and generous in lovemaking than any girl he had known. She also cooked a fine steak and kidney pie. He decided he was in love.

Going after Maisie was a relentless, highly organised pursuit, and it gave him great satisfaction, and it was a turning point in his development, for he knew that no third-year arts person, however bright, could have passed himself off, after a week's study, among the undergraduate mathematicians and physicists who were Beard's colleagues. The traffic was one-way. His Milton week made him suspect a monstrous bluff. The reading was a slog, but he encountered nothing that could remotely be construed as an intellectual challenge, nothing on the scale of difficulty he encountered daily in his course. That very week of the Randolph dinner, he had studied the Ricci scalar and finally understood its use in general relativity. At last he thought he could grasp these extraordinary equations. The Theory was no longer an abstraction, it was sensual, he could *feel* the way the seamless fabric of space–time might be warped by matter, and how this fabric influenced the movement of objects, how gravity was conjured by its curvature. He could spend half an hour staring at the handful of terms and subscripts of the crux of the field equations and understand why Einstein himself had spoken of its 'incomparable beauty' and why Max Born had said it was 'the greatest feat of human thinking about nature'.

This understanding was the mental equivalent of

lifting very heavy weights—not possible at first attempt. He and his lot were at lectures and lab work nine till five every day, attempting to come to terms with some of the hardest things ever thought. The arts people fell out of bed at midday for their two tutorials a week. He suspected there was nothing they talked about there that anyone with half a brain could fail to understand. He had read four of the best essays on Milton. He *knew*. And yet they passed themselves off as his superiors, these lie-a-beds, and he had let them intimidate him. No longer. From the moment he won Maisie, he was intellectually free.

Many years later, Beard told this story and his conclusions to an English professor in Hong Kong who said, 'But Michael, you've missed the point. If you had seduced ninety girls with ninety poets, one a week in a course of three academic years, and remembered them all at the end, the poets, I mean, and synthesised your reading into some kind of aesthetic overview, then you would have earned yourself a degree in English literature. But don't pretend that it's easy.'

But it seemed so at the time, and he was far happier during his final year, and so was Maisie. She persuaded him to grow his hair, to wear jeans instead of flannels, and to stop *repairing* things. It wasn't cool. And they became cool, even though they were both rather short. He gave up Park Town and found a tiny flat in Jericho, where they set up together. Her friends, all literature and history students, became his. They were wittier than his other friends, and lazier of course, and had a developed sense of pleasure, as though they felt they were owed. He cultivated new opinions—

on the distribution of wealth, Vietnam, the events in Paris, the coming revolution, and LSD, which he declared to be extremely important, though he refused to take it himself. When he heard himself sounding off, he was not at all convinced, and was amazed that no one took him for a fraud. He tried pot and disliked it intensely for the way it interfered with his memory. Despite the usual parties, with howling music and terrible wine in sodden paper cups, he and Maisie never stopped working. Summer came, and finals, and then, to their stupid surprise, it was all over and everyone dispersed.

They both got firsts. Michael was offered the place he wanted at the University of Sussex to do a PhD. They went to Brighton together and found a fine place to live from September, an old rectory in an outlying village on the Sussex Downs. The rent was beyond them and so, before returning to Oxford, they agreed to share with a couple studying theology who had newborn identical twins. The Chingford newspaper ran a story about the local working-class girl who 'soared to the heights', and it was from these heights, and to hold together their disintegrating milieu, that they decided to get married, not because it was the conventional thing to do, but precisely because it was the opposite, it was exotic, it was hilarious and camp and harmlessly old-fashioned, like the tasselled military uniforms the Beatles wore in promotional pictures for their sensational LP. For that reason, the couple did not invite or even inform their parents. They were married in the Oxford registry office, and got drunk on Port Meadow with a handful of friends who came for the day. Lieutenant Colonel (rtd) Henry Beard, DSO, living alone in the old house at Cold Norton, did not learn of his son's marriage until after the divorce.

*   *   *

His son was thinking of that time now, forty-one years later, as he waited, jet-lagged at 5 p.m., in the circular bar of the Camino Real hotel in El Paso, Texas, for Toby Hammer to appear. The waitress came by again and Beard ordered another scotch and a second bowl of salted nuts. Under the high, stained-glass cupola, American and Mexican voices echoed and merged and he overheard no one's conversation. He was thinking of that time, the way one does on long journeys when rootlessness and boredom, lack of sleep or routine can summon from out of nowhere random stretches of the past, make them as real as a haunting. And he was almost there now, here, in the dining room of the Randolph, in suit and tie, and the white shirt he had ineptly ironed himself. After a drink he could still bring back fragments of Milton's 'Light'—'and ever-during dark / Surrounds me, from the cheerful ways of men' and something something 'and wisdom at one entrance quite shut out'. He used a poem to get a girl, and she was gone, two years dead from cancer of the liver, in fact. But he had never shaken off the poem. He was thinking how he never took Maisie to meet his father, and never invited the old man to stay at the handsome rectory in Sussex, just left him to his sorrow while the new age dawned and the arrogant, shameless, spoiled generation turned its backs on the fathers who fought the war, dismissing them for their short hair and tidy ways and indifference to rock and roll.

It took more than one drink to arouse guilt in Michael Beard. This was his third, or fourth. He had been waiting more than an hour. Outside in the streets it was forty-three degrees, in here it felt like minus ten. Only the drink kept him warm. He had made the journey and been in this bar many times in recent years. London to Dallas to El Paso, picking up at the airport the outsized SUV, the only kind of vehicle that could comfortably accommodate his bulk. Then recuperating here or meeting up with his associates before the three-hour drive west along the Mexican border to Lordsburg, New Mexico. Today, Hammer was coming in from San Francisco. Freak summer storms were delaying flights over the Rockies. Beard could have gone on without him, but he preferred to wait. He thought he might even stay the night and see Doctor Eugene Parks in the morning and hear the result of his tests. It was a superstition he could not banish, that a wise old American doctor like Parks could be counted on to deliver a clinical judgement with the proper neutrality of a disinterested foreigner, without the moral undertones, the hint of blame or poorly suppressed outrage Beard had come to expect from his medical countrymen. *You may get dressed now, Professor Beard. I'm afraid we really must address your lifestyle*. His lifestyle, he wanted to say as, humiliated, he struggled back into his underwear, was to bring to the world artificial photosynthesis on an industrial scale. If the world with its sclerotic credit markets would only let him.

His drink arrived, piled above the brim with ice cubes, squandered energy in convenient, transparent form, and a half-kilo of nuts on a trencher under a blanket of salt. It was not Doctor Parks's style, to reprimand his clients for the way they lived. And he was sympathetic to Beard's project, being an ardent believer in climate change, and having bought a piece of real estate in Newfoundland which, he was certain, would be capable of sustaining a vineyard within ten years. When the Texan summer temperatures regularly hit fifty centigrade, that would be the time to pack up and head north. There were hundreds, if not thousands, of Americans, he told Beard, now buying up land in Canada.

As he transferred all but one of the ice cubes from his drink to his old glass, Beard saw the blemish on the back of his hand and stared at it, willing it to disappear. Three years ago there had been something there, and it had taken him a good while to go and have it diagnosed. It turned out to be a benign skin cancer, easily frozen off with liquid nitrogen. Nine months ago, it had come back and looked different, and he suspected he would not be so lucky this time. So he did nothing while it grew and darkened to a livid blotch with black edges. Generally, he remembered it when his spirits were low. Such cowardice and irrationality he would once have thought beyond him. Somewhere in Doctor Parks's office, in a file, was the truth in the form of a biopsy report. It could be collected tomorrow, or it could wait until he came back through this way. What would suit Beard best would be to go tomorrow for his general check-up and not be told, unless the result was good. In

America, such things could be arranged.

He had promised to phone Darlene in Lordsburg but he did not feel like it now. On a raised platform in a corner of the bar, two men were settling themselves on chairs by a microphone. One began to tune an electric guitar whose jarring sound of bending microtones stirred a memory. Yes, the name of the married theology students he and Maisie had shared with was Gibson, Charlie and Amanda, and they were devout and intellectual, against the fashion of the time, and studied at an institute in Lewes. Their god, by way of mysterious love, or an urge to punish, had conferred on them two babies of a giant size and type who would easily have snatched the prize from Beard in '47, twins who never slept and rarely ceased their identical piercing wails, who set each other off if they ever failed to start up in step, and who jointly propelled a miasma through the elegant house, as penetrative as a curry on the stove, a prawn vindaloo, but rank like sea swamp, as though they were confined for reasons of religion to a diet of guano and mussels.

Young Beard, working in the bedroom on the early calculations that would lead him to his life's work, his life's free ride, stuffed wads of blotting paper in his ears and kept the windows open, even in midwinter. When he went down to make himself coffee, he would encounter the couple in the kitchen in some aspect of their private hell, dark-eyed and irritable from lack of sleep and mutual loathing as they divvied up their awful tasks, which included prayer and meditation. The generous hallway and living spaces of the Georgian rectory were rendered charmless by the hundred protruding metal-and-plastic tools and devices of modern childcare. Neither adult nor infant Gibsons expressed any pleasure in their own or each other's existence. Why would they? Beard privately swore to himself that he would never become a father.

And Maisie? She changed her mind about a PhD on Aphra Behn, she turned down a job in the university library and signed on instead for social-security benefit. In another century she would have been considered a woman of leisure, but in the twentieth she was 'active'. She read up on social theory, attended a group run by a collective of Californian women, and started up a 'workshop' herself, a new concept at the time, and though, in conventional terms, she no longer soared, her consciousness was raised and within a short time she confronted the blatant fact of patriarchy and her husband's role in a network of oppression that extended from the institutions that sustained him as a man, even though he could not acknowledge the fact, to the nuances of his small talk.

It was, as she said at the time, like stepping through a mirror. Everything looked different, and it was no longer possible to be innocently content, for her and, therefore, for him. Certain matters were settled after serious discussion. He was too much of a rationalist to think of many good reasons why he should not help out around the house. He believed that it bored him more than it did her, but he did not say so. And washing a few dishes was the least of it. There were profoundly entrenched attitudes that he needed to examine and change, there were unconscious assumptions of his own 'centrality', his alienation from his own feelings, his failure to listen, to hear, really *hear*, what she was saying, and to understand how the system that worked in his favour in both trivial and important ways always worked against her. One example was this: he could go to the village pub for a pleasant pint on his own, while she could not do so without being stared at by the locals and made to feel like a whore. There was his unexamined belief in the importance of his work, in his objectivity, and in rationality itself. He failed to grasp that knowing himself was a vital undertaking. There were other ways of knowing the world, women's ways, which he treated dismissively. Though he pretended not to be, he was squeamish about her menstrual blood, which was an insult to the core of her womanhood. Their lovemaking, blindly enacting postures of dominance and submission, was an imitation of rape and was fundamentally corrupt.

Months passed, and many evening sessions, during which Beard mostly listened, and in the pauses thought about work. At that time he was thinking about photons from a radically different angle. Then one night, he and Maisie were woken by the twins as usual, and lay side by side on their backs in the dark while she broke the news that she was leaving him. She had thought this through, and did not want an argument. There was a commune forming in the sodden hills of mid Wales and she intended to join it and did not think she would ever return. She knew, in ways he could never understand, that this must be her course now. There were issues of her self-realisation, her past and her identity as a woman that she felt bound to examine. It was her duty. At this point, Beard felt himself overtaken by a powerful and unfamiliar emotion that tightened his throat and forced from his chest a sob he was powerless to contain. It was a sound that surely all the Gibsons heard through the wall. It could easily have been confused for a shout. What he experienced was a compound of joy and relief, followed by a floating, expansive sensation of lightness, as if he was about to drift free of the sheets and bump against the ceiling. Suddenly, it was all before him, the prospect of freedom, of working whenever he wanted, of inviting home some of the women he had seen on the Falmer campus, lolling on the steps outside the library, of returning to his unexamined self and being guiltlessly shot of Maisie. All this caused a tear of gratitude to roll down his cheek. He also felt fierce impatience for her to be gone. It crossed his mind to offer to drive her to the station now, but there were no trains from Lewes at 3 a.m., and she had not packed. Hearing his sob, she had reached for the bedside light and, leaning over to look into his face, she saw the dampness around his eyes. Firmly and deliberately she whispered, 'I will not be blackmailed, Michael. I will not, repeat *not*, be emotionally manipulated by you into staying.'

* * *

It was a mercy the bar was so large. The two men were singing loudly in unison a comic song in Spanish and there was much laughter each time the chorus came round. For all his time in this corner of the United States, Beard did not understand a word. He raised his hand for another drink and it was with him almost immediately and he was digging it out from under the rubble of ice. Was ever a marriage dissolved so painlessly? Within a week she had left for the hill farm in Powys. In the course of a year they exchanged a couple of postcards. Then one came from an ashram in India, where she remained for three years and from where she sent one day her cheery acceptance of a divorce, all papers duly signed. He did not see her until his twenty-sixth birthday, at which she appeared with a shaved head and a jewel in her nose. Many years later he spoke at her funeral. Perhaps it was the ease of their parting in the old rectory that made him so incautious about marrying again, and again.

With some difficulty, he got to his feet and made his way across the rotunda bar towards the lavatory. By local standards, which were high, he was not an exceptionally fat man. Even now he could see a couple who easily outranked him, a man and a woman obliged by their shape to perch on the edge of their armchairs. But Beard was a fat man just the same, and his knees hurt and he felt dizzy from having stood too quickly. As he crossed the lobby, one of the clerks came out from behind the reception desk and hurried after him.

'Excuse me, Mr Beard, sir? I thought it was you. Welcome to the Camino Real? There was a gentleman looking for you?'

'Mr Hammer?'

'No. It was about a week ago? From England? But he didn't leave a message?'

'What did he look like?'

'I guess, kind of large? And said his name was something like Turnip?'

They would have continued with their questions, but at that moment Beard saw Hammer coming through the glass entrance doors, preceded by the porter with a luggage trolley. As the two men embraced, the clerk moved away with a self-effacing grimace and Beard nodded thanks in his direction.

'Toby!'

'Chief!'

Ever since Hammer learned that this was what Beard was once called, he had taken it up, in an ironic way. Others on the project had adopted it too and Beard, of course, was pleased. It almost made up for having been sacked from the Centre.

He was three years older than Beard, and was lean and strong and had the straight back, the clarity of eyes and skin of a man who had not touched a drink in twenty years. Although he walked bandy-legged, like a saddle-weary cowboy, he still played squash and backpacked alone in the High Sierras. Or he said he did. After time in his company, Beard often put himself on a diet that lasted many hours. Hammer's background was in electronics, but in the early eighties he decided to become a drunk and wreck his marriage and drive all his friends away in the customary manner. Once he was through his recovery and had got everyone back, including his wife and children, he began to develop work that had no clear job description. He knew people and introduced them, and fixed up deals. He introduced Beard to the tax-break lawyers and accountants who knew the state legislature, the go-betweens in Washington who patrolled the vast and vague territory between commerce and politics, and people who had a line to the grant-givers of the big foundations, the venture-capital types who knew people who knew friends of men like Vinod Khosla and Shai Agassi. Hammer steered Beard's patent applications through, secured the lease on the land near Lordsburg with a right to buy, learned to find his way around the solar fraternity and knew the engineers and the materials specialists. He had even squeezed money out of the Bush people in their dying days and, recently, far more from the bounty of Obama.

But Hammer could not protect the project from delay, and progressive shrinkage and, at times, near-complete collapse. There was compromise at every stage. The site in Lordsburg was a fourth choice in the American South-West. There were more sunshine hours per year in parts of Arizona and Nevada, but competition from the big utilities had pushed up prices. Other locations had no water, or no good road or nearby connection to the grid, nor such a friendly local Chamber of Commerce. The company he and Beard and others formed had been forced to reconstitute three times over to qualify for tax breaks. Homeland Security were suspicious of Beard's alien status, and letters from prominent American science academies made little difference in the Bush years. Money was hard, even in the good times. Among the venture capitalists who cared about solar, the consensus was that the two best bets were on the tried and tested routes, solar thermal—focusing the sun's heat to make steam to drive turbines—or photovoltaics—generating current directly from sunlight—and in both cases, concentrating the light with magnifying lenses.

Reliable and cheap artificial photosynthesis was twenty years away, was the general view.

To disprove it, in early 2007 Beard mounted a demonstration to potential backers in a parking lot outside a lab in Oakland, California. The idea was that in full sunshine a large bottle of water would be split into its constituent gases, which would cause a fuel-cell generator to power an electric jackhammer with which a man in a green hardhat would destroy a wall which bore the graffito 'oil'. But certain vital parts failed to be delivered, the meeting was postponed for a month, and then only half of the investors showed up and the project got one third of the money and shrank a good deal more.

The technical difficulties grew as the money declined. Tom Aldous had been correct in his general assumptions, and wrong in certain particulars, though Beard could hardly complain now that he owned seventeen patents. For a long time the little lab model that split water in 2005 could not be scaled up or made to work faster. The light-sensitive dyes that drove the process had to be reconsidered. The catalyst was not derived from manganese, but from a compound of cobalt, and another from ruthenium. Choosing and testing the right porous membrane to divide hydrogen from oxygen should have been easy but was not. The time came at last to design and build the prototype that one day would be mass-produced. An outfit near Paris was chosen. The panel, the glorious achievement, was two metres square and cost three million dollars. It was sent away for testing at the National Renewable Energy Laboratory in Golden, Colorado, and was found to be underperforming by three hundred per cent, and flawed in both design and construction.

They started again with a Chinese company sixty miles from Beijing. The tubes containing the light-harvesting semiconductor, the aqueous electrolytes and the membrane were of plexiglas on top, with a base of conducting stainless steel. The panel that housed the tubes was three metres by two, and each unit cost four million dollars. Once in mass-production, they would cost ten thousand dollars, so the business plan said. According to the lab at Golden, the new panel worked. By then, the world was in recession. Many promises made to Hammer were broken. The option on the land, renewed three times already, was expiring. Toby renegotiated and instead of the four hundred acres, bought twenty-five, right by the water source. There were now two small gas-storage tanks instead of eight giants, only one compressor for the hydrogen, one generator instead of five, and, worst of all, because they were the core and symbol of the project, a mere twenty-three panels tilted skywards instead of one hundred and twenty-five.

But they were finally in place, and the day after tomorrow a new chapter would begin in the history of industrial civilisation, and the earth's future would be assured. The sun would shine on an empty patch of land in the boot heel of south-west New Mexico, strike the plexiglas tubes and split water, the storage tanks would fill with gas, the fuel-cell generator would turn and electricity would be ready to flow to the town in front of friends from Lordsburg, representatives of the national media, people from the power companies, colleagues from Golden and MIT, Caltech and the Lawrence Berkeley labs, as well as a few entrepreneurs from the Stanford area. A press pack, including a special glossy brochure, would be available. All this had been arranged by Hammer and his team. Under a vast marquee that he swore he had got for free from NASA, they would drink champagne, give interviews and talk about contracts. At a given signal, the Nobel laureate would throw a switch and the new era would commence.

Now, in the bright expanse of the hotel's lobby, Hammer gave an account of his trying journey from San Francisco, of a terrifying air pocket that dropped the plane two thousand feet, his neighbour's panic attack, of an inedible sandwich, until Beard's bladder could stand no more and he excused himself. When he came back he found his friend sitting in reception, rattling emails on his laptop.

'*Scientific American* are coming,' he said, without breaking stride. 'And that thin guy from the *New York Times*.'

'This had better work,' Beard said. The electric jackhammer had thrown a long shadow.

'Some local business has put together a giant neon sign that says Lordsburg, exclamation mark. They want to situate it a quarter-mile from us, and have it light up when we turn on.'

'As long as they supply the quarter-mile of cable.'

Hammer put his laptop away. He looked weary, even a little depressed. 'They want it on all night. And the Chamber of Commerce has lined up an army marching band from outside Las Cruces.'

'I thought we were having a girl country group.'

'In New Mexico, or this part of it, you have to have the army first. We also have a fly-past from the air-force base. The girls will play later, and of course, we'll be powering their amps.' In what looked like an effort to appear cheerful, he punched Beard's arm. 'Sunlight, water and money make electricity makes more money! My friend. It's going to *happen*.'

They agreed to have an early dinner and to stay the night and leave straight after Beard had seen his doctor.

'But listen, Chief,' Hammer said as they took their places in the deserted dining room. 'Don't let him make you ill. This is not the time.'

'That's my worry too. A diagnosis is a kind of modern curse. If you didn't go and see these people, you wouldn't get whatever it is they want you to have.'

With wine and water they raised a toast to magical thinking, then they continued a conversation they had been having by email for some months. To an eavesdropper it would have sounded like the essence of commercial tedium, but to the two men it was a matter of urgency. How many orders for panels were necessary to bring the unit cost down to the point at which they could feasibly claim that a medium-sized artificial-photosynthesis plant could generate electricity as cheaply as coal? The energy market was highly conservative. There was no premium for being virtuous, for not screwing up the climate system. Orders for seven thousand panels, this was their best calculation. Much would depend on whether they could reliably power Lordsburg and its environs night and day for a year, through all kinds of weather. And it also depended on the Chinese, how fast they could move, and how plausibly they could be threatened by the prospect of losing the business. In that respect, the recession helped, but it would also depress demand for panels, if not for energy. They went round this topic a few times, quoting figures, plucking others from the air, then Hammer leaned forward and said confidentially, as though the sole waiter on the far side of the restaurant might hear him, 'But, Chief, you can be straight with me. Tell me. Is it true, the planet's getting cooler?'

'What?'

'You keep telling me the arguments are over, but they're not. I'm hearing it everywhere. Last week some woman professor of atmosphere studies or something was saying so on public television.'

'Whoever she says she is, she's wrong.'

'And I'm hearing it everywhere from business people. It seems like it's building. They're saying the scientists have gotten it wrong but don't dare to admit it. Too many careers and reputations on the line.'

'What's their evidence?'

'They're saying a point-seven-degree rise since pre-industrial times, that's two hundred and fifty years, is negligible, well within usual fluctuations. And the last ten years have been below the average. We've had some bad winters here—that doesn't help our cause. And they're also saying that too many people are going to get rich on the Obama handouts and tax breaks to want to tell the truth. Then there are all these scientists, including the one I was talking about, who've signed up to the Senate Minority Report on Climate Change—

you must have seen that stuff.'

Beard hesitated, then called for more wine. That was the trouble with some of these Californian reds, they were so smoothly accessible, they went down like lemonade. But they were sixteen per cent alcohol. He could not help feeling that this conversation was beneath him. It wearied him, like talking about or against religion, or crop circles and UFOs for that matter. He said, 'It's zero point eight now, it's not negligible in climate terms, and most of it has happened in the last thirty years. And ten years is not enough to establish a trend. You need at least twenty-five. Some years are hotter, some are cooler than the year before, and if you drew a graph of average yearly temperatures it would be a zigzag, but a rising zigzag. When you take an exceptionally hot year as your starting point, you can easily show a decline, at least for a few years. That's an old trick, called framing, or cherry-picking. As for these scientists who signed some contrarian document, they're in a minority of a thousand to one, Toby. Ornithologists, epidemiologists, oceanographers and glaciologists, salmon fishermen and ski-lift operators, the consensus is overwhelming. Some weak-brained journalists write against it because they think it's a sign of independent thinking. And there's plenty of attention out there for a professor who'll speak against it. There are bad scientists, just like there are rotten singers and terrible cooks.'

Hammer looked sceptical. 'If the place isn't hotting up, we're fucked.'

As he refilled his glass, Beard thought how strange it was, that after being associates for all these years, they had rarely discussed the larger issue. They had always concentrated on the business, the matter in hand. Beard also noticed that he himself was close to being drunk.

'Here's the good news. The UN estimates that already a third of a million people a year are dying from climate change. Bangladesh is going down because the oceans are warming and expanding and rising. There's drought in the Amazonian rainforest. Methane is pouring out of the Siberian permafrost. There's a meltdown under the Greenland ice sheet that no one really wants to talk about. Amateur yachtsmen have been sailing the North-West Passage. Two years ago we lost forty per cent of the Arctic summer ice. Now the eastern Antarctic is going. The future has arrived, Toby.'

'Yeah,' Hammer said. 'I guess.'

'You're not convinced. Here's the worst case. Suppose the near impossible—the thousand are wrong and the one is right, the data are all skewed, there's no warming. It's a mass delusion among scientists, or a plot. Then we still have the old stand-bys. Energy security, air pollution, peak oil.'

'No one's going to buy a fancy panel from us just because the oil's going to run out in thirty years.'

'What's wrong with you? Trouble at home?'

'Nothing like that. Just that I put in all this work, then guys in white coats come on TV to say the planet's not heating. I get spooked.'

Beard laid a hand on his friend's arm, a sure sign that he was well over his limit. 'Toby, listen. It's a catastrophe. Relax!'

*   *   *

By nine thirty, the two men, exhausted by travel, were ready for their beds and went up in the elevator together. Beard's floor was first. He said goodnight to Hammer, then set off with his luggage down many long corridors at right angles, murmuring to himself his room number to keep it fresh in his mind, and stopping occasionally to bend, swaying, in front of wall plaques with designations like '309–331', while his own, 399, was not mentioned or implied anywhere. So he kept going, eventually arriving from a different direction back by the elevator, or one like it, with a similar brown apple core reclining in a sand-filled ashtray. With a welling sense of victimhood he set off again, eventually passing the elevator once more. He was well into his third circuit before he understood that he was holding the room card upside down and his destination was 663, on another floor. He rode up, found his room, dumped his luggage just inside the door and made for the minibar, from which he took a brandy and an outsized bar of chocolate and sat with them on the edge of his bed.

It was, fortunately, far too late to phone Melissa, and too early to phone Darlene, who would be at work. All he had the strength for was the remote. Before it came on, the TV set gave out a homely, muffled crackling sound of warming electronics, as kindly and familiar as a mother's kiss. But not his mother's. He was tired and drunk and all he could do was surf. Here were the usual, unsurprising things—game and chat shows, tennis, cartoons, a congressional committee, moronic ads. Two women to whom he would at that moment have entrusted his life spoke to each other about their husbands' Alzheimer's. A young couple exchanged a meaningful look that provoked a gust of cackling from a studio audience. Someone said, as though in protest, that President Obama was still a saint, still loved. These days Beard described himself as a 'lifelong Democrat'. He often spoke at climate-change events of the fateful moment in 2000, when the earth's future hung in the balance, and Bush snatched victory from Gore to preside over the tragedy of eight wasted years. But Beard had long ago lost interest in the plenitude and strangeness of America as represented by its television. They had hundreds of channels in Romania now, and everywhere else on the planet. Besides which, if it was on TV, it was no longer strange. But he was too tired to lift his thumb from the channel-up button, and for forty minutes he sat in a stupor with an empty glass and empty wrapper on his lap, then he made himself comfortable on the cushions behind him and fell asleep.

Ninety minutes later he was disturbed by the ring of his palmtop, and came properly awake with it already pressed to his ear as he listened to the voice of the girl whose existence he had done all he decently could to suppress. But here she was, Catriona Beard, as irrepressible as a banned book.

'Daddy,' she said solemnly. 'What are you doing?'

It was six o'clock on Sunday morning in England. She would have been woken by the early light and gone straight from her bed to the sitting-room telephone and pressed the first button on the left.

'Darling, I'm working,' he said with equal solemnity. He could easily have told her he was sleeping, but he seemed to need a lie to accommodate the guilt he immediately felt at the sound of her. Many conversations with his three-year-old daughter reminded him of dealings over the years with various women in the course of which he had explained himself implausibly, or backtracked or found excuses, and had been seen through.

'You're in bed because your voice is croaky.'

'I'm reading in bed. And what are you doing? What can you see?'

He heard her sharp intake of breath and the sucking sound of clean tongue on milk teeth as she considered which part of her newly acquired net of language to cast about her. She would be by or on the sofa which faced the large bright window and a cherry tree in leaf, she would see the bowl of heavy stones which always interested her, the Moore maquette, the neutral colours of the sunlit walls, the long straight lines of oak boards.

Finally she said, 'Why don't you come in my house?'

'Dearest, I'm thousands of miles away.'

'If you can go you can come.'

The logic of this made him pause, and he was beginning to tell her that he would see her soon when she cut across him with a cheerful thought. 'I'm going in Mummy's bed now. Bye.' The line went dead.

Beard rolled onto his back and closed his eyes and tried to imagine the world from his daughter's point of view. Of time, time zones and physical distance she had as yet no proper conception, and she lived with a machine whose wondrous properties she took for granted. At the press of a button she could speak to her disembodied father, as though at a séance to a spirit of the dead, a ghost on the other side. Sometimes she could summon him in person, mostly she failed. When he did show up, he always brought a gift, clumsily chosen in an airport, often inappropriate—a pack of twelve rainbow T-shirts that were too small, a soft toy she thought too babyish but was too kind to say, an electronic game she did not understand, a box of chocolate liqueurs he was obliged to eat himself in one go. Melissa tried to talk him out of bringing presents—'It's *you* she wants'—but Beard's lifelong habit of mollifying girls with surprises buried in wrapping paper was impossible to break. Without a present, he arrived naked, exposed to raw, unpredictable demands, unable to make amends for his absence, required to exert himself in an uncomfortable personal dimension, obliged to engage.

Even at the age of three, Catriona was the kind of person who felt on opening a gift a responsibility towards the feelings of the giver. How could a consciousness so new be so finely attuned? She did not want her father disappointed in her pleasure. The T-shirts, so she reassured him, were not wasted, for one day they would be useful to her baby brother, a tender being whose arrival she anticipated with eerie confidence. She was an intimate, sociable girl of near-unbearable sensitivity. She might hear in a chance remark an inflection, a raised tone, that she took to be a criticism or a reprimand and she would be horrified, and tearful, and then, quite often, she would be sobbing, and not easily reassured. Sometimes, it seemed, she experienced another mind as a tangible force field, whose waves were overwhelming, like Atlantic breakers. This awareness of others was an affliction and a gift. She was bright and confiding, funny and astute, but her emotional delicacy made her vulnerable, and made her father uneasy. Once, some harmless remark of his, some mild expression of impatience, had caused her great unhappiness and brought her mother hurrying into the room to gather the child in her arms. He did not enjoy being made to seem a cad, nor did it suit him, it was constraining, to be sensitive all day long.

Would he have been better off with a bullet-headed, shin-kicking son? Probably not. What bound him to her—at least, as far as he could be bound to anyone—was her insistence, her unconditional, uncritical love. For Catriona, it was simple. He was her father and she claimed him for herself. She understood that his job was to save the world, and since the world was her mother, Primrose Hill, the dance shop and her playgroup, she was fiercely proud. What use Melissa saying that the father did not need to be involved? Catriona would not permit him to defect. She did not care or even notice that he was fat and short and was not very nice and was growing a triple chin, she loved him, and she owned him. She knew her rights. That was another reason why he felt guilt, and brought her presents to distract her from throwing herself at his stomach as he came through the door, and climbing onto his lap and whispering a little girl's secrets in his ear the moment he had sat down after a tiring journey. Like his own father, Beard did not find it easy to be physically affectionate with a child. Like her mother, Catriona was prepared to love unequally, and did not notice his reticence.

In all, he was an irresolute parent and lover, neither committing to nor decently abandoning his family. He clung from habit to a youthful notion of independence that was unusual in a man of almost sixty-two. On arriving back in London he often stayed in the Dorset Square flat, at least for the first two or three nights, until its grime and multiple defects drove him out. Yellowish-grey mushrooms were flourishing along a line where the wall met the ceiling in the kitchen. A gutter outside, which in theory belonged to a neighbour, had cracked and rainwater was penetrating the brickwork. But Beard did not want to confront the belligerent, partially deaf man upstairs, and he did not want to initiate the hacking and plastering, noise and intrusion of a thorough repair. In the hallway the light always failed, however often he changed the bulb. As soon as he turned the switch it popped. In his bathroom upstairs the cold water had long ago run dry. To shave, he ran the hot slowly, and became adept at finishing before the water scalded him. To take a bath it was necessary to fill the tub and let the water cool for an hour or so. These and other small problems required deep attention, and so he preferred to improvise. A large vase collected raindrops in the spare bedroom, an iron foot scraper held the fridge door closed, a frayed and curling length of grubby string substituted for a chain on the ancient lavatory cistern.

But there were no accommodations to be made with the matted, sticky carpets, unvacuumed since his last cleaning lady departed six years back. Nor with the piles of unsorted papers, letters, junk mail and periodicals, the boxes of empty bottles, the odorous sofa, or the grime that seemed to have caked the very air as well as every surface and all the plates and cups and bed linen. He used to tell himself that although the flat was scruffy, it was an office of a sort, it was where he had cracked Tom Aldous's file and reinvigorated his life. At Primrose Hill Melissa and Catriona liked talking to him, whereas here he could sprawl in the lap of squalor and read undisturbed. But that was not always the case now because his ankles itched. The fleas were moving in. There was so much to do to make the place tolerable that no single task seemed worth the trouble. Why refurbish it, why even carry out the dusty scotch and gin bottles and gather up the corpses of flies and spiders when he might, after all, move in with Melissa?

And this hovel, many years back, after he left Patrice, was supposed to be a stopover on his path to the austere and well-lit refuge, as innocently clean as Eden, purged of clutter and distraction, where a free and open mind could range unimpeded. Everywhere he looked in his apartment, made gloomier by unwashed windows, reflected some aspect of himself, his worst, fattest self, incapable of translating a decent plan into a course of action. At any point in the present, there was always something he would far rather do—read, drink, eat, talk on the phone, drift through the internet—than contact an electrician or plumber or a house-cleaning agency, or sort through the three-foot-high paper piles, or answer one of the letters from Tom Aldous's father. It was the same inertia that had forced Beard to stay on an extra year in Dorset Square, the same laziness that had prompted the purchase from the landlord.

When he could stand no more, of himself, of the place, of himself in the place, he retreated northwestwards to the embraces of his lover and their daughter. Cleaned and ironed clothes were waiting for him in Primrose Hill, and a functioning shower and a meal, and two girls who took it in turns to tell him their news and tease him harmlessly about his girth—the Expanding Universe, Melissa named it—and make him relate his adventures in the American desert in his quest to rescue humankind from self-destruction. He would read to Catriona in bed and she would be so awed by the occasion, by the fact it was not her mother but her father intoning, that she lay on her back in a kind of swoon, gripping the duvet beneath her chin, and barely paid attention. Fighting tiredness, she gazed up with contented and possessive love at the bulk of her father sagging over the tiny Beatrix Potter book in his hands. He was all hers. At that time these were the only tales she cared to hear, but Beard was not the man for Potter's dystopia of hedgehogs with ironing boards and rabbits in breeches, and he too struggled to stay awake, and sometimes, mid-sentence, his head would snap forward, and then he would come to and re-engage with affectless voice in the matter, say, of a stolen carrot.

Beard in his Texan hotel room, still on his back with the palmtop in his hand, was thirsty but too weary to raise himself and find a bottle of water. All those miles in the air, all those scotches, and twenty-four hours without sleep were pressing him down into his America-sized bed. He felt waves of virtual movement passing through his back and legs, his body's memory of riding all day the undulations of the stratosphere at three quarters the speed of sound. In this state he was completely without desire but, all the same, he was thinking of Melissa. How did things stand? Generally, after the bedtime story, he would be alone with her at last. At last? These days, he no longer experienced such sharp impatience and urgency, and that was fine, he could concentrate on the food and on hearing about the dance shops. The recession made people feel less like dancing. She was a clever businesswoman, keeping all three shops open by cutting lines, reducing hours but sacking no one. Balletic little girls, in tune with the times, had discovered a taste for black, and middle-aged men no longer tangoed in such numbers, but their wives dropped by for cowboy hats to wear to the line-dancing, which was both unfashionable and popular. Another unexpected boost had been the reality-TV dance contests.

Such talk was soothing, especially in the past frantic weeks, as the on-stream moment for the Lordsburg plant approached. As she chatted he watched her and was certain that in her own, full, rich way, she was as beautiful as ever, and happier than he had ever known her. Motherhood came easily to her. She was warm and relaxed with Catriona, not doting or possessive as she could have been with an only child born three months past her fortieth birthday. Her happiness exceeded anything he had known in his own life, and he thought it had removed her from him partially, placed around her a protective casing that she knew he would never bother to penetrate. She had something magnificent now, a private joy that she thought was not worth the trouble communicating, because he would not understand. She was always pleased to see him, she made love with him as heartily as ever, she encouraged him with Catriona, she even found time to iron his shirts. He gave twenty-five thousand pounds a year to the household, and that was declared more than sufficient. But he suspected that Melissa would have been fine without his money and was just as happy when he was not there.

In effect, she was keeping to the promise she had made many times while they were wrangling over her pregnancy. She would ignore his arguments for an abortion, and in return, she would make no demands. And for his part? He would never have guessed how faithful to himself, how constant he could be. He had made friends with a woman in Lordsburg, a waitress called Darlene, who lived in a trailer on the south side, on the road out to the ghost town of Shakespeare. Darlene was not exactly beautiful, not remotely in Melissa's class, but nor was Beard much to look at now that he waddled a little when he walked and had developed these supplementary chins, the lowest of which hung like turkey wattle and wobbled when he shook his head. When he asked women he did not know out to dinner, they laughed before they said no.

The point about Darlene was that she said yes, and she was good-natured and funny and liked to drink with him. On his last trip to Lordsburg they had got drunk together in the trailer and in a wild moment he had agreed to marry her. But it was while they were making love, it was rhetorical, a mere expression of excitement. The following night, to avoid the scene that would surely accompany his retraction, he got drunk with her all over again, this time in a bar on the north side of town, and he had almost proposed to her a second time. All this meant was that he was fond of her. She was good company, she was a sport, a trouper. But she was currently adding to the general untidiness of his life by wanting to come to England.

The surprise was this: his existence since Catriona's birth was much as before. His friends had told him he would be astonished, he would be transformed, his values would change. But nothing was transformed. Catriona was fine, but it was the same old mess. And now that he had entered upon the final active stages of his life, he was beginning to understand that, barring accidents, life did not change. He had been deluded. He had always assumed that a time would come in adulthood, a kind of plateau, when he would have learned all the tricks of managing, of simply being. All mail and emails answered, all papers in order, books alphabetically on the shelves, clothes and shoes in good repair in the wardrobes and all his stuff where he could find it, with the past, including its letters and photographs, sorted into boxes and files, the private life settled and serene, accommodation and finances likewise. In all these years this settlement, the calm plateau, never appeared, and yet he had continued to assume, without reflecting on the matter, that it was just around the next turn, when he would exert himself and reach it, that moment when his life became clear and his mind free, when his grown-up existence could properly begin. But not long after

Catriona's birth, about the time he met Darlene, he thought he saw it for the first time: on the day he died he would be wearing unmatching socks, there would be unanswered emails, and in the hovel he called home there would still be shirts missing cuff buttons, a malfunctioning light in the hall, and unpaid bills, uncleared attics, dead flies, friends waiting for a reply, and lovers he had not owned up to. Oblivion, the last word in organisation, would be his only consolation.

His final night in London, a mere thirty hours ago, should have been the ripe time when he was reconciled in joy with his tiny family. Few men could have resisted it, and Vasco da Gama himself could not have been unhappy with such a send-off. And at the beginning Beard was happy. Melissa put on an exceptional show. Even Catriona understood that he was going to America to switch something on, and when he did, the world would be saved. She and her mother, dressed in party frocks, prepared a special early-evening meal, the centrepiece of which was a ball moulded by Catriona's own hands, covered in blue icing with green patches. This was the earth, and on top was a candle, which he blew out in one go, to the little girl's rapture. Melissa and Catriona sang a song about ducklings, Beard sang the first few verses of 'Ten Green Bottles', the only song he knew all the words to. His daughter's arms were round his neck for most of the celebrations. Wasn't this bliss? Almost. He had forgotten to turn his palmtop off, and Darlene rang as Melissa was cutting the cake. Automatically, he took the call and said a little too tersely over her opening remark, 'I'll call you back.' He knew that Melissa had heard a woman's voice and the tension in his own, but nothing in her manner changed, there was no clever presentation of suppressed anger that Catriona would not see and he would. She met his eye, she smiled at him warmly, she poured his wine, she celebrated him.

When Catriona was down for the night and they were alone, he poured himself an extra large scotch and braced himself for a scene. It must come, they should confront it. But she kicked her shoes off and sat close to him and kissed him and told him she would miss him. They talked of other things, of travel arrangements, of his return, and all the while his irritation increased. She was playing with him, she was letting him stew in his guilt. But why should he feel guilt? Someone please tell him why. He was not bound to her exclusively, their arrangement was clear. And she was wrong, he decided, to mask her jealousy with kindness and seduction. She poured him another scotch, she moved closer, nuzzled him, put her tongue in his ear, laid her hand between his legs, caressed him, kissed him again. It was an intolerable deceit. She could feel that he was not aroused. How could she pretend she had not heard Darlene's voice, when she knew that he knew that she had?

And then, while she was telling him an unamusing story about something Catriona had said or done, it came to him, an idea as brilliant and plain as any insight he had ever had. She was not jealous at all, she was untouched, she was indifferent. And for that there could be only one explanation.

He pulled away from her and said as levelly as he could, 'Are you seeing someone?'

It was a move born of his silent anger. But another part of himself, the part that had not touched a drink, did not suspect her at all. His question was more of a punishment, and he reasonably expected her instant denial.

In fact, she was affronted. Her lips formed into the pout he found so likeable, before she said in surprise, 'Aren't you? Michael, of *course* I am.'

Oh yes, that. The tired old argument from equivalence. The level playing field. Rationality gone nuts, feminism's last stupid gasp.

After a pause while he ordered his thoughts, he said, 'What is his name?'

She looked away and said, 'Terry.'

'Terry?' He spoke in disbelief. All that was foolish in her was contained in this idiotic name. 'And what does Terry do?'

She sighed. It had to come out. 'He's a conductor.'

'On the buses?'

'Orchestras, symphonies. You know, classical stuff.'

But she hated classical music as much as he did, no rhythm, she always said, not hot-blooded enough, not Tobagan and Venezuelan enough for her. She was sitting at the far end of the sofa, looking as if she wished she had lied.

He said, 'And has Terry met Catriona?'

This made her angry. In a tone of mocking sweetness she said, 'That's enough about me. Let's talk about you. That was her on the phone, I suppose. What's her name, and what does she do?'

He waved the question away. He was not prepared to set his waitress against her symphonic conductor. 'Look, Melissa, there's something you're not getting. You're the mother of our child . . .'

'Oh for God's sake, Michael. And you're the father of our et cetera. I can't believe the crap you talk sometimes. And look . . .'

She seemed on the point of telling him something else, but just then, Catriona wailed from the bedroom and Melissa hurried away to her. When she came back he was standing on the far side of the room, near his luggage.

'That's right,' she said. 'Go. Fuck off. I'm throwing you out.'

'No need,' he said, and picked up his bag and left.

She phoned him in the morning when he was at Heathrow to tell him she loved him. He told her that he was sorry the evening had ended the way it had and blamed himself. They spoke again when he arrived in Dallas and made up a little more. When he thought about it now he was in two minds. He was angry and jealous and wanted to claim Melissa for himself and stuff Terry's baton down his throat. On the other hand, this Terry was his permission, his passport to more fun with good old Darlene. How much fun of this kind did he have ahead of him? And perhaps this was the point—he had the perfect situation after all. But then he thought of this man in Melissa's bed, or reading Beatrix Potter to his daughter, and he realised that he must give up Darlene and get back to London as soon as he could. But then, what about Darlene? Hopeless, to think about it now when he was so weary, when being in Lordsburg tomorrow would clarify everything.

He fell asleep fully dressed on the bed, with the

palmtop still in his hand.

*   *   *

Interstate 10 was quicker, but they preferred the lonely back road, Route 9, that ran a few miles above the Mexican border, straight as a Euclidean line between low hills and the Chihuahuan desert scrub. It was almost midday, forty-four degrees and rising. Ahead, the two-lane road tapered away and dissolved into a mess of heat warp where buckled light showed smooth mirage puddles that evaporated at their approach. In an hour they had seen only three vehicles, all of them white pick-ups belonging to Border Patrol. When one passed, its driver raised his hand in grim salute. Beard drove, and Hammer sat hunched over his laptop, typing and muttering to himself, 'Fucking right they don't . . . that's better . . . but I haven't . . . try apologising, asshole . . .' Occasionally, he offered his companion genuine information. '*New York Times* have cancelled . . . We had two jets for the fly-past, but that war hero with one leg at the Chamber of Commerce, the ex-pilot, knows everyone, so now we have seven.'

Beard drove at a steady fifty-five, the elbow of his steering hand cushioned comfortably on his paunch. In the States, it came easier, to drive at a lordly pace, with the big engine barely turning, almost silent. The country had lived en masse with the automobile longer than any other. People had wearied of the car as a racing device, or penis or missile substitute. They stopped at suburban crossroads and politely negotiated with glances who should go first. They even obeyed the fifteen-mile-an-hour limits around schools. At his untaxing speed, with the faded yellow lines rolling under the SUV, his thoughts turned obsessively, uselessly around the project. He held seventeen patents in the panels. If ten thousand were sold . . . and the conversion rate of water to hydrogen in ideal conditions like these . . . a litre of water held three times the energy of a litre of gasoline. So in a smaller car with the right engine they could have made this journey with two litres of water, three wine bottles full . . . They should have bought wine in El Paso, because the choice in Lordsburg was narrow . . .

His thoughts unfurled like the miles, and he was relaxed and happy, despite his session with the doctor. His sense of freedom was at one with the cloudless sky, blueish-black at the zenith, and the empty landscape before him. Here was the culmination of eight years' work. Travelling to Lordsburg was every Englishman's ideal of America—the open road narrowing to the horizon, the colossal space, the possibilities. Along the route, especially on the southern side, projecting from the tops of sandy banks and hillocks, were piles of stones, some of them five feet high, one stone balanced on another to give a vaguely humanoid aspect. They had a primitive, ancient look, and when he had first seen them he had assumed they were Aztec relics, the local equivalent of menhirs and dolmens. But they were marks of triumph left by Mexican immigrants who had crossed the border and tramped the miles of scrub to rendezvous with their connections. At intervals by the road were Border Patrol observation stations. Elsewhere they parked their pick-ups on strategic rises and watched through binoculars the grey-green expanse of arid ranchland. Who could blame the immigrants? Who would not want to come to a place where a foreigner could be welcomed to launch a revolutionary energy plant with generous local help and tax breaks, and army marching bands and air-force fly-pasts? It would not have been so smooth in Libya or Egypt.

Hammer interrupted the pleasant inward drift of his thoughts. 'There's a message from a lawyer in Albuquerque, been trying to get in touch with you. Says he represents an Englishman called Braby. Wants to talk to you about something in connection with his client.'

'He wrote to me last week, wanting a meeting,' Beard said. 'Ignore it. I don't owe Braby any favours. He's the one who got me sacked from the Centre in England. Remember I told you that story.'

Hammer straightened up and slumped back against the headrest. 'Looking at this screen is making me sick.' He spoke with eyes closed. 'The lawyer's name is Barnard, and he's flying down here tomorrow. He needs to talk to you. You sure there's nothing wrong, something I should know about?'

'Braby's just the sort to kick you in the face, then ask a favour. Ignore it.'

Hammer kept his eyes shut and said nothing for a minute, and Beard thought he had fallen asleep until he said, 'When a lawyer comes some distance unasked to meet you, travelling at his client's expense, you expect trouble.'

Beard let this go. What was there to argue

about? He had been ignoring Braby for years. Let him do the brave thing, and pick up the phone himself. It was not difficult to guess his business. An introduction to the NREL in Golden, access to venture capital for the Centre, or maybe the inside line on solar or on tax breaks. Why worry?

They passed through Columbus, and as the Cedar Mountains rose into view they had one more desultory conversation about their iron-filing scheme. Everything was in place, the investors, the captain, the ship, an option to purchase the filings. All that was missing now was a carbon-trading scheme.

'We've got Obama working on it,' Hammer said. 'We can think about other things, but when it comes, we'll be ready.'

The instrument panel was showing an external temperature of one hundred and twelve degrees Fahrenheit, hotter than either man had ever known. Beard pulled over so they could experience the full blast. It was a mistake perhaps, to go hatless straight from the refrigerated cabin into such savage heat, or perhaps it was his sudden exertion after ninety minutes behind the wheel. As he stepped onto the edge of the road, just as he was about to exclaim to his friend something banal, he felt dizzy, his consciousness partially faded and his knees gave way. If he had not kept hold of the car door handle, he would have dropped to the ground. As it was, he swayed and half stumbled, but managed to stay on his feet as his shoulder swung back hard against the car. His pulse was racing as he struggled with the rear door to look for his hat. He leaned into the relative cool of the back seat and fumbled with his panama and, resting there a few seconds, began to feel better. The episode had taken less than fifteen seconds. Hammer, who was on the other side of the car, saw nothing.

The two men stepped away from the road, marvelling. The heat created a form of synaesthesia. It was loud, vulgar, it towered over them, its weight pressed down on their heads, and it leaped up from the ground and struck their faces. Who would believe that a photon had no mass?

'Here it is,' Beard cried, miming triumph with a raised clenched fist to disguise his strange turn and reassure himself with the sound of his own voice that he was still the same man. 'This is the power!'

'All power to the power!' Hammer said. 'But I've had enough.'

Hammer got back in the car, behind the wheel, and that was a relief, Beard thought as he climbed in beside him. He was still too shaky to drive. Now they were travelling close to eighty and in less than half an hour were through Hachita and Playas, then crossing the Continental Divide below the Pyramid Mountains, in Hidalgo County, in the boot heel of the state. Their site was barely an hour away, on the far side of Lordsburg, and as they got nearer they became noisy and jaunty, more like country boys on their way to a hoedown than men in their sixties with awesome responsibilities. They sang 'The Yellow Rose of Texas', the nearest to a cheerful song about New Mexico that they knew. The way had been long and hard, they had travelled together uncomfortably, sometimes miserably in the Middle East, and tiringly through the American South-

West. The lab work and the office work had driven them apart at times, and now, finally, they were about to share their secret, the ancient secret of plants, and astound the world with their version of cheap, clean and continuous energy. For old times' sake, and because it was their favourite spot, they turned south at the Animas junction and pulled into the dusty parking lot of the Panther Tracks café and parked right beside the local sheriff's patrol car.

Hammer had mythologised Animas as the friendliest rural community in the States. The day it acquired sidewalks, he said, he would stop coming. The café—the finest west of the Mississippi—was a white painted shed with few windows. Stepping out of the heat of the early afternoon, they paused in the doorway to let their eyes adjust. The sheriff and another cop were in quiet conference over mugs of coffee and were the only customers. In the Panther Tracks you did not order what you wanted, but what was available. Today it was pancakes and bacon. The coffee was the specially weak brew favoured across the American South. While they waited, Beard took out his palmtop. It had absorbed new messages that morning in the hotel, but he had not yet opened them. What caught his attention straight off was the name of P. Banner, his fifth ex-wife, Patrice, now married to a cosmetic dentist, Charles, who doted on her almost as much as Beard had nine years ago. She was briefly a headmistress before producing three babies in four years. And all those times she had told Beard that she never wanted children. Not his, anyway. Interesting, that Charles was short, plump and had even less hair than Beard and was two years older. As if marriages were a series of corrected drafts.

A year ago he had bumped into her in Regent's Park with her son, a delicate five-year-old with girlish curls. She was friendly, and he thought she was still beautiful. They sat on a bench and chatted for fifteen minutes. By devious means, Beard managed to pose the one question on his mind. Was she still an unfaithful wife? Yes, she might be, was her equally devious implication, but he did not stand a chance, if that was what he meant.

> Dear Michael, This might not be news to you, but in case it is you should know that five weeks ago, Rodney came out of prison. He tried to get in touch with me. He has all sorts of mad ideas I won't begin to describe. Charles's lawyer went to court and got a prohibitive-steps order that means he'll be arrested if he phones or writes or comes within 500 yards of our house. Now I've just heard from friends of friends that he's gone to the States to look for you. Perhaps he wants to thank you personally for giving evidence against him at his trial! Anyway, I think you should be warned. It's half-term tomorrow and we are all off to the Shetlands in the pouring rain. All best, Patrice.

Yes, that Turnip at the Camino Real hotel. It was one of the quaint decencies of English law that well-behaved murderers served only half their terms. An internet search on Beard's name would lead to Lordsburg easily enough, and to the site. So what? Despite the air conditioning, he felt the pricking sensation of sweat forming above his upper lip, and a tightness across his chest that caused a pain at the base of his throat. The pancakes came, twenty in each stack, the friendly lady said, and a pitcher of maple syrup to douse them with, a pile of streaky bacon six inches high, and a top-up of coffee of palest brown.

'Nirvana!' Hammer said, banging his hands together, still in the mood that had just deserted Beard.

He had always known this moment must come, but he had grown used to knowing it, and he had thought there was a good chance that Tarpin would serve his full term, and that time would dilute everything, and prison weaken him, and that, after all, it was Patrice who obsessed him, that she was the one who did for him at the trial. In fact, Beard's true accomplishment, a masterstroke of self-persuasion, was to half believe that Tarpin, because he was violent, because he had been tried and found guilty and was in prison with other guilty men, was tainted by association, and was indeed guilty, and not only that, but he knew it and was resigned to his fate. Beard, after all, had killed no one, and his story in court was unarguable, his witness from the Institute of Physics impeccable. As the years had passed, those events, on the morning he had returned from the Arctic, had begun to appear dreamlike, unprovable, without consequences. But lying below these appearances, like a stratum of impervious rock, were other assumptions, no, certainties, that in his busy life he had managed not to dwell on. Just as Beard had dreaded that the police and Patrice would assume that he, the jealous husband, had murdered

Aldous, so Tarpin was bound to think so too. Who else would want to frame him with the tools from his bag? So what did an unjustly imprisoned violent man, working out his bitter rage in the prison gym every day for eight years, do on his release? No shortage of cheap flights to Dallas.

As long as the sheriff and his friend were there, on the next table, Beard felt safe. All the same, when the café door swung open with a bang against its frame, he started, and the tightness round his chest intensified. It was a boisterous group of four local teenagers, three boys and a girl, wanting Cokes. The presence of two cops did not subdue them. They greeted each other like family members. Perhaps two armed policemen could do nothing against Tarpin. He might be ready to kill Beard in full view, and spend the rest of his life in the cells, morbidly content with a settled score. No shortage of handguns in this part of the world, and as easily purchased as fishing tackle.

'Off your food, Chief?' Hammer had finished his stack. 'Bad news from home?'

'No, no,' Beard said automatically, though even as he said it, he saw below Patrice's name a message marked urgent from Melissa. 'Just something I need to sort out. But I'm not hungry. It's too hot. Have mine.'

He pushed his plate across and Toby started in on his twenty-first pancake as Beard, after a half-minute's hesitation, opened Melissa's message. He supposed he should read it before he was killed.

'Michael, phone me, please. I need to talk to you about the other night.'

The other night? He struggled with this. Then he remembered Terry, the symphonic lover. She had dumped Terry, or she was marrying him. Beard could not decide at that moment which he would have preferred. If the latter, he would hide in Darlene's trailer. Tarpin would be no match for her. Or he would kill them both. He was not thinking straight, and he was in no condition for a matters-of-the-heart exchange with Melissa. He never would be. He scrolled through the names on the other twenty-seven messages—all but one was work-related, most in the pure, exalted domain of artificial photosynthesis. He opened the one from Darlene.

'Come quick! Something to tell ya!!!'

He did not deserve these distractions. They were encircling him, women, an Albuquerque lawyer, a north-London criminal, the unquiet cells of his own body, in a conspiracy to prevent him making his gift to the world. None of this was his fault. People had said of him that he was brilliant, and that was right, he was a brilliant man trying to do good. Self-pity steadied him a little. He and Toby were due to meet the engineers for a final inspection of the site that afternoon. Then Beard would give a speech to the assembled team. They should get on. But to drive towards Lordsburg was to drive towards Tarpin. The sight of Hammer's pancakes, or rather, the vision of him eating so many, doused in syrup, topped with the partially burned strips of the flesh and fat of pigs, sickened him. Muttering an excuse, he went through the café to the men's room, believing that he might be able to think more clearly if he could be sick. He stood waiting, slightly stooped, like a diligent waiter, over the porcelain bowl. How sparkling clean it was, just when a little disgust, the chocolate arabesque of another man's excrement, might have helped him empty his stomach. But nothing came. He straightened and dabbed at his forehead with a tissue. So what should he do? Either his life was at risk, or he was a hysterical coward. He considered the elemental fact—Tarpin was coming to see him. What good could come of that? Even now he might be sitting on the edge of a bed in a motel room on the Lordsburg strip, oiling his gun. Clearly, he was well motivated. For psychologically, logistically, even financially, it was not easy for an ex-con to fly about the world. He would need to lie about his criminal past on the US visa-waiver form. But no one would know. So it was foolish not to panic. The sensible thing might be to slip away, plead modesty and let Toby handle the opening ceremony, go down to São Paulo, for example, where a woman he knew, Sylvia, a fine physicist herself, would be more than happy to let him stay. He flushed the lavatory, washed his hands slowly, trying to make a decision before going back to the table. Yes, fine, São Paulo, but he could not speak Portuguese. He could not stay down there for ever. He would miss Darlene. So then what?

Hammer was standing to settle the bill. On a smeared plate, four pancakes and one bacon rasher, snapped in two unequal parts, and a toothpick remained. The glass syrup jeroboam was empty. It was a miracle the man was thin. He said, 'We're due in forty minutes and it's forty-five miles. Let's go!'

Beard could think of nothing to say and so, morosely, he followed his friend out into the blinding light of the parking lot towards the car.

*   *   *

They headed north across the grasslands towards the interstate, both men silent, though Hammer at the wheel whistled random notes, as though performing some earnest avant-garde piece. Beard was generally adept at avoiding inconvenient or troubling thoughts, but now that his spirits were low he was brooding about his health, and staring at the reddish-brown blotch, a map of unknown territory, on his wrist. The biopsy was in. Doctor Eugene Parks had confirmed in the morning that it was a melanoma and that it had grown just a half-millimetre deeper into the surrounding tissue than he would have preferred. He named a specialist in Dallas who could remove it tomorrow and start the radiation therapy. But Beard wanted to be in Lordsburg for the opening and told Parks he would come back within the month, as soon as he was free. Parks, in his engaging, neutral manner, told him he was being irrational. No time to lose, on the edge of no return, metastasis a possibility.

'Don't be a denier,' Doctor Parks had said, appearing to refer back to their climate-change chats. 'This won't go away just because you don't want it or are not thinking about it.'

And that was not all the bad news, though the rest was familiar enough. Beard had stripped to the waist and was now, resentfully, buttoning his shirt. The consulting rooms were on the nineteenth floor of a block in downtown El Paso, same floor, Beard remembered, that his mother had died on. Parks, whose people originally came from St Kitts, had minty breath and a wise old leathery face of silvery black. His head projected forward from his shoulders turtle fashion and bobbed kindly whenever Beard spoke. He was the same age as Beard, though some inches taller, and kept in shape by swimming, he said, every morning of the working week, between six and seven, before he saw his first patient. Beard could not imagine being wet, or even awake, at that time of day and knew he could never compete with this boast, could never pay the price of such inconvenience and discomfort to lower his body-mass index.

It was true, the doctor did not lecture or moralise, but he compensated with a disengaged, insulting frankness. With each instance, each looming physical catastrophe, the wise turtle head protruded a little further and he gently tapped his own palm with a pencil. No one, he said, not even Beard, would choose to walk around with a body like Beard's. He was carrying an extra sixty-five pounds, the equivalent of a combat infantryman's full pack. His knees and ankles were swollen from the weight, osteoarthritis was a growing possibility, his liver was enlarged, blood pressure was up again and there was a growing risk of congestive heart failure. His bad cholesterol was high, even by English standards. He was clearly experiencing breathing difficulties, he stood a decent chance of diabetes mellitus as well as advancing the likelihood of prostate and kidney cancer and thrombosis. His one piece of luck—luck, Beard noted, not virtue—was that he was not addicted to cigarettes, otherwise he might already be dead.

The doctor's head and shoulders were framed by a south-facing plate-glass window, a glaring rectangle of hazy white sky suggestive of the oppressive morning heat. Occasionally, an airplane drifted across, taking a turn around the city before landing on the east side. Over the river was Juarez, currently a world capital for murder as drug gangs fought their turf wars and slaughtered along the way soldiers, judges, policemen and city officials. Now the Mexican cartels were hiring unemployed Texan teenagers to do their killing. Clearly, life would push on without Michael Beard. As he listened to Parks enumerate his possible futures, he decided not to mention his recent acquisition of a classic symptom, the occasional sensation of tightness around his chest. It would only make him appear even more foolish and doomed. Nor could he admit that he did not have it in him to eat and drink less, that exercise was a fantasy. He could not command his body to do it, he had no will for it. He would rather die than take up jogging or prance to funky music in a church hall with other tracksuited deadbeats.

When Beard made his vague promise to return within the month, Doctor Parks was for tying him down to dates. Tuesday the twenty-third or Thursday the twenty-fifth, he must take his pick. Beard hesitated, Parks insisted, as though it were his own bloodstream through which liberated cancer cells were about to drift, looking for a new place, a nearby lymph node, to set up home. Beard chose the remoter date, knowing that he could phone Parks's secretary and blamelessly cancel.

Now, as Hammer ceased his terrible whistling and slowed to pass through the minute township of Cotton City, the sanctuary of an obscure clinic in Dallas looked more attractive. But Beard knew that he did not have the strength to run away. The arrangements for tomorrow had a momentum he could not interrupt, not when he was so hungry for public triumph, for that time in the early evening when little Lordsburg with its neon and burger joints and abundant air conditioning became nominally carbon neutral, and American civilisation, which stood for the aspirations of all the world, could continue on its way without the inconvenience of overheating. The eight-year journey from the slow deciphering of the Aldous file to lab work, refinements, breakthroughs, drawings, field tests must be completed. General acclaim was the final stage. Tarpin could do his worst.

Beard fiddled with the radio to catch the on-the-hour news, and there it was, a snappy interview with one of Hammer's PR team explaining that sunlight and water would first power Lordsburg and, one day, the entire planet.

Hammer whooped. 'Beautiful! I trained that girl up well.'

He and Beard never acknowledged, not even to each other in private, that they would not really be supplying electricity to Lordsburg at all. They would be selling kilowatt hours to a local utility company that were the rough equivalent of the town's average consumption over a year. The electrons from their revolutionary plant would swarm anonymously among the rest.

'We'll all be down there,' the announcer said. 'Out on Highway 90, three miles east of 70. Join us at 6 p.m. tomorrow, countdown to switch-on, when Lordsburg leads the world!'

Soon they were heading east on the interstate,

and then swinging north round the town and after a couple of miles turning right for Silver City. Minutes later they came over a slight rise that gave them a view of the site. Beard had seen it many times in the past months, with everything in place and dry runs going smoothly after some initial setbacks. But still, this afternoon he felt a little swoon of pride. Sensing the mood, Hammer slowed.

'Well, matey,' he said, concealing his own strong emotions behind a hideous attempt at cockney. 'Don't it just warm the cockles of your 'eart?'

The twenty-three big tilted panels had a dull gleam under the ferocious sun. They were fed by a mess of pipework and valves. Behind them were the storage tanks for the compressed hydrogen and oxygen, and alongside were the breezeblock sheds housing the fuel-cell generator and the catalysts. Power lines on new poles led to the nearest of the ancient wooden pylons that tottered in succession across the immensity of semi-desert. On the other side of the tanks was a pumping station built over the deep water source, and beyond was a neat brick building that housed the computers.

What was new were the hundreds of people, construction workers, vendors and sound technicians, moving importantly between tasks, and the many hundreds or thousands of Stars and Stripes planted on poles around the panels where the security fence should have been, and in triangular bunting along the top of the giant pale blue marquee and down its guy ropes, around the sound stage, and lining the recently bulldozed half-acre square where the army band would march, and suspended in artfully drooping streamers over the bleachers where the local VIPs would sit, and along the avenue formed by fast-food and cold-drink concessions and, at right angles to it, down an even grander avenue of portable lavatories, and around the perimeter of the parking lot, where there were at least a hundred vehicles instead of the usual dozen, with room for a couple of thousand more. Not a single Union Jack, Beard noted moodily, to honour himself, the inventor and first mover of the project. But he said nothing, and banished the thought.

To one side, on another space cleared of vegetation, and unadorned by flags, were media trucks and satellite dishes. A few hundred yards out into the scrub, on a low rise parallel to the highway, was the unlit neon 'Lordsburg!' sign, in homage to the lettering of the famous Hollywood landmark, all characters erected except the exclamation mark, and even now this thirty-foot-high punctuation was being hauled upright with ropes by men in hardhats.

As they turned off the road onto a dirt track and passed under a proscenium of yet more Stars and Stripes, an aroma of frying fat, chilled by the car's air conditioning, filled the cabin and tickled their noses.

Beard said, 'Toby, you're a genius!'

Hammer nodded in grave acknowledgement. 'I like to bring things and people together. But, Michael. This is your invention. The genius is you.'

Feeling serene now, Beard nodded in return. This was how friendship should be.

Even as they parked, men in T-shirts and baseball caps, some holding clipboards, were hurrying towards them through a dust cloud. This was Hammer's team, or a part of it, and among the group were engineers, hydraulic and computer specialists and other technicians. Beard had done the theoretical work, designed and supervised the experiments in the lab, but the rest, the scaling up, the drawings, the mass-production design, the actual plant layout and construction, the pipes and valves and how they were represented in the software, was not his concern. He knew the principles, he owned the patents, but he could not have given a detailed account of the site. Here on the open plain, he was an eminence, almost a legend, and everybody treated him with appropriate respect, with the intimate politeness at which Americans excel, but no one needed him to come and peer into a trench or adjudicate on spheres of responsibility. The NREL in Golden, Colorado, had examined the prototype and confirmed that the process he had devised worked to a high level of efficiency. The rest was for this friendly bunch of practical men waiting for Toby Hammer, who himself knew nothing about the technicalities or underlying principles, but had a gift for detail and co-ordination and man-management.

So now, as the two men stepped out of their car and engaged in a round of handshakes and backslaps, Beard prepared to slip away. The roasting air was amplifying the appeal of cooking smells, of meat grilling on wood fires, drifting across the parking lot from the concessions. The news about Tarpin had ruined his brunch, but his concentration would remain unsettled until he had strolled down this instant desert boulevard and made a considered choice. Toby, who kept a pick-up on site, handed the car keys over and he and his group headed across the parking lot towards the array.

After barely five minutes' reflection, Beard was sitting alone in deep shade at a trestle table with a paper plate of barbecued brisket, Texan style, with three giant gherkins and a mound of potato salad and a small waxed-paper bucket of draught beer. By the common standards of energy production, the Lordsburg Artificial Photosynthesis Plant, known as LAPP to the engineers, was negligible, a mere toy, barely a prototype. But sitting here, with the blue smoke of grilled chicken rolling past him from the joint next door, and country rock on speakers mounted on poles, and the chefs shouting cheerily to each other of the news that twenty-four hungry men from the 'Lordsburg!' sign-erection team were heading this way for rump steaks, Beard felt himself to be at the centre of the world. How delicious it was, not only the food, but to be here, cosily ignored, in an obscure corner of the American heartland, and to know that the din, the construction, the digital media and soon, jet fighters and marching bands, this imminent industrial revolution, owed their existence at this spot among the palmillas and dried grasses to what he had once conceived eight years ago, lying on a dirty sofa in a basement flat five thousand miles away.

He had his teeth clamped about the fourth piece of succulent brisket when something happened that he had not experienced since his schooldays and even then considered intensely annoying. He felt a presence at his back and before he could turn, warm hands clamped over his eyes, gripping his head tightly so he could not move, and a voice said in a whisper into his ear, 'Guess who?'

A finger of the left hand was pressing uncomfortably on the northern hemisphere of his eyeball and he dared not struggle. His tongue was laden with meat, and in the shock of the moment he was unable to swallow. But still, he managed to say indistinctly, 'Tarpin?'

'She your Chinese girl?' There was merry laughter as he was released.

Darlene, of course, and his irritation vanished as he struggled to his feet, chewing rapidly to empty his mouth, and embraced her. Who could not love Darlene? She was a good-hearted, overweight woman from Nebraska who had waited tables all her life, had married three times, had four grown-up children who appeared to adore or need her, for they phoned constantly, had discovered New Mexico twelve years back and changed her name from Janet. She now spoke fluent Spanish, after living for six years with a Hispanic truck driver in a trailer on the southern edge of town before she threw him out.

And now she had set her heart on Michael Beard. At their first sexual encounter she had told him he was her very first older man. And then, correcting herself, her first much older man. He did not like to think that her own choices, like his, might be narrowing. He was, after all, something of a local hero, honoured by the Chamber of Commerce on East 2nd Street for bringing jobs to the town. He was not such a bad proposition. And she, of course, fulfilled Beard's old fantasy of the grand lowlife. In that way of Americans good-naturedly declaring a class affiliation, she chewed gum, open-mouthed, remorselessly, all day, even while she talked, stopping only in order to kiss him. She never read books or newspapers or even magazines, had never been to church, and disliked wholesome food as much as Beard, and when she doused her plate was fond of evoking Ronald Reagan's celebrated insight that ketchup was a vegetable. Beard was disappointed by her lack of religion. It did not conform to type. But she was staunch. She was not even an atheist, she said, she could not care enough even to deny God's existence. He simply did not 'come up'.

They had met when Beard, with many hours to kill before a meeting, drove out of Lordsburg one afternoon and turned along a track that led to the ghost town of Shakespeare and, faintly bored, afflicted in the spring warmth by formless sexual expectation, wandered down the old main street, from the old saloon to the old general merchandise to the old Stratford Hotel, where Billy the Kid once washed dishes. As Beard was leaving he came across Darlene in the parking lot. She had come out to lend support to her friend Nicky, who was after a job as a tour guide and had just been told she was too unconfident and ignorant to qualify. She was crying on Darlene's arm as Beard, in predatory mode, strolled across and kindly asked if he could be of help. Darlene explained the outrageous rejection while Nicky tried to join in. She was a scrawny, freckly, crop-haired chain-smoker with a stutter, trying to inhale even as she wept, and Beard thought that he himself would not have hired her in any capacity. But this was her third failed attempt in as many days to get a job and so they went back to Darlene's trailer and drank consolatory beers and scotch all afternoon, with Nicky producing cocaine and pot, which he and Darlene refused. To endear himself to Darlene he promised to find Nicky something out at the site (which he did, and Hammer sacked her two days later), and after she had left to see to her children, Beard and Darlene made love in the oak-veneered bedroom next door.

He saw her whenever he came to Lordsburg. There was a bar on 4th Street they liked, and sometimes they partied in his room at the Holiday Inn, but mostly they enjoyed themselves in the trailer, which she kept neatly. There was a small yard at the rear with two lemon trees she cared for like children, trees just big enough to cast some shade in the late afternoon on a couple settling down to drink. After a couple of scotches—she shared that taste with Beard—she laughed a lot, very loudly, and after three or four drinks she loved to go indoors, into the cool throb and rattle of the air conditioning, to make love. For Beard the affair was an unexpected sexual renaissance, with piercing sensory pleasure, much like that near-inversion of agony he remembered from his twenties. A lifetime had swept by since he last shouted out involuntarily like a madman at the moment of orgasm. He never would have believed he would be experiencing such extremities of sensation with a woman of fifty-one, whose body was as slack and tired and inflated, as scribbled on by varicose veins, as his own. He assumed that this might well be his last throw at such ecstasy, and so he cherished her. Just as he took presents from El Paso or Dallas airports to Melissa and Catriona, so he lugged in reverse items for Darlene from

Heathrow. In another town, another country, she might have been considered a noisy drunk. In Lordsburg she was popular and useful, and through her he came to respect the town. Apart from her evening waitressing job at the Lulu Diner, she worked as a volunteer in a grade school, tidying classrooms and cleaning up grazed knees. For two weeks a year she did unpaid menial jobs at a summer camp for autistic kids in the Gila hills. Only rarely, two or three times in a year at most, was she gathered insensate off the sidewalk at night by a neighbour or a patrolman and brought home to the trailer.

Strictly speaking, he did not lie to her about his life in England, but he did not tell her everything. She knew about the five wives, she had roared over tales of the rancid apartment in Dorset Square, which she promised to restore to order and cleanliness for him, if only he would give her the chance. But he refrained from an account of his partner and child in Primrose Hill. Darlene wanted to accompany him to England, and he did not want to heighten her interest in the plan by saying no, or complicate his life by saying yes, and settled instead for vague promises. As eighteen months passed, matters took the usual turn. The very sharpest edges of pleasure and novelty were dulled, but slowly, and only slightly, with many restorative backward steps. At the same time, her thoughts turned more frequently to the future, their future together, an awkward subject, for the time must come when the plant would be functioning and he would no longer need to come to Lordsburg, and he would be setting up somewhere else in the South-West or scattering iron filings in the ocean to the north of the Galapagos Archipelago, or exploiting his patents around the world. But if this divergence of feeling was a problem, Beard was inclined to do nothing. In their easy intimacy, in the heat and fierce shadows of New Mexico, it was easily shelved. The past had shown him many times that the future would be its own solution.

So it was a delight to see her now, and go over to the grill and fetch her a jumbo portion of spare ribs, potato salad and ketchup and a bucket of beer to match his own, and sit with her amid the sentimental din and woozy pedal guitars of the country music, and hear her news and tell her his own. They sat close and, keeping well clear of the private realm, he gave her the latest from the diminutive ancient kingdom across the ocean, where, according to the latest scandal, the hard-pressed citizenry had been obliged to empty their pockets in taxes so that the ruling class might clean their moats, build servant quarters, buy trouser presses and hire pornographic movies. Now, down the smog-shrouded cobbled alleyways of filthy cities and in pestilential thatched villages, there were dark mutterings of revolt. For her part, she told him about Nicky's return to AA, where she had found Jesus for the fourth time and had been off drugs and drink, though not cigarettes, for twenty-two days and still had her job at the pharmacy, though only just.

When Darlene had finished eating, she laid a heavy arm across his shoulders and kissed his cheek. 'But honey, the main news is you. Lordsburg was on NBC last night and CNN were filming on Main Street yesterday right by the

Exxon station, and everyone's talking about tomorrow. I'm so proud of you!'

She was gazing at him with an expression he had not seen before, a look of smug maternal possession that troubled him faintly. But he did not want the moment, and the grander moment that contained it, spoiled in any way. So he kissed her and they drank another beer and shared a chocolate, fudge and peppermint ice cream. Then they stood and kissed again and hugged, and he told her he would see her in an hour. He had a duty to fulfil.

He made his way across the busy site to the control station, where the whole crew was waiting, crowding in around the consoles to hear him deliver the speech of thanks he had mentally rehearsed on the plane from London. Hammer stood solemnly at his side, arms crossed, like a nightclub bouncer. From somewhere outside came the sound of trumpets and a piccolo, and the thump of a bass drum. The marching band, or some of it, had arrived to rehearse.

The team had wrought wonders, Beard began by saying in the bland tones of group exhortation, in bringing what had first been just a dream, then a stream of frenzied calculations, then an exploration by way of laboratory tests, then a set of drawings, to this, an engineering reality here in the desert. What they had built existed nowhere else in the world except for some related workbench experiments in a handful of competitor labs. But the process of discovery and development was far greater than this single project, magnificent though it was. Water was first split into hydrogen and oxygen in 1789, the principles of the fuel cell first discussed in 1839. Countless biologists and physicists had devoted themselves to the continuing elucidation of photosynthesis. Einstein's photovoltaics and also quantum mechanics had played their parts, and chemistry, the science of new materials, protein synthesis, in fact, virtually the whole of the culture of science had contributed in some manner to the triumph that was now almost theirs. And there was a far larger consideration. Everyone here knew that in the greatest scheme of all, spanning billions of years, the capturing and converting of light and the splitting of water by self-organising living forms had generated atmospheric oxygen and had been the engine of evolution. This had been their inspiration, the process they had attempted to reverse engineer.

Beard filled his lungs, then emptied them with a noisy sigh, and showed his open palms in a gesture of abject modesty.

'This is why I can claim nothing for myself. I stood, like Newton, on the shoulders of giants, hundreds of them, and I borrowed slavishly from nature. By good fortune my Conflation helped me see what others could not, though the door already stood ajar. And what I saw was that the most common element in the universe, hydrogen, could be made cheaply, efficiently and in vast quantities by imitating photosynthesis in a certain way, and that it could power our civilisation, just as this beautiful process has powered life on earth by being its principal biological energy input. So now we will have clean energy, endlessly self-renewing, and we can begin to draw back from the brink of disastrous, self-destructive global warming. Some have claimed that my role was vital, that none of this could have happened without me. Well, who knows? All I say is that I was lucky to have had certain ideas, and I was fortunate to be standing in the right place at the right moment in history, at a time of pressing need. My part was simple inevitability. The point is, we're a team and everyone's part was crucial, every last one of you was a vital link. And truly, it has been my great privilege to work with you and come to respect your expertise. And you should know that I owe everything, we all owe everything, to our dear friend here, the human dynamo, Toby Hammer!'

To applause and cheers, Beard clutched at Toby's wrist, scratching the American's skin in the lunge, and wrenched his arm away from his chest and raised it, boxing-ring style.

Unsmiling, Hammer bowed his head to the redoubled cheers. To cries of 'speech, speech!' he declined with pursed lips, and the meeting began to break up.

When there was just a handful left, men who seemed to want to talk to Beard, Hammer shook his head and silently indicated the door to them and after a moment's hesitation they filed out, and the two friends were left alone. Beard sat down at one of the consoles and stared at a screen displaying three graphs with falling curves. They were not identified, but he guessed they showed the regulation of the catalysts.

'What's up, Toby?'

'I'm not sure yet.'

'Still worrying about a warming failure? They're near to breaking the record today down in Orogrande.'

Hammer did not smile. He was leaning against the wall by the door, hands deep in his pockets, staring over Beard's head. Finally he said, 'This guy Barnard called. The lawyer from Albuquerque, acting for Braby and the Centre in England. He's on his way here now. I said I wouldn't see him unless he told me what he wanted. And he did.'

Toby cleared his throat noisily and came away from the door to stand by Beard's side. He put a hand on the Englishman's shoulder.

'Michael, is there anything about this project that I should know that I don't?'

'Of course there isn't. Why?'

'They're filing a claim against your patents.'

'Braby?'

'Yup.'

For several seconds Beard slumped at the console, frowning as he reached back into his grey English past. He brought to mind concrete posts, the smell of the beer factory beside the motorway, the mud between the temporary huts, the makeshift tables piled with foolish dreams. It was as though he were recalling an existence before he was born, before dinosaurs had their dominion, when mists were thick over primeval swamps. And now, as those mists began to clear, he could see. How had he failed to predict it? This was how Braby was going to angle in on the revitalised American renewables scene, not by begging favours for advice or introductions, but with the muscle of expensive litigation. It was threatening behaviour, it was an attempted mugging. He would expect to settle out of court and take a share in future projects. And on the basis of nothing at all.

Beard stood suddenly, feeling energised and

relieved, and, ignoring an attack of dizziness, tapped Hammer on the chest, as though attempting to correct the faulty machinery of his thoughts.

'Listen, Toby. I've seen this kind of manoeuvring before with institutions and patents. Braby thinks, or he's pretending to think, that I did my photosynthesis work while I was at the Centre and that the rights of exploitation belong there. But I didn't get started until I set up at Imperial and by then Braby had got me sacked. And anyway, under the terms of my employment I was free to pursue my own work. I mean, I was only in there once a week. I have the old contract at home. I'll show you.'

'This could slow us down,' Hammer murmured, still gloomily unconvinced.

Beard said, 'When they see the dates, my sacking, my contract, they'll run for cover. We'll counter-sue for harassment, defamation, whatever. The Centre has even less money than we do. They lost nearly everything on a ridiculous wind turbine they were developing. It was a big public scandal.The place runs on a shoestring.'

Beard noticed his colleague begin to relax. Poverty in a hostile litigant was refreshing.

'Michael, promise me there are no hidden reefs, no shocks, nothing you're holding back.'

'I promise. Braby's a damned opportunist. We'll kick his backside across the Rio Grande.'

'Barnard will be here in fifteen minutes.'

Beard made a show of frowning as he looked at his watch. He wanted his spell with Darlene. Only then could he face the lawyer.

'I have a meeting in town. But he can come and

find me at the Holiday Inn this evening. Or in that restaurant across the road.'

As Beard went towards the door, Hammer was already bent over his laptop writing emails and hardly seemed to notice his friend leaving. Normality restored.

* * *

It was invigorating, to come out of the frozen air of the control room into the dry heat of the late afternoon, from fluorescent to golden light, from the murmurings of the servers into the din of preparation and the cacophony of two separate sound systems playing country music in different parts of the site competing with the rehearsals of the army band and the whine of a power drill. It was not only the prospect of heading into town with Darlene that stirred Beard. He was enlivened, uplifted by outrage at Braby's clumsy, unjust claims. They added even greater value to the project. The false friend who had turned on him at the lowest point in his career now wanted some small part of the glory. He could not have it, and it was a joy to contemplate the fact. Beard's step was unusually light and quick as he went through the bustle. He slowed as he passed a stall setting up to sell patriotic souvenirs. He could imagine buying a little Stars and Stripes on a stick and waving it with childish malice under Braby's nose. But no. Let him rot with his tinpot helical turbine in the damp grey confines of southern England.

He was twenty minutes early for Darlene, so he headed towards the parade ground and the silvery trills and foghorn blare of the marching band.

There were twenty or so men in fatigues, not many of them young, standing with their bandmaster in the shade of an awning at one end of the raw, flattened square. On the south side, workmen had finished erecting a set of steeply raked bleachers for dignitaries and press. Again, he marvelled at all that Toby Hammer had achieved with his emails. As Beard made his way around the ground, the musicians were rehearsing, with just a few cranky, misplaced notes, a Beatles medley, and he assumed that this was not a proper army band but some kind of reservist group of local enthusiasts. The bandmaster's white baton conjured an unpleasant association of Melissa's lover. It was already getting late in London and he owed her a call. But this was not the time.

To the strutting tones of 'Yellow Submarine', he walked towards the stand of bleachers, which rose right up from among the brush and palmillas. There was a figure sitting alone, dead centre, and Beard immediately recognised a fellow Englishman. Was it the cigarette, the stoop of narrow shoulders, or the grey socks and black leather shoes and absence of hat and sunglasses? There was a small carry-all at the man's feet and he was hunched forward, chin resting in one hand, staring not at the band, but past it, in the direction of the Gila hills. Rodney Tarpin, of course. His old friend, come all this way to render his account. After the initial shock of recognition, and some minutes of hesitation, Beard decided to go over to him, certain that it would be better to have a confrontation now on his own terms, and in public, than be taken by surprise. Darlene's hands over his eyes had been a warning.

The stand was unreasonably steep and he paused to rest at the centre row before going sideways along it towards his man. In a display of cool, pretending not to notice or care about Beard's approach, Tarpin continued to stare straight ahead as he smoked, even as Beard sat down next to him. He did not trust himself to speak until he had caught his breath, and still Tarpin did not turn to acknowledge him. This was how momentous encounters were presented in certain movies, and Tarpin would have had time to watch a few. He had not wasted much of his eight years in the prison gym. Confinement had shrunk him. His arms and legs were thin, and the builder's proud gut that once held sway above his belt was now a little pot. Even his head looked smaller, the face more mouse than rat, and the impression of taut nostrils, of eager inquisitiveness, had been stamped out. In its place, a passive watchfulness that might have passed, at dusk perhaps, for calm. But in the golden New Mexico afternoon he looked a harmless wreck, a bum sucking too needily on his cigarette, hardly the man to deliver a slap to the face. Beard felt his spirits glow and swell with relief. This poor lag could do him no harm.

The silence was becoming absurd. Beard spoke up briskly, as though to a dim and wayward employee. 'So, Mr Tarpin. They've let you out. What brings you all this way?'

He turned at last, pinching out his cigarette between forefinger and thumb. In the corners of the whites of his eyes were unhealthy egg-yolk smears. There were broken capillaries too running from the bridge of his nose and across his cheeks.

When he spoke he exposed the missing tooth, an upper incisor, that prison dentistry had omitted to fix.

'I thought if I was sat up here you'd be bound to see me.'

'Well?'

'Mr Beard, I need to talk to you, tell you something, ask you something.'

Faintly, Beard's fear revived. He was keeping a watch on Tarpin's hand, and on the bag at his feet. 'All right. But I haven't got long.'

Below them the band ground on through its medley. The final chords of 'Yesterday' dissolved into a chirpy rendition, in strict marching tempo, of 'All You Need is Love'. Hard to credit that millions once screamed and tore at their hair for such staid little ditties.

'I'll come straight to it then. First thing is this. I never killed Thomas Aldous.'

'I remember you saying in court.'

'It doesn't matter you don't believe me. No one believes me. I don't care, because the truth is, I would have killed him if I'd had half the chance. And this is the thing. I told Patrice to do it if she ever saw a way without getting harmed. And I swore to her, if she did it, I'd go down for it, if it came to that. She didn't say nothing, but she must have taken one of my hammers when she was round my place and got him when he was asleep on her sofa.'

'Hang on,' Beard said. 'Why on earth would Patrice want to kill Tom Aldous?'

'I understand you're upset, Mr Beard. I know you got a divorce and all, but this was the woman you loved once and it's not nice, is it, to hear that she's a killer. But she hated him. She couldn't get rid of him. She asked him to leave her alone, but he wouldn't go away. I did what I could, but he was a big bastard . . .'

Beard had half forgotten that he knew the truth and that he had devised Tarpin's misery for him. He hardly knew which objection to raise first. He said, 'Did she tell you she hated him? That she wanted to get rid of him?'

'Many many times.'

'But she told the whole world she loved him.'

Tarpin straightened and spoke with some pride. 'That was later, that was for my motive, you see. Jealous! I was ready to do anything for her.'

'For God's sake, man, then why didn't you plead guilty and get a shorter term?'

'Some cocky little lawyer said he could get me off, and I believed him.'

'So you planned all this out together?'

'I couldn't get to her once Aldous was dead. And then I was arrested. So we had to sort of work it out as we went along without actually speaking. But we knew what we were doing.'

The band had given all it could to the Beatles and was taking a rest. Brass players were decanting condensate onto the desert sand from their instruments. The bandmaster was striding away with a cigar in his mouth.

Beard said, 'But surely, if you had gone to see Aldous yourself, you could have frightened him off.'

Tarpin laughed bitterly. 'Tried that, didn't I? Right at the start. Went round to his place in Hampstead, took a tyre iron just for effect. He had it off me first stroke, threw me all over his garden, put my back out, fractured my kneecap, held my head under his pond, dislocated my arm. And did this. Look.'

He pointed to the gap in his teeth.

Beard could not help a fierce proprietorial pride in Tom Aldous. What a physicist! He said, 'Paying you back, I suppose, for blacking Patrice's eye.'

'I apologised for that, Mr Beard,' Tarpin said huffily. 'More than once, if you want to know. And in the end Patrice accepted my apology.'

'So you went to prison for my wife. And she came to see you, wrote you beautiful grateful letters?'

'It wouldn't look right, would it, visiting her lover's murderer. After a year I started writing to her. Every single day. But I heard nothing. Nothing in eight years. I didn't even know she was married again till I came out.'

The poor deluded sap stared away towards the mountains beyond Lordsburg. Looking at him, Beard was pleased that he himself had never fallen properly in love. Not if this was what happened to a man's reason. He had come closest with Patrice, and what an idiot that had made of him. In the circumstances it was not possible, but he would have liked to press Tarpin about the murder weapon, the hammer with the narrow head. Had he really forgotten that he had left a bag of tools in Belsize Park? What an ass, and how convenient.

Tarpin said, 'I can't stop thinking about her, and you're the only one I can talk to. We've both loved the same woman, Mr Beard. You could say our fates are entwined. She won't let me come near her, won't even talk to me for five minutes on the phone. But I still love her.'

He repeated himself, with greater force, so that

two workmen walking past the stand glanced up in their direction.

'I ought to be bitter, I ought to be furious at the way she let me down. I ought to break her neck, but I love her, and it makes me feel good just to say it out loud to someone who knows her. I love her and if it was ever going to stop, it would have happened a long time ago, when I realised I wasn't going to hear from her. I love her, I love . . .'

'Let me get this right,' Beard said. 'You came all this way, you concealed your criminal record from Homeland Security, just to tell me that you still love my ex-wife?'

'You were the only other player, if you see what I mean. You're the only one I can say it to and it means something, that Patrice killed Aldous, and I paid for it with eight years of my life. And I owe you an apology, treating you the way I did when you came round to my house. But I was under a lot of stress, you see, with Patrice going to see Aldous in the evenings because she didn't dare upset him. But I am truly sorry about hitting you like that.'

Beard said, 'I think we can let that one go.'

But there was a purpose to Tarpin's apology. 'There was another reason I came. I've thought about this really hard. I've got to do something with myself. I can't spend the next ten years just thinking about Patrice. Mr Beard, I want a fresh start, somewhere far away from where she is. I saw about your thing here on the TV. You're the only one who knows this situation and I know you'll understand. I'm asking you to give me a job. I've still got the skills, plumbing, wiring, bricklaying, labouring. I'll pick up litter, if that's what's on offer. I know how to work hard.'

Beard's thoughts were running ahead. He had found something for Darlene's Nicky, even though she lasted only two days. There were ways round Tarpin's illegal status. And the man was a fantasising fool who possibly deserved a break. It was unfortunate for Tarpin, however, that minutes before, Beard's mood had dipped at the memory of those dark days, when he watched from a first-floor window as his wife, in new frock and shoes, went down the garden path to her Peugeot and her evening assignation. Wasn't eight years enough? Wasn't his punishment complete? It probably never would be, Beard thought as he stood and extended his hand and resumed his official tone.

'Thank you for coming to see me, Mr Tarpin. I don't know whether I believe your story, but I've enjoyed it. As for a job, well, you had an affair with my wife and you encouraged her to murder my close colleague, or, who knows, you killed him yourself. All in all, I don't exactly feel I owe you any favours . . .'

Tarpin stood too, but he refused the handshake. He sounded astonished. 'You're saying no?'

'Yes.'

He moved at speed from whining petitioner to aggressor. 'Because I went with your wife?'

'Mostly that, yes.'

'But you didn't love her. You fucked everything in sight. You didn't look after her. You could have had her all to yourself, but you drove her away.'

Now that he was angry, he looked more like his former self, with the colour back in his cheeks and that old ratty look. He was gaunt, but in possession perhaps of some wiry strength. And though he had shrunk and aged, he remained taller and younger than Beard.

'I didn't go looking for an affair,' he said loudly. 'Patrice came on to me as a way of getting at you. I had my own problems. My wife ran off with my kids. You wrecked your own fucking marriage. That beautiful woman. You broke her poor heart!'

Mindful of the possibility of violence, Beard was edging away along the line of bleachers. He was no Tom Aldous, adept at cracking kneecaps. He said from a judicious distance, 'There are some patrolmen down by the highway. Clear off now or I'll invite them to come and discuss your tourist visa with you. They're not so gentle with illegals in these parts, you know.'

'You bastard! You cowardly bastard!'

Beard descended the stand as fast as he was able, then strode away. Even when he had reached the far side of the parade ground and was heading back towards the Texan-style barbecue, he could hear the diminishing cries, 'Cunt! Coward! Cheat! I'll get you!' Heads of upright citizens turned to look, and there were disapproving glances in Beard's direction too. Some minutes later, after a wrong turn, he found himself in the grand colonnade of green portable lavatories and slipped inside to make lingering use of one. When he came out and looked around, he saw Tarpin in the distance, right down on the highway, waving his thumb at the passing traffic.

Beard was late for his rendezvous with Darlene, but he was tired and hot, and there was much to think about, so he dawdled. Tarpin, not Aldous, was the lover whom Patrice could not shake off, and she made up a story to escape another black eye. But what had stopped the bullying was the thrashing Aldous delivered. Even if Beard had strangled Aldous with his bare hands, Tarpin would have stepped up to take the blame, such was the reach of his obsessive delusional state. Beard's past was often a mess, resembling a ripe, odorous cheese oozing into or over his present, but this particular confection had congealed into the appearance of something manageably firm, more Parmesan than Epoisses. He was reflecting cheerfully on this formulation—it reminded him that he was still peckish—and was in sight of the Texan barbecue when he felt his palmtop trembling in his pocket. Melissa, the screen told him. Calling before she turned in for the night. But when he put the phone to his ear he heard the sound of a car's engine and, faintly in the background, Catriona singing.

'Darling,' he said quickly, before she could speak. 'I've been trying to reach you.'

'We were on the plane.'

Running off with the conductor, taking his child, was his immediate thought. 'Where are you?' he said peevishly, expecting her to lie.

'We're just leaving El Paso.'

He paused to take this in. 'How can you be? I don't understand.'

'We're on our way. It's half-term, Lenochka is taking care of the shops and, as you know, Catriona and I have got something to discuss with you.'

'Like what?' Beard said, feeling nameless guilt. What had he done now?

She said, 'Someone called Darlene phoned to tell me you two are getting married. Before you do, your daughter and I would like a word.'

That. In memory the occasion was as vague as a half-forgotten dream, but he knew the moment, some weeks ago in the trailer bedroom. Darlene had not mentioned it since.

He said, 'Melissa, believe me, there's no truth in it.' As if by saying so he could make her turn back to London and leave his evening free.

She said, 'Hold on, I've got to take this exit . . . One other thing I want you to know before we meet. Terry.'

'Yes.'

'He doesn't exist. I made him up. It was a way of saving face, and it was stupid. It made things worse.'

'I see,' Beard said.

And he did. She had uninvented Terry, and now he would be expected to do the same for Darlene. He heard Catriona singing or shouting in the background.

Melissa said, 'We'll see you soon. And you belong to us.' She rang off.

He remained where he was, leaning against a pole that supported a loudspeaker. Thank God it was silent. Around him the site was emptying as the sun lowered and men came to the end of their shifts and headed for the parking lot. As he recalled it, he and Darlene had been making love after drinking one hot afternoon, and the air conditioning was at its highest setting, rattling like a madman at the bars of his cell. Seconds before he came, she cupped her hand around his balls and asked him to marry her and he had said, or shouted, yes. Perhaps the notion of such wild folly and abandon was what brought him on. How could he have meant it when he was already not married to Melissa? No one would believe a man at such a moment? The point was that Darlene had discovered his other life, and like the bold player she was, she was forcing his hand. Someone, or everyone, would be disappointed. Nothing new there.

Beard reached for his infrared car key, whose reassuring solidity seemed to contain all the miles he wanted to put between himself and Lordsburg. It would be sensible to slip away now, find lodgings along the interstate in Deming, avoid Darlene and Melissa all day tomorrow in order to concentrate on his world-historical event, then face them afterwards, together or separately. Anything but face them this evening. But as he turned to walk towards his car, he felt great sadness at losing the promised hour with Darlene. The old parliament of his selfhood was in uproarious division. An eloquent voice of experience rose above the din to suggest that denying himself a long-awaited release could be even more damaging to his concentration. He ignored this voice and continued walking. Sometimes a man had to make sacrifices, for science, for the well-being of future generations.

But then came deliverance. He had taken barely thirty steps when he heard his name called behind him. She had come out from under the Texan-barbecue awning into the thoroughfare just a hundred yards away, and was running towards him in a jiggling, splayed-arm manner, and he felt relieved. They would go straight to his motel room. The decision was out of his hands.

For reasons of her own, she did not ask him why he was heading in the wrong direction. They strolled companionably arm in arm down the boulevard of green latrines towards the parking lot. When they were there she thought it would be better if she left her car and came in his. He could think of no good reason why not, except that he would be bound to her company, tomorrow morning as well as tonight. That was surely what she had in mind. As he drove towards Lordsburg she slid her left hand across his lap, and she caressed him the whole way while she told him what she would do when they were indoors. He was in a trance, no other thought in his head, as he turned into the motel drive and pulled up outside his usual room. He went robotically to the office to check in. Soon they were reclining their excited naked bulks on cool sheets behind a double-locked door. Only ten years ago, when he still thought he could rescue himself with exercise, he would have been shocked by his own pneumatic form, by his concertina of chins, and by the ribbed contours of the woman he was stroking, and by the sweaty scent of newly cut grass that arose from armpits, groins and crooks of knees, heavily enfolded regions that rarely saw air or light. Yet everything was as thrilling as it had ever been. She was a kind and ingenious lover, who sucked and licked and teased and drew him wetly in, but when his moment came, he remembered to refrain from giving himself away in marriage.

Afterwards, they lay closely side by side. She lifted her weight onto one elbow and, gazing down on him fondly, played with the few tufts of hair that survived behind his ears. His eyes were closed.

'Michael?' she whispered. 'Honey?'

'Mm.'

'Did I ever tell you that I love you?'

'Yes . . .' He had been thinking, with strange lucidity of his old friend, the photon, and a detail in Tom Aldous's notes about the displacement of an electron. There might be an inexpensive way of improving a second generation of panels. When he was back in London he would blow the dust off that file. He said again, contentedly, 'Yes.'

'Michael?'

'Mm.'

'I love you. And d'you know something?'

'Mm.'

'You belong entirely to me and I'm never letting you go.'

He opened his eyes. Post-coitally, it troubled him, that women could not instantly discard their intimate pre-coital personalities, but lingered instead in an oppressive continuity of feeling. He, on the other hand, was luxuriating in the rediscovery of his unshareable core, in nurturing that private little part that was a man's closest approximation—was this ridiculous?—of a foetus. Ten minutes before he had felt he belonged to her. Now, the idea of belonging to anyone, of anyone belonging to anyone, was stifling.

He was roused to accusation. He said, 'You phoned Melissa.'

'I sure did! More than once.'

'And you told her we were getting married?'

'You bet.'

She was still completely naked, but from somewhere she had produced a stick of gum—she never chewed while they made love—and set her jaws in their easy circular motion, and at the same time grinned good-naturedly down at him, waiting for his outburst, and enjoying herself.

'How did you get the number?' An irrelevant question, but her jauntiness had thrown him.

'Michael! You called her from my place while I was at work. You think it doesn't show up on the phone bill?'

He was about to speak but she laughed and clutched his elbow.

'Do you know what happened when I called that number first time? A little child answered and so just to make sure I said, "Sweetheart, can I speak to your daddy?" and do you know what she said?'

'No.'

'Real serious. "My daddy's saving the world in Lordsburg." Isn't that cute?'

It was no longer possible to have such a conversation naked. He went to the bathroom and fetched a dressing gown, and when he came back he was surprised to find her getting dressed. She still looked cheerful. He sat on a chair by the bed, watching her as she stepped into her skirt and bent with a grunt to fix her shoes.

Finally he said, 'Darlene, let's be clear. We're not getting married.'

She spoke as she pinned her hair in a mirror by the TV set. 'I have to get home to shower and change. I'm helping out at the school tonight for an hour. But don't worry. Nicky gets off work at the pharmacy in ten minutes and she'll give me a ride.'

She was ready to leave and came and sat by him on the edge of the bed. She smiled ruefully and patted his knee. He was already feeling some rising regret that she was going. Was it self-love, this appetite for such a voluminous woman? His life had been a steadily mounting curve, Maisie to

Darlene.

She said, 'Listen to me. A list of things you ought to know. One is, you're not an entirely good person, nor am I. Two, I love you. Three, I always assumed you were married. You didn't talk about it, I didn't ask. We're consenting adults. Four, when I spoke to Melissa I found out there was no Mrs Beard. Five, there have been times when you made love to me you said you wanted to marry me. Six, so I've decided. We're getting married. You'll kick and scream, but my mind's made up. I'll wear you down. No escape, Mister Nobel Laur-ee-ate. The stagecoach is pulling out and I do believe you're on it!'

She was so merry, so hopelessly optimistic and well disposed. So *American*. He started to laugh, and then so did she. They kissed, then kissed deeply.

He said, 'You're magnificent, and I'm not marrying you. Or anyone.'

She stood and took her bag. 'Well, I'm marrying *you*.'

'Stay a little longer. I'll drive you home.'

'Uhuh. I just got dressed. You'll make me late. I know you.'

She blew him a kiss from the door and was gone.

* * *

He remained in the chair wondering whether to phone Hammer and find out how the meeting with the lawyer went. The conversation would be easier from his own point of view, he decided, if he took a shower first. He thought he might watch the local TV news to see if the project was getting full coverage, but the remote was under a pillow, under one of many, on the far side of the bed, and he did not feel like stirring, not just yet. He was so lethargic that it crossed his mind that it would be a fine thing to move, or be gently moved on a hospital gurney to another room where the bed was made and his clothes were not sliding off the chair and the contents of his suitcase were not advancing across the floor. Not possible. He belonged here, in this world. So he would take a shower, now. But he did not get up. He thought about Melissa and Catriona approaching him along the Interstate, driving into the sunset, and how wise he had been, not telling Darlene of their arrival. She would want them all to have dinner together and discuss the future. He wondered where Tarpin was staying, and then he reminded himself he should be feeling excited about tomorrow, which made him think again about Hammer. And so his mind turned soporifically through the complications of the evening, so that when it came, the explosive knock or kick against his door, his startled surprise took the form of an involuntary leap from the chair and a jolt of pain through his chest. Then it came again, two powerful blows resounding against the hollow plywood.

'All right,' he shouted. 'I'm coming.'

Pulling open the door sucked the dry asphalt warmth of the evening into the motel room and revealed Hammer against an orange sky, and behind him a large figure in a suit.

'I'm not even asking,' Hammer said flatly. 'We're coming in.'

Beard shrugged as he stood back. Why then

should he apologise for the state of the place?

Hammer looked pale, his face was rigid. He said in the same unmodulated voice, 'Mr Barnard, Mr Beard.' It was usually 'Professor'.

Beard shook the man's hand and gestured towards the chaotic bed, the only place to sit, and he returned to his chair. Barnard, who carried a document case, brushed the sheet with a fastidious flick of his hand, reasonably concerned about bodily fluids getting on his grey silk suit. Hammer sat beside him, and the three were hunched close together, like children plotting in a bedroom on a rainy afternoon.

Barnard, big, square-jawed, thin-lipped, with heavy-framed glasses, six three at least, and bursting out of his shirt, gave an initial impression, by the way he perched his case on his knees and kept his ankles together, of a meek-mannered fellow in a tough guy's body, more of a Clark Kent type, and apologetic about it. Toby at his side looked to be in a state of shock. There was a novel tremor in his right hand, and he kept swallowing hard, sending his Adam's apple up with an audible click. This should have been the kind of occasion when he sought out Beard's gaze for a conspiratorial or satirical exchange. Lawyers! But he would not meet his colleague's eye. Instead, he stared at his clasped hands as he said, 'Michael, this is bad.'

In the silence Barnard nodded sympathetically and waited, and then said in a voice pitched a little too high for his form, 'Shall I begin? Mr Beard, as you know, my firm is instructed from England in the matter of various patents granted to you. I'm going to spare you the legal language. Our intention is to settle this reasonably and swiftly. Our immediate wish is for you to cancel tomorrow's public event because it is prejudicial to our client's case.'

Beard's mind's eye, like a studio camera on a wire, was moving smoothly through the Dorset Square flat looking for the pile in which his old employment contracts were concealed. He said through a pleasant smile, 'And what case is that?'

'Sweet Jesus,' Hammer said softly.

'In the year 2000 my client personally made a copy of a three hundred and twenty-seven page document which we know to be in your possession. These were notes written by Mr Thomas Aldous before his death and while he was employed at the Centre for Renewable Energy, near Reading, England. This copy has been examined by reputable experts, top physicists in their field, including Professor Pollard of Newcastle University, and they have also examined your various patent applications. From their conclusions, parts of which have been seen by Mr Hammer here, we have every reason to believe that those applications were based not on original work by you, but on the work of Mr Aldous. Theft of intellectual property on such a scale is a serious matter, Mr Beard. The rightful owner of Mr Aldous's work is the Centre. These were the clear terms of his employment, which you can read for yourself.'

Beard maintained his engaged, kindly grin, but privately he registered this threat or setback in the form of an uncomfortable rippling of his pulse, like a syncopated drum roll, that did not simply distort his consciousness, but interrupted it, and for a second or two he might have passed out.

Then his heartbeat steadied, and he seemed to return to the room and adopted from nowhere a no-nonsense tone. 'Disrupting tomorrow's event would be highly prejudicial to our own interests and those of the locality and is clearly out of the question. It's virtually impossible anyway.' He leaned forward confidentially. 'Have you ever tried cancelling a US Air Force fly-past, Mr Barnard?'

No one smiled.

Beard continued. 'The second point is this. As I remember, the cover sheet of Tom Aldous's notes is marked confidential. For the exclusive attention of Professor Beard. I believe this confidentiality has been breached. Thirdly, before his death, Mr Aldous and I worked intensively on artificial photosynthesis. He used to come to my house, so often in fact that, as everybody knows, he ran off with my wife. When we were working together, I did the thinking and talking, Tom did the writing. In our democratic times, Mr Barnard, science remains a hierarchical affair, unamenable to levelling. Too much expertise, too much knowledge has to be acquired. Before they become old fools, senior scientists tend to know more, by objectively measured standards. Aldous was a lowly post-doc. You could say he was my amanuensis. And that was why the file was marked for me, and no one else. I have scores, if not hundreds, of pages of my own notes covering the same material, all properly annotated and dated, and certainly pre-dating the Aldous file. If you insist on wasting the Centre's resources coming to court, I'll make them available. But you will be paying my costs, and I shall take advice on whether to sue Mr Braby personally for defamation.'

Toby Hammer's slumped back had begun to straighten a little and there was hope, or the beginning of hope, in his eyes as he watched his friend.

The lawyer continued much as before. 'We have letters Aldous wrote to his father describing his ideas and his intention of putting them before you in this file. He wanted you to use your influence to get funding. We know from many sources that your interest at the time was confined to a new kind of wind turbine.'

'Mr Barnard,' Beard spoke in the falling tones of gentle, steely admonition. 'My life's work has been in light. Since the age of twenty, when I learned by heart the poem of that name by John Milton. Some twenty-five years ago, I received the Nobel Prize for modifying Einstein's photovoltaics. Do not try to tell me my interests are or were confined to wind turbines. As for Tom's letters, he would not be the first ambitious young man who made grand claims about his achievements to a father who was still supporting him.'

Beard drew his dressing gown around him, and nodded reassuringly at Hammer.

Barnard conceded nothing. He simply moved to his next point. 'This is not central to our case, it merely corroborates it. We have transcripts of a recording of a speech you gave in the Savoy Hotel, London, in February 2005. We find that it was mostly derived from various paragraphs in Mr Aldous's file.'

Beard shrugged. 'And those paragraphs were derived from me.'

'We also have,' Barnard said, 'notes made by Mr

Aldous in the year before he met you, and these demonstrate a deep interest in global warming, ecology, sustainable development, and various calculations, the sort of things that were developed in this file. And before you tell me, Mr Beard, that he must have got these from you somehow, even though he didn't know you, you should be aware that our office has researched thoroughly every public lecture, radio talk, media interview, newspaper opinion piece, every course you gave at university, and there is nothing of yours that touches on artificial photosynthesis, nor is there a single mention by you of climate change or renewable energy in the months and years before Mr Aldous died and his file came into your possession. Hardly what one would expect, is it, Mr Beard, from a public figure like yourself making breakthrough discoveries in the field?'

Hammer had slumped again, and at last Beard was angry. What was this ludicrous man doing in his room, sitting so primly on the bed which minutes before had supported the glorious form of Darlene? Beard was on his feet, one hand holding his dressing gown in place over his private parts, the other jabbing a finger towards Barnard's face. 'Climate change? You're conveniently forgetting that I was head of the Centre before I ever knew Tom Aldous. No win, no fee, is it, Mr Barnard? Looking to get rich? Well, take this back to your Mr Braby. Tell him I know a shabby opportunist when I see one. We've made something beautiful here and he thinks he can hitch a ride. He's also stupid enough to think that a court will believe that this is the kind of work a graduate student can dream up alone. Tomorrow our site will be delivering clean low-cost electricity to Lordsburg. Tell Mr Braby to watch it all on TV, and we'll see him in court!'

Barnard had also stood and held his briefcase against his chest. He was shaking his head, and when he spoke his voice was tight with a new emotion, indignation or pride or some blend of the two. 'There is one further development you should be aware of. Mr Braby is no more. Last month was the Queen's birthday and to mark the occasion as special she invited him to become her knight of the realm. He is now Sir Jock Braby.'

Beard moaned in exasperation and made a show of clapping his hand to his forehead. But there was a look of panic in Hammer's eyes. If Braby had the Queen of England on his side, what possible chance did they have in an English court of law?

Beard said, 'It's all crap, Toby. Don't listen. This is the Queen's Birthday Honours List. She doesn't choose it, she knows fuck all about it, and they all scramble to be on it, every booby and arriviste from science and the arts and the civil service who wants to strut about the place hoping to be taken for a member of the minor aristocracy.'

There was a silence after this outburst, and then Barnard sighed and took a step around the bed towards the door. 'Shall we assume then, Mr Beard, that Her Majesty hasn't gotten round to choosing you?'

Beard said crisply, 'I'm not at liberty to say.'

Barnard let his briefcase swing down and dangle at his side. Toby was now on his feet. Barnard said, 'Well, on behalf of Sir Jock Braby and the National Centre for Renewable Energy, I want to put it to you one last time. If you agree to call off tomorrow's media event and agree to revisit the patents situation, you'll find us sympathetic collaborators who will certainly find a role for you in the development of a technology which rightly belongs to the Centre. If not, then our first move will be to go to court to freeze all exploitation until this matter is resolved.'

Hammer, turning to Beard, looked like he was about to go down on one knee. 'Michael, that could take five years.'

Beard was shaking his head. 'No, Toby. I say no.'

Barnard said, 'The British government has deep pockets, at least in this affair. They're keen to see the Centre own the patents and show the taxpayer a decent return.'

Hammer clutched at the lapels of Beard's dressing gown. 'Listen, we owe a lot of money. No one's going to sign with us until this is straightened out. We can't afford lawyers.'

'We've put in all the work,' Beard said as he pushed Hammer's hand away. 'If we roll over now, we'll be lucky if they take us on as lavatory attendants.'

'Gentlemen,' Barnard said. 'I'm pretty sure we can offer you something better than that. And Mr Hammer's right. When news of our legal contest becomes public, people will not want to do business with you. Surely it's in your interests too, not to make a splash tomorrow.'

'I'm putting this as politely as I can,' Beard said. 'Please leave.'

With the faintest pursing of his thin lips, Barnard turned and opened the door. Over his shoulder the orange desert sky was fading through yellow to luminous green.

Hammer, usually a cool type, wailed on a rising note, 'Michael, we've got to keep talking! Mr Barnard, wait, I'll come out with you.'

The lawyer inclined his head regretfully. 'Sure, but it's Mr Beard's signature that we want,' and he stepped out into the dusk, and Hammer hurried after him. The door swung shut, and Beard heard the voices of the two men retreating across the parking lot, with Toby's suddenly growing louder, beseeching, begging for time, then giving way to Barnard's insistent murmur.

He was slumped in the chair just as before, still wondering about a shower. The episode appeared like a playlet staged for his benefit. For the moment he was numb to its implications. He was aware that a great wall obstructed the progress of his life and he could not see past it. His thoughts were stilled. His only concern was that Melissa and Catriona would arrive in less than an hour and he should be dressed to greet them. After many empty minutes he went to the bathroom and got under the shower and stood there blankly, barely conscious, with hot water drumming on his skull. At a sound, he put his head out of the cubicle and listened. There was a loud knock on his door, then another. There was silence, then his palmtop began to ring from the bedside table as the knocks resumed and grew louder. Hammer called out his name many times. No doubt desperate to come in and persuade him to be Braby's minion.

Beard retreated under the shower, and when he was sure that his friend had gone away he stepped out and began to dry himself. Hot water on his skin had done the trick. He was refreshed and knew what must happen. It was all down to attitude.

Tomorrow's opening must go ahead. The rewards might be snatched away, but the world would see what he had accomplished. He would go out in a blaze. Or better, persuade someone with money to back him through the courts in return for a part share. Their most important visitors were already in their hotels in El Paso, and some were coming through Silver City. The sun would rise, the panels would makes gases out of water, the gases would run the turbines, electricity would flow, the world would surely stand amazed. Nothing must interrupt the Beatles medley and the screaming low-level jets.

With a towel stretched round his waist, whistling 'Yellow Submarine', he came back into the bedroom, rummaged in his case and pulled out a shirt, which he shook free of the laundry-service cellophane and cardboard. The sound of plastic wrapping was a reminder of one more animating factor, his hunger. Having refused his brunch, and replaced it with his lunch, he was running a meal deficit which he was about to address. He found clean underwear and socks—strange to think back to the days when he could put his socks on while standing up—and unfolded his best non-crease suit. Of course, he was dressing for Melissa. At the thought of her, while dousing himself with cologne at the bathroom mirror, he went back into the bedroom to spend some minutes straightening out the bed. And at the thought of Darlene, and how and where everyone would sleep and what would get said, his mind reared up like a skittish horse and went off in another direction. Which was alcohol. The restaurant across the road did not serve it. From a compartment inside his suitcase he brought out a silver and calfskin hip flask filled with Dutch gin, Genever, easily good enough to be drunk at room temperature, and indistinguishable from water. He took a shot now and put the flask in his pocket. Then he paused before the door and drank a longer shot, and stepped outside.

Always a delicious moment to be savoured, and never to be had in the British Isles, when, showered and perfumed and wearing fresh clothes, one steps out from the air conditioning into the smooth, invincible warmth of a Southern evening. Even in the denatured neon glow of the Lordsburg mini-strip, the crickets or cicadas—he did not know the difference—went on singing. There was no money in stopping them. And no means of preventing or franchising the neatly etched half-moon that hung above the gas station.

Tonight, however, his pleasure was marred. Parked thirty feet away from his motel-room door was a black Lexus, and climbing into the driver's seat was Barnard. Standing on the passenger side, waiting to get in, with that same bag at his feet, was Tarpin. As he opened his door he noticed Beard and half smiled and made a knife of his forefinger and drew it across his throat. The engine started, the headlights came on, Tarpin got in with his luggage and the car reversed from its space and pulled out of the parking lot. Baffled, Beard watched them go, and remained on the spot after they had disappeared. Then he shrugged and went over to the office to tell the receptionist to let Melissa know where he could be found, then walked across the road to the Blooberry and arrived with his good mood partially restored. He was not going under.

He could make a case that there was no better or happier place to eat in the United States than the Blooberry Family Restaurant—speciality, a steak skillet breakfast. The unreflecting atheist was bound to find interest and instruction in the Mennonite tracts on a table by the entrance. 'A Happy Home', 'A Loving Marriage', and nearer his own field, 'Caring for the Earth'. By the checkout was a gift shop where in the course of eighteen months he had bought more than two dozen T-shirts for Catriona. The restaurant floor was large, the waitresses all seemed close versions, merry cousins, of Darlene. Off-duty cops ate here, and Border Patrolmen, truckers, hollow-eyed interstate travellers sitting alone, and families, of course, Hispanic, Asian, white, often in large spreads across three or four tables pushed together. But even when it was crowded, the Blooberry was dignified and subdued, as though it quietly craved a drink. The place was soothingly anonymous. Not once had he been recognised as a regular by the jolly staff. Interstate 10 was close by and turnover was high.

The food happened to suit him. As he waited to be seated he had no need to reflect on choices—he always ate the same meal here. There was no point in straying. He was led to a booth in the farthest corner. To help settle his impatience for the starter to arrive, he poured a stiff measure of gin into his empty water glass and drank it down like water, and poured another. Everything was terrible, but he was not feeling so bad. At least this Terry no longer existed. Or was that such a good thing? Melissa and Darlene, a serious mess. He could not face it, he could not bear to think about it. But it would be faced. And poor Toby. He knew he should phone him to explain why the demonstration must go ahead, but for the moment he could not be doing with another argument.

To keep his mind off his order—fifteen minutes had passed, and it usually took less than five—he looked through his emails, and here were a couple of items that made him exclaim with pleasure. The first was an informal approach from an old friend, an ex-physicist now working as a consultant in Paris. A consortium of power companies wanted Beard to bring his 'wide experience of green technologies to the task of steering public policy in the direction of carbon-free nuclear energy'. On offer was a salary well into six figures, along with an office in central London, a researcher and a car. Well, of course. The argument could be made. The CO_2 levels went on rising and time was running out. There was really only one well-tested means of producing electricity on a scale to meet the needs of a growing world population, and do it soon, without adding to the problem. Many respected environmentalists had come round to this view, that nuclear was the only way out, the lesser of two evils. James Lovelock, Stewart Brand, Tim Flannery, Jared Diamond, Paul Ehrlich. Scientists and good men all. In the new scale of things, was the occasional accident, the local radiation leak, the worst outcome possible? Even without an accident, coal was daily creating a disaster, and the effects were global. Was not the 28-kilometre exclusion zone around Chernobyl now the biologically richest and most diverse region of Central Europe, with mutation rates in all species of flora and fauna barely above the norm, if at all? Besides, wasn't radiation just another name for sunlight?

The second email was an invitation to address a meeting of foreign ministers at COP 15, the grand climate-change conference in Copenhagen in December. He would be at one with its spirit and he was, he supposed, the perfect choice. He would be there. His starter arrived, orange-coloured cheese, dipped in batter, rolled in breadcrumbs and salt and deep-fried, with a creamy dip of pale green. Perfection, and in such quantity. As soon as the area around his booth was clear of waiting staff, he poured the remains of the Genever. He ate rapidly and was down to his last three lozenges, and beginning to wonder if some of them were filled with mushroom, not cheese, when the palmtop vibrated by his plate.

'Toby.'

'Listen. I've got all kinds of bad news for you, but the worst has just happened, minutes ago.'

Beard noted the strained tone of controlled hostility in his friend's voice.

'Go on.'

'Someone's taken a sledgehammer to the panels. They've gone down the rows and taken them all out. Shattered. We've lost all the catalysts. Electronics. Everything.'

There was no taking this in properly. Beard pushed his plate away. Builder's work. What would Barnard have needed to pay Tarpin? Two hundred dollars? Less?

'What else?'

'We won't be meeting again. I don't think I could bear the sight of you, Michael. But you might as well know. I'm talking to a lawyer in Oregon. I'll be taking action to protect myself against what are rightfully your debts. We, you, already owe three and a half million. Tomorrow's going to cost another half million. You can go down there yourself and explain to all the good people. Also, Braby is going to take you for everything you have and will ever have. And in the UK that dead boy's father has persuaded the authorities to move against you on criminal charges, basically theft and fraud. I hate you, Michael. You lied to me and you're a thief. But I don't want to see you in prison. So stay out of England. Go somewhere that doesn't have an extradition treaty.'

'Anything else?'

'Only this. You deserve almost everything that's coming to you. So go fuck yourself.' The line went dead.

This time he did not conceal the flask as he shook it over his glass. Two drops fell out. His waitress was standing by his elbow with a heaped plate. She was a solemn teenager with hair in a prim ponytail and on her teeth were braces studded with colourful glass beads. It cost her a lot to say what she had to.

'Sir? We have a no-alcohol poss . . . policy on these premises?'

'I didn't know. I'm terribly sorry.'

She took away the bowl with the three cold lozenges and set the main course down before him. Four wedges of skinless chicken breast, interleaved with three minute steaks, the whole wrapped in bacon, with a honey and cheese topping, and served with twice-roasted jacket potatoes already impregnated with butter and cream cheese.

He stared at it a good while. The destination of

choice, as the cliché ran, to avoid extradition was Brazil. Was he to buy a ticket to São Paulo and stay with Sylvia? She was a lovely woman, and interesting too. It might not be so bad. But impossible. To soothe himself he took up his knife and fork and was immediately distracted by the sight of the lesion, the melanoma on the back of his hand. It was larger, he thought, since he last looked, and was an angry purplish-brown under the Blooberry's fluorescent lights. Was he really going to deal with this now, along with everything else? He thought it unlikely. It would take care of itself. Nor would he go to the site tomorrow to speak to the angry crowds. Nor would he be saving the world.

He set the cutlery down unused. What he wanted most was to go alone to a bar and sit at the counter with a scotch. It was a short walk down to 4th Street. But he would take the car. He was about to call his waitress over for the check when he heard a commotion on the far side of the restaurant. He turned and saw Melissa with high colour in her cheeks and wearing one of her vibrant Caribbean dresses of big green flowers against a red and black ground. She was striding past the 'Please Wait To Be Seated' sign, and right behind her, surprisingly, was Darlene, and both women looked stormy, furious and rumpled, as if they had just had a fight outside. Now they were looking for him. Ahead of them by several feet was Catriona, carrying a little girl's backpack designed to give the impression that a koala bear was clinging to her shoulders for a free ride. She saw her father before the women did and was running towards him, coming to claim him, calling out something indistinct, skipping between the crowded tables. As Beard rose to greet her, he felt in his heart an unfamiliar, swelling sensation, but he doubted as he opened his arms to her that anyone would ever believe him now if he tried to pass it off as love.

Appendix

Presentation Speech by Professor Nils Palsternacka of the Royal Swedish Academy of Sciences

(Translation from the Swedish text)

Your Majesties, Your Royal Highnesses, Ladies and Gentlemen,

That you see me standing before you is a tribute to the photopigments in your eyes that capture light. That we are all feeling pleasantly warm, despite the chilly weather outside in the streets of Stockholm, is by grace of leaves in Carboniferous forests that captured sunlight with their photosynthetic pigments and left us a residue of coal and oil. These are simple examples of how the interaction of radiation and matter underpins life on earth. In the late nineteen forties, a deep physical understanding of this interaction was achieved by Feynman and Schwinger, and by 1970 it seemed to most physicists that this was a finished chapter and that exploration of fundamentals had moved on either to a more cosmic scale or to events deeper within atoms. Yet there was a surprise in store.

The Solvay Conference is an event of great importance in the physics calendar. At the 1972 gathering, well into an afternoon session, a cry was heard from the back of the hall. Heads turned to see Richard Feynman holding a bundle of papers aloft in his hand. 'Magic!' he cried, and advanced to the front, and, apologising to the speaker, seized the stage. In five minutes of intense, gesticulating argument he explained how a problem that had long baffled him had been solved by a young researcher named Michael Beard.

The Solvay 'magic moment' has of course gone down in history, and it is not hard to see why the ideas in Beard's paper appealed so strongly to Feynman. They showed how certain diagrams that described the interaction of light with matter obey a new kind of subtle symmetry that greatly simplifies calculations. In popular perception, quantum mechanics describes the very small; and indeed it is true that only very small systems can easily maintain coherence, in the sense that they preserve their isolation from the environment. Yet Beard's theory revealed that the events that take place when radiation interacts with matter propagate coherently over a large scale compared to the size of atoms; furthermore, the manner of their propagation resembles the flow diagram for a complicated system, the sort of picture an engineer might give of the workings of an oil refinery, say, or of the logical steps in a computer program. This has transformed our understanding of the photoelectric effect to such an extent that we now speak of the Beard–Einstein Conflation, a spine-tingling hyphenation for any physicist, placing Beard's work proudly in a lineage originating from Einstein's revolutionary 1905 paper.

With his genius for popularisation, Feynman contrived a party trick to demonstrate the principles behind the Conflation. This requires six belts or straps that are interwoven in an attractive pattern. Six people then take two free ends each and hold the knot out for inspection. Anyone may verify that a very intractable knot has been created and there is no hope of untying it unless the participants release their ends. Next the participants perform a sort of country-dance pirouette with a neighbour, an operation that seems to increase the intractability of the knot. But then, at a signal, all the participants pull, and to the amazement of the gathering the belts fall apart. Feynman's Plaid has become a favourite with all physics lecturers, and there is probably no physics undergraduate who has not participated in it, and in some cases met his or her future spouse in the happy melee.

Here we see the topological essence of Michael Beard's conception: the action of the group (the exceptional Lie group E_8, one of the bulkier residents of the Platonic realm) that disentangles and choreographs the complicated interactions between light and matter, unfolding them into a succession of logical steps. It is the interplay of these operations that constitutes the essential magic, the wave of the enchanter's wand, and it brings to mind Einstein's description of Bohr's atomic theory as the highest form of musicality in the sphere of thought. In the words of the philosopher Francis Bacon:

> *The sweetest and best Harmony is, when every Part or Instrument, is not heard by it selfe, but a Conflation of them all.*

Professor Michael Beard, you have been awarded this year's Nobel Prize in Physics for your profound contribution to our understanding of the interaction of matter and electromagnetic radiation. It is an honour for me to convey the warmest congratulations of the Royal Swedish Academy of Sciences. I now ask you to step forward to receive your Nobel Prize from the hands of His Majesty the King.

ACKNOWLEDGEMENTS

I am grateful to David Buckland and Cape Farewell for inviting me on a trip to Spitsbergen in February 2005—this novel had its beginnings on a frozen fjord. Dr Graeme Mitchison of the Centre for Quantum Computation in Cambridge gave generous guidance on mathematics and physics. Any remaining errors are mine. He also kindly unearthed the citation for Michael Beard's Nobel Prize. I owe thanks to Professor John Schellnhuber, Director of the Potsdam Institute for Climate Impact Research, and Stefan Rahmstorf of the same institute, to Dr Doug Arent, James Bosch and Professor John A. Turner of the National Renewable Energy Laboratory in Golden, Colorado, Malcolm McCulloch of the Department of Engineering Science, Oxford, Professor Mike Duff of Imperial College, Philip Diamond of the Institute of Physics, Tim Garton Ash and, as always, Annalena McAfee. Thanks to Dan Boekman for lending me a house in New Mexico, and to Greg Carr for his house in Sun Valley, Idaho. I am indebted to innumerable books and papers on climate science and related matters, and to an exchange between Steven Pinker and Elizabeth Spelke on Edge.com. I was a grateful and admiring reader of Edward Slingerland's *What Science Offers the Humanities*. Above all, I owe a debt to Walter Isaacson's fine biography *Einstein*.